HELL DIVERS III

DELIVERANCE

D1571337

BOOKS BY *NEW YORK TIMES* BESTSELLING AUTHOR
NICHOLAS SANSBURY SMITH

HELL DIVERS III

DELIVERANCE

NICHOLAS SANSBURY SMITH

**BLACK
STONE**
PUBLISHING

Copyright © 2018 by Nicholas Sansbury Smith
Published in 2022 by Blackstone Publishing
Cover and book design by Kathryn Galloway English

Printed in the United States of America
Originally published in hardcover by Blackstone Publishing in 2018

ISBN 979-8-200-92412-7
Fiction / Science Fiction / Apocalyptic & Post-Apocalyptic

Version 1

CIP data for this book is available
from the Library of Congress

Blackstone Publishing
31 Mistletoe Rd.
Ashland, OR 97520

www.BlackstonePublishing.com

To my good friends and partners at Blackstone Publishing, thank you for helping me bring the Hell Divers series to life. I'm honored to work with each and every one of you.

"A very great vision is needed, and the man who has it must follow it as the eagle seeks the deepest blue of the sky."

—Crazy Horse

ONE

Lightning forked through the center of a massive storm brewing above the badlands. The bowl of cracked dirt seemed to continue forever in all directions. The constant stream of light illuminated a roadway that twisted through the barren terrain. Hundreds of years ago, fields of crops would have framed this road, but now there were only two living creatures here, leaving tracks in the dust.

A man and his dog trekked over the broken asphalt. The man wore a black radiation suit, with an olive scarf wrapped around the area where the crest of his chest armor met the bottom of his helmet. Long ago, the metal of his armor had shone, but years of exposure had faded everything to a dull gray. He walked with a slight limp in his gait—a product of injuries and bad joints.

The man motioned for the dog to join him by his side as they plodded down the decaying road. While the sixty-pound Siberian husky kept his crystal-blue eyes on the path, the man kept his eyes on the swirling storm clouds.

They were both searching—the dog for hostiles, the man for something he could hardly remember. Squinting, he studied the shape of a swollen cloud that reminded him of an oversize beetle. He halted on the road and lowered his rifle, tilting his head as memories flooded through his tormented mind.

"What you're looking for doesn't exist anymore," he said in a scratchy whisper. "They're all gone now."

The dog glanced up at him questioningly and then trotted ahead. The man remained standing in the gusting wind, scarf blowing like a pair of wings behind his helmet, as he tried to recall his past. No matter how hard he tried, he simply couldn't remember certain things. Important things. Things such as who he had been in his old life, before he was left behind. But he could remember his name. It was scribbled on the first page of a dog-eared book he kept in a plastic sleeve inside the breast pocket of his vest.

"You are Xavier Rodriguez." He swallowed, forcing saliva down his dry throat. "You are X," he said, louder this time. "You are the last man."

Miles looked back at him. The plastic of the dog's radiation suit whipped back and forth as he wagged his tail. X felt a tingle at the edges of his lips. It was the closest he had come to smiling in . . . how long? It took him a moment to realize he couldn't remember the last time.

"Keep moving," he said to himself. The words became a mantra that he repeated in his mind as he navigated the shattered asphalt that had once been a highway.

His path was the road. It connected the cities of the Old World, where humanity had once thrived. In the distance, the skeletal husks of scrapers reached for the storm clouds. A child who had never seen a city wouldn't guess that the structures were made by humans. Someone who had never set foot down here would have thought they were part of the earth.

And in some ways, they were, just like the bones of the

humans and animals that had once lived here. But X knew all too well what the ancient cities were—and what dwelled in the networks of interlacing streets. This city would be no different. It had once been home to millions of people, but now it was the lair of mutant beasts such as the Sirens—genetically engineered humans that had evolved into monsters.

He no longer had a permanent home. His home was wherever he decided to stop and rest. Sleep came whenever his body needed it. With no one to talk to and nothing to do but trek across the blasted land, he had fallen into a routine that made him feel more machine than human.

X walked.

He didn't know how long he had been walking. He had lost track of time. In the wastes, time was everything, and time was nothing. He had learned this long ago, but how long, he couldn't say. In truth, he didn't want to know. Like the grit whirling around him, memories of his old life surfaced and then blew away. Images and sounds were nearly impossible to recall. But something from his past kept him going.

His destination was the place where water stretched across the horizon. The memory of that sight haunted him, called to him. He had forgotten the name humans used to call it, but he remembered from dives just how cold and dark it was. That seemed a lifetime ago. But so did his journey across the wastes. How long had he been traveling since he left Hades? Four years, or was it five? Could it be longer than that?

Lightning lanced into the ground in the distance, searing the scarred earth. The boom of thunder rattled his visor. The wail that followed stopped him in midstride. Miles halted, ears perked inside his helmet.

The screeching of the wind sounded just like them—a Klaxon that signaled danger and death on swift wings. It was a sound X never forgot, a sound that always made him raise his battered carbine and point it at the irradiated landscape. He searched for the shadowy forms of the Sirens but saw nothing.

Cold fingers of wind sneaked through the holes in his tattered boots and his clothing. Another draft blasted his side. The grit collected in layers beneath his suit and armor. No matter what he did, he couldn't seem to keep the dirt out.

He threw the strap of his rifle over his back and pressed down on the loose duct tape flapping over his wrist. It had come undone and exposed his dark skin. He studied his flesh as if seeing it for the first time. The dirt caked his body like an extra layer of skin. He couldn't remember the last time his body was clean, but he had stopped caring. All that mattered was keeping out the radiation.

X sucked in a long breath of filtered air, filling his lungs. Sometimes he forgot how exhausted he was from walking from city to city all this time, raiding old structures for anything he could use to survive as he searched for the ocean.

That's what they called it, he thought. *The ocean.*

He tightened a string over his wrist to hold the tape down and then reached for his rifle. It caught on his rucksack. The massive ruck contained everything he owned, from the water purification kit that he pissed into each night to the blocks of calorie-rich synthetic food that gave him and the dog the energy to continue.

The weight was a burden on his shoulders, but nothing like the weight of not knowing whether he was the last man on earth.

He pressed forward, forcing his legs to carry him a few more steps. *Keep moving.* His eyes flitted back to the storm clouds disgorging bolts of electricity. The bright tendrils speared downward, licking the ground to the west. Another strike lashed the dirt to the east. In the interval between flashes, an oddly shaped light emerged across the dome of clouds, like a lightbulb with a dying power source.

This wasn't lightning.

He studied the rays with a sense of awe. Where there should have been the blue residue of lightning, he saw a warm orange.

"It can't be," he mumbled.

Miles tilted his helmet to look at this new, anomalous sight.

By the time X realized it was the sun, clouds had swallowed the warm glow. He hadn't seen the sun in a long time and had almost forgotten how beautiful it was.

He exhaled, noticing he had been holding in his breath. Seeing something from the past sometimes helped him remember other things. Closing his eyes, he tried to visualize the smooth beetlelike contours of the airship he had once called home. Next, he pictured the interior. In his mind's eye, he saw the silhouettes of passengers walking through the narrow corridors. As in all the other times he tried to remember, these people had no faces.

Pulling out his journal and a pen, he prepared to jot down anything he could recall. But the mental image was gone again already.

A bolt of lightning slashed the earth in front of him, raising the hair on his neck, and rain began to pelt his body. He quickly placed the precious book and pen back in their waterproof sleeve and stowed them in his vest. Then he raised the scope of his rifle to his visor and slowly raked the muzzle over the landscape, searching for shelter.

There wasn't much out here besides the occasional trunk of a dead tree, or the retaining wall of a building long since destroyed. But to the east he noticed patches of red poisonous weeds. Beyond the field of foliage that thrived in the radioactive conditions, a rocky hill shielded the brick foundations of an old community.

It would have to do.

X lowered the scope just as a flash of movement darted from one of those foundations and vanished into a hole in the ground.

Lightning flashed above him, but he didn't so much as flinch. His gaze was locked on to a single spot. Out here, the movement could be anything from a dust storm to a mutant monster. Most of the beasts fed on plants, but they would happily feed on him and his dog if he got close enough.

Thunder boomed above—another threat barreling down. He raised his left arm and checked the rad meter, which looked like an oversized clock. The radiation here was minimal. Then he scanned the sky again for any sign of the Sirens. He hadn't seen any of the winged monsters in a long time, but he never let his guard down, always aware of the threat and listening for their otherworldly wails.

"Come on, boy," X said.

He left his night-vision goggles off to conserve the battery and flicked on his flashlight instead, directing the bright beam at the dirt to the right of the road. Using the light to guide them, he fell into a run, with his only friend in the world by his side. Everywhere he looked, cracks and holes marred the earth like deformed flesh.

X didn't like to stray from the road. It was safer to stick to the path. The road didn't move. It was the one thing on the cursed earth that seemed to remain constant.

A beetle half the size of Miles poked a pair of ropy antennae out of a cavern in the dirt. X slowed and watched the black chitinous shell emerge. It skittered forward, antennae wobbling back and forth. Like many creatures on the surface, it had no eyes.

Again he was reminded of the airship in the sky. But he was also reminded of all the things that lived underground, from the badlands to the desert he had once crossed. Snakes large enough to swallow a human hunted in the dunes, their scaly armored flesh tunneling beneath the sand. His first meeting with them had nearly cost him his life.

Usually, the insects were harmless, but he didn't take any chances. Using his boot, he kicked the creature aside, sending it scuttling for cover.

He continued, eyes flitting over the cracks and holes in the ground. He was more concerned with falling in a crevice and breaking an ankle than with anything that might crawl out of the ground. That would be bad. And sometimes the holes harbored bigger things than insects. That would be worse.

The ground was solid here, at least. Trekking across sand was something he never wanted to do again.

"Stay close, boy," he said to Miles.

The rocky hill grew larger as they approached. It was a natural bluff, not a mound of scree or debris from a destroyed building. Even better, there was an overhang that would shield him from the wind and rain.

He jogged faster, anxious to set out his tracking gear and start a fire. Lightning sizzled across the sky to the west, and the rumble of thunder followed an instant later. The field of poisonous plants retreated in the sudden downpour of rain, curling into holes in the ground.

Drops of rain hit his visor, sluicing down the thick glass. X shut off his flashlight and chinned his night-vision goggles back on as he approached the hill. Miles halted, too, but not for lack of light. Unlike the man, the dog had genetic modifications that allowed him to see in almost complete darkness.

"What is it?" X asked, bringing up his rifle.

They stood in silence for a few moments, sheets of toxic rain beating their radiation suits. The dog finally trotted onward, and the man lowered his rifle, following cautiously.

Brick foundations traced the ground two hundred feet ahead.

The bluff rose three or four stories into the sky. He used the side of his boot to scrape mud off an old street that carved through the terrain. Streets were good. Not as good as the road, but they didn't play tricks on the eye the way the dirt did.

Metal poles protruded out of the dirt at odd angles, like arrows carelessly dropped along the street. Hundreds of years ago, they had provided power to this small community, but the wires were long gone.

X navigated the wet, ruined settlement, wondering whether this place had survived the initial bombs that destroyed most of the Old World. He stopped and bent down to look at something else sticking out of the soil. He brushed the dirt off the skeletal remains of a human hand. Plucking a ring off one of the fingers, he examined it with his flashlight before slipping it into his pocket for later. Then he covered the shallow grave with fresh dirt, which was quickly turning to mud.

Standing, he scanned the area once more, looking for the hole where he had seen something dart away. That creature was bigger than a beetle, and he didn't like surprises. It took him only a few seconds to identify the sinkhole. He motioned for Miles and then trained his rifle on the entrance as he approached, listening for the electronic noises of the Sirens but hearing nothing besides the boom of thunder. At a hundred feet, he stopped and brought up his hand.

The dog sat on his haunches, waiting for orders.

Reaching into his back pocket, X brought out an old can full of coins he had collected on his journey across the wastes. He dropped the ring inside and secured the lid. After making sure the thin cord was attached tightly to the top, he tossed the can. It vanished in the hole, clanking as it fell.

The cord caught in his hand, and he began pulling it back toward the surface. Another sound replied to the echoing metal. It started as a squawk but rose to a high-pitched squeaking.

X pulled the cord until the can reemerged. It clattered over the dirt as he yanked it a few more feet. Then he raised the rifle and aimed it at the lip of the hole, waiting for his bait to draw whatever lurked there out into the open.

He could hear the creature's claws scraping rock on its way to the surface. This was no beetle. Miles' tail dropped between his legs, but X remained steady, keeping the rifle barrel trained on the opening.

A deformed head with a spiky flesh Mohawk popped out of the opening, focusing a pair of bulging bloodshot eyes on the can. It sniffed the air with a nose that was little more than holes in the middle of its face. Then it glared at X, undeterred by the rain striking its crazed eyeballs or, apparently, by the sight of a man.

The beast heaved itself from the hole with two long arms covered in hardened scales like a sort of organic armor. The raised plates ran the length of its body, covering broad shoulders, a wiry torso, and powerful back legs.

X had never seen one of these before. Not wanting to waste precious bullets, he studied the beast for weak spots. It stood on all fours, its arched back lined with ridges and several fins. At its throat, a collar of thicker armor opened and closed like a vent as the beast breathed.

Miles growled a warning, and X aimed at the gill-like feature. The creature tilted its head toward him just as he pulled the trigger. The round lanced into the soft flesh in the opening of the collar, blowing out gore that painted the rain-soaked ground. The blood looked green, but then, so did everything else in the view of his NVGs.

Unable to cry out, the creature flopped silently on the ground as it choked on its own blood. X lowered the rifle and pulled his knife. By the time he reached the body, the abomination was dead.

He looked toward his dog. "You think it tastes good?"

Miles trotted over, sniffed the body through the breathing filter around his muzzle, and walked away, uninterested.

"Yeah, me neither," X said. He pushed the carcass back into the hole and pointed the rifle barrel into the green-hued darkness. The lizard-like monster hit the bottom a few seconds later, the thump and crunch echoing up from the hole. The sound faded away, leaving the man and the dog once again alone in the downpour.

X lowered his gun and walked over to the shelter of the bluff, where he took off his rucksack and rested it on the ground. He checked his rad meter again, and seeing that the area was still a green zone, he took off his helmet. Then he bent down and removed Miles' helmet for him. Next, he pulled out three foot-long stakes attached to the side of his backpack and handed one of them to the dog.

Miles gripped the stake in his mouth and trotted off into the pouring rain. X followed with the other two stakes. Working together, they stuck the poles into the dirt at three different locations, forming a triangle around their camp. When they finished, X raised his wrist computer and activated the network. If anything tried to sneak into the area, a warning alarm would sound on his HUD, beeping in his helmet.

He checked the data on his wrist monitor, and seeing that everything looked good, he returned to his pack and pulled out his metal pot. Next, he put his ministove on the ground and ignited the flame powered by a long-lasting fuel cell.

X walked out from beneath the overhang and put the pot on the ground, then shook open the telescoping catchment funnel and set it over the pot. Rain began to trickle down the broad conical structure and in minutes the pot was full. He brought it back to the stove and set it on the burner. Then he dropped in a pill that would purify the water of radiation and kill any toxins that weren't boiled away. He was running low on the precious pills, but he and Miles had to eat.

Finally, he pulled out a block of synthetic food from his pack. Using his knife, he lopped off a chunk of the bar and dropped it into the water. The brown block expanded into something that looked like a nest of snakes. A few minutes later, they had a pot of noodles and broth.

X sat his aching bones down on a smooth boulder. He waited for the contents of the pot to cool, then reached inside with his gloved fingers. He pulled out a strand and handed it to Miles, who wolfed it down without bothering to chew.

With the dog's blue eyes locked on his, X raised another noodle to his lips and sucked it down. A memory flashed through his mind. He was in his old quarters on the airship he had once called home, sharing a meal with a boy wearing a tinfoil hat. The son of his best friend. *Aaron*, he remembered. *Aaron Everhart and his son, Michael Everhart.*

In the memory, X had watched Michael, who went by "Tin," slurping down a plate of food. But as with most of the memories, the boy's features were blurry, like a broken video screen.

X pulled out his journal and jotted down the memory anyway. It quickly faded in his mind, like all the others, but this time he was able to capture it on the page.

A new memory emerged as he finished writing the first one down. It was the moment Tin had handed him a piece of paper, just before that last dive stranded X on the surface.

Face your future…

X winced. The scars on his body stretched over his tired muscles.

"Without fear," he said with an exhale, finishing the quote as he wrote it into his journal.

Times like this, when he could remember what someone had

said, or the words scrawled on a piece of paper, were rare. So rare that he couldn't recall the last time he'd had such a vivid memory.

Lightning webbed across the sky in the distance, and a third memory surfaced. This one he had no trouble recalling, for it haunted him often as he tried to fall asleep in this blasted wasteland. He felt himself falling through the clouds, a Siren's leathery wings wrapped around him. He saw blue battery units—the beating heart of a Hell Diver. Three featureless faces looking down at him—fellow divers, one of them the woman he once loved— as they ascended toward the *Hive* and he fell back toward hell.

It wasn't a memory he wanted to put in his journal.

X growled as the memories faded away like the afterimage of the lightning. He put his book back into its sleeve and finished his dinner. Then he rolled out the blanket attached to the bottom of his backpack, and Miles curled up beside him.

"Good night, boy," X said. He reached for his helmet and brought it over by the blanket, catching a glimpse of his reflection in the mirrored visor. The flickering fire illuminated a haggard face he almost didn't recognize.

A stranger, a ghost.

X brought his gloved fingers up to the thick, graying beard over a square jawline. With his finger, he traced over a scar forming a ravine up his right cheek and through his eyebrow. Dark eyes framed by crow's-feet stared back at him, the irises almost lost to the fathomless black pupils.

He set the helmet down, unable to look at himself anymore. Bones aching, he grunted as he rested his head on the blanket. The glow of the fire filled the cracks in the stone overhang. Rain pattered down outside their shelter. The sound was calming, and he didn't fight the wave of fatigue sweeping over him.

Minutes later, he was asleep, dreaming of events and people from his past. But not even in his dreams could he remember faces or voices. The dreams, like reality, were mostly just fragments.

A beeping sound entered his dream. His eyes sprang open to darkness as the chirp of the alarm snapped him awake. He saw a silhouette to his left. Miles stood growling and staring out beyond the perimeter.

X fumbled for his helmet, cursing his stupidity. He had forgotten to put it back on before drifting off to sleep. As soon as he slipped it over his head, he saw several contacts on the minimap in the upper-right corner. They were what had set off the alarm.

Cursing, he grabbed his rifle and angled it out toward the abandoned settlement, scanning for targets. His eyes flitted from the map on his HUD to the green hue of the terrain, but nothing moved in the sheets of rain.

What the hell?

Miles growled behind X, but the dog wasn't looking at the settlement. He was glaring, teeth bared, at the wall behind them.

X slowly raised his rifle at the tower of stone, half expecting a Siren or some other beast to come skittering down the side.

"What is it, boy?" he whispered. He checked his HUD again. The contacts were coming from the right. Miles continued growling at the rock, and X moved slowly, rifle shouldered, over to examine the sloped wall.

A crunching sounded, and a cascade of rocks crumbled down the side. He gasped as a pair of massive eyeballs blinked from inside what appeared to be a solid wall. A limb the size of a man reached directly out of the rock. Then a chest emerged, followed by the rest of the body.

Swallowing hard, X scrambled backward as the beast peeled away from the wall and dropped down. The impact of the seven-foot-tall monstrosity shook the ground as dust puffed around its hooves.

"Run!" X shouted.

Miles turned and ran as the beast staggered toward X. He raised his rifle and aimed at the creature's chest. Three rounds smashed through the rocklike armor covering flesh and vital organs.

The rock monster let out a deep howl and swiped with a long arm. Its massive paw hit the muzzle of the gun and knocked it free. X staggered backward and reached to pull his blaster from the holster on his thigh, like a gunslinger preparing for a showdown.

He pointed the gun at the beast's forehead and pulled the trigger.

Click.

His heart thumped against his ribs. Contacts beeped on his HUD. More of the monsters were out there, awakening from their hibernation.

The creature in front of X took another step forward and raised its thick, muscular arms. The flesh looked exactly like weathered stone. X continued to retreat from the camp. He flipped open the break of his blaster but then decided just to run.

The beast followed, opening its wide maw and releasing a roar that boomed like thunder. The rocky ledge shook as four more of the beasts dropped to the ground.

Miles barked at them and then looked to X for orders. He eyed the rifle, then the rucksack still tucked against the wall. They would have to come back later for the gear.

"Go, Miles!" X shouted. He motioned for the dog to follow him into the toxic rain. They could fight another day.

TWO

The launch bay reeked of sweat and fear. Captain Leon Jordan hated that smell. It was the bouquet of the *Hive*—a scent he had breathed his entire life.

Normally, technicians, engineers, and Hell Divers preparing for a descent to the poisoned surface would have crowded the bay. But today there were no flashing lights or countdowns warning of an imminent launch. That didn't mean the space was empty, though—far from it.

For the first time in the documented history of the *Hive*, there weren't enough Hell Divers to make a jump. Only three remained. Two of them were in the sick bay—one with a broken back from a mission years ago, and the other with cancer. The third diver, Jordan's former lover Katrina, sat in the brig.

Instead of the predive bustle, hundreds of citizens had squeezed into the launch bay to mourn the loss of the men and women who hadn't returned from the last dive. They all stared across the room at the smooth plastic domes like giant eggs covering the launch tubes.

Only a few knew that the divers hadn't all perished at the

Hilltop Bastion and that Jordan had chosen to leave them behind. The divers might very well have still been alive when he gave the order to leave them down there. But the traitors had made their choice—and paid the price.

"Today, we gather to honor the divers who gave their lives on the last dive to the Hilltop Bastion," Jordan said, his voice booming through the vaulted room.

Every face turned in his direction as he stepped out from the crowd and walked toward the launch tubes. Stopping at the first plastic dome, he turned and scrutinized those gathered.

At the front of the crowd, Lieutenant Hunt, Jordan's new XO, and Ensign Ryan both stood stiffly. They knew the truth about what had happened at the Hilltop Bastion, but as loyal soldiers, they would protect the truth with their lies or face the consequences. There were several others who knew what had happened. Men such as Ty Parker, who were not so trustworthy as Ryan and Hunt. The technician was now cooling his heels several cells down from Katrina. Jordan still wasn't sure just what Chief Engineer Samson knew, but the man had remained loyal so far, and he was far too valuable to throw into the brig—or jettison out of an air lock.

Jordan continued his scan of the crowd. Right of Lieutenant Hunt stood Sergeant Leonard Jenkins, commander of the militia. He also knew the truth. In fact, he knew more than any of Jordan's crew—especially about the false prophet, Janga. And while he had been loyal thus far, Jordan was starting to suspect that Jenkins didn't like the way he was running the ship. It was in the subtle things—the vaguely insolent slouch in his stance, the second of hesitation before following an order.

He would need to do something about Jenkins, but first he had to get everyone else in line. After letting out a rueful sigh that could be heard throughout the room, Jordan began the speech he had been planning for several days.

"Commander Michael 'Tin' Everhart, Commander Rick Weaver, Magnolia Katib, Rodger 'Dodger' Mintel, Layla Brower, and Andrew 'Pipe' Bolden might not have returned with fuel cells or supplies for the *Hive*, nor did they find a habitable place for us to set down, but their sacrifice was not without worth. Their loss, though regrettable in the utmost, proves a point that many of us have had a difficult time accepting."

He waited a few seconds before continuing. "They proved there is nothing down there awaiting humanity besides death. No miraculous green zone—no radiation-free area where we can sow new crops. Nothing... but... death."

He paused again to let the words sink in. Among the crowd were several lower-deckers, as evidenced by their poor hygiene and tattered clothing. A few of them shed tears; others held their heads high, choosing to honor the memory of the divers without showing any emotion. Jordan respected them for that. He had never trusted anyone who was overly emotional. People like Captain Ash, who put her heart before her brain. Doing so compromised a person, making it impossible to be rational.

One thing was certain: he had the unwavering attention of everyone in the room. Good. He was sick of the traitors, thieves, and snakes. The only way humanity would continue to survive on the *Hive* was through complete obedience. He would tolerate nothing less. The time for niceties was over.

"If anyone in this launch bay still believes there is something down there for us, feel free to step forward. I will happily instruct our technicians to give you a one-way ticket to the surface so that you may investigate further." Jordan gestured toward the launch tubes.

"Does this mean we're giving up the search entirely?" asked a deep voice.

Jordan searched the crowd to find the man who had

interrupted him, but he saw no one obvious. "Step forward if you wish to speak," he commanded.

The sea of passengers parted down the middle to disgorge a haggard-looking Cole Mintel.

"Are you saying my son gave his life just to prove a point?" he asked.

Jordan considered his response for a moment. The last thing he wanted was to make a scene with the disgruntled father of a dead Hell Diver. Besides, Rodger had played his part perfectly, using the Industrial Tech Corporation card Jordan had given him to reveal what was really down there.

"Your son died for far more than that, sir," Jordan said, opting for the truth. "Your son died by discovering what awaits anyone who sets foot on the surface."

Cole folded his muscular forearms, honed by countless hours of woodworking, across his chest. Confused faces centered on Jordan. He still had their attention. He was in control of the crowd, but to keep it, he would have to tell more of the truth than he had planned on. The truth about the world they feared, and the idea of a home that some still believed possible.

"Rodger and the other Hell Divers entered the Hilltop Bastion because of bogus information from Captain Ash," Jordan said. "Their deaths are on her shoulders, not mine. She had hoped that the Hilltop Bastion might be an area we could turn into a new home, but as I suspected, the bunker was nothing more than a tomb overrun by creatures out of a nightmare."

Cole remained standing in front of the crowd, with his dark eyes locked on Jordan. It was going to take more than this cryptic explanation to convince the father that his son had died for a noble cause.

Running his hand over the smooth plastic surface of a launch tube, Jordan said, "Captain Ash was right, in a way. The Hilltop

Bastion *was* a good place for humans to wait for the radiation to clear on the surface. But then the Sirens and other mutated beasts claimed it as their own home. Thanks to the information your son and his fellow divers retrieved, we can now focus on avoiding places like this and surviving in the skies."

"If you knew there were these Sirens down there, why did you send my boy?" Cole growled, lowering his arms and clenching his fists.

"You misunderstand," Jordan said. "I didn't know for sure." His eyes flitted to Sergeant Jenkins, who glared at Cole, ready to silence the man at a moment's notice. Jordan didn't want it to come to that. He wouldn't let anything disturb the fragile peace aboard the ship. The loss of so many divers at once had united the upper and lower decks for the first time in as long as he could remember.

"I'm truly sorry for the loss of your son," Jordan said, "but Rodger's death has reaffirmed what most of us already believed. Life will continue in the sky for the next two hundred and fifty years, until the radiation and electrical storms have finally abated."

He patted the launch tube one last time. Once, it had dropped the very bombs that destroyed the surface. Now it dropped the men and women who kept the ship in the air.

After a half minute of silence, Jordan forced a smile. "I was going to keep this confidential, but your son sent a final message to the *Hive*."

Cole squinted at him as if looking for the lie. "What did my son say?"

"He wanted his discovery of the monsters at the Hilltop Bastion to embolden us. He said he wanted more men and women to follow his lead and fight tooth and nail for the future of humanity."

Jordan waited a beat and then added, "Rodger knew that his death and the deaths of the other divers would leave a void, but in his final moments he sent a message of courage—and a challenge to those of us still breathing."

Jordan saw the bob of Cole's Adam's apple as he swallowed. His balled fists fell limply to his sides, and he slipped his callused hands into his pockets.

Jordan almost smiled. He had turned the tide with yet another beautiful lie. He pressed his advantage.

"Today, we're gathered not only to mourn the lost Hell Divers but to honor them as well. And in keeping with Rodger Mintel's final request, I humbly ask for volunteers. Who of you will accept his challenge? Who will step forward and become a Hell Diver?"

If the airship had a nerve center, Michael Everhart was sitting directly in the middle of it.

The smooth charcoal-gray bulkheads rumbled quietly throughout the bridge of the ITC airship *Deliverance*. Monitors and touch screens flashed data all around him. The bridge was a third the size of the *Hive*'s, and instead of split levels, it consisted of a singular circular space, with all stations positioned around a central island that served as a desk.

Bulkhead-mounted monitors surrounded the space, and a single leather chair sat facing the largest screen, at the helm, with a row of chairs behind the captain's. The one thing Michael missed from his old home was the ship's oak wheel. Here, there were modern flight controls for the captain and supporting pilots.

The differences in subtle details reminded Michael that this wasn't home and never would be. *Deliverance* was simply a vehicle that he would use to find Xavier Rodriguez before returning to the *Hive*.

He couldn't quite believe that X was still alive down there, but he also had trouble believing they had escaped the Hilltop Bastion in a brand-new ship. Well, *most* of them had escaped. Not everyone had been so lucky.

Commander Weaver and Pipe had lost their lives. And for what? To be used as pawns in Captain Jordan's private agenda? Their blood was on Jordan's hands, and Michael was going to make sure the son of a bitch paid for their deaths.

But first, he needed to figure out how they were going to survive.

He focused on the screens, taking in as much information as possible, but his expertise was with the systems of the *Hive*. *Deliverance* was much more sophisticated, a newer model than the ancient airship he had grown up on. And after a few hours of cleaning dust off the bridge, she shone as she must have coming off the assembly line two centuries ago.

He tapped the holographic screen in front of him and pulled up the flight data. Unlike the *Hive*, *Deliverance* relied heavily on turbofans and thrusters. It also had a single nuclear engine, and no helium gas bladders at all, which explained the smaller size. *Deliverance* also came equipped with the first artificial intelligence that Michael had ever met. Timothy Pepper, manager of the Hilltop Bastion, had transferred his consciousness to the sentient program upon his death. That program was now running the airship.

According to Timothy, this was *Deliverance*'s maiden journey. That didn't inspire confidence. Michael, Layla, Magnolia, and Rodger had spent the past two days working on a host of problems ranging from mechanical to electrical issues. Every time they fixed something, another alarm would beep, indicating a new crisis. Currently, they all were off working in different compartments.

"Timothy, can you give me a sitrep on our operating systems?" Michael asked.

"One moment, Commander Everhart," Timothy replied over the PA system.

Michael continued scanning the data while he waited, unable to relax his tired muscles in the firm leather seat. For the first time in his life, he was actually sitting in something "new."

"The nuclear engine is operating at eighty-five percent, and the energy grid is at seventy-five percent," Timothy said. "But several secondary systems are not functioning properly. Life-support systems are currently at fifty-one percent and dropping. Only three of six thrusters are working, and the turbofans are—"

The oval hatches to the bridge whisked open, and footsteps clattered across the metal platform, stopping Timothy in midsentence. Michael twisted in his seat to see who it was. Layla, his lover and best friend, stood silhouetted in front of the open hatch. By her posture, he could tell something else was wrong.

"There you are," she said.

The overhead lights flicked on, spreading a blanket of bright white over the room. Layla's freckled face was covered in grease, and her braided blond hair was draped over one shoulder. Pulling her hands from the pockets of the baggy blue sweatshirt that hid her athletic body, she caught his gaze.

He hurried over to meet her. "Hi," he said. "What's up?"

She smiled warmly. "Are you okay?"

"Yeah." He raised one brow. "You?"

Her deep-brown eyes flitted to the metal platform as some thought or memory passed through her mind, casting a cloud over her normally sunny features. She met his gaze again and sighed. "I'm hanging in there."

Before he could reply, she wrapped her arms around him in a tight embrace. "I guess I just missed you."

"I've missed you, too," he whispered back. Since leaving the Hilltop Bastion, neither of them had found much time to talk.

When they weren't working, they were sleeping, too exhausted to make love during the scant time they had alone together.

"Timothy was just giving me a report on the secondary systems," Michael said. "It's not good."

They pulled apart as the AI's translucent form solidified over the platform beside them. The computer-generated version of Timothy mimicked the real man, from the old-fashioned suit to the neatly trimmed hair and beard.

"Would you like me to continue that report, sir?" the AI asked.

"Not right now. How far are we from Commander Rodriguez's coordinates? And how long will it take us to get there?"

"I require additional parameters. At what speed do you intend to fly?"

Michael rubbed the bridge of his nose. Timothy looked and sounded like a person, but he was still a machine. "Obviously, I want to get there as fast as possible," he said, frustration bleeding into his voice.

"Until the secondary systems are functioning properly and at least one more thruster is working, I do not recommend flying at full speed," Timothy said.

"At our current trajectory, then. How long until we get to X?"

"It depends on weather conditions, Commander. The ship's meteorological systems are not functioning at optimal levels, either, which—"

"Just give me a number," Michael said.

"Sixty-two hours, fifteen minutes, and thirty-two seconds," Timothy replied.

Layla reached out and a put a hand on his back to rub his aching muscles. "We have time," she said. "X has survived this long. A few days extra isn't going to matter."

"But what if it does?" Michael asked, pulling away. He wasn't trying to sound rude, but she simply didn't understand. "We left him down there ten years ago. Can you imagine what that's been like for him? He's been all by himself the whole time."

Michael had thought of little else since learning that X was still alive. Days of wondering what he would be like now—or whether he would be able to forgive them.

"We have to get to him as quickly as possible, Timothy," Michael said. "To hell with optimum efficiencies. Full speed ahead."

"Understood, Commander."

Layla reached for Michael's hand. "Listen, I get how you feel..."

"Do you?"

She dropped his hand and shook her head. "I'm trying to help, but you're not doing a very good job of letting me."

"I'm doing my best to keep this mission going, Layla."

She looked back at him, her eyes filled with equal parts frustration and love. "I know. With Weaver gone, you're in charge. You hold rank. That means Mags, Rodger, and I are counting on you to make the right decisions for all of us."

"Meaning what, exactly?"

She sighed. "Meaning that tearing the ship apart just to reach X a few hours earlier is selfish. I'm sorry, but it's true."

Michael drew in a quick breath, intending to defend his position, but suddenly the passionate fire that heated his veins only moments before eased, cooled by her soft touch. She was right. He entwined his fingers with hers. "I'm sorry. I won't put our lives in jeopardy. I need to be patient. It's just..."

"You blame yourself for X."

"Yeah."

She kissed him, a light brush of her lips across his. "Michael, X being left behind is not your fault. It's Jordan's, and he *will* pay. Come on. Let's go find the others and get something to eat."

"Timothy, belay my previous orders," Michael said. "Keep us at a safe speed."

"Copy that, sir."

Michael followed Layla out of the bridge, his thoughts troubled. They were getting so close to the man who had been a second father to him, the man everyone had given up for dead. A few days ago, X had been nothing but a ghost, but in just over sixty hours, Michael could be reunited with the most legendary Hell Diver ever. What would they say to each other after all this time? Would X even recognize the man Michael had become? And, more troublingly, would Michael recognize X after his long ordeal on the surface?

The oval hatch whispered shut behind them. Lights along the floor illuminated the black metal bulkheads. Absent were the bright paintings and graffiti that covered the *Hive*. Michael was already missing the scenes that he used to look at every morning on his way to work. It was odd to walk through a passage that hardly anyone had ever used before.

"This place gives me the creeps," he said.

"Don't be a ninny, Tin," Layla said, chuckling.

"Really? You're still calling me that?"

"'Tin' or 'ninny'?"

A warning sensor cut the teasing short. "What's that?" Michael asked.

Timothy's smooth voice replied a moment later, "A minor fluctuation in the electrical grid. It is now at seventy percent."

They continued walking down the corridor. It was going to take a long time to search each of the quarters for supplies, but for now his focus was on getting the ship working properly. They passed the hatches of officers' quarters, then the berthing areas for the rest of the crew.

"This place is freaking massive," Layla said, "but it doesn't look like it was designed to hold as large a population as the *Hive*. There aren't enough cabins."

Michael pulled his shoulder-length hair back and looped a tie around it as he moved. "Seems that way."

"I guess it looks a lot bigger with just us four."

Timothy cleared his holographic throat.

"Us *five* aboard," Layla corrected herself.

"Thank you," replied Timothy's voice over the PA system.

Layla smiled. "Glad to hear you have a sense of humor." She whispered over to Michael, "Still don't trust him, though."

If Timothy heard her, he didn't reply.

Michael slowed when they reached the largest hatch on the ship. A sign that read WEAPONS COMPARTMENT crested the bulkhead. After losing most of their weapons and ammunition back at the Hilltop Bastion, this was the top room on his list of places to investigate. Michael tried to spin the wheel handle, but it wouldn't budge.

"Won't open?" Layla asked.

He shook his head and looked up at the closest of the black balls that served as Timothy's "eyes."

"Can you unlock this for me?"

"One moment," Timothy replied. A second later, he reported, "I am sorry, Commander, but the hatch is protected by an encrypted password."

Michael scratched the stubble on his chin and looked at Layla. She shrugged again.

"Can't you override it?" Michael asked.

"I do not have the appropriate permission," Timothy said. "These quarters were locked by General Stan Lorn on March 15, 2075. Overriding the system could trigger a self-destruct mechanism."

"What the hell is he talking about?" Layla asked. "The ship will blow up if we try to open that door?"

"We'll figure it out later. For now, let's leave it." Michael pointed with his head, and they continued to the engine-room hatch. Layla spun the wheel handle, and Michael helped her swing open the hatch. A dimly lit spiral staircase extended several floors down. Hot air blasted his face as he followed Layla into the bowels of the ship.

Halfway down, he wiped the beads of sweat off his forehead. The temperature continued to rise the deeper they descended. Near the bottom, he heard voices. *Loud* voices. An argument, from the sounds of it.

"I told you we don't have enough!" Magnolia shouted.

"We *do* have enough, but barely," Rodger replied. "You need to trust me!"

Layla stopped at the open hatch below Michael and flung a glance up at him. He motioned for her to keep walking and followed her out into the engine compartment. Catwalks stretched across the second level, overlooking the generators and engines.

"So you're going to be the one to tell Commander Everhart?" Magnolia asked. "Because I sure as hell don't want to break the news."

Magnolia and Rodger were standing near a wall of lockers, and she held what appeared to be a parachute. The hum of machinery filled the lull in their conversation.

"What's going on here?" Michael asked.

Magnolia whirled to face him. She brushed a strand of blue hair over her ear and snorted, pointing at Rodger. He wiped his forehead, then looked in Michael's direction. The tape holding the rims of his glasses together had come undone, and one of frames sagged over his eye. He pushed it back up, then used his sleeve to wipe the grease off his forehead. When he didn't reply, Magnolia spoke for him.

"We only have enough material to make two parachutes, but

Rodger thinks we can extend it to three, maybe even four, which I say is dangerous as hell."

Confused, Michael looked back to Layla. "Why do we need parachutes?" he asked.

She sank her hands in the pockets of her baggy sweatshirt and looked away. Michael turned back to Rodger, knowing he would get a straight answer out of the man—Rodger couldn't lie to save his life.

"Tell me why we need parachutes," Michael asked again.

Timothy's hologram suddenly flickered in the space between Michael and Rodger. Everyone looked at the AI.

"Commander Everhart, I do apologize for not telling you earlier, but it is not safe to land *Deliverance* at the coordinates Mr. Xavier transmitted, due to a massive electrical storm."

"And you didn't tell me this because…?" Michael said.

"I would have earlier, but you cut me off."

"I thought you said the weather sensors aren't working properly."

There was a pause. "Is that a question?"

"Yes."

"Then that is correct, Commander," Timothy said. "The meteorological sensors are not working properly, but radar has picked up a storm covering one hundred square miles over the source of the last distress signal. In order to reach Mr. Xavier's location, you will need to dive through the storm or proceed on foot for approximately fifty miles over radioactive territory."

THREE

Xavier Rodriguez watched the storm from the safety of an ancient vehicle stranded at the edge of a cliff. Thunder rumbled—a constant din that shook the metal bulkheads around him. For hundreds of years, the armored truck had sat on the crest of a hill once covered in thick forest. The former occupants, a pair of soldiers, were now buried beside the deflated tires. X had decided to honor the old way of putting humans to rest by digging holes in the earth and covering them with dirt.

He was safely back inside the rusty armored truck now, sitting behind the steering wheel, in a cracked leather seat, with Miles curled up next to him. The interior was surprisingly well preserved, considering its age. It had also provided one of the best finds ever: maps showing military bunkers across the United States. These weren't ITC facilities, and he hoped they would have power cells, food, weapons, and perhaps even other people.

Leaning forward, he examined the lettering on the bulkhead. It was some sort of model number. What little he knew about the Old World was from experiences like this. The vehicle was called a Stryker and had served as a mobile command center for troops during war. While the electrical and mechanical systems had stopped working long ago, one of the scopes still functioned, and he was confident he could get the radio back online.

Through the thick glass window, he watched the bowl of the storm swirling over the flattened city. Yellow light churned deep inside the guts of the clouds.

A scratching noise made him jump, and Miles looked up as a spider with purple legs skittered over the glass. It pecked at the bulletproof glass with its beaklike jaws and then looked at X with a dozen bulbous eyes.

"It's okay, boy," X said. "Just a bug."

The creature pecked at the window again, then moved to the upper right corner, where it attached itself to the glass with limbs tipped by suction cups.

"Looks like we have a new friend," X whispered.

He didn't mind, as long as it stayed outside. Suddenly, a vision of a bite wound filled his mind. Venom from the wound melted the man's skin, slowly consuming the entire leg. The scene was from twenty years ago, when X had been forced to watch a fellow diver succumb to a bite from a spider like the one outside. The mutated arachnid could kill a grown man in seconds with a single bite.

The storm belched webs of electricity over the city below, lashing the decaying structures over and over. From this vantage point, X could see a huge crater on the other side of the city. The bomb had leveled almost everything, leaving behind nothing but twisted metal and concrete foundations. The hill the vehicle sat on was burned bald, with not even a tree stump left behind. Rocks and boulders peppered the steep slope, their surfaces glazed and sooted even now, centuries after the nuclear explosion.

It was only a guess, but perhaps these soldiers had driven to the top of the hill to assess the damage after the blast. For some reason, they never left the vehicle again, dying inside the mobile command center. Perhaps it had been from radiation poisoning or some other illness. The bodies had been too badly decomposed to tell.

At least the monsters didn't get them.

In the strobe flash from several lightning strikes, a flitter of motion caught his eye. He followed the movement to a sinkhole in one of the streets. The silhouetted form slithered into the opening and vanished. The openings in the streets led to vast sewer and rail systems under the city, and he avoided them at all costs. A human and his dog had no place setting foot down there.

Still, he would need to find a way across the debris field sooner or later. They couldn't wait here much longer. He was low on food again and down to two blaster shells and one magazine for his rifle.

Miles looked up, sniffed the air, and reoriented his furry body. They had been hiding inside the vehicle for several days, maybe more. X had lost track of time again.

The sporadic boom of thunder continued. It was calming, in a way. X wished he could stay sheltered here longer, but he still had hundreds of miles to go before he reached the coast.

He looked at the spider once more and then flipped the hatch down over the inside of the window. Darkness filled the interior. He lit an emergency candle and placed it on the dash before climbing into the command center behind the front seat, where he lit a second candle. The flames cast a warm glow over the monitors and radio equipment. Several bucket seats faced the equipment, all of them covered in fine dust.

Miles followed X into the compartment and sat at his feet while he reached into his vest and pulled out the book. In the dim light, he scanned its contents. A picture fell out. He held up the image of palm trees swaying in the wind on a beach. Teal water slapped the edge. This was where he was headed, although he knew it wouldn't look the same.

Two years earlier, as X was starting to lose his mind, he had found the image during a raid of an abandoned bunker. He had also found the book then. The pages had been empty, but now they were filled with his words and other things he had collected over the years.

The book helped him remember those he had lost: Rhonda, his wife, and Aaron Everhart, his best friend. It also contained descriptions of the people he was still searching for: Michael Everhart, Magnolia Katib, and Katrina DaVita. He had described them to the best of his memory so he might never forget.

There were also pages dedicated to the people he had some serious questions for. People such as Captain Maria Ash and Lieutenant Leon Jordan—the people who had left him behind.

After recording a note to himself about the spider's venom, he set the book on the bench, next to the candle, and reached into his pack. He took out a power pack and set it by the radio, then connected them with the attached cord. He then used a second cord to patch his wrist monitor into the power pack.

Miles watched curiously as X jabbed at the cracked touch screen of his wrist computer. As the radio equipment charged, he tapped into the system that would allow him to transmit on any open channels.

"Maybe Captain Ash will hear this one," he mumbled to himself.

Miles wagged his tail at the sound of X's voice. X reached out and stroked the dog's soft fur. If he didn't have Miles, he wasn't sure what he would do. He looked up, trying to remember how old his dog was now. They had been together since Hades. For an entire year, he had resisted the temptation to break into the cryogenic chambers and choose a companion for himself, and then he and Miles had stayed another year in Hades. They had left that city around four years ago. That put Miles at about five years old. Had it really been that long since X last saw another human? Six entire years?

He went back to petting his dog, hoping that the genetic

modifications ITC had made to his DNA would keep him healthy for many years to come.

A deep wistfulness passed over him. X had no such modifications, and every day that passed, he grew older and weaker. The radiation exposure and injuries had taken their toll. He wasn't sure how much longer he could keep going.

You have to keep going. You can't ever stop.

If he died, Miles wouldn't be able to survive in the wasteland. X had selfishly chosen to break the dog out of his cryogenic sleep, so it was his responsibility to take care of him.

The radio equipment suddenly crackled, and the screen flashed blue. Data began scrolling across it.

"We're in business, Miles," he said with a satisfied nod. Using his wrist computer, he pulled up their current coordinates. The database revealed they were in the foothills of a place that had been called Asheville, North Carolina. The name meant nothing to him, but he scribbled it down in his book so he could remember it later.

"Asheville. Asheville, North Carolina," he said. "A town made of ash."

The dog wagged his tail again. He didn't care about the words; he was just happy to hear his friend's voice.

Reaching for the radio receiver, X repeated the ritual he had performed at dozens of locations over the years, relaying the same starting message. "If anyone's out there, this is Xavier Rodriguez, currently broadcasting from Asheville, North Carolina. I'm heading toward the coast."

From time to time, he also added the coordinates of locations he had raided that yielded food, water, weapons, or fuel cells, just in case someone *was* listening—someone like Magnolia, Weaver, or Katrina. If X could help them, he would, even if it also helped the bastards who left him for dead.

He lowered the receiver and waited, listening to the hiss of white noise from the ancient speakers. They crackled loudly, sparking Miles' attention. The dog tilted his head at the radio, then let out a low whine.

X tuned to a different frequency, repeated the same message, and continued the process. On the fifth try, a sound answered. It started as a high-pitched wail that X almost mistook for the radio. Almost, but he knew better by now.

He shut off the device and scrambled out of the command center, into the front seat. Just as he opened the hatch to look outside, a boom of thunder sent a tremor through the metal bulkheads.

Miles followed him, tail between his hind legs.

"Keep quiet, boy," X said.

He pressed his visor up to the hatch and held in a breath as a brilliant flash of lightning captured the shapes of long-limbed beasts racing through the streets. Darkness once again reclaimed the land, and X waited for another flash.

The next strike was even more vibrant than the last, illuminating the debris field directly below the bluff—and more Sirens, skittering over the foundations of old buildings near the bottom of the hill. Eyeless leathery faces searched the darkness for prey. Most had already homed in on the vehicle.

Each flash of electricity showed the beasts advancing. It wouldn't be long until they reached the slope and began to climb.

X swallowed and looked away, taking a moment to think.

He could make a run for it with Miles, but they wouldn't likely get very far. Perhaps it was safer to stay here, sealed inside. He returned to the command center and checked that the hatches were secure. Both were rusted thin, but they would hold.

A second later, the bone-chilling screech of the beasts cut through the rumble of thunder. The fur on Miles' back stood straight up, like the spines along the creatures' backs. X slowed and deepened his breathing, preparing for the attack.

The wait wasn't long. A Siren smashed into the side of the Stryker, the clank of bone on metal echoing inside. Another jumped on top, claws scratching over the armor. Two more slammed into the side.

The sound of a beast pulling on the hatch handle above froze X to the core. He pulled the blaster from his thigh holster and pointed it overhead. His other hand grabbed the rifle and propped it against the bulkhead. Then he unsheathed his blade. If the beasts somehow found a way to open the hatches, he would make them work for their dinner.

For the next hour, the creatures crashed into the Stryker and pounded against the rusty armor. Their angry cries rose into an electronic howl that made X's ears ache as they became more desperate to get inside. Miles hunkered on the floor, blue eyes wide with fear. X wanted to comfort the dog, but he dare not say a word. Maybe the beasts would leave.

But that was wishful thinking, and he knew it. The Sirens knew they were here, could sense them somehow, whether by scent or by sound. Whatever the case, they weren't going to give up easily.

Maybe this was what the soldiers had felt like years ago. Trapped, at the mercy of a threat they could not see.

As the minutes ticked by, X lowered his blaster and knife to ease the strain on his shaking hands and arms. He had stopped flinching each time the Sirens knocked against the vehicle.

Just as he was about to whisper words of encouragement to Miles, the onslaught stopped.

The silence was short-lived. Several squawks sounded, short and sharp. X had heard them act this way only a few times before. One would cry out, and another would answer in their other-worldly language.

The Sirens were planning something.

A heavy body crashed into the back hatch, sending a vibration through the vehicle. X nearly fell off the bench. He raised his rifle at the metal door.

Another jolt hit from the rear, rocking the entire truck. Two more Sirens and then a third slammed into the hatch all at once, and this time X did fall onto the floor.

Before he could get up, the vehicle rocked again from the impact of more bodies. The force pushed the vehicle several feet.

"Oh, shit," X whispered.

Flipping open an armored peephole, he could see the monsters working together to push the Stryker over the cliff. One stood on its hind legs, extending its wings. Its black lips opened and released a high-pitched wail.

As if on cue, a half-dozen Sirens charged from a hundred feet away. They came running all at once, their bony heads angled downward, fins cutting through the air. Several more swooped in from above. They smashed into the back of the Stryker.

X staggered backward. He quickly righted himself and grabbed Miles. He put the dog in a bucket seat and buckled the harness across his body, then sat beside him and clicked a belt across his chest armor.

The next impact pushed the vehicle to the very edge of the bluff. The front seemed to dip, and X held in a breath.

The beasts hit harder the next time, and he felt the vehicle teeter on its undercarriage. There was a sickening lurch, and for a second, all sense of motion vanished.

Miles let out a whimper as the vehicle accelerated down the slope. The front of the Stryker smashed into rocks, jerking X back and forth with each impact.

Through gritted teeth, he said, "Hold on, buddy."

FOUR

Captain Leon Jordan tried to shake off the recurring nightmare as he walked through the dimly lit passages of the *Hive*. In the dream, Xavier Rodriguez would slice Jordan's throat from ear to ear with a rusty blade. Jordan tried to plead for mercy, but that only made X push harder on the blade until it hit bone.

Jordan always woke up bathed in sweat, breathing heavily and reaching for his throat. And now he didn't even have Katrina to comfort him in the early morning hours. She had betrayed him, which hurt worse than the torture of the nightmares.

Holding up his wristwatch, he checked the time. 0600 hours.

Almost everyone on the ship was still asleep, but he had a feeling Katrina would be wide awake by the time he got to the brig. Deep down, he still held on to hope that she would change her mind, that she would see that he only wanted to save the human race. That everything he had done was to secure a future for her and their unborn child.

Two guards flanked him as he worked his way through the winding passages of the ship. Rusted steel hatches covered the portholes on the bulkheads, and in the faint glow of the overhead lights, he studied the bright drawings of fluffy white clouds, blue skies, and happy sun faces painted on them. Ever since he was young man, having put aside childish fantasies, he found the artwork disturbing. Why hide the truth?

He halted for a moment and then turned to the guard on his right.

"Ensign Lore, I want these hatches removed and used for scrap," Jordan ordered. "People should see what's really out there."

Lore scratched at the back of his neck but didn't say anything. He didn't need to; reluctance was written across his face.

"Those have been here for a hundred years, sir," said the other guard, a thickset man named Del Toro. "My grandfather helped paint—"

Jordan took a step closer to both guards, staring them down without saying another word.

"Yes, Captain," Lore said. "I'll... we'll make sure of it."

Jordan continued around the next corner, the two guards hurrying to catch up. Ahead, two women from the lower decks emerged from an open hatch. He examined the contents of their baskets as he passed. A handful of undersized tomatoes, some of them still green, which told him things were getting even more desperate below. The women avoided his gaze and walked in the opposite direction, toward the trading post, while Jordan and his escort continued to the brig.

Red helium pipes snaked across the overhead. The gray fins of sea creatures cut through the faded blue ocean scene decorating the pipes. The images reminded him of Janga's prophecy. She had claimed that a man would lead them to a new home near an ocean filled with strange fish. The dangerous rhetoric had forced Jordan into the position he was in now, with most of the lower-deckers hating him and everything he represented. He took a moment to imagine her body smashing into the surface twenty thousand feet below. The image filled him with grim satisfaction. He no longer had to worry about Janga, at least.

"I want this artwork . . ." Jordan paused. "I want this *shit* removed."

Lore nodded. "I'll add that to the list, sir."

Jordan continued walking toward an intersection. The bridge was to the right, but he turned left instead. Many of his staff lived in this wing, but he hadn't been here for a while. Over the decades, the occupants had added little decorations to the bulkheads and hatches.

He recalled long ago, when he was just a child, scribbling his own drawings along this passage. His mother was dead by then, and his father spent most of his time in the water treatment plant where he worked, or at the Wingman, drinking his sorrows away, and hadn't been around to teach him right from wrong.

He walked slowly toward room 789 and stopped outside the hatch. Memories flashed in his mind's eye as he reached out to touch a faint picture of a star-filled sky. He ran a fingertip down the metal to a sketch of a stone castle. He had seen something like it in a book—a place surrounded by white walls with fields of crops, and pastures where he could ride a horse, and streams where he could skip stones or fish for food.

Everyone on the *Hive* had imagined an ideal home at some point, a fantasy cobbled together from pictures and old videos along with rumors and daydreams. But none of those places existed anymore. The closest thing to a castle on the surface, Jordan knew, was the Hilltop Bastion, a concrete bunker that housed only monsters, not knights and princesses.

He yanked his hand away from the hatch as if it had burned his flesh. There were no fairy-tale castles. No safe havens. No heaven.

Only hell.

Children needed to grow up knowing the truth instead of holding on to dreams of the past.

"I want the *Hive* purged of every single painting, sketch, drawing, and graffito," Jordan said. "I want the bulkheads and everything else scrubbed clean. Anyone caught defacing the ship will be subject to loss of rations, or time in the brig. Repeat offenders will be dealt with harshly."

The guards nodded, their faces expressionless, and prepared to follow Jordan, but after a few steps, he halted in the middle of the passage.

"Del Toro, I want that order carried out immediately," Jordan said. "Lore, follow me."

"Aye, aye, Captain," Del Toro said.

Footfalls receded in opposite directions as the men parted ways. Jordan continued toward the brig, but when he got there, he didn't stop. Lore remarked on the change of route this time, but Jordan ignored him. Three turns later, they stopped.

"Stay here," Jordan said.

He opened the wide doors to the launch bay and stepped inside. Across the room, past the launch tubes, four silhouetted figures paused their routine of push-ups and stood. While most of the ship still slept, the new Hell Divers trained.

Sergeant Jenkins stood watching with his sleeves rolled up to midbiceps, showing off old muscle covered in militia tattoos. Jordan wasn't sure exactly how old the man was, but he had to be nearing sixty—a venerable age aboard the *Hive*. In many ways, Jenkins was a legend, much as X had once been.

The soldier lowered his arms to his sides and stiffened as Jordan approached. He saluted. The divers followed his lead.

"Good morning, Captain," said the sergeant.

"We'll see about that," Jordan said.

He stopped to scan the new divers. Jenkins had been tasked

with vetting the three volunteers from the ceremony and scouting two more individuals for a complete dive team. So why did Jordan see only four divers?

"Form a rank," Jenkins said gruffly.

Jordan walked through the maze of launch tubes and stopped ten feet from the new divers, who were now standing side by side. He knew their names already but decided to let them introduce themselves.

"Name, age, and occupation," Jordan said. He paused for a second and then added, "And tell me why you're here."

Jordan nodded at a thin man dressed in black pants and a button-up blue shirt.

"Tom Price, age thirty-four, assistant cook," the man said. "I volunteered to be a diver because my wife and daughter could use the extra rations."

Jordan nodded, unimpressed. His eyes flitted to the next diver, a short woman with dreadlocked hair and piercing blue eyes. She reminded him a bit of Magnolia.

"Jennifer Hodge, forty-one, farmer. I'm here because my daughter was diagnosed with cancer and she needs treatment."

She held Jordan's gaze, and he could tell she was angry. Whether it was directed at him or at her situation, he wasn't sure. She would need to be monitored.

Next came Lester Mitchells, the tallest man on the entire ship. The tuft of thinning brown hair on the top of his head reminded Jordan of some sort of extinct bird.

"Les Mitchells, but most people call me Giraffe," he said with a wry smile. "I'm thirty-five years old and have been an electrician my entire life."

Jordan waited for him to continue, but Mitchells simply looked at him.

"Why did you volunteer?" Jordan asked.

"Oh, right." Mitchells scratched his scalp. "I'm here because I ain't got no choice. My boy got caught stealing, and Sergeant Jenkins said my service will reduce his sentence. My wife is sick and needs meds—something I can't afford. I was promised help in return for service."

Jordan glanced at Jenkins. The sergeant's reluctance to meet his gaze did not inspire confidence. Was Jenkins hiding something? Was he *planning* something?

The more Jordan thought about it, the more his unease grew. After Katrina's betrayal, he had no one left he could fully trust—not even the loyal sergeant who had served in the militia for almost as long as Jordan had been alive.

You can trust yourself—and only yourself.

Jordan looked at the final recruit, a well-built man with thick strawberry-blond eyebrows that seemed to be trying to make up for the lack of hair on his bald pate.

"I'm Don Olah, with the militia. I'm here because I want to continue serving my ship and my captain. I feel diving is the best way to do that, sir. I will happily give my life so humanity can continue in the sky."

Jordan nodded at him, acknowledging his bold words. *Finally, a man worthy of being a diver.*

"While I appreciate those of you who volunteered, I will remind you that this is not a job. Diving is a *duty*—a duty that men and women have done for hundreds of years. Most of you are here because you want to help your families, but I suggest you start thinking like Ensign Olah." Jordan paused and added, "If you fail, your families will die—along with all the rest of us. You are humanity's last hope."

Olah saluted, but the other three just stared blankly ahead, either too afraid to speak or too overwhelmed by the burden of the captain's words to muster up a salute of their own.

"Since you're all new, we're going to start with green-zone dives," Jordan said. "I've got a list of places I want you to scavenge."

"Sir, could I speak to you in private for a moment?" Jenkins asked.

Jordan looked at the divers once more before following Jenkins over to the operations room. As soon as the door was shut, Jordan let out a sigh and said, "This is the best we have left on the ship?"

"No, but the best all hold important jobs," Jenkins replied. "We can't afford to take men out of engineering or the water treatment plant right now. It's a matter of bodies—we don't have many left."

"We have four hundred and eighty-four passengers, and you're telling me we don't—"

"Sir, with all due respect, have you been to the lower decks lately?"

Jordan paused and then shook his head.

"Most everyone below our boots is starving or sick. They don't have the energy to train, and they definitely don't have the energy to dive. Most of them aren't educated, either, and it would take too much time to explain how all this works."

Jordan cursed. Losing Michael Everhart and the others had come at a heavy price. With their deaths, the *Hive* had lost not only experienced divers, but engineers as well.

"What about the fifth diver I asked for?" Jordan said. "Certainly you can find one more. I eventually want two teams again, maybe even three."

"I'm still working on it, sir. Thought maybe we could make some sort of an arrangement with that technician, Ty Parker."

"Negative," Jordan said. "Parker is a traitor, and I don't trust him. He knows too much. I can't afford to let him out of the brig."

"I say give him the ultimatum: dive with a chute as long as he keeps his mouth shut, or dive without one."

Jordan eyed the collection of framed photographs, some of them dating back decades, that covered one wall of the operations room. Dozens of Hell Divers stared back, their expressions ranging from cocky to scared, to stoically noble. "As it happens, I've taken matters into my own hands."

Jenkins raised a gray eyebrow. Jordan pushed the black bead of his headset comm link to his lips. "Lieutenant Hunt, send our recruit to the launch bay."

"Roger that, Captain," Hunt replied over the channel.

"Our fifth diver will be here in a moment," Jordan said. "Is there anything else you wanted to report?"

"Yes, sir. There's one other thing."

Jordan clasped his hands behind his back and waited.

"Sir, you tasked me with *finding* the divers, but I have no idea how to train them. I'm a militia man, not a Hell Diver."

"That won't be a problem," Jordan said. He studied the wall of photographs and stopped on Aaron Everhart, Michael's father, who had died on a mission over a decade ago.

Jenkins looked confused. "Lane and April are the only two divers left, and they're both out of commission. Unless you mean to release Katrina?"

Jordan looked next at the photo of Katrina, pinned up beside Xavier Rodriguez, the ghost that haunted his dreams. The two had been lovers, and he had to admit they made a good-looking couple. For years, Jordan had wondered whether Katrina still missed X, but now it didn't matter. She hated Jordan, and he doubted there was anything he could do to convince her he wasn't a villain.

Still, he would protect her. Not in the hope of rekindling their relationship, but for their child.

"Not Katrina. She's pregnant, and she is . . . unpredictable. I won't have her train these divers. I've found someone else—someone who went through the training and even has several dives under her belt."

As they left the operations booth, the fifth and final diver walked into the launch bay.

"There she is now," he said.

Turning, Jordan studied the sergeant's features. His face had gone slack with shock at the sight of the short, dark-skinned young woman walking across the bay. She moved quickly with a stride that exuded confidence.

"Erin?" Jenkins said. "What the hell are you doing here?"

She raised a hand and said, "Hi, Dad."

*   *   *   *   *

"This is the biggest damn storm I've ever seen in my life," Magnolia said. She stood in front of the radar station with Michael, Rodger, and Layla. The island of radar and operational equipment chirped, beeped, and flashed data.

They had finally managed to fix the third and fourth thrusters, increasing the ship's speed, but Magnolia still had a laundry list of other things to get back online. Her gut growled. The ship wasn't the only thing running low on power.

"Looks like a real queen bitch," Layla added after taking another look at the screen. "I never saw anything like it."

Rodger leaned down for a closer look. "This is one hell of a monster. It's got to stretch over a hundred miles of coastline."

"One hundred and thirty miles of coastline, approximately," Timothy confirmed. "The weather sensors are online now, so I can break it down in feet and inches if you would like."

"No, that's okay," Michael said. He massaged the bridge of his nose and drew in a breath. "We're going to have to put down on the edge and trek in. No way in hell we're going to dive through that."

Rodger nudged Magnolia in the side. "See? Told you, Mags."

She rolled her eyes. "That's actually not what you said."

"Sure, it is. You never listen to what I—"

Michael snapped his fingers. "You're too smart to be that dumb, Rodger Dodger. Now, stop arguing for a damn second. I know you're all tired, and we're still grieving, but Weaver and Pipe sacrificed their lives so we could continue with this mission."

"I'm sorry," Magnolia said.

"Yeah, sorry, Commander," Rodger said.

Michael nodded. "There are still multiple secondary systems that aren't working, and we're running low on food and water. This isn't the *Hive*. There's no farm or water-treatment plant."

"I don't mean to be a nag," Rodger said, putting a hand on his gut, "but I'm really hungry. Not sure I can work much more without eating something."

"We all are," Michael said. "So let's stop complaining and suck it up." He looked over at Timothy's hologram. "Bring up a map of the area. I want to identify the best LZ."

"One moment, Commander." The hologram vanished and then reappeared at the helm. A map bloomed across the white surface. The divers gathered around behind the leather chairs that faced the island.

"This is the source of the SOS," Timothy said.

A red X marked the map. The irony wasn't lost on Magnolia. The spot was where their own X had last transmitted from.

"It is an old city called Miami," Timothy said. "The storm covers much of what's left of the eastern coastline."

"What do you mean, 'left'?" Michael asked.

"I've retrieved the most accurate map I could find in the database. But much has changed since that map was created. Most of what was once southern Florida is now permanently underwater."

"So how the hell did X get there?" Rodger asked.

"He's X," Magnolia said with a shrug. "If any human could make it across a place like that, it's him."

"He's still alive," Michael said firmly. "I can feel it."

There was a moment of silence. Magnolia had a feeling that Rodger and Layla weren't necessarily believers, but it didn't matter now. They had come too far to give up.

"I have identified several potential landing zones," Timothy said. Three more red marks showed up on the map. "No matter which one you choose, you will have to traverse at least thirty miles through swampland."

"Sounds lovely," Layla said.

Magnolia had heard tales from other divers—legends passed down from the time when there were more airships in the sky—but no one from the *Hive* had ever traveled there. The thought of exploring it made her heart quicken from fear and excitement.

She reached for Rodger's hand but stopped short and slipped her hand into her coverall pockets instead. She had spent her entire life being afraid of getting close to people after losing her family, her lover, then X, and now Weaver. Everyone she had ever cared about ended up dying.

Not everyone, she thought. *X is still alive.*

Her eyes flitted to Michael and Layla, who stood side by side, studying the topographical holo map over the center island. They had found each other when they were just kids. Somehow, they were still together—much longer than most couples. And while Magnolia felt a connection with Rodger, she didn't have room in her heart after it had been shattered so many times.

"I'd like to study the potential LZs before I make my decision," Michael said. "In the meantime, we need to find food and water. Without supplies, we won't be able to trek three miles, let alone thirty."

Magnolia followed the others around the stations in the

central island. She stopped when she saw motion on the radar screen. Something was moving near the right edge, in or over the ocean, which made no sense.

"What the hell is that?" she said loudly enough to make Michael stop and look over his shoulder.

"What the hell is *what?*"

When Magnolia looked back down, the blinking dot on the radar had vanished.

"Timothy, are you picking up any contacts in that storm?" she asked.

"Negative," said Timothy's voice over the PA system.

"Mags, stop messin' around," Rodger said.

"I thought I saw something," she said. She checked the radar one more time, brushing a strand of blue hair behind her ear, then joined the other divers in the spacious cabin adjoining the bridge.

They all had been living in the captain's quarters for the past few days. Although Magnolia didn't say it, she was too afraid to sleep alone.

Inside, several bunks and two desks were pushed together. On the metal surface were the supplies they had salvaged after fleeing the Hilltop Bastion.

"We have three rifles, three blasters, and four revolvers," Michael said. "We're down to five flares, fifteen shotgun shells, three magazines of 5.56-millimeter rounds, and twelve .45 rounds for the revolvers."

Layla picked up a canteen. "We've got about a pint of water left between the four of us, and we've got one meal if you count these calorie-rich bars from the *Hive*."

"How are we doing on battery power?" Michael asked, pointing to his armor unit.

Rodger shook his head wearily. "Not good. Our batteries are

all below thirty percent. I think I can rig up the system to charge them, but I need time."

"I can help with that," Magnolia said.

Michael leaned on his palms over the desk. Several rebel strands of hair fell over his face and he brushed them behind an ear as he looked down at their gear.

"Timothy, have you finished your search of the ship's database for other weapons?" he asked.

"Yes, Commander." Timothy's hologram reappeared at the other end of the table. "The armory is stocked with hundreds of weapons of various calibers, and tens of thousands of rounds of ammunition. In addition, there are—"

"Let me guess," Rodger interrupted. "We can't get to any of it without triggering the alarm that will in turn set off the self-destruct system."

Timothy dipped his translucent head in agreement.

"What about water and food?" Magnolia asked. "Have you found anything in the quarters we haven't searched yet?" She knew there had to be rations somewhere on this ship, but so far, they hadn't found any.

"My memory unit is still damaged from the Hilltop Bastion," said Timothy, "and there are certain places I cannot access. I can, however, tell you which rooms may contain supplies, given the number of lockers present."

"Good," Michael said. "We'll split up and start searching. As soon as we're done, I want Rodger and Mags to start working on the batteries, but right now, food and water are our priority. If it's on the ship, we need to find it."

"A word of caution," Timothy said. "I do not believe you will find what you are looking for."

Michael had already turned away from the table, but he halted and glared at the AI. "Why is that?"

"Because *Deliverance* was not built to support passengers for long periods of time. That was never its primary purpose."

"Neither was the *Hive*," Rodger replied, "but we retrofitted it."

"There was no reason to retrofit *Deliverance*," Timothy said, "nor was it ever used for its primary purpose."

There was a moment of silence. Magnolia squinted at the shimmering image, trying to make sense of what he was saying.

"Wait," she said, her gut tightening. "What else is in the armory? You were going to say something before Rodger cut you off."

"The armory contains twenty-five mega nuclear warheads. They are one thousand times more powerful than a normal warhead. Each of them would produce an explosion large enough to destroy twenty-five hundred square miles."

Magnolia had never been good at geographic distances, but even she could visualize how big an area that was. It was hard to imagine a weapon that could create a fireball of that magnitude, and while she had seen the results—the charred surface and the storms raging in the skies—she would never understand why humans had destroyed their beautiful world.

"This is a warship," Magnolia whispered. "A world ender."

Everyone looked at her, even Timothy, who said, "Precisely, Miss Katib."

FIVE

Les Mitchells felt uneasy as Erin Jenkins led the new divers to their lockers in the launch bay. Her reputation preceded her: strong, smart, beautiful, and aggressive. And she was also the sole survivor of her former Hell Diver team, Wolf. Years ago, they had been caught in the middle of a dust storm that impaled one diver with a steel pole, crushed another, skinned a third alive, and broke the back of the fourth.

If the rumors were true—and Les had no idea whether they were—then Erin had survived through ruthlessness, not luck. People said she had left her teammates to die while she saved her own skin. Mitchells wasn't sure about that. So far, he liked her. But he didn't have a lot of confidence in someone not yet thirty with only a few dives under her belt.

She's also here to train your sorry ass, he thought as he approached the lockers. Even from here, he could see the stickers, sketches, and engravings left on the lockers by their previous owners.

"Claim one," Erin said, "but respect the divers who came before you. We don't remove anything from these lockers." She opened a door marked with a picture of a Wolf.

He stepped up to a locker and bent down to look at a picture of a bird with yellow eyes, a hooked beak, and black head with white wing feathers.

"Team Raptor," Erin said, nodding. "That dynasty ended with the deaths of Michael Everhart and his team at the Hilltop Bastion."

Mitchells thought about choosing another locker, but he didn't want to appear weak. Besides, he rather liked the fierce-looking bird, and the crest on its head reminded him of his own hair.

She looked to the other divers. "To honor tradition, we'll come up with our own team name and symbol, but not right now. Today, we're going to get acquainted with the gear."

"You got anything to fit Giraffe?" Tom Price, the cook, asked. He grinned, revealing two missing front teeth.

Les shrugged a shoulder. He was used to the ribbing about his height, but he was worried about the same thing. At nearly seven feet tall, his body wasn't designed to fit on an airship with low overheads and tight quarters, and no armor was going to fit him without major modifications.

Les opened the locker and ran his finger over the pictures left by previous owners. On the interior door was an image of a smiling Hell Diver with his hand on the shoulder of a boy wearing a shiny foil hat.

"Aaron Everhart," Les whispered as he recognized the father and son.

Erin leaned over and peered inside. "He was a good man."

Les nodded. "I was in school with Aaron a long, long time ago. He always wanted to become a Hell Diver. I'm not surprised his son became one, too. My boy, Trey, looked up to Michael. He's a few years younger, but they liked each other."

"Aaron wasn't just any diver. He was one of the best." Erin studied the picture. "So was Michael."

She stepped away, and Les watched the other new divers shuffling through the contents of their lockers. Tom pulled out a partly charred leg guard with his finger and thumb as if picking up a dead rat.

"Most of this gear is very old," Erin said, noticing Tom's expression. "Divers are expected to take excellent care of their armor and weapons."

"This guy did a pretty lousy job," Tom said. He tossed the piece of armor back inside, shut the door, and moved to another locker.

Les went back to going through the equipment in Aaron's old locker. The suit didn't look all that small when he held it up. The armor, however, would definitely need significant modifications. The chest piece, which should have come down to his belt, came down only as far as his navel.

Don Olah watched him struggling and laughed. "You'll be a hell of a target for lightning...and the Sirens."

Les chuckled at the first part, but the second made him pause.

"Won't be any Sirens where we're going," Erin said. She winked at Les as if to say, *Trust me.*

He continued struggling with his chest gear, trying to forget the stories about monsters living on the surface. The Hell Divers weren't supposed to talk about it, but every once in a while, one of them would spill the beans, and the tale would spread through the decks of the *Hive*.

"All right," Erin said. "Close your lockers and join me in the operations room."

Les shut the door with a click. He could tell by the look on Erin's face that she had bad news. The others, some of them halfway out of their new armor, were all looking at her.

"Screw it, I'm just going to tell you now," Erin said, running a hand over her short, curly Mohawk. "We have three days to get you ready for something that most divers spend months, even years, training for."

"Three days?" Tom asked. "We're supposed to dive in *three frickin' days?*"

Les didn't know what to think. He had volunteered to help his family, but he hadn't figured on ending up dead. His daughter was too young to work, his son was in the brig, and his wife was too sick, which left him as the sole provider.

"Captain's orders," Erin said. "Come on, let's get moving."

Too shocked even to grumble, they finished stowing their new gear in silence. Erin jerked her head at the lockers they were leaving behind. "One hundred and thirteen, if you're wondering," she said. "That's how many divers have come before you."

"And they're all dead?" Jennifer asked.

Erin nodded. "Everybody but me, Katrina, and the guys in the med ward."

"Is that supposed to inspire confidence?" Tom replied. "I would think you'd try to make us feel better or something, especially after you just told us we're diving in three days."

"It's to put things in perspective," Erin said.

They walked past several launch tubes and stopped outside the entrance to the operations room.

"We're going to focus on green zones and storm-free skies," Erin said. "Easy stuff. No Sirens, no giant beetles, no carnivorous plants."

Jennifer muttered under her breath, "Shit, there's plants that *eat* people?"

"Will you be diving with us, ma'am?" Olah asked.

Erin hesitated for a moment and looked over her shoulder. Les assumed she was checking to see whether her dad, Sergeant Jenkins, was in the room.

"Yes," Erin said, "I'll be diving with you. But Command doesn't know that yet, so keep it between us."

Les blinked. He had assumed that Jenkins and Jordan would have worked out some sort of deal to keep Erin safely aboard the *Hive*. Some said she had been yanked from active Hell Diver duty after her daddy pulled some strings, and he was surprised that she planned to join them on the surface. Surprised—and a little worried. He couldn't forget the other rumors he had heard about her and the fate of her old team.

Erin clapped her hands together. "Let's get to it. In three days, we're diving to an ITC facility that's apparently flush with fuel cells and other parts the *Hive* desperately needs. There's a lot to do before then."

Jennifer raised a skeptical brow at Les. He grinned back at her. He didn't know Jennifer well, but he could tell they were going to get along—even if it wasn't for very long.

Olah, eager as ever, looked at the other divers. "You heard her, let's move it, people."

Les wasn't sure about the militiaman. He seemed to have some grandiose idea about dying for the *Hive* out of duty. Not Les. He was more like Tom and Jennifer, who were here to help their families. The idea was *not* to get killed.

For the next several hours, in the ops room, they ran through the module training that simulated a typical dive. It turned out diving involved much more math than Les had originally thought. That was okay; he was pretty good with numbers.

"Running calculations while diving through a storm is not easy," Erin said. "In fact, it's next to impossible, especially when your HUD is offline. That's a *heads-up display*, in case you didn't know. You won't be able to communicate or use your night-vision goggles. You must use this." She tapped her skull.

"Our suits will protect us from lightning, right?" Jennifer asked.

"There's a synthetic layer built in that will help deflect electricity, but it won't save you from a direct strike. We're not diving through the really bad storms, so you won't have to worry about that."

The launch bay doors creaked open, and the divers all turned to look out the ops room window. Two militia soldiers walked into the bay with Captain Jordan.

"I'll be right back," Erin said. "Run through the simulation again while I'm gone."

She left the divers behind to sit and stare at the screens.

"*Three days* before our first dive?" Jennifer said after a moment, flipping a dreadlock over her shoulder. "This is fucking crazy."

Tom tapped the table. "I hope they include firearms training, because the only weapon I've ever used is a knife, and that's only to butcher guinea pigs and chickens in the kitchen."

Jennifer snorted. "I didn't sign up to die in three days. I thought it would be a while before we actually dived."

"We're going to be fine," Olah said. "I'm trained on many different weapons, and I'll show you how to use them. I don't know about you, but I personally plan on breaking Xavier Rodriguez's and Rick Weaver's records. Look at this as an opportunity, not a death sentence."

Les wanted to laugh, but he managed to keep a straight face. He wanted to tell Olah the truth: that the overeager ex-militiaman would likely be the first to splatter on the surface or get torn apart by some mutant beast.

In his experience, people who wanted to be heroes usually ended up dead.

*   *   *   *   *

"Your parents think you're a hero, Rodger Dodger," Magnolia said. "Try to stop worrying. You *will* see 'em again."

"You can't know that." He sulked for a moment longer, then looked up and said, "I miss my parents so much, and I still can't believe Jordan used me. That worm-eaten pile of goat shit!"

Magnolia looked over her shoulder as they walked down the passage. "Doesn't surprise me in the slightest. Bastard tried to kill me by cutting my chute."

"I'm going to wring his neck," Rodger growled, bringing his hands together around an imaginary throat.

Magnolia halted in the dark passage and turned. "No one touches Jordan but me," she said, poking Rodger in the chest. "You got it?"

Rodger swallowed and nodded. Not that Magnolia scared him, but he didn't want to do anything to upset her. She finally seemed to be warming to him, and he didn't want to blow it now. The elephant he had carved for her peeked out from a side pocket of the small pack she carried over her shoulders, and he eyed it with a smile.

Nice work, Rodgeman. Nice work, indeed.

She walked away, and Rodger did his best not to gaze at her backside as he followed her into another wing of the ship. Clusters of crew quarters branched off from the main corridor. They would need to search them all, for a prize could await behind any one of these doors.

"I don't understand why the residents of the Hilltop Bastion didn't retrofit this ship and take it into the sky," he said.

Magnolia smirked. "*Really*, man? You're smarter than that. It's pretty clear to me why."

Rodger didn't like her condescending tone. "Why's that, then?"

"Everyone was already living belowground. And they didn't need a warship, because the whole world was already destroyed."

"Oh." Rodger shook his head. "So *Deliverance* just sat there waiting all these years, still armed with enough bombs to blow up the world a second time?"

Magnolia raised a brow. "Yup. Now, come on. We have to get to work. You take the hatches on the left; I'll take the right."

Rodger threw a salute and grinned, but Magnolia didn't return either gesture. Clearly annoyed, she walked over to the closest hatch and spun the wheel until it clicked open.

"Good luck," she said.

"You, too."

Rodger opened the first hatch on the left. He entered, took in a draft of stale air, and flipped on the bank of overhead lights. Only one bulb flickered to life, revealing a small room furnished with a desk, bed frame, and couch. The desk drawers were already open, and the bed had been stripped of sheets. He checked the closet, pulling back a drape to find two metal cases, both of them open and empty.

It looked as though someone had already raided these quarters. But how was that possible? Rodger went back out to the passage and tried the next hatch, with the same result. The third and fourth were also empty—not so much as a towel or pillowcase left.

The fifth hatch was stuck. He braced his shoulder against the metal and pushed with all his strength. Inside, something groaned and scraped, like the sound of metal grinding against metal.

"Come on, Rodgeman," he whispered.

Grunting, he shoved the hatch open and stumbled into the room. The entrance had been blocked off from inside with the desk, bed frame, and several chairs. He flipped on the light. The grate covering the vent had been removed and lay in the center of the floor. Bending down, he examined some deep parallel gouges in the floor. It was as if someone had dragged a pitchfork over the metal.

Feeling uneasy, Rodger stood and backed out of the room. The next room was also blockaded, and he could shove the hatch open barely more than inch. He peered inside. A streak of something brown was smeared across the floor, and he decided that he didn't want to get inside after all.

"Mags, I found something you got to see," Rodger called out.

When she didn't reply, he jogged down the final stretch of passage and rounded the corner. Magnolia stood outside another hatch, grunting as she tried to twist the wheel.

"Help me with this," she said, her face red from the strain.

"Hold on, I found something back—"

"Just help me, Rodger Dodger."

He hurried over, grabbed the handle, and tried to spin the wheel. It wouldn't budge.

"There must be something good in here," Magnolia said. "Something worth protecting." She stepped away from the hatch and looked up at the overhead. "Hey, Timothy, can you unlock this hatch?"

Timothy's hologram suddenly appeared. He approached the bulkhead to examine the dusty number.

"Room ninety-one," he said quietly. "I...I remember this place."

Magnolia exchanged a glance with Rodger.

The locking mechanisms clanked inside the hatch. Timothy stepped to the side and gestured for the divers to enter.

"If you would, please," he said. There was something else in his tone beyond politeness. It made Rodger hesitate.

Magnolia grabbed the wheel handle and spun it until the hatch clicked open. The draft of air that came from the room smelled slightly different from the stale scent of the other quarters.

When Rodger turned on the lights, he quickly saw why. He took a step backward from the human remains and bumped into Magnolia so hard, she slapped the back of his shoulder in protest.

"Ouch!" he grunted.

Her eyes widened when she saw why he had stumbled into her. Timothy drifted into the room, brows crunched together.

Rodger moved out of the way so that Magnolia and Timothy could have a full view of the three dried-out bodies lying face-down on the floor. They were clothed, but their skin and flesh had shriveled over the years. To the right, the legs of a smaller body protruded from under one of the beds. Something dark had spattered the bulkheads.

"I told you I found something," Rodger said. "The Sirens, or maybe something even worse, must have found a way onto the ship, and some of the residents in the Hilltop Bastion must have hidden in this cabin. Maybe we should get out of here."

"These people died a very long time ago," Magnolia said. "Whatever did this is long gone."

Timothy knelt in the center of the room, a few feet from the boots of the first victim.

"I recognize this place," he said. His normally smooth, calculated voice sounded strained. "I know these people."

The AI glanced over his shoulder at Rodger and Magnolia. "I knew them."

Magnolia nudged Rodger gently in the side and widened her eyes as if to ask, *Is he all right?*

"Can you please help me?" Timothy's holographic form flickered. "Can one of you turn these people over?"

Rodger pulled his gloves out of his back pocket and put them on as he walked over. Bending down, he moved the first corpse with the utmost care, revealing the mummified face of a dark-skinned woman. At least, that's what it looked like, though the body was so old it was hard to tell. Wispy hair tangled around her head. Her eyes were gone, and she had a small bullet hole in the center of her forehead.

Timothy let out a whimper as he leaned closer to the woman. Rodger hesitated but then flipped the next body. It was another woman, this one much younger than the other but with the same dark skin.

"No," Timothy moaned. "It can't be."

Rodger had studied the science of AIs aboard the *Hive*, so he knew they were capable of displaying emotion, but this seemed over the top. He looked at Magnolia, who stood wide-eyed in the doorway.

"Please," Timothy said, lips trembling. "Show me the faces of the others."

Rodger grabbed the small shoes of the body under the bed and pulled it out into the light with a horrible crackling sound. It was a child, maybe eight or nine years old.

Timothy let out a wail, his hands coming up to his mouth.

Rodger looked at Magnolia. She gave him a wary nod. He continued to the fourth body. It was larger than the rest, dressed in dark pants and a button-down shirt. In its bony hand, the corpse gripped a pistol.

When he turned the body over, Rodger gasped.

Although the face was shriveled, there was no mistaking the perfectly groomed beard. Rodger quickly scooted away, looking from Timothy to the body and then back again.

"It's...That's..." Rodger tried to say.

"Me," Timothy replied. "This was my family. This is where we died."

SIX

X awoke to the scent of something burning. He had a thudding headache. Beyond the ringing in his ears came a sound that snapped him alert. The distant wail of emergency sirens was bad enough, but an even more troubling noise came from inside the Stryker: the yelp of an injured dog.

Frantic, he tried to stand up, earning himself a jolt of pain in his right shoulder. The crash had dislocated it.

"*Shit,*" he grumbled. Sucking in deep breaths to manage the pain, he grabbed the harness with his other hand. The belt around his chest armor had saved him from smashing into the controls across the room.

Thunder boomed, rattling the bulkheads. Blood sang in his ears, and his head continued to pound, but he finally managed to focus on the immediate space around him. What he saw made no sense. The floor was now the ceiling. The truck had landed upside down. He blinked away the stars and glanced over at the seat next to him, and then at the ceiling—now the floor—where Miles sat on his haunches. Blood trickled from the husky's muzzle and down the front of his white coat.

"It's okay, boy," X whispered. He didn't like lying to the dog, but there was no sense in scaring him.

Miraculously, one of the emergency candles had survived the crash without going out, and still filled the compartment with an orange glow. But as his vision cleared, he saw that it wasn't just the light of a single candle. The book where he kept his memories was on fire, too. The flames had already charred the outside edge of the pages.

"NO!" he yelled.

With his left hand, X unbuckled his belt. The fall to the ceiling wasn't far, but he cried out in pain when he hit the metal overhead. The impact had done the trick, at least, and popped his shoulder back into place. But the fall had also caused another problem. The metallic taste of blood filled his mouth. He had bitten right through the side of his tongue.

Miles limped over and licked X's face as he heaved himself up onto his knees. He crawled away from the dog and grabbed the book, the flames licking his gloves. He blew on the cover, but that only made the flames grow stronger.

Desperate, he clutched the burning book against his chest armor and then smothered it against the floor. Smoke puffed out from under his body, filling the compartment. He coughed and turned away, eyes stinging.

The candle wick burned in a wax puddle a few feet away from the hatch. Blinking, he saw, in the flickering glow, something moving he hadn't noticed earlier. The hatch was open. The rusty locking mechanism had broken in the crash.

X forgot about his book, leaving the smoldering pile on the inverted roof. He wasn't sure how long the airtight seal had been broken, but neither Miles nor he was wearing his full radiation suit and helmet. Given the rad levels in this area, even a few minutes of exposure could make them sick, and he was all out of the rare pills that would protect him and Miles. He could almost feel the gamma rays cooking his insides.

X scrambled for his helmet and slipped it over his head. He chinned on the NVGs, grabbed his rifle, and crawled over to put out the candle. In the green hue of his optics, he examined the hatch. He tried shutting it several times, but it wouldn't latch.

"Shit, shit, SHIT!" X slammed his armored fist against the hatch.

The screeching of the Sirens filled his ears, and the sound of Miles yelping made his blood boil. Would their journey end here, like this? Were they really going to die in this rusty old-world shit can?

Fuck that.

He wasn't going to die tonight, and he sure as hell wasn't going to let the monsters get their claws and teeth on his dog. X had questions to ask the people in the sky, and a score to settle with those who had left him down here for dead.

He pushed the hatch open and drew his blaster. A squeeze of the trigger sent a flare streaking across the dirt. It exploded, red blossoming over a field of debris. In the ruddy glow, the long shadows of four-legged creatures came down the slope, their spiky backs raised, conical heads down, bounding over the toxic dirt.

Lightning cracked against the foundation of an ancient building to the left of the Stryker, rattling him for a moment. He holstered the blaster and grabbed the rifle.

Ducking through the hatch, he brought the weapon up, holding the buttstock right where it hurt worst. Too damned angry to care about the pain, he fired a round at the lead beast, a monster with a wrinkled white hide. The Siren crashed to the ground in a mangled heap of limbs, blood spurting from a chest wound.

"Stay here, Miles!" X said. He closed the hatch and pivoted toward the hill to see the slope crawling with the creatures. At least a dozen Sirens were skittering down the dark terrain to avenge their fallen comrade.

Behind X, the electrical storm raged above the crater that had leveled everything within fifty miles. Nets of lightning blasted the rubble.

It was a toss-up whether the lightning or the beasts would get to him first. If he survived those, he still might get radiation sickness. Miles was genetically modified to handle brief exposure to higher doses, but X still needed to take out the Sirens and get him back into his suit.

He picked out a Siren scrambling down the slope and fired a round that hit it in its sinewy torso. Losing its footing, it pitch-poled down the hill, somersaulting in a cloud of black dust and ash.

Three more came leaping over the rusted carcass of an old-world vehicle. He took two of them down with well-aimed shots to their misshapen heads.

Lightning struck the ground between him and the third beast, sending it galloping for cover. He shot it in the spine before it could retreat.

Several more of the creatures took to the air in his peripheral vision. He checked the targets still on the ground, counting four. They were fanning out across the bottom of the slope, preparing to make a run across the two hundred feet of rubble that separated X from them.

Scratching sounded on the hatch behind him, but he didn't turn. It was Miles, trying to get into the fight.

X fired three more quick shots at the advancing monsters. They were close enough that he could hear the popping noise as the rounds cut through their leathery hides. Blood painted the mud as the creatures fell one by one.

And yet the beasts still came, flapping overhead, hurtling down the slope with their black maws open, running across the flat.

Bringing up his rifle, X fired the final rounds of his last magazine into the sky, scoring hits to the wide wings of a Siren. It cartwheeled to the ground, screeching in its high-pitched alien wail.

Lightning flashed near the two remaining airborne Sirens, and they swerved away. He slung the rifle over his back and unsheathed his machete. Holding the blade in his left hand, he drew the blaster with his right.

Four of the Sirens were almost on him. He fired the final shotgun shell into the biggest one as it charged on all fours. The blast took out its left arm, separating it at the elbow.

The other three charged, screeching with rage. He stared at the eyeless faces, listening to Miles clawing at the hatch, and the rumble of thunder over the dead city. X readied himself, dropping the blaster and pulling out his combat knife. Raising the two blades, he dropped into a loose, ready stance with his boots firmly planted.

The first beast leaped into the air, claws extended and jaws open. Saliva webbed across its jagged teeth. X jabbed the knife into its mouth, spearing through the soft palate and into the brain.

An edge of the knife had lodged in bone, so he let go and moved out of the way. The creature slammed to the ground with the blade stuck inside its brain. When the second Siren turned to check on the plight of its kin, he swung the machete, slicing a deep gash in its back and exposing ribs. It screamed in agony and scrambled away, making way for the third and final monster to plow into X.

They thudded to the ground in a mass of tangled arms. Air burst from X's lungs. He had landed on his back, with the machete between his armor and the creature's flesh. He pushed up on the blade, cutting into the Siren's torso. Wailing and writhing in pain, it reared back, gripping its side to keep its entrails from falling out.

X didn't give the thing a chance to run. He hacked at it over and over again, spraying his armor with its blood. The sickening crunch of each stroke rang out until the beast finally crashed to the ground.

He wiped the gore off his visor.

Another screech sounded behind him, and he turned to see the creature he had wounded earlier lunging for him. There was no time to avoid the claws. Elongated nails raked over his armor, and one of them sliced through his suit, opening one more gash on his scarred flesh.

He winced in pain. It slashed again, but this time X jumped to the side. The creature fell onto all fours, and X swung the machete down on the exposed back of its neck, cutting so deeply that the head hung by strands of sinew. Another slash, and the head fell away.

Gasping for air, he staggered away from the carcass as blood jetted from the stump. He looked out over the killing field of dead beasts, their blood steaming in the darkness. Flashes of blue illuminated the reddened mud.

He dragged himself back to the vehicle and opened the hatch. Miles jumped out, but X herded him back inside. He had to get them both patched up and their suits fixed before the monsters returned.

As he secured the hatch behind him, he looked at the shattered radio. He hoped his message had gotten through to someone before the crash. Then he saw the remains of his book— the picture of a beach and palm trees, his precious words, and the other memories now nothing but ash. He gripped his bleeding side, telling himself that the tears prickling his eyes were from the physical pain of his injuries.

He gritted his teeth and stuffed the maps of military bunker locations into his vest. Those just might end up saving his life in the future. There was no time to despair over the words he was leaving behind. All he could do was keep moving.

*   *   *   *   *

Michael dashed down the corridor, losing Layla in his wake. With the ankle she had sprained several days earlier on the surface, she simply couldn't keep up. He knew he should wait for her, but he couldn't afford to slow down. He was too anxious to see what Rodger and Magnolia had discovered.

His and Layla's search had uncovered nothing but empty quarters. Someone had already been through the ship, stripping it of valuables and supplies.

It took him another ten minutes to get to room 91, and by the time he reached the open hatch he was winded—not from the fast pace, but from lack of food. He was exhausted, and without proper nutrition, he was running on fumes.

Michael stopped to catch his breath, and Layla caught up with him. Her face was even paler than usual and slick with sweat. They both were young. It shouldn't be this tiring to get from one side of *Deliverance* to the other.

"You okay?" he asked.

Layla simply nodded and walked past him, into the room where Rodger and Magnolia were standing over Timothy's flickering form.

"What the…?" Layla said. "Why are there mummies in here? Who are they?"

Timothy let out a racking sob, the hologram blinking in and out. Translucent tears dripped from his eyes, fizzling into nothingness before they could reach the floor.

Michael hadn't known that AIs could cry.

"Commander, may I speak with you?" Rodger asked.

Michael pointed with his chin down the corridor, and Rodger joined him outside while Magnolia whispered soothing words to the distressed AI.

"We have a problem," Rodger said.

"I can see that," Michael replied. He grabbed the hatch and quietly shut it so they could talk in private.

"Apparently, those corpses were his family, and...I don't even know how to say this." Rodger looked back into the room. "That's Timothy's body in there."

Michael let out a breath. "Holy shit," he said. "Wait, I thought he was the final survivor of the Bastion and transferred his consciousness to the AI program."

"Apparently, that was *after* he killed his entire family," Rodger said.

Michael eased the hatch open a sliver to peer inside, eyeing the pistol in the original Timothy's dead hand.

"I'll be damned," he said. He unconsciously reached for his own holstered pistol as he considered what would drive a man to do such a thing. Facing similar circumstances, could he ever shoot Layla? The idea made him sick, but he could imagine scenarios where it would be better than the alternative.

"He must have wanted to end things his way," Michael whispered. "To keep his family from being ripped to shreds by the Sirens."

Rodger saw him reach for the gun but didn't understand the reason. "Don't worry, Commander, the Sirens are long gone. This all happened hundreds of years ago."

Timothy stood and finally turned to face Michael, holographic tears still streaming down his face.

Michael relaxed his grip on the pistol and let his hand fall to his side. He pushed the hatch open and walked inside with Rodger.

"I'm very sorry, Commander," Timothy said. "My memory was damaged when Rodger and Magnolia activated my program at the Hilltop Bastion. Some of the older memories are just now coming back. It appears my programming suppressed them for obvious reasons. Seeing the bodies brought them back."

Timothy winced, his brow furrowing as if he relived his painful last moments. He reached up and put a hand on his head. With his other hand, the AI pointed to a bookshelf propped against the right bulkhead. "Commander, would you please move that?"

"Is that real oak?" Rodger said, stepping over to take a look.

"Just give me a hand," Michael ordered.

Together, he and Rodger moved the shelf to reveal a four-foot-high door built into the bulkhead and secured by a touch-screen keypad. Michael tried to open it, but it was locked.

"One moment," Timothy said.

A click sounded, and the door popped open, revealing shelves stacked full of supplies.

"We came here to hide from the beasts while most of the other residents hid inside the facility," Timothy said. "But when the Sirens entered the ship, my family…we decided to end things quickly. We never got a chance to use these supplies, but perhaps they will help you."

Michael reached in and pulled out a container of dried food. Blaster shells, flares, food, and containers of water in sealed packages were arranged neatly on the shelves. It would keep Michael and his team alive for weeks, if not longer.

"I'm sorry about your family," he said, turning from the shelves. "Sorry you had to see them like this."

Timothy dipped his head, and when he looked up, it was as if the storm of emotions had never happened. He met Michael's gaze. "Will you do me one favor when I drop you off on the surface, Commander?"

"Sure, Timothy. Whatever you need."

"Will you please bury my family? They deserve that much, and in my current form, I am unable to give them a proper burial."

*   *   *   *   *

"Your daughter won't have to dive as long as you do your part, Sergeant," Jordan said. "That means carrying out every order without so much as a flinch. You got that?"

Sergeant Jenkins stood across from Jordan's desk in the office inside the bridge. He nodded solemnly. "Yes, Captain. You have my word."

Jordan met the soldier's gaze, searching for the lie. The last thing he needed right now was to worry about Jenkins plunging a knife into his back.

But Jordan had a contingency plan in case Jenkins betrayed him.

"If you do decide to ignore this conversation, Erin will dive again—without a chute. Got it?"

Jenkins nodded again, his nostrils flaring with anger. That was okay with Jordan. Who wouldn't be mad?

"It's nothing personal, Sergeant. I'm just trying to ensure the survival of everyone on this ship. We need your daughter to train the new recruits, and I need to make sure you don't get any bright ideas."

"I wouldn't dream of that, sir."

Jordan took another few seconds to study Jenkins before dismissing him. As the hatch swung open, he saw Ensign Ryan, waiting for him on the platform outside the office. Ryan shifted his glasses higher on his nose—a nervous habit that told Jordan something was wrong.

"What is it?" Jordan asked.

Ryan glanced over his shoulder to make sure no one was

listening. The platform was empty, and the officers stationed on the levels of the bridge below them were all focused intently on their screens, monitoring everything from the water pressure to the electrical storms.

"Captain, I've intercepted another message from Xavier Rodriguez," Ryan said quietly. "I'm not sure how old it is, but this one is from a different location than the others."

Jordan gestured for Ryan to enter the office. The hatch sealed them inside, and Jordan opened a desk drawer. He retrieved a map marked CLASSIFIED and spread it across the small table across from his desk. On the map were dozens of locations where they had picked up X's transmissions over the years. Jordan had kept the project a secret, revealing it to only two other people aboard the *Hive*.

"Go get Lieutenant Hunt," he ordered.

Ryan left the room, and returned a few minutes later with the XO. Leaning down, Jordan examined the locations of the other messages. They formed a squiggly line away from Hades, toward the coast.

"Where was he transmitting from this time?" Jordan asked.

"A place called Asheville, North Carolina. He claimed there's an ITC facility with more of that synthetic food. You know, the kind that looks like strings."

"Yes," Jordan said, annoyed. "I'm aware of what it looks like. What else did he find? I'm not risking a dive for food that will last us only a few months."

"Fuel cells and livestock embryos," Ryan said.

Jordan straightened his back and massaged the wrinkles on his forehead. "We are in desperate need of more chickens."

"Here are the coordinates," Ryan said. He pulled out a piece of paper and placed it near the map, then took a pen from his uniform and circled the location.

Jordan had never taken the time to memorize the old states until he started following X's journey. Now he could practically draw the map from memory.

"Damn, he's getting close to the ocean," Jordan said. He walked over to his desk and sat down in front of his monitor. He touched the screen and brought up another map that showed the radiation levels across the continent.

"Looks like Asheville is in the middle of a red zone," Jordan said. "I'd be amazed if he made it out of there alive. It's got to be crawling with Sirens."

"He's surprised us before, sir," Hunt said.

Jordan looked around the monitor at Hunt. "Excuse me?"

"Sorry, sir," Hunt said. "I'm sure you're right."

There was no trace of sarcasm in Hunt's tone, and Jordan turned his attention back to the monitor.

"The facility is on the outskirts of the city," Jordan said. "It looks like it's in a yellow zone." He checked the current location of the *Hive*. "We're about two hundred and thirty miles west of Asheville. I had planned on checking out several green zones with the new divers, but this is one hell of an opportunity."

"Sir, you'd send novice divers into a red zone?" Ryan asked, sliding his glasses up his nose.

"It's a yellow zone," Jordan said with a shrug, "and if they die, I can always recruit from the lower decks. I've also got Ty Parker in the brig. Jenkins seems to think we should let him dive. His daughter would be a better option, but I made him a deal, and I'm going to honor my word."

"Parker is a risk," Hunt said.

"Tell me something I don't already know, Lieutenant."

"Sorry, sir."

"I've made my decision," Jordan said. He looked up from the map. "Change our course for these new coordinates."

Hunt nodded. "Yes, sir."

"And if anyone asks why, tell them we found something in the database about this location. You will not mention the transmission. Clear?"

A second nod from Hunt, and a "yes, sir" from Ryan.

"That's all. Dismissed." Jordan plopped back down in his leather chair and studied the radiation map on his monitor as the men left.

This wasn't his first time searching facilities X had visited. Each one had turned up supplies. The irony wasn't lost on him. The diver he had left behind continued to keep the airship in the sky by providing locations of areas with food, fuel, and weapons. Jordan would continue to use the man until his luck finally ran out.

SEVEN

Almost two days after discovering the remains of Timothy's family, they reached the edge of the massive storm. The AI was now preparing to set *Deliverance* down on the very surface it had been designed to destroy. Magnolia and the other divers stood in the cargo hold at the stern, watching through the starboard portholes.

"I like the new look," Rodger said, gesturing with his eyes toward Magnolia's hair.

She gave her freshly cut locks a casual toss and winked at him. Last night, she had gotten sick of the way her hair was always falling in her eyes, and asked Layla to help her hack it off. She hadn't been able to touch up the cobalt streaks in her hair, but she rather liked the way they had grown out and faded. The tips were a soft blue—the color the sky was supposed to be.

Two miles to the east, the colossal electrical storm rolled across the horizon in every direction. Magnolia always thought of the storms as living beasts. The flashes were constant, lighting up the monstrous belly. The churning clouds parted briefly to reveal the yellow heart of the storm. There was no way they could fly through the storm, and diving was out of the question.

"The surface will be safer than the sky," Michael said as if reading Magnolia's mind. He turned from the view to look at the divers in turn. He got two nods in reply, then a low belch from Rodger.

"Sorry," Rodger said, wiping his mouth. "I . . . really don't feel so good."

Magnolia clapped him on the shoulder. "Suck it up. If X can survive a decade down there, you can push through a stomachache."

Rodger burped again.

"You good to go or not, Rodger?" Michael asked.

"Good to go, Commander."

Michael said to the AI, "All right, Timothy, start the descent. Everyone else, let's gear up."

Timothy's hologram vanished after acknowledging the order. Since encountering his own corpse, the AI had kept to himself, only answering direct questions or helping when beckoned, and today was no different. He was turning out to be very human, expressing emotions beyond what Magnolia could possibly have expected from a computer program.

The corpses lay in state on the loading platform at the other end of the cargo bay. Blankets covered them, and a shovel was on the floor beside them for when they landed. It was the old way of burying people, during a time long before the *Hive*. Timothy had asked them to follow the old tradition.

Magnolia forced her gaze away and circled around the only furnishing in the entire cargo bay: a metal table bolted to a bulkhead, where they had set out their diving gear and supplies. The dull black armor that had saved her life countless times was waiting for her to put it on. She fastened the clasps on both sides, tightening them an extra notch for the weight she had lost.

"I had to do the same thing," Rodger said with a grin. He patted the black armor covering his belly. "I've probably lost ten pounds in the past week."

"You were too skinny to begin with," she said. "And you could use a shave."

He scratched his straggly beard. "I thought ladies liked a man with a little scruff on his chin and chest."

Magnolia took a swig of water from her bottle before holstering the canister on her duty belt. For the first time in days, she felt refreshed, but she was still nervous about the long trek across the radioactive landscape, especially through a swamp—even if it was to find X.

The divers continued donning their armor, working together to clip the tricky pieces. They completed the routine by inserting the battery units into the socket in their chest armor. The blue glow from the heart of each suit warmed to life, spreading across the room. Michael's glowed red, due to modifications he'd made before his final dive from the *Hive*, giving his battery a longer life than the others'.

Rodger fished in his pack and handed out four black patches. "I made these from material I found in the engineering wing. It's a synthetic polymer—very rare."

Layla held hers up. "Where's it go?"

"Over your battery unit," Rodger said with a roll of the eyes. He slapped his on his chest. "I even added some magnets so they lock on to our armor."

"Okay, so why do we need these?" Michael asked.

Rodger looked at the commander the way he might look at a slow child. "They'll lessen the energy footprint that our suits give off."

"So these things make us invisible," Michael said.

Magnolia examined the patch, impressed. Rodger was without a doubt one of the smartest men on the *Hive*.

"Nice work Rodger Dodger," Layla said, slapping him on the shoulder.

Rodger smiled and pushed his broken glasses farther up

on his nose. "I was also able to fully charge all the units," he announced proudly. Magnolia threw him a glance, and he added, "Thanks to Mags."

"Good job," Michael said. He tied his hair back and then pulled up the ship's database on the touch-screen monitor attached to the table.

"I picked the closest LZ to the signal, putting us within twenty-five miles," he said. "There was a road here at one point. My hope is we can take it to Miami and avoid most of the swampland, but we won't know until we set down."

A hologram shot out of a center console, displaying a translucent image of the landscape twenty thousand feet below.

Rodger scratched the back of his head nervously. "Any idea what kind of radiation levels we should expect down there?"

Everyone looked at Timothy, who had reappeared by the bodies resting on the liftgate. The AI bent down and reached out as if to touch them. Magnolia had some concerns about his behavior. Her heart broke for the program, or man, or whatever he was now. No one should have to see their family like that. But they still needed Timothy to do his job.

Michael seemed to have the same thought. "Timothy, are you okay?" he asked.

The AI nodded, finally turning back to the team. "Yes, Commander."

"You're sure?" Layla asked.

Timothy shifted his gaze from Michael to Layla. "I am functioning within normal parameters."

His words didn't seem to convince Michael, who gestured for the AI to join him. They stepped aside to have a private chat.

"Let's finish up here," Magnolia said to Rodger.

"He's off his rocker, man," Rodger whispered. "Can AIs lose their shit? Because—"

"Let Commander Everhart deal with Timothy," Magnolia said. "You just focus on not puking, okay?" She grabbed two long curved blades that looked like double-edged sickles off the table and slid them into sheaths that buckled across her chest armor. The new weapons would replace the knife she had lost at the Hilltop Bastion. She had already rewrapped the old metal hilts.

Next, she stuffed flares and extra shotgun shells into the front of a nylon bandolier around her thigh armor.

Rodger chose an ax from their gear—another tool they had found on the ship. He had cut it down into a more practical weapon by removing half the handle.

"I'm honestly more worried about what we're going to find on the surface," Layla said quietly. "Assuming we survive the radiation and monsters down there. What if we've come all this way for nothing? What if X is just a skeleton?"

"He's alive, trust me," Magnolia said. "You were too young to remember him, but he—"

"Bullshit," Layla said, stepping up within inches of Magnolia's face. "I remember him just fine."

Michael returned before Magnolia could reply. His youthful features were strained, and she could tell he was nervous about more than the expedition to find X. He didn't need Magnolia picking a fight with his girlfriend.

"Something wrong here?" he asked.

"Nope, we're good," Magnolia said firmly. Layla held her gaze for a second before backing off.

The hull suddenly creaked, and the floor vibrated as the ship began to lower through the clouds.

"Initiating landing procedures," Timothy announced. "We're at twenty-two thousand feet. We will arrive at the landing zone in ten minutes."

"You heard him," Michael said. He pulled the blaster out of

his thigh holster and dropped a flare and two shotgun shells into the break. The other divers finished their final preparations, with the clatter of magazines being slapped into weapons.

It wasn't exactly predive jitters, but Magnolia felt a messy combination of fear and adrenaline working through her system. The ship jolted again as they lowered through the sky. Lightning flashed outside the portholes, but they were too far away from the storm for the distant thunder to rattle the bulkheads.

"Ten thousand feet," Timothy announced.

"Start scanning the LZ for heat signatures," Michael ordered. He watched the map on the center console. A green overlay appeared, but not a single heat signature blinked back during the first scan. It looked as though the ground was clear. Michael folded a map on the table and slipped it into a waterproof sleeve while they waited for Timothy to finish the scan.

"Radiation levels are in the upper tiers of the yellow zone," Timothy said. "No contacts in the general vicinity."

Michael grabbed his helmet and slipped it over his head. "Okay, Raptor, time for a systems check."

Magnolia slung her rifle over her back and put on her helmet—the final step of their gear prep. One by one, the HUDs flickered on, revealing their beacons on the minimap in the upper right corner.

"Raptor One, online," Michael said.

"Raptor Two, online," Layla said.

Rodger tapped the side of his helmet several times. "Oh, there we go," he said on the third try. "Raptor Three is A-OK."

"Raptor Four, online," Magnolia said.

"Open the doors," Michael ordered.

The hydraulics hissed as the top of the loading door opened. A light wind gusted into the bay, puffing up the sheets that covered the corpses on the platform.

Michael grabbed a backpack from the table and set it at his feet. "Timothy, as soon as we move under that storm, we're probably going to lose contact," he said. "Wait for us in the sky here unless another storm rolls in. Once we link up with X, we'll transmit for evac. I expect it will take us several days to complete the mission."

"Understood, Commander. I will be here waiting for you." The AI smiled, displaying a perfect set of holographic teeth, but his expression seemed forced.

Magnolia's stomach knotted. What if Timothy left them out here? He might look like a man, but he was technically a machine—and an unpredictable one at that.

The loading door continued opening as the Hell Divers approached, standing side by side. Lightning forked through the swollen storm clouds, leaving behind blue afterimages that quickly faded. The skies to the south were mostly calm.

"Six thousand feet," Timothy said.

Magnolia chinned on her night-vision goggles and waited for her eyes to adjust to the green view. Wind continued to whistle into the cargo hold. A rogue gust flipped the sheet off Timothy's deceased daughter. The fabric sailed away, flying past Magnolia as if the girl's ghost had finally departed.

Timothy's hologram faded in and out before solidifying again. The bulkheads vibrated as the ship suddenly picked up speed. Magnolia reached out for something to hold on to, stumbling.

"Timothy, hold us steady," Michael called out.

"Warning," announced an automated female voice over the PA system. "Warning," she repeated in a calm and professional manner. "Threat level rising."

Timothy started walking toward the bodies, ignoring both the alert and Michael's order. The door was almost completely open, and as they picked up speed, the drafts grew more violent, rippling the exposed parts of Magnolia's suit. A second sheet blew away.

"Timothy!" Michael yelled.

"Warning," the female voice said a third time. "Thrusters three and four are offline."

Deliverance tilted slightly, enough to throw Magnolia off balance. The following jolt, amplified by the speed of their descent, sent her crashing to the floor.

"Threat level critical," the maddeningly calm female voice said over the PA.

"Timothy, what the hell are you doing?" Michael screamed.

Layla and Rodger remained standing, their arms flung out for balance. The lift door finished opening with a metallic click as Timothy's holographic projection bent down next to his dead daughter, the wind whipping her thin hair. The sheet over his wife had flipped up, exposing her leathery face. He reached down to cover her back up, to no avail.

He's gone haywire, Magnolia realized as he kept trying to pull the sheet back over her face even as the ship crashed.

The Klaxon wailed from the speakers, and the female voice continued to warn them of the impending crash. "Emergency. Threat level critical. All thrusters are offline. Ship integrity threatened. Please move to life-support units."

The airship tilted again, and Magnolia scrambled for the platform. Her eyes had adjusted to the optics, and in the green hue she glimpsed the terrain below. There didn't appear to be a road— only what looked like vibrating earth.

She tried to get to the corpses, thinking that if she could just cover them, Timothy might snap out of it, but the ship tilted again before she could reach the liftgate. The bodies began to slide toward the edge of the platform. The shovel slipped over the side.

Timothy remained on his knees, swiping determinedly at his dead daughter with his see-through hands.

Rodger let out a high-pitched wail as he hit the ground and

began sliding. Magnolia tried to grab the raggedy shoes of the nearest corpse.

"Timothy, you have to calm down," she said. "You're going to kill us all. That's not what you want, is it?"

She reached out and put a hand over his. It slipped through the holographic projection. "What was her name?"

That got his attention.

"Susan," Timothy mumbled, still grasping ferociously at the flapping sheet that half-covered his wife. "We called her Susie Q."

"Susan wouldn't want you to do this, would she? She'd want you to save us."

The ship continued to plummet through the air without slowing. Cracks and groans echoed throughout the cargo bay like snapping bones. The ship was advanced, but it wasn't designed for a free fall. It would take only forty seconds or so to hit the dirt at this rate, and they were still picking up speed. Magnolia found it more and more difficult to move. It was almost like diving.

"Three thousand feet, and we're picking up speed!" Rodger shouted, his voice distant.

"Threat level severe," said the female voice. "Please evacuate."

The Klaxon wail was almost drowned out by the roar of wind.

"Timothy, please," Magnolia begged, her entire body shaking. "Susan would not want this. She would want you to help us."

"Two thousand feet!" Rodger yelled.

Michael and Layla were crawling toward the table bolted to the bulkhead behind them, but Magnolia knew there was no way they would be able to stop the ship now. Their fate rested in Timothy's hands.

A flash of motion came from behind her, and she looked over her shoulder to see Rodger holding out the missing sheet.

"Help me with this!" he yelled.

Magnolia reached out, and together they draped the flapping sheet over Susan's remains. Timothy's hands stilled.

"Now, turn the goddamn thrusters back on!" Magnolia shouted.

Timothy tilted his head and looked at her for a moment, almost as if he had forgotten who she was.

The thrusters kicked back on, jolting the ship so hard that Magnolia and Rodger were pressed against the floor.

Pain raced through her knees and wrists, but she managed to push herself up. The ship leveled out and then continued its now-gradual descent, slowly lowering them until they were just above the ground. The thrusters had shut off, but the turbofans whirled below, allowing the ship to hover.

"Threat level stabilized," said the female voice. The Klaxon shut off, and silence filled the cargo bay.

Magnolia glanced up at her HUD. They were only a hundred feet above the ground, hovering with the turbofans. Outside, the dirt seemed to be moving again. She pushed herself up to find that the brown, swirling terrain wasn't dirt at all. The turbofans sent air drafts over a brown swampland, blowing ripples out across the sludge-colored water.

Timothy rose to his feet and looked curiously around at the chaos of the launch bay. "What just happened here?" He shook his head from side to side as if he had just woken from a deep sleep.

"You just about killed us, and I just about pooped myself again," Rodger said. "That's what just happened."

"Holy shit," Layla said, breathing heavily. She wasn't looking at Timothy—she was looking out the open cargo door. Michael joined the three divers on the platform next to the corpses.

Below, the swampland seemed to stretch forever. A beeping sounded behind them, and Magnolia turned to see the monitor on the table across the room flashing, red dots moving across the translucent LZ.

Michael raised his rifle. "Everyone on alert. We've got company."

Les Mitchells bent down to clear the low bulkhead over his daughter's bunk. It wasn't the first overhead his skull had gone to war with, and he had the scars to prove it. The worst was from getting knocked unconscious by a pipe when he was a gangly six-foot-nine teenager. Since then, ducking had become part of his daily routine.

"Daddy?" Phyl whispered as he leaned down. She opened her eyes and let out a moan, rolling over in her bunk to look at Les.

"Hey, sweetie, I'm sorry if I woke you. I was just going to give you a kiss goodbye."

"What time is it?"

"Five in the morning," he said, kissing her on the forehead. "Go back to sleep."

"Are you going to work?"

"Yes, but I'll be back tonight and I'll bring you a treat."

"What kind of a treat?" Phyl said, trying to sit up.

Les brushed her long brown hair from her face. "It's a surprise."

"Okay, Daddy."

He kissed her again on the forehead, his heart hurting at the thought of her in pain. She had no idea he had joined the Hell Divers. She thought he was heading to his old job as an electrician.

A cough rang out, filling the small quarters. Katherine, his wife, broke into a fit, her lungs crackling with fluid.

Les pulled the sheets back up to Phyl's chin. She was tall already, and at only seven years old, she had a long way to go.

"I'll see you later, baby girl," Les said. Ducking down, he walked across the room and sat in the chair by his wife's bed. There was a glass of water on the bedside table, and he handed it to her. She drained half of it as she gradually regained her breath.

"Looking good, Les." She coughed with a hand over her mouth. "I like the uniform."

Les looked down at his red coveralls and smiled. He held out his arms to show how the sleeves came halfway up his forearms. Then he raised a leg to show off his ankles.

Katherine smiled and took another drink of water. She was a petite woman with blue eyes, dirty-blond hair, and a contagious smile. Les was the towering gentle Giraffe, who had charmed her when they were just kids. Back then he had fallen for her hard, and his love never wavered over their fifteen years of marriage. In his eyes, she was and always would be the most beautiful woman on the *Hive*, even though the illness had robbed her of her youth and vitality.

Katherine brought her hand up and coughed into her sleeve again, holding his gaze in the candlelight.

"You're going to be okay," he said. "We're going to get you medicine, and we're going to get Trey out of the brig. I promise."

"None of that will matter if you're dead," Katherine said. She lowered her voice so Phyl couldn't hear. "We can't go on without you."

"You have to trust me." Les looked away, guilt setting in. He still hadn't told her they were planning on diving tomorrow. "Jordan promised me medicine. Once you're well again, you can go back to work. If something happens to me, you can at least take care of the kids."

"Stop it," Katherine said, reaching out but stopping just short of touching him. "You can't leave us. I won't let you."

He smiled at that. She was still strong—even now, despite

being thin, sick, and exhausted. Her eyes softened, and she pulled her hand back.

"Daddy, will you read me that story about trains?" Phyl asked.

"In a minute, baby." Les kept his focus on Katherine. He hated to see the love of his life suffering. It also made him even more determined to learn the ins and outs of diving, so he could stay with his family. Nothing, not even a bolt of lightning or a swarm of Sirens, could yank him from this world.

"How many dives do you have to do before they help us?" Katherine whispered.

"Daddy, I have the book." Phyl held up a blue hardcover with the picture of a train on the cover. The images had always disturbed Les. What kind of person drew a human face on a train?

"Be right there," he said, turning back to his wife.

"How many dives?" she repeated.

"I'm honestly not sure, but they're all green-zone dives, so don't worry. We're not going through any storms or into any radiation zones."

"How many divers do they have?"

"There are five of us for now."

"That's it?"

He nodded and glanced at the ground.

"I know that look," she said. "What are you keeping from me?"

"I think this will be a long-term gig, sweetie. I don't think it's something I just get to retire from. You know how it works."

A tear fell from her eye, and she wiped it away, trying to be strong. Les wanted more than anything to lean in and kiss her, but he couldn't risk getting sick. If he caught her respiratory infection, then they would starve. And he couldn't lie to her. She deserved to know the truth.

"Tomorrow, I dive so our family survives."

EIGHT

After nearly a week in the brig, Jordan decided it was finally time to go talk to Katrina. He hoped she'd had enough time to rethink her betrayal, but he had his doubts. She had always been a stubborn woman.

"Hunt, you have the bridge for the next two hours," Jordan said. He pushed at the armrests and rose from the captain's chair that over a dozen men and women had held before his tenure. They had helped preserve the human race for over 250 years in this old, rusted tub of an airship.

He would not let them down. He refused to be the final captain of the *Hive*.

Jordan felt a renewed sense of purpose as he walked up the stairs. Officers in their white uniforms were working intently at their pod stations, avoiding his gaze by remaining focused on their holo screens. Ensigns Lore and Del Toro, his new personal bodyguards and errand boys, were waiting for him outside the hatch.

"Where's Sergeant Jenkins?" Jordan asked.

"In the launch bay with the new divers," Lore replied.

"Tell him to meet me at the brig."

"Yes sir." Lore set off down a connecting corridor while Del Toro and Jordan walked toward the brig. Just ahead, several workers in green coveralls were scrubbing away the painting of the ocean. Their wire brushes scraped off the blue paint, exposing the dark metal skin of the *Hive*.

Around the next corner, more workers were sanding the graffiti off a bulkhead. Two groups of technicians in yellow coveralls had already removed the hatches from half the portholes. The scrap would be put to good use, bolted to the areas where radiation leaked through in the lower decks. Other pieces would go belowdecks to the junkyard, where they would wait to be reused or recycled. Nothing on the *Hive*, from plastic bottles to broken lightbulbs, went to waste.

He walked past the trading post, where the dinner crowd were bartering their goods. Jordan caught a whiff of freshly baked bread, and his stomach growled. He briefly considered getting a loaf for Katrina but decided against it. He didn't have time to stop.

But the next corridor was blocked by a sea of people, and he was forced to slow. Del Toro saw the crowd gathered outside the entrance to the farm and immediately reached for his baton. It wasn't unusual to have people loitering here, but for once they weren't shouting about food.

"Stop!" a man yelled.

"You can't take that down!" shouted another.

Militiamen had already gathered with their batons and crossbows. The sight of the weapons didn't seem to deter the crowd.

"Why didn't I hear about this?" Jordan asked Del Toro.

"Not sure, sir. Let me find out what's going on."

Jordan put a finger up to his earpiece. "Lieutenant Hunt, do you copy? This is Captain Jordan."

"Copy, sir."

"We have a situation outside the farm. Why wasn't I informed?"

After a slight pause, a static crackled in Jordan's ear.

"Sir, I wasn't aware of the situation, but it looks like the militia has deployed a unit to take care of it. They are sending a second unit to the lower decks just in case there's trouble there, too."

"I want this taken care of quickly and quietly," Jordan said. He cursed when he saw more passengers join the crowd watching the workers scrub away the paintings outside the farm.

Jordan motioned with his head down the opposite corridor. "Let's go, Del Toro."

A shout stopped them. "Captain Jordan!"

Jordan turned as Cole and Bernie Mintel led a small group of people down the hallway. They all wore tattered clothing, and he could smell them from where he stood.

"What's the meaning of this?" Bernie asked. She brushed her long gray hair over her shoulder while Cole rolled back his sleeves, revealing muscular forearms and a clock tattoo.

"Sorry, but I'm quite busy, Mr. and Mrs. Mintel," Jordan replied. "Please check with your representative to learn about the renovations." He turned away, but Cole called out after him again.

"*Renovations?* You're taking down our heritage! This is history!"

Del Toro struck the end of his baton against his palm, the metal making a loud smack against the leather glove. "Back off, Cole," said the ensign.

Jordan dipped his head politely as if they had just had a pleasant conversation, and continued down the next corridor. He had known that the plan to take down the art wouldn't be popular, but he was surprised to see the fury in the eyes of Cole and the others. Still, he would not be deterred. Like many of his plans, the current operation was geared toward long-term change, and in the end, people would look back and agree with him. Their resistance was the burden every leader had to endure when making unpopular decisions.

They made it to the brig a few minutes later. Sergeant Jenkins was waiting outside the hatch with Ensign Lore.

"Sergeant, you're neglecting your duties," Jordan said.

"Sir?"

"There was nearly a riot outside the farm. You should have been there."

Jenkins pulled at his collar anxiously. "I'm doing my best, sir, but you also tasked me with making sure the new Hell Divers are trained properly."

"Do better," Jordan said, moving through the open hatch into the brig.

Behind the metal desk stood Lauren Sloan, a mean-looking woman with a buzz-cut head and a lazy eye. She never said much to Jordan, but that damned eye seemed to follow his every movement. He couldn't tell whether she wanted to sleep with him or stick a knife in his heart.

"I'm here to see prisoner nineteen," Jordan said. It felt a little odd using a number for a human being, especially for the woman carrying his child, but the ship survived by a system of rules and protocols, and he wasn't going to break any of them for Katrina unless she swore loyalty.

A wall-mounted speaker beeped as Sloan let them in. The hatch leading to the cells clicked open, and Jordan stepped inside. Sloan and Jenkins followed him into the dim-lit passage. Metal trays sat outside the cells, all of them licked clean by the prisoners—except one, halfway down the hall.

As he walked toward it, a banging sound made him flinch. He looked to his right to see one of the most infamous criminals on the ship. Raphael Eddie—brother of Travis Eddie, the man who had unsuccessfully tried to lead a mutiny a decade earlier—was staring out at him through the small glass window.

"Morning, Captain!" Raphael said, rearing his head back to let out a crazed laugh.

"Shut up," Sloan said. She walked over to the hatch and closed the aluminum shutter over the window.

"Remind me why we waste resources keeping him alive," Jordan said.

"His brother had a lot of supporters from the lower decks," Jenkins said. "Killing him would cause a riot. His sentence is up in a year, anyway."

"If he survives that long," Jordan said.

Jenkins nodded reluctantly at Jordan's subtle order. It was a good test. If Raphael should pass away in his cell, Jordan would know that the sergeant was still loyal enough to keep around. It would take only a drop of poison to make the death look natural. He trusted Jenkins to figure it out.

The prisoners watched in silence as Jordan walked down the passage. They knew their place. One of them, a teenage boy named Trey Mitchells, even saluted.

At least Les' kid knew something about respect, although Jordan had heard the young man was close to Michael Everhart. That made him wonder; maybe the salute was just a facade.

Jordan stopped outside the cell of Ty Parker, the technician who had once worked with many of the great Hell Divers. Parker sat on his bunk looking down at the floor, head in his hands. That was good. The traitor should be thinking about what he had done. If not for his unique skill set, Jordan would already have jettisoned him from one of the air locks, but he needed Ty to continue working—under militia supervision, of course.

Ty glanced up, but Jordan moved on to the cell with the full tray of slop sitting on the floor in front of it.

"She's been refusing food, sir," Sloan said.

"For how long?" Jordan asked.

"Two days."

Jordan bent down and picked up the tray of reeking slush. The prisoners were given a combination of old stew and bugs grown on the farm to help with the crops. Most people didn't realize it, but bugs were a healthy part of the ecosystem and high in protein.

Sloan unlocked the hatch and opened it for Jordan. After taking in a discreet last breath of fresh air, he walked in and nodded for the guard to seal them inside.

"You're not eating," Jordan said.

Katrina sat cross-legged on the floor, her back to him, braided hair falling over her shoulder.

"I lost my appetite," she said without turning. "Did you come to kill me?"

Jordan sat on her bunk and placed the tray on the floor beside it.

"No, I came to tell you I love you."

A snort was her reply.

"And I know that deep down, you love me, too, Katrina."

The single overhead light cast a glow on the letters and numbers carved into the metal bulkhead above the bed. Jordan couldn't help but wonder how many prisoners this cell had housed over the history of the ship. He waited anxiously for her to say something, anything. But when she didn't, he decided to try a different approach.

"You have to eat," he urged. "If not for you, for the baby."

She snorted again, and Jordan stiffened. Katrina had always been stubborn, but this was crazy. She wasn't thinking clearly.

"I'm also here to make you an offer," he said. "An offer to reinstate your position as XO. All you have to do is promise you won't speak of what happened at the Hilltop Bastion. You don't have to love me, but you do have to eat. That's not negotiable."

Katrina picked up the tray and slammed it against the wall, smearing the slop all over the bulkhead. Some of the splatter landed on his face.

Jordan stood and wiped it away.

"You just don't get it, Katrina. X and the other divers are dead. They betrayed me, and they betrayed the *Hive*!" His voice grew louder. "You may not want to see it, and you don't have to like it, but I won't let you kill our baby out of spite."

Katrina whirled to face him. "Not *our* baby, Leon. You lost your right to the child the moment you killed everyone I cared about."

Jordan stood his ground. "You'd better be careful with your next words, Katrina," he said, lips quivering and heart pounding. "I came here to offer you a way out of this. To give you a second chance."

Before she could reply, he added, "I'm working on a project that will cleanse the ship and refocus its people on the right priorities."

She narrowed her gaze at him, crow's-feet crinkling around her eyes. "Cleanse?" she said.

Jordan raised his wristwatch and nodded. "In a few minutes, a riot team will raid the library to seize all materials about the Old World. Crews are working around the clock to remove the paintings, graffiti, and sketches from the bulkheads. In a few hours, the ship will be purged of the past to pave the way for the future. What doesn't get reused will get sent back to the surface."

Katrina's jaw dropped. "Do you even *hear* yourself? People will mutiny. They won't accept this."

"I've already ordered Professor Lana to revise the curriculum. From here on out, our focus will be on teaching survival, not history."

Katrina dropped her hand to her belly and closed her eyes for a moment.

"Join me, Katrina. We'll save this ship together."

Her eyelids opened, and she slowly shook her head.

"I'll *never* join you, Leon. You're insane. You can't just erase the past. All these years, it's the one thing that has given us hope. If we forget where we came from, the future will be lost to us forever."

"We'll see about that," Jordan said. "Or maybe not. It depends on how well you behave after you give birth to our child."

*　　*　　*　　*　　*

Michael stood at the edge of the open door, looking down at the swamp. *Deliverance* skimmed the surface of the turbid water as he searched for a new landing zone. The temperature here was a chilly forty degrees, and the radiation level was in the yellow zone. Lightning speared the horizon, and the resulting thunder clapped loud enough to shake the metal bulkheads.

"I don't like this, Tin," Layla said.

Michael didn't bother telling her not to use his nickname. He had a dozen things on his mind, none of them pleasant. Multiple heat signatures were coming from the swamp, indicating that more than one beast lived under the water. And Timothy's meltdown had rattled Michael to the core. There were a lot of ways the mission could end in failure, and he was beginning to wonder whether he had made the right decision.

"You're out there, X, I know it," Michael whispered as he scanned the horizon.

"There!" Layla yelled. Michael followed her fingers toward an island in the vast swamp.

He pulled his binos from the vest covering his armor and zoomed in on the small piece of land in the middle of the brown sludge that seemed to cover most of the area. There appeared to be a chain of islands in that direction.

"That's our new LZ," Michael said. "Good eyes, Layla."

The ship changed bearing, gliding to the northeast as the turbofans directed them through the calm sky. Michael used the moment to check on Timothy, whose projection stood next to the corpses of his family, watching over them as *Deliverance* began its descent. He seemed to be functioning normally now that the bodies were covered up, but Michael couldn't trust him anymore after what had happened on the descent.

Rodger grabbed a handhold on the side of the cargo bay and leaned out the side as they glided over the water. "Do we have any idea what those things are down there?" he asked.

"Stay back if you don't want to find out," Magnolia said.

Rodger took a hasty step back.

"Whatever they are, they can swim," Layla said.

Magnolia cradled her rifle across her chest. "Hopefully, they can't walk or fly."

"Setting down in T minus thirty seconds," Timothy announced.

Michael pulled his attention back to his team. "Okay, this is it, everyone. I know you're all scared, but if X found a way across these swamps, we can, too."

"Be nice if we had a boat," Rodger said.

"No way in hell I'm taking a boat through that shit!" Magnolia exclaimed.

"Neither would I, then," Rodger said.

Michael tried to think what X would do in this situation. "Cut the shit and focus." After making sure he had everyone's attention, he said, "There's a way across, and we're going to find it no matter how long it takes or whatever's out there. Got it?"

"Yes, sir," the other divers said together.

Michael centered his binos on the island. It seemed to be

several square miles, surrounded by a network of land bridges that spread like veins across the swamp. In the center of the mass were the crumbling shells of buildings.

"Looks like there's some sort of ruins down there," he said, zooming in on the structures. "Timothy, can you do another scan?"

"The LZ appears clear, Commander," the AI replied a moment later. "No heat signatures are present on the land mass."

"All right, set us down."

Timothy deployed the landing gear and then shut off the turbofans as the massive feet connected with the dirt. The ship groaned. A bridge extended from the platform, angling twenty feet down until it sank into the mud.

Michael and the other divers scanned the area for any creatures that the sensors may have missed. The muddy field stretched a quarter mile to the bottom of a hill. Hunks of sheet metal, a refrigerator, and several rusty vehicles peppered the marshy landscape.

"Looks clear," Michael said. He turned to the AI. "I'm going to fulfill my promise to you, Timothy, but you have to promise me you're not going to leave us down here."

"You have my word, Commander."

Timothy's reply seemed sincere, but Michael simply didn't trust him. Still, what other option did he have?

"Come on," Michael said to his team.

Working together, the divers gently carried the corpses from the platform to the ground. Michael took another moment to scan the area for hostiles while Rodger ran back up to find another shovel.

From the ground level, Michael didn't see anything moving in the muddy terrain aside from a few armored centipedes scuttling across the hull of an old pickup truck.

Satisfied they were alone, he grabbed the shovel and started digging while Layla and Magnolia held security.

A light rain fell on the divers as they worked. Taking turns, Michael and Rodger dug for an hour, scooping out the wet soil and tossing it into a pile. By the time they had excavated four graves, Michael was covered in sweat beneath his layered suit and armor. Gently, almost tenderly, he and Rodger set the corpses inside the graves.

Timothy stood in the open cargo bay looking down. "Thank you," he said. "Thank you for finally putting my family to rest."

Michael gave a nod and began shoveling dirt back into the graves. Once they were filled, Magnolia bent down and placed something above Susan's.

"I hope you don't mind, Rodger," she said, glancing up.

Rodger bent down to look at the wooden elephant statue he had carved for Magnolia.

"It's yours to do with as you wish," he said.

"Thank you," Timothy repeated. "That was very kind."

The turbofans clicked back on, and the divers retreated as a vortex of grit and mud whipped through the air of the landing zone.

Michael wiped his visor dry and watched the hologram in the open doorway looking down, remaining there as the ship rose into the sky. Timothy raised a hand in farewell to the divers, or perhaps his family—Michael couldn't be sure.

Michael returned the gesture. "You'd better wait for us, Timothy Pepper of the Hilltop Bastion."

NINE

The crooked sign hung from rusted poles on the side of the road. WELCOME TO FLORIDA, THE SUNSHINE STATE. Blue weeds grew between the cracks in the concrete. They were oddly beautiful, but Xavier Rodriguez knew to stay away from them.

He led his dog around the mutated foliage, careful not to get snagged by a tentacle. The plants mostly fed on cockroaches and other bugs, but they might try to snare the husky.

X walked over to the sign, trying to read through the rust that made the surface look like a hunk of moldy cheese. The only thing he could make out aside from the letters was the faded image of a sun integrated with the letter o in FLORIDA.

It had been a long time since he saw the real sun.

He looked up at the black sheet draped over the atmosphere. Not a single ray of light could penetrate the darkness. Raising his wrist monitor, he checked the temperature: fifty degrees Fahrenheit.

That was a sauna compared to most places on the surface. He would have taken his helmet off if not for the rads. They were high here, and getting worse with every step.

He looked at the sign once more, thinking of the picture that had burned in the Stryker vehicle. It was that image that brought him here, but this place looked nothing like the picture.

X stepped over a two-foot-wide crevice that had split the road in half. Blue tentacles writhed in the air, reaching for him. He didn't know whether heat or movement attracted them, but whatever the reason, his presence was riling them up.

X navigated around the carnivorous vegetation and raised his rifle scope to glass the area for bigger threats. A wide array of monsters dwelled in the wastes. Since their journey began in Hades, the man and his dog had battled stone beasts in the desert, and in the cities he fought the Sirens as well as big lizards and one-eyed birdlike abominations. From overgrown poisonous plants to man-eating worms, just about everything down here on the surface was out to eat you.

Lightning forked into the ground, reminding him that the swirling, bulging dome of storm clouds could be as deadly as any monster.

But the monsters and the storm would not stop him. Somewhere out there, not far from here, was the place he'd been searching for. The place from the picture.

The place he had risked everything to reach.

"We're almost to the ocean," he said with what might have passed for a smile.

Lowering the rifle, he pulled out his maps and shuffled through them till he found the military map from the Stryker. Not far from their location, underneath an airfield, was a bunker. Sliding the precious maps back into their sleeve, he started walking again.

Soon the journey would be over. They would find a home, a place where they could stay until the end. He wasn't exactly sure where that place would be—only that it would have a view of the ocean.

This was the one thing he had managed to hold on to. He had lost almost everything else, some of it more than once. His gear. His weapons. His book of memories. But he had held on to this dream.

These days, he spent most of his energy just staying alive. He was tired. Exhausted. The years of traveling and fighting had taken their toll, and his skin was a canvas of injuries, some of which had never quite healed.

Miles, on the other hand, was still cavorting around like a young dog, just as he had when X unfroze him back in Hades. It was hard to believe that was eight years ago.

But their journey was almost over. The ocean wasn't far now.

He looked back up at the sky, and a distant thought of the people who had left him down here to die flitted through his mind. The memories were as muddy as the dirt on the side of the road.

That life is over. Let it go.

X had forgotten their names. After his journal burned and his messages went unanswered, he had finally decided to give up—both on those he loved and on those who had betrayed him.

There was nothing for him in the sky now, just the long road and the loyal dog that trotted by his side.

They kept moving, one step at a time. X was low on food, low on ammo, low on water, and low on energy. But he could do this. He would reach his goal, and then he could rest.

Several days of traveling south along the road had led them past the ruins of civilization. X had seen similar sights on his journey across what had once been the United States of America. The crumbling towers and flattened buildings looked pretty much the same wherever he went.

But on the third day of the trek through Florida, X saw something new. He almost broke down at the sight.

"It can't be," he croaked. He tried to swallow, but his throat was too dry.

Miles sat on his haunches, unconcerned. But the man didn't believe what he was seeing. This couldn't be the ocean, could it? The water was brown and muddy, like sewage. There were no whitecaps, no beaches. And a terrible smell filtered through his helmet.

Lightning flashed through the storm system, illuminating the water for as far as X could see. Several islands and spurs of land stretched out into the muck. He reached into his vest and pulled out the maps again. They were over 250 years old, but the tattered papers had served him well this far.

This time, however, either the map was wrong or the land had changed, or else he was lost. He tucked the sleeve back into his vest and unslung his rifle. The cracked leather strap nearly snapped. Like everything else, it was barely holding together.

"Come on, boy," X said, his throat burning with every word. He knew that something was wrong, but he had no medicine.

Miles looked up, concern in his gaze. *That* was what the ocean was supposed to look like, X thought, looking into the dog's bright blue eyes. Not this brown shit.

The road curved out through the water, framed on either side by a half-eroded landmass a hundred feet wide. Miles followed him toward the bridge, both of them alert for threats. He raised his wrist monitor to check the radiation levels. They were still in the yellow zone, but the rads continued ticking higher and higher.

He stopped when they got to the land bridge. Several chunks of concrete had broken off and slid down the sides. More debris littered the slopes. Hulls of old-world vehicles, rebar, and hunks of metal. He leaned over the side to see human skeletal remains covered in red moss and half protruding from the mud. Purple and blue plants grew along the road and in the cracks. One plant sprouted through the grinning jaw of a skull.

X put one boot on the bridge and kept the other on the road

behind him. Something was strange about the remains below. The skeletons looked...different.

Miles remained where he was, his helmet angled toward the water. They both stood there for several minutes, listening to the clap of thunder and the gurgle of the water.

Looking through the scope on his rifle, X confirmed the skeletal remains below weren't all human. Some of them were machine. He could tell by the smooth bones. Human remains didn't age like that.

There were plenty of robot skeletons in the wastes, but X had never seen a graveyard like this. Whatever had happened to the bots below didn't matter now though.

He placed his other boot on the bridge, waited a moment to see whether it would hold, and then gestured for Miles. Rifle up, X scanned the slopes to either side. Miles' masked muzzle sniffed the path as they walked, following the curved road deeper into the swamps. Thunder boomed louder, shaking the concrete beneath his boots. To the east, lightning zapped the water. The insulating layers in their suits would protect them from anything short of a direct hit, but X had made sure they wouldn't attract the charge by adding a second layer of rubber.

He stepped over to the edge of the road and looked down. There was no way to tell how deep it was, and it was so murky, he couldn't see whether anything lurked below the surface.

The storm boomed in the distance, and shock waves rumbled across the ground. Miles let out a whine.

"It's okay," X said. "Just keep going."

They pushed onward, the din of the storm pounding like great drums in the clouds, growing louder with each step. Another thunderclap rumbled through the ground. The sound faded, but the concrete continued to shake.

The vibration grew more violent. X could feel it in his bones now. This was more than thunder.

Miles halted, sat, and howled. Now X knew that something was wrong. The dog had a sixth sense about danger.

"What is it?" X asked.

Miles barked back at him.

X looked down the road and then back the way they had come. He didn't want to turn back, but Miles wouldn't budge.

Before X could move, a section of dirt on the right side of the bridge crumbled away, splashing into the water. Cracks webbed across the road. Miles nudged up against him, nearly herding him off the road. X finally realized what was happening. He had lived through dust storms powerful enough to skin you alive and ice storms that could freeze you where you stood, but he had never been in an earthquake before.

He didn't know what to do besides run. Miles ran after him down the bridge, toward solid land. More cracks broke across the road, and a piece the size of a truck tumbled down the left side and splashed into the brown water.

The entire area must be some sort of sinkhole. Maybe it had always been this way, but he suspected that the bombs had made things even more unstable.

He hopped over part of the buckling street. Miles followed with a graceful leap. For several minutes, they ran at full speed, the quake still rocking the land bridge. They weren't far from where they had started. Ahead, the curved road connected with solid ground. Water sloshed along the side of the bridge as the groaning earth shook beneath them. X glimpsed movement under the dark surface, but lost sight of it when his boot caught a chunk of concrete. He fell, scraping his kneepads on the road, and dropped the rifle.

He paused long enough to grab the weapon and then continued running after Miles. The dog was still bolting for safety, and X didn't bother calling after him. The dog would reach safety, even if X didn't. That was something, at least.

Move it, old man!

Breaking into a run, he glimpsed another flash of movement in the sewage-colored water. This wasn't from the quake. This was alive. A curved red back squirmed like a snake beneath the surface and then vanished.

The land bridge suddenly shook so hard that a fissure opened up a few feet ahead. Miles tried to stop but slid toward the widening crevice splitting the bridge in half.

X ran harder than he could remember running, as the dog slipped over the side. Miles managed to turn and claw at the top with his front paws, but his hind legs had gone over the edge.

Throat and lungs burning, X sucked in air, forcing his tired muscles to pump faster. He bent low and prepared to slide toward Miles when a massive coiled body rose from the water on the left side of the bridge. A bright red tentacle flicked out and grabbed Miles.

X screamed in wordless rage and horror. He dropped his rifle and ran full speed for the edge of the road. As he prepared to jump, he unsheathed his knife, then propelled his body into the air.

"I'm coming, boy!" he yelled.

His boots sank into the fetid muck as he splashed into the water. The world went dark for a flitting moment. He kicked above the surface and turned from side to side to search the murky water for Miles or the beast. His muffled screams filled his helmet.

"Miles, Miles!"

Another tentacle whipped in front of him, slamming into his side. The twenty-foot-long creature had Miles in its grip. X kicked toward him and swiped with the blade, slashing through the rubbery hide. The wound did not bleed but instead disgorged pinkish spheres the size of apples from the *Hive*'s farm. He slashed again as the creature twisted its boneless body through the water.

This time, his blade sliced through the bulging midsection, letting out more of the balls that, X realized, must be eggs.

The gravid monster let Miles go and whisked about to face X. A halo of spikes rose around the creature's head, and it opened a maw lined with sharp teeth. Then the serpentine nightmare clamped its mouth shut and squirmed away as X jabbed at it.

He sucked in filtered air and tried to watch the beast circling. The cloudy water made it nearly impossible to see anything, and the weight of the armor made treading water difficult.

A flash of motion alerted him at the last second as the monster darted through the murk. X moved left and jabbed again with the knife, but the blade missed, and the creature wasted no time throwing a coil of its muscular body around his chest armor and squeezing.

X's arms were still free, and he plunged his blade into the thick hide as it continued coiling its body around his legs, pulling him deeper into the water. He couldn't see Miles anywhere, and then he couldn't see anything at all as the monster dragged him below the surface.

*　　*　　*　　*　　*

PRESENT DAY

Les Mitchells and the other divers watched Erin Jenkins enter the wind tunnel. The noise drowned out the raised voices outside the launch bay. Les tried not to get distracted by the civil unrest in the corridors. He wasn't sure what was going on outside, but he canceled it out the best he could and focused on training. The wind tunnel was the closest they were going to get to diving before being launched from one of the tubes.

"You really think you're going to fit in that thing?" Jennifer teased. She jabbed Les in the ribs hard enough that he shot her a glare.

"I'm not a freaking—"

"Giraffe?" she finished with a grin.

Les laughed. Then he reached out and pointed at her hair. "You're probably going to need to cut those to fit in your helmet."

"Yeah, yeah." She pushed her dreadlocks over her shoulders and focused on the wind tunnel. Don Olah and Tom Price both had their arms crossed over their red coveralls, watching Erin get into position.

They all were beat from training eleven hours straight. After the wind tunnel, they were heading to the armory for weapons simulation.

And tomorrow they would put it all to use.

Les still couldn't quite believe they were going to dive so soon. The thought sent a chill through his long body. The wind tunnel clicked on in front of him, pulling him back to reality. Erin rose into the air, arms out. Bending her knees and putting her elbows at right angles, she moved gracefully in the upward draft. She drew her limbs in a little and dropped almost to the grate below.

"This is the stable fall position," she said over the comms. "This is what you'll be doing for most of a dive."

She held the position for several minutes.

"You will nose-dive only if we're in a hurry," Erin said. "And usually that happens only if the *Hive*'s weather sensors missed picking up a storm. The quicker you get through it, the less likely you are to get fried by a lightning strike."

Les watched her go through the moves, but the hundred other things on his mind made it hard to concentrate. Phyl, Trey, and Katherine were all counting on him to take care of them. He was used to pressure and stress, but this was on an entirely new level.

In his mind's eye, he kept imagining the aftermath of his death. Trey would end up rotting away in the brig, his wife would succumb to her illness, and Phyl would grow up an orphan—if she got a chance to grow up at all.

"You're going to save them," Les said out loud.

Don, Jennifer, and Tom all looked in his direction.

"You okay?" Jennifer asked.

"Sorry," Les replied, his cheeks warm with embarrassment.

Erin did a backflip inside the tunnel and continued speaking over the comms to explain her moves and how to execute them. Les shook away his worries and watched, knowing he would be up soon.

A few minutes later, Erin ordered Olah to shut off the fans. The wind jets clicked off, and she lowered to the grate and took off her helmet. Erin stepped out of the glass tube and ran a hand over her Mohawk.

"Who's first?" she asked.

Olah stepped up. He was always first to volunteer.

"He's definitely going to be the first to die," Jennifer whispered to Les.

My thoughts exactly.

Erin moved out of the way to stand beside Les and the other two divers while Olah secured his helmet and stepped into the tube.

"You okay, Giraffe?" Erin asked.

"I'm good," Les said.

"I've got a question," Jennifer said. "Something we've all been wondering about."

Erin nodded. "Okay."

"What happened to Team Wolf all those years ago?"

The question blindsided Les—and Erin, too, judging by her face. It contorted as if she was remembering something awful.

After a brief pause, Erin said, "Fair enough. Eight years ago, not too long after we lost X and a handful of other divers to Hades, my team was sent on a routine salvage mission."

"And?" Jennifer prompted.

Erin sighed. "And we were caught in the middle of a dust

storm. We had the supply crates full of supplies and ready to deploy. Lane—Commander Bricken—should have ordered us to take shelter, but he wanted to get the crates in the air to beat the storm."

She paused again, massaging the surface of her Wolf ring. "We lost four divers that day, along with our supply crates. I helped Jon Tormund escape, but at a cost. He broke his back after the storm flung him into a rock. He lived only a few years after that."

"Wasn't Lane your boyfriend?" Jennifer asked.

Erin shot the other woman an icy look. "You ask a lot of questions."

Jennifer lifted one shoulder. Les wasn't sure whether it was an apology or a shrug.

"Anything else you guys want to know?" Erin asked.

A shout sounded in the corridor outside the launch bay doors, and Les turned to see people running past the small windows.

"What the hell's going on out there?" Tom asked.

Erin let out a sigh. "It's getting worse."

"What is?" said Jennifer.

Les looked over at Erin. He couldn't quite read the expression on her dark, freckled features.

"Captain Jordan ordered all history purged from the ship," Erin said. "Paintings, vids, books—everything."

Jennifer lowered her hands to her sides. "You have to be kidding."

"I wish I were. My dad told me last night."

"But...without all that stuff, the *Hive* is just a rusted hull and a couple of gas bladders," Tom said, looking thoughtful.

"Captain's orders," Erin said.

"Damn right it is," Olah said over the comms from inside the wind tunnel. "Captain Jordan must have had a good reason to issue that order."

"May I?" Les asked, nodding toward the button that activated the wind tunnel.

Erin nodded, and Les walked up to the tunnel with a grin. "Good luck, Olah." He pushed the button and stepped back to watch.

"Shit, shit!" Olah said, holding his arms out as the air took him. He rose halfway up the tube before losing his balance and flipping over.

Jennifer and Tom both laughed, but the sounds were lost under the shouting in the corridors.

"That sounds bad," Les said. "What if the other passengers tear the ship apart while we're gone?"

"Don't worry about that," Erin said. "My dad will keep things under control up here."

Olah continued to struggle in the tube while they talked, and Les couldn't help but chuckle. The guy had no sense of balance whatsoever. He wobbled in the updraft like an overweight bird, arms and legs flapping.

"We still need to pick a name for the team," Erin said. "Something new. Something different from any of the other teams."

Les looked at the flash of her silver ring as she reached up to scratch her head. He liked the name Wolf but understood why she wouldn't want to use it again.

"What about *Phoenix*?" he said.

"Why Phoenix?" Erin asked.

Les shrugged. He had picked it because he loved mythology, and naming the team after something culturally significant seemed like a big *screw you* to Jordan without actually saying it to his face.

"I'll run it by the other divers," Erin replied.

More shouts broke out from the corridor, and the divers all turned toward the launch doors. A group of lower-deckers ran past as militia soldiers in riot gear gave chase.

"Damn fools," Les muttered. The one good thing about his son's being in the brig was that he couldn't get hurt. Knowing the boy, he would be the first to throw down with the militia.

"Don't worry," Erin said. "The ship has had problems like this before, but we always make it through. My dad will make sure of it."

"Your dad's not the one I'm worried about," Les said.

TEN

Rodger decided he didn't much like the swamps. Too much water, too much mud. And it smelled like an old sock full of manure.

"What do you think happened to this place?" Magnolia asked.

"Boom," Rodger said, miming an explosion.

"I'm talking about the swamps," Magnolia said. "Where the hell did they come from?"

"Doesn't matter," Michael said. "Now, be quiet. I'll take point. Layla and Mags, you take rear guard. Rodger, get behind me and shut your trap. Eyes up and ears out."

Rodger hurried to catch up with Michael, who had already taken off at a trot. The young commander didn't have as many dives under his belt as Magnolia, but he was a natural leader who knew when it was time to joke around and when it was time to get down to business.

Rodger knew he needed to learn a thing or two about that. Lately, he was always saying or doing the wrong thing. For a while, he seemed to be finally getting somewhere with Magnolia. But then she dropped it—the gift he had made for her with his own hands and carried through a city full of monsters to deliver—onto a stranger's grave.

Maybe he should make her something else.

"Look alive, Rodger," Michael snapped, bringing his attention back to the task at hand.

Michael had an AK-47 rifle trained on the buildings above, while Rodger had been entrusted with only a small-caliber pistol. He pulled the ax from the sheath over his shoulder and held both weapons in his hands.

The distant whir of the turbofans pushing *Deliverance* into the sky reverberated in the clouds above them, but he kept his focus on the buildings ahead. Empty windows, the glass long gone, looked out over the vast swamps. It was hard to imagine that two and a half centuries ago, the occupants would have been looking through swaying palm trees at a sunny sky. Rodger had seen Florida in old prewar vids. It was never supposed to look like this.

His boots crunched over the muddy, debris-strewn ground. Almost constant flashes of lightning made the dark landscape visible, but it was nothing like sunlight. The divers kept their NVGs off and used the blue glow to guide them toward the ruins.

The path led up a steep slope with several stone and brick structures at the top. A steeple rose above the other buildings. Beams arched over what remained of the roof, framing the swirling storm.

"Looks like a nice place," Rodger muttered.

"I'll check it out," Michael said.

"Just be careful," Layla said.

Michael started up the muddy slope, and Rodger followed close behind, using the same footholds to avoid falling on his ass. At the top, they looked out over an ancient city. A single metal chair sat in the middle of the road ahead. The sight gave Rodger a chill. Who had sat here all those years ago to watch the world burn?

Crooked brick foundations and stone walls framed a street leading across the island. Pools of water filled gaping craters in the sunken pavement. Thunder boomed, rattling his armor.

"Keep sharp," Michael said. He pulled out his binos while Rodger chinned on his NVGs. The green hue flickered over the ruins, but nothing moved. He took a few steps away from Michael to look at a brick building to the east. A hole in the wall provided a glimpse into the guts of the structure.

"Looks clear," Michael said. He turned back to the edge of the slope and flashed hand signals to Magnolia and Layla.

They continued down the street, with Rodger angling his pistol at the east side and Michael searching the west with his rifle.

"You see these messed-up foundations?" Rodger whispered. "Must have been some sort of geological event to make the ground shift like that."

Michael halted and brought a finger to the front of his helmet.

Okay, I get the point, Rodger thought.

Magnolia and Layla caught up with them as they approached the largest building, the one with arched roof beams and a steeple at the other end. A wide stone staircase led up to the front entrance. A massive set of double doors had once led into the building. The right door was missing, but the left appeared to be mostly intact. It looked like oak, maybe maple. Definitely not pine. Nothing as soft as pine would survive in conditions like this.

"This was a church—a place of worship," Magnolia said. "I've seen these places in the picture books on the *Hive*."

They walked cautiously up the stairs. The door on the left was carved with intricate designs that reflected the skill of a talented craftsman. Shards of colorful glass littered the dirt along the wall. Michael moved through the door and into the building. Rodger nearly ran into him as he followed. The commander had stopped in the entrance, his left hand in a fist.

Rays of blue light from the storm penetrated the clouds, cutting through the rotted rafters. The glow illuminated the inside of what had been a holy place, now covered in vines and roots. At the other end, the thick trunk of a tree had grown through a raised platform and up into the steeple overhead. Spiky branches with barbs on the ends extended over the rafters like some sort of palm tree out of a bad dream.

Magnolia stepped up behind them. "Holy shit," she whispered. "I saw something like this back in Charleston. Don't get close."

She raised her rifle and aimed at the center of the tree. Rodger didn't understand—it was just a tree, not a Siren.

"Hurry, let's get out of here before it notices us," she said quietly.

"*Notices* us?" Rodger said, turning around to look at her.

As soon as he moved, the bark of the tree began to vibrate. Cracking and creaking sounded as vines rustled and branches swayed.

Rodger gulped. "Oh, shit."

The web of interconnected vines and branches shifted and peeled away from the walls. Pieces of stone fell and shattered on the ground.

"Move it!" Magnolia said.

Everyone retreated except for Rodger. He remained in the doorway, watching as the strange tree began to glow. The thick foliage lit up all at once, flashing pink on the first pulse and then an angry red.

Someone grabbed him by the back of his armor and pulled him outside.

"You want to be plant food?" Magnolia said. "When I say move, you *move*!"

Rodger pulled his gaze away just as the center of the tree split open, revealing something that looked a lot like an animal mouth with teeth the size of his arm.

He stumbled backward and then loped down the stairs with Magnolia. Vines shot out of the entrance, wrapping around the door and pulling it back into the church.

"No!" Rodger shouted.

A crunching came from the interior as the mutant tree destroyed the ancient wood. More vines snaked outside and writhed across the steps.

Michael held up a hand. "Hold your fire," he said.

Slinging his rifle over his shoulder, he pulled out a large blade instead. Magnolia followed suit, exchanging her gun for the two curved blades. She swiped at a vine that stretched toward them, slicing through it with a quick motion. A beat later, Rodger holstered his pistol and gripped his ax in both hands. He hacked another limb in half with the sharp blade. Green blood sprayed the pavement.

The tree inside the church answered with the crunch of more branches, and the interior lit up like a flame. Michael and the other divers sliced their way through to the center of the street as more vines tried to grab them. Layla leaped over one, crying out in pain when she landed on her injured ankle. Michael ran over and put his arm under her shoulder while Magnolia and Rodger kept the barbed appendages at bay.

"They're everywhere!" Magnolia yelled. She wielded her two blades expertly, shearing off the limbs before they could touch her. She was much faster and more agile than Rodger, who hacked away with his ax. The limbs were tough and pulpy, some so thick it took several swings to chop through them. For every vine he cut to pieces, five new ones appeared.

"Don't let them flank us!" Michael yelled. Layla was still leaning on him as a crutch. Rodger wasn't sure how badly she was hurt, but she was slowing them down.

He fought harder, swinging madly at the vines and branches

that now spilled from the interior of virtually every building. Pulsating red light bathed the four divers as they struggled down the street.

Lightning slammed into the city. Sparks showered down. The thunder banged away in a constant din, making it nearly impossible to hear anything else.

Rodger lost track of time. He felt the sweat trickle across his skin, and his muscles began to ache with fatigue. A barbed vine streaked across his chest armor and wrapped around his calf guard, jerking on his leg so hard, he hit the ground.

"Get it off! Get it off!" he yelled. The limb yanked him toward a building. His armor scraped across the concrete.

"Help!" he screamed, flailing for something to hold on to.

Magnolia jumped over a branch, then sliced through the needle-covered tentacles. Thick green fluid gushed over the ground. She vaulted onto the hood of a rusted vehicle and then leaped toward Rodger. Wielding one of the sickles, she severed the branch holding his leg.

"Get up!" she yelled.

Rodger grabbed her arm and jumped to his feet. Not bothering to wipe off the green fluid that oozed down his legs, he ran toward the other divers. Layla and Michael were fighting off the vines on the opposite sidewalk. They came together in the center and fought their way toward the end of the street.

"I think they're talking to one another!" Magnolia shouted over the boom of thunder.

"No way!" Layla yelled back. "Plants can't do that."

Michael slashed at a vine that tried to trip him up. "Just keep them back!"

They struggled for another mile until Rodger finally saw the city limits. His stomach sank at the sight of the brown swamp water slapping the banks of the eroding island. Get torn apart by vines, or drown in something that looked and smelled like sewage? Neither option appealed to him. He was really starting to wish he had stayed on the *Hive*. He could be eating dinner with his parents right now.

The tree-things pursued them out of the city, but they could reach only so far. The divers lost them as they crossed into an open field. Before them lay the forbidding swampland.

"We're going to need one of those," Layla said, pointing at the rusted stern of a boat resting on its side fifty paces away.

Lightning fired the shore nearby, illuminating a dozen holes in the boat's hull. The team moved along the edge of the water. Tires, a bathtub, chairs, and other junk littered the beach.

Rodger turned to look at the branches behind them. They were twisting and curling, unable to reach any farther. They reminded him of fingers reaching toward them.

They were trapped here between the swamp and a city infested with mutant trees. How else could things go wrong?

An electronic wail answered his thought.

He wasn't the only one terrified by the sound. The limbs and vines suddenly twisted away, crawling back toward the buildings they had left behind. The red glow faded, leaving the divers alone in the flashing blue light of the storm.

Again came the high-pitched call of a Siren. The divers stood together, armor clinking back to back as they sheathed their blades and pulled their guns. They all knew what was out there, and it was much worse than man-eating trees.

* * *

The trading post reeked of body odor, but it also smelled of boiled cabbage and onions, which Jordan loved. His mother had made a cabbage soup that he would never forget. He hadn't tasted anything that good since he was seven years old, not long before she died.

He walked through the large room with his hands clasped behind his perfectly ironed white uniform. Sergeant Jenkins and Ensign Lore followed close behind. They kept their hands on their batons as they walked.

The lower-deckers made a path when they saw Jordan. He rarely visited this place, but today he had a special reason. He continued through the sea of passengers. Buyers, sellers, and hustlers loitered everywhere he looked. Despite the nostalgic smell of cabbage and onions, he wanted to leave here as quickly as possible to escape the resentful glares from the throng of haggard faces.

Most of them didn't see the captain who had risked everything to save them from joining the rest of humanity in the graveyards twenty thousand feet below. They saw a privileged elite who didn't give them enough food, water, or medicine. He had given up trying to win their hearts and minds. He cared only about preserving the ship and providing a future for these people and their descendants, even if they despised him for it.

A woman in a colorful coat stitched together from scraps held out bottles of herbs. "Will cure all of your ailments, only…"

She darted away when she turned to see Jordan and his entourage. Two more loiterers turned and hurried through the crowd as he passed.

"That's what I thought," Jordan muttered. He despised the so-called healers peddling their fake medicines. Janga had been one of those. In fact, he thought the multicolored coat might actually have belonged to the old woman. No matter how thoroughly he tried to erase the damage she had done belowdecks, Janga's legacy kept creeping back.

They passed a makeshift stall where jars of clear liquid were on display. The vendor was trying to hide them under a cloth, but he wasn't fast enough. Jordan motioned for Ensign Lore. "Go talk to Jimmy and confiscate his supply."

"Yes, Captain," Lore said.

The crowd grew thicker, and Jordan was at last obliged to have Jenkins clear the way. The sergeant pulled out his baton and waved it, yelling, "Out of the way, everyone!"

Jordan followed him through the parting throng until they arrived at his destination, a booth with a crooked sign that read DRAGON. The bulbs had all burned out, leaving the rusted shack draped in shadow. The owner, a man with curly red hair named Dom, stepped up to the counter. He blinked several times as he tried to focus on Jordan in the weak light.

"Oh, uh. Well, hello." The clearly nervous shop owner smiled unconvincingly. "What can I do for you, sir?"

"An order of your famous orange noodles," Jordan said, looking over his shoulder, "and make it quick." A group of lower-deckers were gathering nearby, watching him. He motioned for Jenkins, who stepped out with his baton, slapping the stick against his palm.

"Go back to your business," Jenkins said.

Jordan focused on Dom, who had retreated into the booth. He turned on a stove burner, grabbed a skillet and pot, and set them over the flames.

"Just a few minutes, Captain," Dom said.

Jordan nodded and folded his arms across his chest, waiting impatiently.

"Didn't know you were a fan of my noodles," Dom said.

"I'm not," Jordan replied. "These are for ... a friend."

Dom nodded and peeled a small orange, dropping the sections into a pot with freshly cut vegetables.

"Your friend got a name?" he asked, reaching up for a jar of spices. "I know most of my customers, and I remember exactly how they like their noodles. Some like crunchy, some like soft, some like—"

"Katrina," Jordan said, cutting off his chatter.

Dom glanced over, holding the skillet in one hand. "Ah. How is she? I haven't seen her for a while."

"She's been busy," Jordan said. He turned to see how Jenkins was holding up.

The busy marketplace had grown subdued since their arrival. Gone were the shouts from hawkers and hustlers, replaced by hushed voices and glares from resentful passengers, all of them focused on Jordan and his bodyguard.

"Hurry up," Jordan said to Dom.

"Katrina likes her noodles crunchy. If I hurry, they're going to be too soft. She's like X—very particular about the consistency."

"What did you say?" Jordan snapped.

Dom flipped the veggies in the skillet without looking at him. "I said Katrina likes her noodles crunchy."

"After that."

"She's very particular—"

Jordan cut Dom off a second time. "Why are you talking about X? He's been gone for a decade."

Dom froze in midflip, losing several vegetable bits in the process. Onions and other ingredients sizzled on the stove, and several fell to the filthy deck. Cursing, he scrambled to put the burner out.

Jordan let out a sigh as he watched Dom try to salvage the meal. When he had finished cleaning up, he apologized and said, "Sir, I didn't mean to upset you. I..."

"Just give me the food so I can be on my way."

Dom handed Jordan a small container of the steaming noodles. "This one's on me, sir," he said.

Jordan didn't bother thanking the man. After that fiasco, Dom was lucky he didn't lose his food license.

"Let's go, Sergeant," Jordan said. He followed the soldier out of the trading post, ignoring the onlookers.

By the time they reached the brig, Jordan had started to calm down. But the thought of X remained on his mind as he walked through the corridors and steeled himself for what came next.

At the brig, Sloan stood guard at the metal station inside the lobby. She straightened her hunched back when she saw Jordan and Jenkins arrive.

"I'm here to see Katrina," Jordan said.

Sloan ran a hand over her shaved scalp. Her lazy eye made her hard to read, but she looked shifty today. Something was wrong.

"Is that going to be a problem?" Jordan asked.

"Yes, Captain. I'm sorry, but she's been transferred to the medical ward."

"*What?* When did this happen?"

"A few hours ago."

"Why?" Jordan snapped. "What's wrong with her? Is it the baby?"

Sloan hesitated, her hard features softening. "She had a miscarriage, Captain. I'm really sorry."

Jordan stared at Sloan for a moment, the words not seeming to quite sink in. She bent down with Jenkins to pick something up from the ground. Looking down, Jordan saw the mess of noodles he had dropped on the floor.

ELEVEN

X was being pulled deeper and deeper into the filthy swamp water. He glimpsed the mud-caked bones of buildings and houses forming an underwater city all around him. He slashed at the reptilian coils gripping his body, but they continued to tighten, squeezing his armor against his ribs. The pressure made breathing difficult. Blood sang in his ears. The breathing apparatus in his helmet kept him from drowning, but that wouldn't matter if he couldn't breathe or if his helmet took on water.

At least Miles had escaped. Although it wouldn't matter if X didn't survive. The genetic modifications enabled the dog to survive in harsh conditions, but without X, he wouldn't be able to get food or water.

X twisted and squirmed to no avail. The only way out of this was to fight. He had maneuvered his knife around and was sawing away at the thick hide when he noticed flashes of movement in the cloudy muck. The struggle had attracted other creatures.

Sucking in what little air he could get into his lungs, X fought back with the last of his strength. He angled the tip of his blade into the gap between the coils and his chest armor before it could tighten even more. He had barely nicked the gigantic snake, but it suddenly unwrapped itself, leaving him to sink slowly through the water. He filled his lungs with a long breath as the tail whipped away, vanishing into the cloudy depths.

Something massive and covered in gray scales rushed through the murk in front of him, churning the water and hitting him with a wake that knocked him backward. He drifted, still trying to catch his breath.

There was something else down here—something worse than the snakelike monster.

Pulling with his arms, X kicked toward the surface. He wasn't the best swimmer, but fear inspired him. If the snake thing was retreating, then it wasn't the top of the food chain here—and X had no illusions about where he fit in, which had to be somewhere near the bottom.

It took him an entire minute to haul himself back up to the surface. When he finally broke through, he wasn't even close to land. The snake had pulled him deep into the swamp. Five hundred feet away, Miles paced and barked at the water's edge.

I'm coming, boy. Hang on.

He swam toward the embankment. The quake had churned the calm water into scum-choked waves that slapped the shoreline and knocked him about. The armor weighed him down, and the radiation suit clung to him, impeding his movement in the water.

He sank below the surface for a moment, kicked back up, and kept swimming. Every few strokes, he would force his body back into a horizontal plane by kicking hard with his boots. But even adrenaline and determination couldn't keep him above water for long. Halfway to shore, he continued to struggle, dragged downward again and again by his armor, boots, and helmet.

Thunder boomed and lightning sizzled as he treaded water to

catch his breath. He glanced over his shoulder just as a reptilian head and upper body slid through the surface fifty feet behind him. Maybe it was the same one that had tried to kill him, not that it mattered. For a moment, the eyes seemed to fix on his, but then it was sucked back down into the water as if by an unseen force.

The creature gave a loud hiss before it vanished in the churning brown foam. A massive dorsal fin sliced through the waves. X flung himself toward the shore. The time for rest was over.

He straightened his body and timed his strokes and kicks, trying to get a rhythm going. Swimming was a part of Hell Diver training, and though he was rusty, the thought of becoming fish food kept his aching body moving.

As X narrowed the distance to shore, Miles, unable to help himself, jumped into the water, trying to meet him halfway.

X saw movement in his peripheral vision, but he didn't turn. After pulling a few more yards, he spotted the dorsal fin up ahead. It appeared to be moving toward shore.

Toward Miles…

X stopped to tread water and wave his hands in the air.

"Over here!" he shouted. "Come get me, you slimy bastard!"

The fin changed tack, heading right for X. He continued treading water. Water had leaked into his helmet, and it smelled worse than any shit pot aboard the airship he once called home.

Of all the things to remember, he thought.

X didn't have time to celebrate having resurrected the name of the ship from his desolate memory banks. He pulled his knife out and faced the wide, scaly back of the abomination barreling toward him. The tail rose up and then slapped down on the surface. The fin alone was the size of his body, but he couldn't see the rest of the monster.

Just as it was about to reach him, he dived below the surface and rolled to look up. At last, he could see the monster's head.

It had a bony face with mandibles where teeth should be. Those serrated jaws would crush him, armor and all.

He thrust the knife upward into the pale gray belly passing overhead. The blade skittered across scales tougher than his own armor.

The huge tail fin whipped, hitting him so hard he choked on a mouthful of the putrid water in his helmet. He kicked back to the surface and pulled for shore, still a hundred feet away.

He swam until his feet hit the muddy lake bed. Righting himself, he waded as fast as the sticky muck would allow. The fish lurked in deeper water, watching. It finally slapped the water with its tail and turned to swim through the shallows. As it got closer, the fearsome mandibles opened. It could consume X in a single bite.

Panting and trying not to retch into his helmet, he slogged up onto the shore and motioned for Miles. He moved up the slope. Behind him, ten feet from shore, the monster beached on the shallow bottom. A wave hit the shore in a spray of brown muck as the beast struggled to free its massive body.

After putting some distance between himself and the shore, X collapsed onto his back. Miles nudged up against him and tucked his helmeted head under X's arm. The floundering monster clacked its mandibles together, staring at X with eyeballs the size of porthole covers, before it finally broke free of the mire and vanished.

He wasn't sure how long he lay on the road, but at some point after dumping the swamp water from his helmet, he dragged himself up and continued his trek toward the bunker on his map, limping and grunting like an injured beast. Despite the pain, he had no choice but to keep going. He walked in a daze, unsure of anything except the stark reality that if he stopped moving, he might never get up again.

Three days after the earthquake and the attack from the swamp creatures, X finally found the refuge under an old airfield. Using his wrist monitor, he hacked his way in. A long tunnel led him to a garage, but he ignored the old-world vehicles and searched the rest of the small bunker. When he finally sat down and peeled back the bandages covering the wound on his leg, he could see that it was infected. And he had developed a fever from swallowing the fetid swamp water. Adding to his misery, his throat was now so raw, he had trouble swallowing.

He found water and preserved food, all of it engineered to last for ages. That didn't mean the food tasted good, but he didn't care. Once he had fed Miles, he unfolded a cot and collapsed on it. He rested there, breathing heavily, his lungs crackling and his shaking body covered in a sheen of sweat. Miles licked the salt off his skin.

"I'm okay, boy. I'm okay."

X downed some antibiotic pills he found in the bunker's medical supply, hoping they would break the fever. When he was well enough, they would cross the final stretch of land to the ocean. After reaching that goal, if he was to die, then so be it.

Through the open door, he looked out over the garage. It was one of three rooms in the smallest bunker X had ever found in his journey across the ruined United States. Several old-world motorcycles and armored vehicles sat in the dark space, waiting for drivers long since dead.

His eyes went to the map, which showed a network of old roads leading to the coast. Then he looked back to the vehicles.

One of them will take you there.

As soon as he could sit up without blacking out, he would start restoring one of them. If he could get a working motor vehicle, it would make the final leg of his journey much easier. But first, he had to survive the fever.

Shivering, he swallowed a sip of water, his throat burning as the liquid ran down his swollen throat. A wave of lightness washed over him, and for a moment he had that weightless sensation he used to feel during the first seconds of a dive. He laid his head back and closed his eyes, hoping he wouldn't dream of monsters or memories.

PRESENT DAY

Michael kicked a rock. It skidded across the dirt and dropped into the swamp with a plop.

"Dangers on all sides," he muttered, looking out over the water. His gaze shifted to the city. The mutant foliage had retreated, but the Sirens were out there, stalking them.

The mission to find X had gotten off to a lousy start. They were still alive, though, and they hadn't wasted any ammo. He scanned the sky to the south, where Timothy had dropped them, and wondered what X would do in his shoes.

He would fight. He would do what it takes to survive.

Michael looked over at Layla's profile. Every decision he made affected her, Mags, and Rodger. They were his friends, his family. And they all were looking for him to lead them through this wasteland.

He chinned on the radio frequency for *Deliverance*. "Timothy, this is Michael, do you copy? Over."

Static crackled into his helmet. Either the storm was blocking the signal, or Timothy wasn't responding. Either way, they were stranded without an evac.

"I still can't reach Timothy," Michael said, "so we're going with plan B."

"Plan B better not involve boats," Magnolia said.

"Or man-eating trees," Rodger said.

Michael turned his binos back to the swamps, scanning for a way across, but only saw small islands barely big enough for one of them to stand. They had already plumbed the water's depth. Wading wasn't an option.

They needed transportation. Again he eyed the rusted boat. Judging by the holes in the hull, it wasn't going anywhere. But maybe there was another way...

"Sorry, but my plan includes both those things," Michael said.

Layla stepped closer to him and put her slender hand on his shoulder. Things between them had been different since Weaver's death. She had been burdened with grief, while he had been grappling with the responsibilities of command. It felt good to know she still supported him. He had missed holding her in his arms more than he wanted to admit.

"We're going to have to head back into the city to find transportation across the water," Michael said. "I don't want to hear any protests. Let's get it done, Team Raptor."

Normally, he would have asked for opinions, but he already knew what the other divers thought, and there was no time to argue. He waved the group after him, and they set off across the field separating the banks of the swamp from the ruins.

Lightning speared through the sky. In the cold flash of light, Michael glimpsed a Siren. The winged monster sailed under the cloud cover with a vine in its claws. The severed tentacle wriggled like a snake in its grip. An otherworldly call echoed over the island, stopping the divers in their tracks. The beast swooped into a building, where it disappeared.

"Six o'clock," Rodger said. He raised his pistol toward the sky, where another Siren hunted. It glided back to the south, taking no notice of them.

"Anyone else have eyes?" Michael asked. So far, he had seen

only three of the creatures, but the island was surely home or hunting ground to more.

"Got nothin'," Layla said.

"Me, neither," said Magnolia.

Michael flashed the signal to advance, and they continued toward the city. He took point and ran in a low hunch along the brick wall of the closest building. He didn't know where the hell they were going to find a boat, but he wasn't picky. All he needed was something that would float. If it came down to it, he would swim to find X.

Crouching, he peered around the corner. The vines had writhed back into the broken structures, but he could see spiny branches rising through the tops of several buildings.

"Rodger," Michael hissed, motioning Rodger forward. Rodger darted over and knelt beside Michael. "I want you to stay here and watch over Layla, okay? She's injured."

Rodger hesitated before nodding. Michael knew that he would rather be with Magnolia, but the man's ridiculous crush didn't figure into the decision.

Michael moved over to Layla. "I'm sorry, but you're staying here with Rodger. I'm taking Magnolia."

She raised a hand to protest, but he cut her off.

"Mags is faster, and you're hurt. Sorry, babe."

"If you said you need me to stay here and babysit Rodger, that would make me feel better," Layla said with a wry smile.

Michael grinned and pressed his helmet against hers. "I love you."

"Love you, too, Tin," she said. "Be careful."

Magnolia crawled over and waited for Michael to give the all clear.

"Just you and me this time," he said. "Show me how fast you are."

"Fearless, fast, and—" Rodger began before Michael cut him off.

"Radio silence unless necessary."

"Sorry," Rodger said. "Be careful out there, you guys."

Michael crept around the wall to look for contacts a second time. Seeing the empty street, he tilted his head for Magnolia to follow. She took off running down the street behind him. The nuclear blast had mostly spared this area, but Mother Nature had done what the explosion had failed to do, leaving most of the man-made structures broken.

A raucous thunderclap rattled the ruins as they crossed the street. Michael gritted his teeth and looked up at the swirling beast of a storm above them. He tried to reach *Deliverance* again.

"Timothy, this is Michael. Do you copy? Over."

More static. What the hell was going on?

Michael pointed toward a three-story building on the left side of the street. Branches stuck out of the third-floor windows, but the first floor looked clear. He stepped up to the open doorway and peered left, then right. The ceiling had caved in, dumping a bathtub, sink, and toilet on the floor.

"No good," he said.

They moved on to the next building and continued their search. Inside, the vines and trees had lost their pinkish glow and were a dark brown, camouflaged to blend with the rest of the drab landscape. The vegetation looked dead, but they were careful to avoid it, just in case.

The first block turned up no boats—and, happily, no Sirens. Just the filthy interiors of houses where his ancestors had once lived in peace. He led Magnolia onto the next block, where several shop fronts faced the road. Old-world vehicles rusted under downed power lines. An ash-covered electrical cable stretched across the sidewalk like one of the carnivorous vines.

Michael stepped over a faded sign that read COFFEE AND ESPRESSO.

What the hell was espresso?

It was hard to imagine what this place had once looked like. On other dives, he had never paid too much attention to artifacts. His mind was always focused on the dangers, not the treasures.

Today was no different.

He ignored another sign that promised something called "seafood," and directed Magnolia toward a building across the next street. A large metal door covered the storefront, suggesting that something inside might have survived intact. They ducked into an alleyway to look for a back entrance.

Lightning smacked down a block away. The tremor rumbled across the dirt. Michael braced for the mighty crack that followed, rattling his body and hurting his ears.

Magnolia stepped up to a metal door in the brick wall of the alleyway and tried the handle. Locked. She slung her rifle over her back and pulled out her tool kit while Michael stood guard. He couldn't see much of the sky, and the thunder made hearing difficult, but there was still no sign of the Sirens.

"Layla, how you doing back there?" he asked over the comms.

There was a short wave of white noise. "I'm fine, but Rodger won't sit still."

"Take a seat, Rodger Dodger," Michael ordered.

"Yes, Commander. Whatever you say."

When he returned, after he and Layla stole a few moments for themselves, he was going to have a talk with Rodger about a few things. The man had no respect for rank, and while he considered Rodger a friend, Michael was also his commander. He needed to know that Rodger would follow orders without questions—or sarcasm.

Michael raised his AK-47 as Magnolia opened the door. He chinned on his NVGs and moved inside, raking the barrel over the damp walls of what had been some sort of workspace. Industrial equipment was mounted on long tables in a room the size of the trading post on the *Hive*. The ceiling appeared mostly intact, aside from a few holes that had allowed water in. Pools had collected in several places.

He motioned for Magnolia to check the right side of the space while he cleared the left.

They weren't going to find a boat here, but perhaps there was something that would help them. He spotted a rust-caked sign on the wall. This one didn't have any text—just the symbol of what looked like a computer.

He stepped around a table stacked with equipment he didn't recognize, and ducked down to check underneath. Several tools and cans lay on the ground, but nothing looked useful. He stood and kept moving, checking on Magnolia's progress.

"Find anything?" he asked over the comm.

"Nothin'. You?"

"Negative."

They cleared the room in ten minutes and met back at the entrance. Stepping back out into the alley, they moved to the next block, where the recent lightning strike had ignited a pile of trash on the side of the road. Smoke threaded into the sky.

Another large door sealed off the entrance to a building not far from the fire. An old-world pickup truck sat in the driveway, reduced to rust, glass, and cracked rubber. Above the vehicle, a crooked sign beneath an overhang showed pictures of sailboats and palm trees.

Magnolia pointed, her eyes alight, and they bolted across the street to the gate.

"Wait for thunder," Michael said.

A trident of lightning blazed overhead, and as the thunder boomed, Michael and Magnolia grabbed the handles and lifted the door. The screeching metal was hardly audible over the noise.

With the door open, they both stepped back and leveled their rifles at the interior of the garage. It took a moment for Michael's eyes to adjust to the green hue of his NVGs, but when they did, he saw the mother lode arrayed before them.

The long space housed several fiberglass boats, and others of aluminum. He recognized them from old books and vids in the *Hive*'s library: canoes, kayaks, and even a sailboat. To the left, surfboards hung from the wall.

"Holy shit!" Magnolia breathed. "We actually found—"

A screech cut her off.

Michael whirled around, looking up, but the alien wail seemed to be coming from all directions.

"You got eyes?" he asked calmly.

Magnolia's armor hit his with a clank, and her reply came in a garbled mess. "What the shit ... Oh, no, not these fucking things again."

Michael turned back toward the garage and followed the barrel of her rifle toward a bulbous cocoon hanging to the right of the surfboards. Bristles like giant eyelashes covered the central opening.

"Nests," she whispered.

An eyeless face poked out of one of the openings, and gooey liquid sloshed down the wall. Bony hands widened the gap, allowing the Siren to push its body out past the thick bristles.

Michael watched in horror as more of the nests began to stir and twitch. He counted an even dozen.

"They're just babies," Magnolia said quietly. "Maybe we can sneak out before the parents get back."

Michael unholstered his blaster and flicked the selector to the flare. He had aimed the barrel at the ceiling and prepared to torch the bastards when another conical head suddenly poked through an opening in the roof.

The Siren that looked down at them was no baby. It squeezed its body through the gap and dropped to the floor between the two divers, separating them from the nests—and from the precious boats.

"Watch out!" Magnolia shouted.

Michael aimed the blaster back at the ceiling as the beast folded its wings over its spike-ridged back.

"Fire!" he shouted.

His flare streaked into one of the nests. The blaze ignited the flammable soft tissue and quickly spread to the other cocoons.

The Siren let out a screech louder than thunder, nearly bringing Michael to his knees. Magnolia squeezed the trigger, riddling the pale, stringy flesh with two three-round bursts. The eyeless creature jerked back and forth as bullets ripped through and out its back and peppered the walls, killing the babies crawling out of the nests to escape the flames.

"What's going on!" Layla shouted over the comms.

The Siren fell back onto a canoe, flopped once or twice, and went still. Michael stepped forward and lifted the end of the boat, dumping the carcass off.

"Get ready to paddle!" Michael replied over the open channel. "We're getting the hell off this island!"

TWELVE

Jordan sat in his dark office, looking at the ceiling. Whatever remained of his heart had died inside him.

Maybe it's for the best, he kept telling himself. *Maybe this is what you needed to focus you back on your duty to the* Hive *and humanity.*

He shook his head and closed his eyes. He had hoped Katrina would give birth to a boy who would carry on his legacy as captain, that eventually their son would create his own family. Generations of Jordans would continue aboard the *Hive* until the day it was finally safe to return to the surface.

But his dream was not to be.

His child was lost, and Katrina was, too. It was her fault the baby had died. She had refused to eat, refused to care for herself. She had killed their child as surely as if she had driven a knife into her own belly.

He opened his eyes and stalked over to the door, stopping momentarily to look at the sword hanging on the bulkhead. He turned on the overhead light to examine the one piece of history that he would not be removing from the ship.

Since the launch of the *Hive*, the blade had been handed down from captain to captain. It was a ceremonial weapon, but there were stories of a captain actually using it in a rebellion a century ago. Since then, the sword had remained on the wall in the captain's quarters. His predecessor, Maria Ash, had never liked it, which made Jordan appreciate it even more. It had hung useless on the wall for too long. It was time for a captain to carry it again.

He reached out and took the metal sheath in both hands, raising it from the wall mount. Using a clip on the sheath, he fixed it to his belt. Then he pulled the sword out, holding the blade aloft in the overhead lights.

He traced a finger along its edge. The blade was as dull as a dinner plate. *Harmless*, he mused as he sheathed the blade. But that could be fixed.

He flicked off the lights and walked out onto the bridge. Several officers, including Hunt, looked in his direction, their eyes flitting to the sword and then back to his face.

He wasn't sure how many of them knew about Katrina, but it didn't matter. They all would know soon.

"Hunt, you have the bridge," Jordan said. "Radio me if you need anything."

Ensigns Del Toro and Lore were waiting for him on the platform near the exit.

"Sir," they said in unison.

"Let's go," Jordan said. "I'm headed to the library and then to the launch bay."

Lore's thin lips moved as he if wanted to reply, but he stiffened and nodded silently instead.

"Is there a problem with that?" Jordan asked, looking at Del Toro. He had more spine than Lore.

"Sir," Del Toro said. The thickset officer drew in a deep breath through his nostrils, as if he needed to gather his courage. "It's not safe to go to the lower decks right now without a squad. I'm sure Sergeant Jenkins would agree."

"I would," said a voice.

Jenkins ducked through the open hatch and joined them on the platform overlooking the bridge.

"We've got a major problem, Captain," Jenkins said. He wiped his nose, smearing blood on the brown sleeve of his uniform. "The raid on the library did not go well. The librarian put up quite the fight."

"Jason Matthis?" Jordan raised a brow. "He's an old man, and practically blind! Explain to me how he put up a fight."

Jenkins lowered his hand to his side, and Jordan noticed the scraped and bleeding knuckles.

"What the hell happened, Sergeant?" Jordan said.

"Sir, with all due respect, what did you think was going to happen when our crews started taking down paintings and pulping books? The people are rising up."

Jordan took three steps until he was inches from Jenkins' face. Fueled by rage and grief, he didn't even try to hold back.

"I didn't ask you for your fucking opinion, Sergeant. I asked you what the hell happened." The sergeant held his ground and the captain's gaze.

"Do you not remember the oath you swore to the *Hive*? Do you not see where you are right now? You're on the fucking *bridge*!" Jordan gestured with his arms wide. "You are not here to question me. You exist to follow *my* orders."

Jordan felt the gaze of every officer burning into his back. He turned away from Jenkins and yelled, "Get back to work!"

All faces dropped back down to their stations, and Jordan turned back to Jenkins.

"I'd ask you again what the hell happened, but I'm going to

see for myself." And with that, he brushed past, his sword sheath bumping the sergeant in the side.

Footfalls echoed across the platform, which told Jordan his guards were following. He halted right before he reached the open hatch.

"Put an edge on this." Jordan unfastened the sheath from his belt and handed it to Del Toro. "I want it sharp enough to shave with. Then bring it back to me."

*　　*　　*　　*　　*

Sergeant Jenkins pulled out a key and unlocked the armory. He wore his matte-black padded armor and carried his helmet in the crook of his arm.

Don Olah was first to walk into the room. The other divers followed, with Les Mitchells ducking under the overhead. A bank of lights clicked on, illuminating racks of weapons mounted to the bulkheads.

"Holy shit," Jennifer said.

Rifles, crossbows, pistols, blasters, and shotguns were lined up neatly on the racks, but most of the mesh lockers were empty. Only a few helmets and armor suits remained inside. Several of the weapons racks were also empty. Most of them were in the hands of militia soldiers. On the way to the armory, Les had spotted dozens of them patrolling the corridors, armed to the teeth and outfitted in full riot gear. For now, the ship was quiet, but he feared that an uprising was near. Purging the history had caused an uproar the likes of which Les hadn't seen in over a decade.

The hatch behind them closed, and the soldier on the other side locked it with a click.

"Welcome to weapons training," Erin said. She gestured to her father, who glowered at them with his burly arms folded across this chest. For an old guy, he was buffed. "Sergeant Jenkins will be taking over this portion of your training."

"Most of you have never fired a weapon in your life," Jenkins said. "Ensign Olah has, but we all know he's not the best shot."

Olah's cheeks reddened.

"I wasn't a great shot when I started, either," Erin said.

"But you're not diving, so it doesn't matter," Jenkins replied.

Her smile vanished, and she caught Les' gaze. He realized in that moment that she hadn't told her father about her plan to dive with them, and Les wasn't eager to see how that conversation went.

"Today, we're going to train you in how to use the weapons that may very well end up saving your life when you land on the surface," Jenkins continued. "The most dangerous part of a dive are the creatures that dwell down there."

He plucked a blaster off the rack. "This is your primary weapon," he said, opening the break and showing it to each diver in turn. "There's room for two shotgun shells and a flare. Flicking the button up allows you to fire a flare. Flicking it down allows you to fire the shotgun shells."

The sergeant replaced the gun on the rack and grabbed a rifle.

"This is an AK-47 that fires a thirty-round magazine. We also have M4s, M16s, and various other models salvaged over the years. They're antiques, but they're good, reliable weapons. Only two of you will be assigned rifles on this next dive: Olah and whoever ends up as the best shot in simulation training today."

Jenkins pointed at the pistols next. "Everyone else will have a handgun and a blaster."

"Go ahead and familiarize yourself with the grips of each weapon," Erin added. "Then we're going to get in the simulator for live training."

Les picked up a shiny-barreled pistol with a wooden grip.

It felt heavier than he had thought it would, and raising it, he couldn't help but imagine what it would feel like to fire it at a living creature. He had never in his life killed anything bigger than a bug.

Erin led the team through another hatch. Smiling warmly and eagerly, she turned and gestured for Les and the others to follow. Les hadn't trusted her up until now, but after hearing the story about the fateful dive that ended Team Wolf, he was starting to get more comfortable with her. Losing her friends and her lover explained her standoffish reputation—heck, anyone would be scarred by such an experience. The next time he heard folks talking about Erin behind her back, he planned to give them a piece of his mind.

The lights flipped on in the next room, revealing two desks with virtual-reality headsets, and three firearms with red tips on the barrels.

"This is how we're going to train to shoot?" Jennifer asked.

Olah glared at her. "What did you expect? We'd let you waste real bullets? Besides, most of you would end up blowing holes in the gas bladders."

Les ducked into the room and stepped up to the first desk.

"Olah is correct," Sergeant Jenkins said. "We have always trained this way, both the divers and militia. Every bullet is precious."

He looked about to continue his lecture, but then he reached up and placed a finger on his earpiece, turning his back to the divers to listen to a message.

"Roger that, Lieutenant," he said after a short delay.

"What's going on?" Erin asked.

"More crowds are gathering outside the trading post. I need to go. I'll get back when I can."

The sergeant hurried back into the armory, where he stopped to grab a crossbow. He unlocked the hatch leading to the corridor outside and vanished. Les heard the commotion as the hatch swung shut.

As soon as Jenkins left, two more people entered the armory: a woman with a shaved head, and a man wearing orange coveralls.

"Is that who I think it is?" Jennifer asked.

Erin turned to look. "Ah, they're early," she said.

Lauren Sloan, the hard-looking guard of the ship's brig, pushed a thin man into the training room. The man kept his head down, and Les couldn't see his face in the dim light.

"What the hell is this traitorous lump of shit doing here?" Olah asked. Apparently, he recognized the prisoner even if Les didn't.

"He's not to be given a weapon," Sloan said. She unlocked the cuffs and patted the man on the shoulder in a surprisingly tender gesture. "Remember the agreement."

"We have a guard posted outside," Sloan said. "If you need anything, just holler, but I don't think he'll be giving you any problems."

"I'll take care of him if he does," Olah said.

Sloan rolled her good eye and left the room. All five divers stood looking at the prisoner. Eyes downcast, he was chomping on a calorie-infused herb stick.

Ty Parker, Les thought. *I'll be dipped in hog puckey.* He had thought the man was dead.

He looked halfway there, anyway. His face was covered in yellow bruises and scabbed cuts. He was thin as a whip, with sharp cheekbones and hollow eyes. The calorie-infused herb stick he was chewing on didn't seem to be doing much good.

Les didn't know the former technician well, but he had heard stories. Everyone said he was a good man to have at your back. He wasn't sure what had happened between Ty and Jordan during the launch that left the other divers dead at the Hilltop Bastion, but Les had a feeling it wasn't Ty's fault. It seemed that a lot of things he had heard on this ship were turning out to be lies.

*   *   *   *   *

Rodger had taken cover behind a tumbledown brick wall with Layla. Standing side by side, they fired their pistols at the Sirens rising into the sky. His gun had quite a kick, and the hammer bit into his glove.

"Shit!" he grumbled, shifting his grip. His next shot missed the Siren. It swooped down, claws extended and leathery wings rippling in the air. Three of the beasts were trailing Michael and Magnolia out of the city. The storm illuminated the obstacles in their way: a metal guardrail, several rusted vehicles, a fence of downed power lines, and upended slabs of concrete.

Slowing them down were two small boats. They dragged the boats across the dirt, stopping every few yards to fire into the sky. Only a quarter mile of rocky terrain separated the divers from Rodger and Layla, but the Sirens were closing in.

"Keep them off us!" Michael yelled over the comms.

Layla and Rodger continued firing, empty casings dropping to the mud. The near-constant flash of blue light from the storm gave enough illumination to see the creatures, but flying targets were nearly impossible to hit with small-arms fire from this distance.

Rodger gripped the handgun in both hands, closed one eye, and trained the barrel ahead of the Siren diving toward Michael. The ugly creature had its wings pulled back into a delta, leading with its eyeless conical head.

As Rodger pulled the trigger again, he couldn't get past the fact that these things had evolved from humans. There wasn't much that was human about them anymore, but that shared ancestry somehow made the creatures even more terrifying.

The shot nicked the upper part of the creature's wing, but it continued streaking down toward its prey. Rodger squeezed off another shot, but the monster was undeterred. A second one joined it, the beasts flanking Michael.

"TIN!" Layla screamed at the top of her lungs.

The first beast clawed at Michael's helmet while the second plowed into his torso, knocking him to the ground. The third Siren circled above, biding its time.

Magnolia dropped her boat and ran over with both curved blades drawn. She struck from behind, lopping the scabrous head with a double strike. Then she sheathed the blades and unslung her rifle to fire at the second creature, which was coming in for another run. Rounds tore into the sinewy body, blood gushing from the holes as it spiraled into the loom of power lines.

Magnolia made killing look easy. And sexy.

Focus, Rodgeman.

In the distance, more Sirens rose into the sky, flapping like monstrous bats above the buildings. It took them only a few seconds to home in on the divers.

"We have to help them," Layla said. She moved away from their position behind the brick wall, limping out into the mud to fire her semiautomatic pistol.

"Get back here!" Rodger shouted. He bolted after her, reloading his weapon as he moved. One of the bullets fell into the mud, but he didn't waste time to bend down for the precious round.

Thumbing back the hammer, he raised the revolver and searched for a target. Only one of the original three Sirens remained. It continued circling at a safe distance, calling for reinforcements in a high-pitched wail that made Rodger shiver.

Michael had pushed himself to his feet and was now dragging the long blue boat across the dirt again. He appeared unharmed, but he might just be too stubborn to realize he was hurt.

Layla limped farther out into the muddy field, navigating the trip-me hunks of concrete and tangled rebar jutting out of the ground. She slipped, righted herself, and kept moving.

Seeing her press on like a madwoman reminded Rodger how much she cared for Michael. For the first time in his life, Rodger, too, was fighting to save someone other than himself or his friends. His feelings for Magnolia had grown into something bigger and stronger than he had ever felt before. He needed to tell her, but first they had to live through the Siren attack.

"On my way, Mags!" Rodger called out.

She dropped her boat and knelt behind a rock to aim at the next flight of Sirens coming in from the city. There were six, all of them full-grown with eleven-foot wingspans. Their hellish screeches rose into a macabre chorus.

Rodger slipped and fell in the mud, hesitating there when he saw the Sirens move into a V formation. The beasts were expert hunters and had survived, even thrived, in the apocalyptic wastelands. How could the divers fight such aberrations of evolution?

Get up, Rodger! Magnolia's in trouble.

He pushed himself back up and jogged after Layla, who was already halfway to Michael and Magnolia.

The beasts were preparing to dive toward the field. Their wings flapped through the air, and their clawed feet hung low, ready to grasp and tear.

Layla stopped to fire, and Rodger followed suit. Their pistols spat .45 rounds into the sky, but neither found a target.

"Get back to the swamp!" Michael shouted.

Layla ignored the order, and Rodger ran after her a beat later.

Michael's frantic voice surged over the channel a second time. "Timothy, are you out there?"

By now it was obvious to Rodger that the AI had left them. The storm couldn't be blocking out *all* their transmissions. The broken program was probably off sulking somewhere, having taken their only means of escape with him.

"I never trusted him," Layla said.

Rodger didn't reply. He was too focused on the monsters moving in.

He planted his boots the best he could and picked out a target. With the barrel lined up, he held in a breath, closed one eye, and led the beast in his sights.

The bullet hit the creature in the spine. It somersaulted limply through the air. Amazed, Rodger watched it crash into the foundation of an old building.

"I got it!" he yelled.

"Then get another!" Layla shouted back.

Magnolia and Michael were almost to their position now, but the other five Sirens were still flying undeterred beneath the storm clouds. Michael had the kayak on his shoulders and ran without glancing back. Magnolia continued dragging hers.

The Sirens all dived at once, as if a signal had coordinated them. Magnolia dropped her boat and fell on her butt. She pulled her rifle and raked the barrel back and forth, spraying bullets into the sky. Several found targets, disrupting the formation and sending the Sirens flapping in different directions.

Lightning lanced through clouds, and the thunder overwhelmed the eerie electronic shrieks.

"Stay here!" Rodger said. He sprinted past Michael until he reached Magnolia.

"You shoot; I'll carry the boat," he said.

She nodded and stood with her rifle aimed into the sky. Rodger holstered his pistol and bent down to grab the paddles from the boat. It took some coordinating, but he managed to get it on one shoulder and keep the paddles in his other hand. The crack of gunfire followed him as he ran across the sludge of radioactive dirt. A human skull poked out of the mud ahead, and his boot crunched through it.

A quarter mile away, he could see the border of the swamps. They were almost there. He ran harder, eyes on his goal. Layla grabbed Michael's rifle and took over, firing as she backpedaled.

"Changing!" Magnolia said.

In the lull of her fire, high-pitched wails filled the air. He could picture the beasts swooping down and pulling him into the sky, but he couldn't turn his head to look without losing the kayak.

Do not piss yourself, Rodger!

He wasn't used to fighting eyeless freaks that wanted to eat him alive. He was a carpenter and engineer, not a soldier. He should be back at home on the *Hive*, working on his latest carving or having dinner with his family. He should never have volunteered to be a Hell Diver. He wasn't cut out for adventure and danger.

A memory of being dragged across the water treatment plant by the monsters back at the Hilltop Bastion surfaced in his mind. The thought of it made his skin crawl, and he filled the piss container in his suit to the brim.

A burst of automatic fire from Magnolia's weapon snapped him out of his trance. They were almost to the edge of the swamp now. Michael lowered his boat and slid it down the slope into the brown water.

"Got one!" Magnolia shouted.

That left three, if Rodger had counted correctly.

He made the final push across the field, dropped the boat on the ground, and pulled his pistol back out. Three Sirens remained, flapping into the darkness away from the wall of fire the four divers had put up, but there were more shadowed figures back in the city. Smaller creatures.

The youngsters.

The sight evoked another memory of the water treatment

plant. If not for Weaver, he would have ended up eaten alive back there. Thoughts of the brave old diver who had given his life for the others fired Rodger with new confidence.

"Conserve your ammo!" Michael ordered.

Rodger holstered his pistol and pulled the ax off his belt. The three adult Sirens were coming back in for another run, with their children on both flanks.

"Let's get in the water!" Magnolia shouted.

Rodger hefted the ax and watched the squadron of monsters coming at them. Magnolia stepped up to his side. She was working the action of her rifle, trying to free a jammed round.

"Son of a bitch," she growled.

Behind them, Layla and Michael were pushing both boats out from shore.

"We have to stand our ground here," Rodger said. "We get out there, and we'll end up drown—"

A flash of motion came from the left before he could finish his sentence. A Siren had flanked them. It leaped toward Magnolia, but Rodger pushed her out of the way at the last second.

The beast slammed into him, knocking him backward. He landed on his back and found himself staring into the monster's mouth opening. It struck at his helmet, cracking the glass.

Blood sloshed over the visor, and the body pinning him to the ground went limp. A hand gripped his and pulled him to his feet.

"You okay?" Mags asked.

Rodger wiped the gore from his cracked glass and nodded. Magnolia grinned. "Good. Now, get out of the way."

Pivoting to face the Sirens swooping toward them, she opened fire. The fusillade cut through the beasts, sending them flopping to the ground less than a hundred feet away.

The others suddenly wheeled away. Slowly Magnolia lowered her weapon.

"Is everyone okay?" Michael asked, panting.

Rodger looked down at his suit. He didn't see any tears or feel any injuries, but he raised his wrist monitor to make sure. Several agonizing seconds passed before he got the reading.

Suit integrity: 100 percent.

"I'm okay," he said.

"Let's get in the water," Michael said.

Working together, the divers pushed the two long boats out into the swamp and put their gear inside.

"Timothy, do you copy?" Michael asked again. "This is Commander Everhart. We're heading into the swamps to continue the search for X. If you're listening, please respond!"

Rodger got into the boat with Magnolia and grabbed a paddle. She suddenly let out a gasp and pointed at a long humpbacked creature rising from the water. It ducked back under the surface, sending out ripples.

Perhaps the Sirens weren't fleeing the divers after all, Rodger realized. Maybe they just didn't want to tangle with whatever beasts lived beneath the murky waters.

THIRTEEN

Xavier Rodriguez coughed up something that looked like an egg yolk, and spat it on the cold concrete floor of the military bunker.

His fever had broken, but his throat wasn't getting any better. It hurt to speak, and each breath felt like sandpaper. He didn't say much these days anyway, even to Miles—because of the pain mostly, but also because he didn't have much to say.

Raising his arm, he wiped his mouth on the sleeve of his new camouflage jacket and continued down the hallway toward the supply room. The small bunker consisted of only three rooms. He was headed for the smallest: a large closet filled with neatly stacked rows of vacuum-sealed items ranging from medicine bottles and high-calorie food bars to water purification equipment, soap, bedding, stacks of clothing, and batteries.

Most of what he had salvaged was already in the saddlebags of the motorcycle he had been working on, but he wanted to do a final check to make sure he wasn't leaving anything useful behind.

X grabbed a bottle of anti-inflammatory medicine he had overlooked earlier, and returned to the garage. Parked inside were two motorcycles, a jeep, an armored truck, and a pickup truck. He had managed to get only one of the old-world vehicles to work. He selected a wrench from the wall of tools and walked over to his new ride.

The motorcycle was finally rust-free after several sandblasting sessions and had a new coat of matte-black primer. The garage was equipped with every tool needed to restore the vehicle. He had patched the old tires and filled them with air, salvaged enough fuel cells from the armory to power the bike, and overhauled the engine, replacing the valves and piston rings. But the most impressive feat was the wheels.

X bent down to examine the foot-long blade jutting from either end of the front hub. They would slice through poisonous foliage, and if any beasts got in his way, they would get a nice haircut.

He checked the gears next. The highest gear still needed replacing, but that was fine—traveling at 150 miles per hour on a highway that hadn't seen maintenance for over two centuries didn't sound like the brightest idea anyway. He finished tightening the final bolt on the seat he had built for Miles, and stepped back to admire his work.

Two saddlebags hung from the sides, stuffed full of gear, supplies, and food. Miles even had his own compartment, which X had welded onto the back of the bike using spare parts, even padding it with pieces of carpet. Everything was set. All he needed to do now was finish packing his gear.

X moved out of the garage and into the office that had served as his bedroom. Miles, who had been snoozing on the cot, looked up and wagged his tail.

"You ready to go, boy?" X asked. His voice came out scratchy. Something caught in his throat, and he bent over, coughing. He hacked and spat, and this time there was blood.

X reached up with one hand and placed his fingers on his

throat. His pulse was racing. There was something wrong with his body that radiation pills and antibiotics couldn't fend off.

He stared at the blood for another moment. Miles whined, sensing that something was off.

"I'll be fine," X tried to say, but the words sparked another coughing fit.

He forced down one of the anti-inflammatory pills with some water. The cool liquid felt good on his throat, though he doubted the medicine would do much. After nearly a decade in the radioactive wasteland that once was Earth, X feared that his time was almost up. He just needed to hold it together long enough to finish his journey.

X grabbed his armor and their radiation suits and motioned for Miles to follow him to the garage. Once they were secured in their suits, helmets on, he picked Miles up and placed him in the back. Hot breath steamed the inside of Miles' helmet, but he seemed comfortable enough buckled into his makeshift seat.

After heaving open the garage door, X stepped back to check the long tunnel that sloped up nearly three hundred feet to a second blast door. He had already opened the outer door earlier this morning to check for contacts. Sporadic blue flashes glowed at the top of the ramp. The violent storm hadn't let up at all in the days since he found the bunker.

He hopped on the bike and turned the key. The engine purred. He had tested the vehicle on the tarmac aboveground a few times, laying it down only once while learning how to ride it. He was still nervous, but hey, it couldn't be any more dangerous than diving.

X coughed as he steered the heavy bike to the garage door. Before leaving, he paused to look at the radio equipment at the other end of the room. A partially intact skeleton—the only human remains X had found in this place—sat in the chair facing it. He considered trying to send a message to those who had left him behind. If they were somehow still up there, they could use the supplies in this bunker.

No. They're gone. It's just you and Miles.

X gunned the engine, accelerating out of the garage and up the slope toward the open blast door. Lightning flashed across the skyline. Miles let out a bark that X could hear over the rumble of the bike.

"It's okay!" X shouted. His throat was still scratchy, but the water had helped soothe it for now.

The bike wobbled a little, but he was still getting the hang of riding. He slowed as he approached the door, and brought the bike to a stop to look out over the landscape. The map he had used to find this place showed an interstate system that should eventually bring him to the ocean. He checked his rifle in the scabbard he had mounted on the side of the bike. The blaster was holstered on his thigh, and the pistol in the duty belt around his waist. If they met any Sirens, he had plenty of firepower within easy reach.

There was no reason to linger, but for some reason, X couldn't bring himself to drive onto the tarmac. He stared at the remains of an old airship nearby, now nothing more than aluminum ribs. This wasn't the first time he had seen it, but it made him think of the people in the sky again. Maybe he should send that message after all and let them know there were more fuel cells and rations down here.

His brain flashed through fragmented memories. Blurred faces, distant voices, and a word…

Tin.

The word didn't mean anything to him, yet it made him inexplicably sad. In his mind's eye, he saw a locker with a picture of a bird over it, but the image faded, replaced by a winged monster pulling X down to the snowy surface of Hades. Funny how he had no trouble remembering the name of hell. That was something he would never forget, no matter how much time passed.

For several minutes, he sat in the entrance to the bunker, staring at the wreck of the ancient airship. The pain of isolation had never truly healed. But it had transformed into anger. Anger at being left behind. Anger at the devastation the human race had wrought on the surface. Anger that Miles had to live in a radiation suit instead of being able to run and play.

He would not send a message about the supplies this time. The bastards didn't deserve it. Instead, he twisted the throttle. They shot out onto the tarmac. Miles barked behind him, but he kept his focus on the road and on the speedometer that he had linked to his HUD. The numbers ticked upward.

Thirty miles an hour...forty.

He gave the engine more juice and felt the jolt of sudden acceleration. Miles stopped barking, and X looked over his shoulder to see that the dog had hunkered down.

Fifty miles an hour.

His eyes flitted from his HUD to the broken road. The tires thumped over the cracks, and he maneuvered around a plate of broken asphalt. He was rapidly closing in on the ruined airship. The flayed exterior provided a clear view into the guts. It was like looking inside the belly of a massive, rotting sea creature. Despite the damage, the destroyed ship looked eerily familiar.

He found himself staring at the charred bulkheads instead of focusing on his HUD and the road. Memories flashed through his mind again, blotting out the present.

No, he thought. *Not right now...*

In the blackened wreck, he saw the apparition of a boy wearing a tin hat. The child waved and smiled at X as he passed. In a room near the bow of the ship, another specter appeared. A woman with electric-blue highlights in her hair stood on a platform.

No...they're gone. They're all dead.

X shifted gears and twisted the throttle as far as it would go. The numbers on his HUD ticked up to sixty miles per hour. The tires rumbled over the cracked pavement and started the bike wobbling and threatening to dump. He gripped the handlebars tightly and steadied the bike as they passed the bow of the airship. He kept his eyes on the only thing that mattered: the road. He was almost to the ocean now, and nothing short of a nuclear blast was going to stop him from getting there.

*   *   *   *   *

PRESENT DAY

Jordan lay in bed, listening to the quiet hum of the ship. The bulkheads creaked and groaned all around him. These had always been comforting noises, ever since he was a child. The *Hive* was the mother and father he had never really had growing up.

He rarely thought of the woman who brought him into this world. She had died long before he was old enough to remember her, and his father hadn't been around much before he, too, was gone.

Although Jordan didn't have much guidance in his youth, he had always known he wanted to be captain. He had spent most of his childhood fascinated with the *Hive*, learning all he could about it: how it stayed in the air, how it supported the people who lived aboard it. In some regards, he was a lot like Michael Everhart. His path had been set for him from an early age.

After Captain Maria Ash passed, Jordan became one of the youngest captains in the history of the *Hive*. Now, at forty-four, he was determined to make his mark. His years of study and service as second mate to Maria had taught him almost everything he needed to know about how to operate the vessel. It was the only home he had ever known, and he would die to defend it.

The people could curse him; they could talk behind his back; they could riot. It didn't matter. He would never give up fighting for their future, no matter how much it cost him.

He swung his legs over the side of his bed and put his feet on the cold floor. It still felt odd not having Katrina by his side, but he shook away thoughts of her and their lost child.

Focus. Just keep the ship in the air one more day.

The touch screen across the room warmed to life, displaying the time and temperature at his voice command: *0600 hours / 75 degrees Fahrenheit.*

He grabbed his uniform off a hanger in his closet and draped the perfectly ironed shirt and pants over his chair. He dressed quickly, but as he was lacing up his boots, he glanced up and caught a glimpse of himself in the mirror. A haggard, dispirited face stared back at him. New lines framed his eyes and mouth, and gray streaked through his slicked-back dark hair.

He turned on the sink for two seconds, just enough to fill his palms with cold water. Then he splashed it on his face. There was nothing like it to wake him up in the morning. He looked back up at the mirror, but the bracing dash of water hadn't changed his appearance.

"You earned the right to serve these people," he said. "You deserve your command, and you *will* save them."

He clipped the sword onto his belt and opened the hatch to his quarters. Del Toro and Lore were waiting for him in the corridor. Neither man looked as though he had slept.

"Do you have a sitrep?" Jordan asked.

"Things calmed down overnight," Lore said, "thanks to the strong militia presence in every corridor. The curfew seemed to work, too. We made zero arrests."

"Good. Let's get going."

Jordan walked through the passages and admired the recently

scrubbed bulkheads and overheads. All the paintings were gone, leaving behind only dark metal and red helium pipes. Seeing the ship cleaned of the images from the past filled him with a refreshing sense of rebirth. He could see the *Hive*'s skin now, and its veins of helium pipes.

But just as a body needed food, the *Hive* needed Hell Divers.

The ship was almost in position, and in a few hours they would be dropping the divers over a yellow zone.

Lieutenant Hunt waved at Jordan as he approached the launch bay.

"Stay here," Jordan ordered his guards.

Lore and Del Toro stood sentry outside the launch bay as Jordan crossed the room, avoiding the gazes of the technicians and divers. He was too tired to talk to anyone but his XO.

Hunt closed the operations booth door behind Jordan. "Good morning, Captain," he said.

"Is it?" Jordan replied.

The lieutenant shook his head. "No sir. It's not. We picked up a garbled transmission early this morning. It seems to be an active one, and although I can't make out any of it, the voice does sound oddly familiar."

Jordan raised an eyebrow, trying to keep his mind focused on the dive despite the news. "Could it be X? Or is it someone else?"

"It's not X," Hunt said. "I'm certain of that. The voice is more youthful."

"Is it possible Commander Everhart is still alive at the Hilltop Bastion?"

"Maybe, but the transmission is coming from somewhere over Florida."

Jordan paused to think, then shrugged. He had bigger things to worry about. "Keep me updated." He turned to head back into the launch bay but stopped when Hunt called him back.

"There's something else, sir," Hunt said quietly.

"Great," Jordan said. "What now?"

"During the raid, the militia found something in the library that you need to see."

Jordan's thoughts were interrupted before he could ask any questions. Through the glass window of the operations room, Sergeant Jenkins and several of his men walked into the launch bay. Even at a distance, their faces appeared rough and exhausted from a long night of keeping order on the ship.

Jordan opened the door and stepped out to meet the sergeant. There was fire in Jenkins' eyes as he marched onto the platform. But he wasn't focused on the captain.

"Erin, what the hell are you doing?" Jenkins shouted across the room. His angry voice echoed, attracting the attention of all.

Jordan looked to the divers preparing outside their launch tubes. He hadn't even noticed that Erin was dressed to dive. She carried a helmet in the crook of her arm. An image of a fiery bird was painted on the helmet. For the Hell Divers, Jordan had made an exception to the mandatory art removal, since the emblems were part of the *Hive*'s history, not reminders of humanity's existence on the surface. But usually, they chose actual animals that had once existed. He wasn't sure he approved of such fanciful nonsense.

"I'm going with them, Sergeant," Erin said. "They are my responsibility."

Jenkins looked toward him. "We had a deal, Captain. She isn't supposed to be diving."

"She clearly made her choice," Jordan replied. "I had nothing to do with it."

The technicians and militia in the room went on about their business, while the divers crowded around, along with Hunt, Jordan, and Sergeant Jenkins.

"I'm not a kid anymore," Erin said. She put a hand on his shoulder and smiled warmly. "I'll be fine. I've done this before."

"And I made sacrifices so you wouldn't have to do it again." He snorted like a bull and looked at Jordan. "She isn't going. I'll go instead."

Jordan shook his head. "I need you on the ship, Sergeant."

"You don't even know how to dive," Erin said.

"Neither do we."

Jordan looked up at the tall diver they called Giraffe.

"And that's exactly why I have to do this," Erin said. "They need me."

"Personally, I don't care if she goes or not," Jordan said, "but figure this out." He motioned to Hunt to indicate they were leaving. He stopped just short of walking away.

It was his job to wish the divers well, but Jordan hadn't followed the traditions of the previous captains. Captain Ash would have told them all, "Good luck and Godspeed." Jordan said, "Oh, and come back with those supplies or don't come back at all."

FOURTEEN

Les Mitchells waited in his launch tube, heart pounding in sync with the countdown crackling over the launch bay's speakers. He should be thinking about the dive. In a few minutes, he was going to be dropping through twenty thousand feet of darkness, into a world he'd never seen before.

A world overrun by mutated monsters, poisonous plants, sinkholes, earthquakes, electrical storms, dust storms, snowstorms, ice storms...

Shut up, Les.

He suppressed the fears racing through his mind and thought about the reason he was doing this: his family. Phyl, Trey, and Katherine were counting on him to come back. He hadn't even been able to say goodbye to Trey. A kiss on Phyl's cheek and a squeeze of Katherine's hand were all he could manage.

Captain Jordan wanted the launch to happen, and there was no arguing with the man. But what really rankled Les was that the arrogant bastard hadn't even wished them good luck. What kind of a captain didn't even take the time to do something that simple?

A captain that doesn't give a shit about his people.

Les exhaled his rage and tapped the minicomputer on his left forearm. Normally, he prided himself on being a mostly happy person, but the stress and fear had really gotten under his skin.

The control panel warmed to life, and he activated his HUD. The subscreen in the upper right corner showed five other blips. Jennifer, Ty, Olah, Tom, and Erin were all online.

"Phoenix systems check," Erin said.

Les finished looking over his data and said, "Phoenix Two online."

"Phoenix Three online," Tom said.

"Phoenix Four online," Olah said.

"Phoenix Five online," Ty said.

"Phoenix Six online," Jennifer added.

"Phoenix One, this is command," came Hunt's voice. "Skies are clear and ready for dive."

Les crunched the numbers as he waited. Statistically, one of them was bound to die on Team Phoenix's debut launch—or at least suffer serious injury, which, for Les, was just as good as being dead. He couldn't help his family if he couldn't walk or work.

"In position," said the lead technician, a man named Harvey. In the past, it would have been Ty at the controls, but now he was in a dive tube.

Les wasn't happy about Ty diving with them. The former technician had betrayed Captain Jordan and disobeyed orders. That didn't exactly inspire confidence.

A red light flashed inside the metal cocoon, bathing Les' long body in a red glow. The first real surge of adrenaline rushed through him as he watched the mission clock on his HUD.

He took in a long breath that smelled of sweat and plastic. The Klaxon screamed, making him flinch. Erin had gone over the launch procedures, but none of it had seemed real.

"Holy shit," Tom said. "I can't believe this is happening."

"Everyone, just relax," Erin said. "I'll be here to guide you the entire way to the surface."

Despite the rumors of what happened on the dive that killed most of her team, Les believed Erin's words and her version of the story. She had been a good teacher, and it was damn brave of her to suit up with them now when she could be kicking back on the bridge and monitoring the mission from the skies.

One of the first lessons she had taught them was to stay calm. But no matter how hard he tried, he couldn't keep his heart from racing. He imagined that command was monitoring their heart rates. The monitors would all be beeping out of control right about now. He continued trying to manage his breath as he looked down at the swirling black clouds beneath his boots.

"One minute to drop," Hunt announced over the comms.

Tom panted heavily over the network.

"Phoenix Three, cut the floor noise," Erin ordered.

The labored breathing quieted. Les felt the sweat beading across his forehead. He looked down at the pistol holstered on his duty belt, the knife, and the blaster strapped to his leg. He had never used any of them for real—just practiced in the simulations yesterday.

Oh, shit. Is this really happening?

"Thirty seconds," Hunt said.

"I'm going to puke," Tom said.

"Take a deep breath, Phoenix Three," Erin said.

"This is crazy," Jennifer muttered. "This is fucking crazy."

Erin growled out her response. "Phoenix Three and Six, keep it together. You're going to be fine. Once we jump, follow my lead and I promise you'll be okay."

The red lights shifted to a cool blue. Les wasn't sure whether it was some effort to calm the divers, but it didn't work for Tom. He gagged over the comms, throwing up inside his helmet.

"Let me out of here," Tom moaned. "I've changed my mind. I want to go—"

His words cut off as the final alarm buzzed. Before Les had a chance to steel himself, the glass doors under his feet whisked open, and he plummeted into the black abyss.

He tried to scream, but all that came out was a hoarse croak. The blue glows of the other battery units shifted around him as the team cut through the clouds.

"Stay calm," Erin said, her voice crackling.

Les did what he was trained to do, and made a half barrel roll into a back-flying position. A shiver rippled through him as the wind took his long legs to the side, breaking the position. He tumbled head over feet, screaming in terror.

"Hard arch, Phoenix Two!" Erin shouted. "Then pull into back-flying position."

He caught a glimpse of her—at least, he thought it was her. The silhouetted shape wasn't in back-falling position, either. She was diving headfirst through the clouds to keep up with the others.

He checked on the other blue dots. Three of the divers were falling erratically. The only person who seemed to be doing okay was Ty.

Lightning flashed in the distance, and bile rose up in Les' throat. He struggled to gain control of his fall and managed to stop rolling. Now in an arch position, he slowly maneuvered his body the way Erin had taught him—arms and legs bent, helmet slightly downward.

The floor of cloud cover wasn't much to look at, and doing so made his guts clench. He focused on his HUD instead, trying to ignore the scalloped gray mattress beneath him.

The electrical interference was minimal, allowing the system to operate normally. He was already at fifteen thousand feet and falling at a rate of a hundred miles per hour and ticking upward.

"Phoenix Two is in position," Les reported.

"Phoenix Six is, too."

"Phoenix Five is good."

"Roger," Erin said. "Phoenix Three and Four, how are you doing?"

Tom and Olah both answered at the same time.

"I can't control it," Olah shouted.

Tom's garbled voice sounded like the caterwauling of some wild animal.

Les checked his HUD. *Twelve thousand feet.*

Lightning illuminated the interior of a shelf of clouds to the east. The thunder rattled his suit and shook his brain inside his helmet. He bit down on his mouth guard as a pocket of turbulence jerked him about. He fought to keep his mass in a stable position.

All the other team members had disappeared into the cloud cover, but he could see their beacons flashing on his subscreen. Everyone was still alive.

"Tom, bring your arms and legs out," Erin said.

The gurgled response made no sense. Was he choking?

They were at eight thousand feet and 110 miles per hour. Les tilted his head back to look up at the sky. Even in the green hue of his night-vision optics, he couldn't make out anything but clouds. Where was everyone else?

The world seemed to bend around him, the darkness shifting. He felt as though he was falling into an endless pit. There was no longer any sense of up or down—just darkness, and a terrible pressure against his limbs. The sporadic lightning didn't help.

Five thousand feet.

Les' entire body seemed to quiver as his speed continued to increase. His muscle fibers stretched, and his joints groaned.

Lightning flashed under his flight path, and he instinctively jerked to his right, rolling and flipping out of stable position.

Shit, shit, shit.

He fought around into a back fall while Erin continued talking Tom and Olah through the dive. The militia soldier seemed to be doing okay for now, but Tom couldn't form a coherent reply. His voice sounded as though he was gasping for air and choking at the same time. Maybe the poor son of a bitch had inhaled his own vomit. That'd be a hell of a way to go.

Back in a stable position, Les looked up at his HUD.

Three thousand feet.

They had only a few seconds to deploy their chutes.

When Les looked down, he saw something he had never seen before: the actual surface of the earth. The checkered brown terrain was the strangest, most beautiful thing he had ever seen. In the distance, rolling hills surrounded the ruins of an ancient metropolis. The buildings looked like jagged teeth.

My God, people really did live down here.

Part of him had always wondered whether it was true, or the surface was just a myth. Now here it was for real, yawning up at him.

"Get ready to deploy chutes, Phoenix," Erin said.

Les checked his HUD to identify the drop zone. They weren't far from where the beacon blinked. Several supply crates were already there, waiting with the gear they would need after they landed. They would send the crates back up with any supplies they found.

"Pull your chute," Erin ordered.

Les pulled the ripcord and felt himself yanked upward as the suspension lines went taut. He reached up for the toggles and gripped them, keeping his eyes on the surface.

Hundreds of buildings waited below, all of them skeletal,

NICHOLAS SANSBURY SMITH

165

rusted structures. Les could all too easily imagine being impaled on those ragged spikes if he missed the DZ. His heart caught in his chest when he saw the crater in the distance. Was that where one of the bombs had detonated?

"Phoenix Two, deployed," he remembered to say.

All the other divers replied except for Tom.

Les looked up into the sky to see five of the flickering blue lights break through the cloud cover. Each trailed an open or opening chute—all of them but one.

Tom's body was falling limp through the sky—and he was headed right for Les.

Pulling on the toggles, Les steered left, swinging his body out of the way just as Tom flew past.

"Pull your chute, Tom!" Erin shouted.

But Tom either couldn't hear or was too out of it to reply. He plummeted toward the surface.

"TOM!" Erin shouted.

The other divers all yelled over the comms, but it was no use. Tom hit the earth a few beats later. There was no sound—just a poof of dust where his body landed.

Les stared as his chute lowered him toward the ground. To his right, Jennifer had just flared her chute and was stepping down out of the sky. Olah was about to do the same. But Les couldn't bring himself to move. Tom was dead. Not even five minutes into their first dive, Phoenix was down a man. It could as easily have been Les. Even now, he could imagine Sergeant Jenkins delivering the news to his wife.

"Phoenix Two, prepare for landing!" Erin yelled.

Les snapped out of his trance. He performed a two-stage flare, just like in training, but out here, with the wind whipping his body, it was nothing like the simulations.

The brown floor rose up to meet him, and his boots hit the

ground way too fast. He tried to run out the momentum, but his legs couldn't carry his body fast enough. He tripped on a clump of dirt and crashed to the ground, sliding on his belly.

Shouts filled the comms. It sounded like sobbing. Was that Jennifer?

Les rolled to a stop, wrapped up in his chute and tangled in the suspension lines. He fought his way to his knees, nylon fabric billowing around him. Reaching behind him, he found the thick riser and popped the capewell, spilling the wind from his chute so he could wad it up and stuff it in the supply crate.

With the chute out of the way, the first thing he saw was a corpse. The impact had half-liquefied Tom's body and shattered his helmet. Blood, brain matter, and vomit spattered the cracked visor.

Erin offered Les her hand, and he took it, rising to his feet.

"You okay?" she asked.

Les could only nod.

Jennifer joined them while Olah ran over to Tom's body.

"Shit," Erin said, kicking the dirt. "He wasn't ready."

"None of us were," Jennifer said.

"We should see what we can salvage," Olah said.

"So we're just going to strip him and leave him here?" Jennifer asked.

Olah looked up. He had already plucked the battery from the center of Tom's chest armor. "What else are we supposed to do? He doesn't need this gear anymore, but we do."

Ty bent down next to Olah and began removing weapons and other gear from the body. Jennifer just stood beside Les and watched.

Lightning cracked overhead, and Les slowly took in his surroundings, seeing the world down here for what it was: rusted, gray, and dead.

A voice pulled him back to Tom's mangled body. Olah looked up at Les and Jennifer. If Les didn't know better, he would think he saw a smirk on the soldier's face.

"You guys thought I was going to be the first to die, huh?" Olah said.

Michael's paddle stroked through the swamp water, roiling the brown muck. He forced himself to scan the water constantly for hostiles, but he could hardly keep his eyes open.

Rodger stabbed at the water to the right, his stroke doing little to move the two boats, which had been roped together. They all were exhausted, having been on the open water all night and into the morning. The islands out here had turned up nothing, and despite the long hours of paddling, they had traveled only about five miles according to his wrist monitor.

"Timothy, do you copy?" Michael mumbled into the black bead of his mike.

"He's not coming back for us," Magnolia said. "Give it a rest, Commander."

"I never trusted him," Layla added from her perch in the stern of their kayak.

"You're supposed to be sleeping," Michael said.

Layla looked over her shoulder. "The thunder kind of makes that impossible, Tin."

The storm continued to rage overhead, its nearly constant lightning illuminating the way as they paddled across the swamps.

"You got eyes on anything, Rodger?" Michael asked quietly.

Michael scanned the water, looking for the snakelike beasts they had spotted several times throughout their journey. So far, the creatures had left the divers alone, but it was only a matter of time before one of them grew brazen enough to attack.

"I don't see anything," Rodger said. "This place is terrible, and no matter what I do, I can't get the stink out of my helmet."

"That's not this place," Magnolia joked. "It's you."

"Hah!" he replied. "The Rodgeman smells fantastic."

Referring to himself in the third person was a nervous tick that Michael had noticed Rodger doing more and more when he got embarrassed or scared. As with so much of Rodger's personality, Michael couldn't decide whether it was endearing or annoying. "Hold us steady for a few minutes, *Rodgeman*," Michael ordered.

Rodger stopped paddling and checked the rope connecting the boats, while Michael pulled out a map and compass. His eyes flitted from the tools to the minimap in the upper screen of his HUD.

"We're about seventeen miles from the source of X's last transmission," Michael said after a few minutes. "At this pace, it's going to take us at least another day to get there if we can't find land."

"My hands are already covered in blisters," Rodger said.

"I'll take over," Magnolia said, sitting up. She stretched her arms and reached back for the paddle, but Rodger held it out of her reach.

Michael's eyes were drawn to a ripple of water to the right of the boats. A long, sinuous shape breached the surface before vanishing back into the soup.

"Everyone quiet," Michael said.

He gently placed the paddle back in the boat and grabbed his rifle. The weapon was already charged and ready to fire, saving him the trouble of pulling back the bolt. He slowly scanned the water in all directions. Another hump-backed body appeared on their left.

"We're being surrounded," he murmured.

He flashed several hand motions, and the divers held their weapons at the ready, covering all quarters.

"Timothy, this is Commander Everhart reporting our coordinates." Michael continued to relay the information to the AI just in case he was listening.

Water slurped against the sides of the boats as lightning rippled across the sky, backlighting more spurs of land that spread across the horizon. The earthquakes had turned most of Florida into wetlands and provided a home to a type of beast Michael had never seen before.

Something darted through the water in front of Layla. She flinched and trained her gun on the ripples.

"Hold your fire," Michael whispered.

He heard another beast behind their boats but didn't look in time to see it. The wake from the creature's movements hit the side of the boats, rocking them and pushing them slightly through the murky water.

Rodger let out a high-pitched yelp as a red tail suddenly shot out of the water and wrapped around him. It yanked him backward, but his knee caught on the stern. Magnolia reached for his legs and grabbed hold while Michael aimed at the ropy coils looped around Rodger's neck. Rodger dropped his pistol, the weapon clanking on the bottom of the boat as he reached up to grab the beast.

"Use your blades," Layla said to Magnolia.

Before Michael could fire a shot, another snake emerged from the water. An elongated skull on a thick neck tilted to look at Layla and Michael in turn, studying them as a sharp black tongue flickered out at them. Spikes flared around its head, forming a crown.

Michael fired a round point-blank to the center of its head, right between the almond-shaped eyes. The impact flung the creature back into the water.

Rodger let out a scream as a second snake cinched around his arm and tried to drag him out of the kayak. The beast pulled hard enough to yank both boats backward, and the rope between them fell slack. Layla reached out to grab it as a third snake wrapped around the front of her boat, yanking it in the opposite direction.

"Fire!" Michael shouted. Anger boiled through him, giving his fatigued muscles a new surge of energy. While Layla hacked at the snake holding on to the bow, he turned and fired two shots into the closest snake pulling Rodger toward the water. The rounds cut through the rubbery flesh, nearly severing the head.

Rodger let out a wail. "Don't shoot me; shoot *him*!"

Michael aimed carefully and pulled the trigger at the body still holding on to Rodger. The round sliced through the stringy flesh, and Rodger jolted forward with a length of red-orange tail still wrapped around him.

Magnolia, both blades out, whirled to strike the beast at the bow of Layla and Michael's boat. Together, they cut through its coils, leaving the front of the blue boat covered in gore and slick blood.

The serpentine bodies undulated up and down in the water around the divers. Michael followed one in his sights and fired a three-round burst, sending the creature back under the surface. As he scanned the water around them for another target, a snake burst up from the deep and curled around his chest. Its face loomed right in front of his visor, the halo of spikes flicking up around its head as it opened its mouth and let out a loud hiss. The creature's tongue flickered over his visor, obscuring his view with gooey saliva.

Layla was screaming Michael's name, but he didn't have the breath to reply. He tried to squirm, but the motion just made the coils wrap tighter around his chest, arms, and stomach.

A whipping sound emerged in the distance that sounded almost like flapping wings. Or was it just in his mind?

Layla disappeared from view as he was yanked backward, out of the boat. The snake pulled him deep into the murky swamp, tightening its grip around his body so he couldn't even squirm. Water churned inside his helmet. It smelled awful and tasted worse. He spat it out, trying his best not to swallow any.

"Help!" he shouted into the comm.

Static crackled in reply.

He could see the lightning flash above, and the outlines of the two boats. But the darkness quickly surrounded him as the snake writhed deeper into the water. There wasn't much he could do now. The creature had him wrapped so tightly, he couldn't even squirm. The farther downward he was pulled, the more he didn't want anyone risking their lives saving him.

"Stay put!" he yelled into the comms.

"Tin!" Layla's voice crackled back.

Michael closed his eyes, focusing on the memory of her face. If he was going to die in a fetid, stinking swamp, at least his last thoughts would be of something beautiful.

"I . . . love you," Michael choked. The water bubbled over his mouth and nose as he was pulled into the darkness.

FIFTEEN

ONE YEAR AND NINE MONTHS EARLIER

X knew he was close to death. He had been here several times before, teetering on the edge between life and whatever came after. But of all the threats he had faced over the years—diving through electrical storms, battling stone beasts, and running from Sirens—cancer was the last thing he ever thought would finally get him.

Miles sat by his side as X lay on the mattress in the small apartment. Dogs were magnificent creatures. Especially Miles. He could sense pain, smell adrenaline, hunt in almost total darkness, and had saved X from countless monsters over the years.

X wished he could squeeze out a few more years with his best friend. He would even take a few extra months, or weeks, despite the pain of the cancer eating at his throat. He remembered watching a woman slowly die from the same kind of cancer. She had long red hair and was dressed all in white. For some reason, thinking about her made him angry. Had the woman betrayed him? He couldn't recall anymore. All his memories were nothing but dust and ash.

Ash. Was that the woman's name? Had she been the one who left him here to die?

X let the fragment of memory go. It didn't matter now who

had betrayed him. The only steadfastly loyal creature in his entire life was a dog.

X looked over at Miles, sleeping with his head on his paws. An eyelid flickered open, exposing a blue eye. The dog closed it again, going back to sleep.

He had taken every measure to see that Miles lived on after X succumbed to the cancer, but there simply wasn't enough food and water to leave behind for the dog. Without him, Miles would die within weeks. The thought broke his heart. Miles had been created by the same shortsighted fools who blew up the planet, making it impossible for even a genetically engineered superdog to survive here. It was a cruel twist of fate.

"I'm sorry, boy," he whispered.

He lifted his hand to pet Miles, even as pain wracked his body. The survival instinct that had kept him moving all these years was slowly fading away. But it was still there, like old muscle, and a part of him didn't want to give up.

He carefully stripped the blanket off his half-naked body and gritted his cracked teeth as he sat up. His muscles strained and clenched beneath the scarred flesh. His clothes, radiation suit, and diving armor rested on a chipped dresser across the room. The remains of a mirror were piled neatly beside the door, where Miles wouldn't step on them. X was glad he couldn't see his own face in the mirror.

Miles jumped up with X and followed him over to the dresser, wagging his tail. He nudged up against X's tattered pant leg and licked at the bottom of his hand.

X crouched down, doing his best to hold in a cough. He stroked the husky's thick coat, and its tail beat the air harder. Then he straightened and grabbed a long-sleeved shirt off the dresser.

He wasn't going to die today.

Today, they were going outside to look at the ocean. It was

the reason X had fought so hard to get here, to see a place like the one in his old picture.

X pulled on his shirt and then helped Miles into his suit. The dog's tail wagged again in eagerness. They had spent the past few days sitting in the cramped, cold apartment, listening to the otherworldly calls of monsters outside.

After X finished securing Miles in his helmet, he reached for his own gear. A tickle in his throat heralded a cough. Lungs crackling, he tried to massage his burning throat, but that didn't work and he doubled over to cough up bloody spittle.

The violent fit left him exhausted. He grabbed a bottle off the floor and forced the cool water down, though it did little to soothe his throat. Miles gave a whine and nudged up against his leg. He knew that X was sick. If X could speak, he would reassure the dog, but a pat on the head would have to do.

When X finally felt steady enough to move again, he wiped his bloody lips on his sleeve and finished putting on his radiation suit. Reaching for his helmet, he hesitated.

Why put it on? Why not see the world with naked eyes? The bloody phlegm on the floor proved he was as good as dead anyway. But the mission that had brought him here was finally complete. He had reached the ocean.

He staggered out of the bedroom and into the central room. It was furnished with four chairs, a dining table, and the boxes of supplies X had carried up to the twenty-fourth floor of the high-rise overlooking the city once known as Miami. His rifle rested against the wall. He grabbed it on his way over to the plastic sheeting that covered the broken balcony door.

Miles whined and pawed at his leg. X tried to speak, but what came out was a raspy whisper. He reached for his throat and closed his eyes as he swallowed. The pain was intense, as if he were swallowing molten lava. Not even the painkillers helped anymore.

He pulled the industrial tape away from the double layer of plastic sheeting and led Miles out onto the platform. Their apartment had a magnificent view of what had once been a beautiful skyline. He imagined this was where the old-world equivalent of upper-deckers had lived in wealth and privilege.

While most of the city had been leveled by the bombs, signs of Earth's former glory were everywhere. The condo where he had taken refuge was littered with fancy furniture and other relics of the past. In the kitchen, he had found dozens of plates and cups, all pure white and so thin he could almost see through them, and a drawer full of silverware that gleamed after he cleaned it.

X could picture the previous occupants sitting at the table to eat dinner as a family. Compared to what little he remembered of his life aboard the airship, the people here had lived in almost unimaginable luxury.

He approached the metal railing to look east, where the ocean lapped at the shoreline. The chilly wind rustled his thinning hair as he raised the binos. He tried to picture the bright sun the way it must have been, the golden glow warming his skin. He imagined the palm trees waving in the wind, and the teal water lapping onto the beach. He had seen a picture like that years ago, an image his mind became obsessed with during his journey, before it burned in his journal.

But all he saw now were the poisonous weeds and carnivorous trees growing along the beach, and the cold gray water breaking on trash-littered sand. Instead of the sun, the never-ending storm brewed overhead, shitting lightning over the ruined city.

Much of the ancient metropolis was flooded by ten to twenty feet of water, and many of the buildings were nothing more than twisted steel and chunks of concrete. He couldn't see it from here, but twenty miles past the fence of half-destroyed scrapers was a bowl of water a hundred feet deep—the result of the bomb that had leveled Miami. The radiation in sections of the city was at red-zone levels, and he had driven the motorcycle as fast as possible over the bridge to get clear of it.

X knew this landscape like the back of his hand. Staring out from the balcony had been his entertainment since he arrived here several months ago. His favorite sight was the fishing ship stuck horizontally between two apartment buildings. Thick purple vines with barbed suckers hung like octopus arms out of a jagged hole in the side of the hull. Despite all odds, the ship had remained here over all these years, keeping the structures from toppling. It was a miracle any of the buildings were still standing—a true testament to human engineering.

The apartment he now stood in was missing its left wall, which had been blown away by the heat wave from the nuclear explosion. The steel struts still held the structure together, like a spine keeping a skeleton from falling to pieces.

He looked back to the coast, where another of his favorite landmarks stood in the field of destruction. The lighthouse with a red dome was the flame of Miami, a bright pop of color in a gray world. The bottom third of the stone structure was submerged in water, but it was still standing. He zoomed in on the windowless observation tower at the top. A red metal railing surrounded the platform that hadn't been used in over two and a half centuries.

The trees and bushes on the beach suddenly lit up, their limbs flashing pink. He zoomed in to see a Siren munching on the foliage. In a matter of seconds, an entire section of coastline lit up like an emergency light as more of the Sirens joined the feast, ripping and tearing the vines. The plants were no doubt fighting back with venomous barbs and suckers.

As he watched, another cough brewed inside his chest. He forced saliva down his tight throat and fought the wave of fatigue sweeping over him. Just a few minutes of standing out here had taken so much out of his body.

He stepped away from the railing, preparing to go inside and lie down, but halted when he saw shadowy figures flapping across the skyline.

Miles saw them, too. The dog bared his teeth but held back a growl. He slowly retreated into the apartment with his tail between his legs, eyes on X as if to say, *Let's go, old man!*

But instead, X stayed to watch the beasts streaming out of the destroyed roof of a building on the other side of the city. From this distance, they looked like bats, fluttering into the air with their long, featherless wings. He knew that the longer he stayed out here, the more radiation he would take in, but it didn't matter now.

Instead, he watched an aberrant branch of human evolution flock over a city that had once been home to mankind. The Sirens were coming from the ITC facility across the city. They may have evolved to survive in these conditions, but they hadn't the intelligence of a human being—at least, not that he could see. They didn't build things or create anything. Their instincts were basic and predatory.

X supposed that was the point, but he couldn't escape the irony. The corporation that had tried to save humanity had doomed it instead. They had created the monsters that killed the survivors on the surface.

There was one final hope for X. Inside the facility were cancer drugs that could save his life. They were rare, and X had seen them only on one dive, long ago. Journeying to one of these secured facilities was, in itself, a death sentence. And how could he ever fight dozens of the beasts in his current condition? He could hardly get out of bed without feeling dizzy. X was done fighting. He should just let the disease run its course. It wouldn't be too much longer.

Gripping the railing, he continued to watch the beasts circling the city, hunting for their next mutant meal. Their hellish wails grew closer, and he finally stepped back inside the apartment.

Miles was waiting for him inside, his blue eyes filled with concern. He rushed over and pressed against X's legs.

You can't give up, X thought. *Miles needs you.*

He closed the sheets and sealed the tape. Winded, he took a seat in a chair facing the supply boxes. He opened the medical crate and pulled out a small box of syringes. Inside was medicine that would get him where he needed to go—or it might stop his heart for good.

A shot would keep him moving for several hours and could provide him with enough energy to get to the ITC facility and fight the Sirens. But this trip was too dangerous to take Miles with him.

He leaned down to take off the dog's helmet. Then he kissed the husky's soft fur and hugged him for several minutes, feeling Miles' heart beating and his sides rising and falling with steady breaths.

"I love you, boy," X mumbled in a faint, scratchy voice.

He stood and grabbed his helmet, put it on, and secured it with a click. Then he gathered his supplies and weapons. When he was ready, he pulled back one glove, exposing a vein in his filthy arm. He inserted the tip of the syringe into the vein and pushed the liquid into his body.

A wave of heat washed over him. He grabbed two more of the syringes and then set off down the staircase to the garage below, where the bike waited.

Time to live or time to die, he thought. *Time to fight one more time.*

*   *   *   *   *

PRESENT DAY

"We have a confirmed KIA, sir," Hunt whispered to Jordan.

The captain stood on the bridge of the *Hive* with his hands on the oak steering wheel. The news wasn't surprising, but he gave a rueful nod to keep up appearances.

"Tragic, but just the one death?" Jordan asked, playing the part. He kept his eyes on the wall-mounted monitor. Storm clouds moved across the screen, and lightning rickracked through the darkness.

"As far as we know, sir," Hunt replied. "I'll go talk to Ensign Ryan to see if he has more information."

Jordan listened to the XO's footsteps clanking up the rungs. He closed his eyes for a moment, trying to picture Katrina in the medical ward. Deep down, beneath the anger, he still loved her. He wanted to go to her, to comfort her and mourn the loss of their child.

No. She betrayed you.

His job was to keep the ship running. His life was his work. He breathed a long sigh.

"Electrical disturbances are making communication with the surface impossible right now, sir," Hunt reported when he returned. "Tom Price's beacon went off during the dive. We're not sure what happened."

Jordan nodded and looked to the weather data screen.

"That storm is growing stronger," he said. "I want an estimate of when it's going to hit us."

"Yes sir," Hunt replied.

Jordan went back to studying the storm on the monitor at the front of the room. The cameras positioned on the stern, hull, and bow of the *Hive* provided a glimpse of the skies from every direction. A bulging cloud flashed lightning on the horizon. If he steered too close, the strikes would tear through the synthetic hide of the airship and could even puncture a gas bladder.

"Ascend to twenty-two thousand feet," Jordan ordered.

Hunt cleared his throat. "Sir, that will take us out of broadcast range. We'll lose contact with the dive team."

"That won't matter if there's no ship for them to return to, will it, *Lieutenant*?"

After a short pause, Hunt shook his head. "No, it will not, sir."

"Give me full power to the turbofans," Jordan said. "I'm bringing us to safe altitude."

"Aye-aye, Captain."

A slight jolt rocked the bridge as the ship began to climb through the clouds. Pockets of turbulence rattled the bulkheads, but the massive, beetle-shaped *Hive* powered through, just as it always had and always would.

Jordan slowly turned the oak wheel, watching the front monitor for any sign of a rogue storm cloud that the sensors and cameras might have failed to detect. Just when he thought things were running smoothly, a raised voice came from the top of the bridge.

"We've got a problem in compartment nine!"

Jordan's earpiece crackled a beat later. "Captain, this is Sergeant Jenkins, do you copy?"

"Copy," Jordan replied. "What is it?"

"Over two dozen lower-deckers have gathered outside the trading post," Jenkins said. "Several of them are armed with knives."

"What do they want?"

"Your head, sir," Jenkins said. "Listen to this."

The radio crackled with static, followed by angry shouts. "We want a new captain! We want a new captain! We want a new captain!"

Jordan's face burned with anger. He gripped the wheel harder and jerked it hard to the left, jolting the ship.

A warning sensor flicked on, spreading a swirling red light over the clean white bridge. Several officers cried out in alarm.

"Sir!" Hunt yelled.

"They want a new captain?" Jordan said through clenched teeth. "Tell them to get to their fucking stations!"

Before Jenkins could respond, Jordan heard another voice from the crowd. "Katrina DaVita for captain!" someone yelled.

Jordan ground his teeth. Why bother trying to save these people when they were so stupid?

"Because it's your duty," he said out loud. Looking over his shoulder, he found Lieutenant Hunt. "I want everyone to get to their assigned shelters, NOW!"

"Understood, sir," Hunt said, though his face had gone white.

The Klaxon rang out, echoing through the entire ship. If the militia couldn't get the crowds under control, then Jordan would force them into submission.

"Jenkins, report to the bridge," Jordan ordered.

He continued to steer the ship through the clouds, climbing higher and higher, away from the storm. When they were at twenty-two thousand feet, he put the system on autopilot.

"We'll move back into broadcast distance once the storm passes," he said as he walked away. "Until then, bother me only if there's an emergency."

Jordan loped up the stairs, avoiding the gazes of his crew. He retreated to his office and flipped on a single light over the bulkhead. The book Hunt had given him from the raid on the library sat on his desk. He took off the sword, plopped down in his chair, and pulled the book into the light.

At first glance, the red and black binding of the hardcover book didn't appear to be anything special. He rotated it to read the title: *ITC Protocols*.

He thumbed through the yellowed, dog-eared pages. Fifteen minutes into his search, he had found nothing of interest. What the hell was so important about this book? It read like an instruction manual on how to survive nuclear war.

Before Jordan could read any further, a knock sounded on the hatch. Hunt entered the room looking nervous.

"Sorry to bother you already, sir," he stuttered. "I wanted you to know the crowds have retreated to their assigned shelters."

Jordan nodded, but Hunt didn't leave. "Well, what is it, Lieutenant?"

"That garbled transmission we picked up this morning—I think I found out who it is."

Jordan sat up straighter. "And?"

"It's Michael Everhart, sir. He's alive and . . ." Hunt shook his head incredulously. "If I'm not mistaken, he's trying to hail another airship."

Jordan slowly stood at his desk.

"The *Hive* isn't alone, sir," Hunt continued. "Captain Everhart has found a ship called *Deliverance*."

SIXTEEN

Limp and pale, Michael lay on the cargo bay floor while Layla sobbed by his side. Magnolia leaned in for another breath while Rodger pushed down on the commander's chest. Working together, they were doing everything they knew to save his life after pulling him from the swamp. His crushed armor lay in a heap on the floor.

"Please, please let him be okay," Layla cried. She shook Michael's arm. "Tin! Tin, wake up!"

The glow from Timothy's hologram illuminated the scene. Magnolia still couldn't believe it, but the AI had flown the ship low over the water to save them. If not for that, Michael would be dead.

He is dead, Magnolia realized. They had pulled him from the water nearly five minutes after the snake hauled him out of the boat. Not long after, Michael had lost consciousness, and then he had stopped breathing altogether.

"Hold on," Timothy said. The bulkheads and floor rattled as the ship accelerated. He was taking them back to the original LZ, but they were smack in the middle of a storm.

Magnolia prepared to give Michael another breath, but it caught in her chest. She couldn't believe it. After everything, they were heading right back to square one. Their short journey had come at a terrible cost.

"Come on," Rodger muttered as he doggedly continued the chest compressions.

Magnolia breathed into Michael's mouth again, and Rodger pushed down on his chest. They continued trying to resuscitate him, but it didn't seem to be doing any good. Layla grabbed Michael's hand and squeezed, tears flowing down her cheeks. She leaned down and whispered something into his ear.

The white illumination from Timothy's hologram vanished as the ship continued to pick up speed. The liftgate door had sealed shut, locking them inside. Outside the portholes, lightning flashed like a hand reaching out for the ship.

Magnolia flinched as a bolt struck the overhead. The raucous crack boomed like a blaster shot. She hit the floor hard but fought her way back to Michael and breathed air into his lungs.

"Warning, power surge detected," announced a female voice over the PA system.

Magnolia focused on Michael. There wasn't anything she could do right now to fix the ship. Their fate was in Timothy's hands—a terrifying notion. She trusted the AI more than she trusted Jordan, but that wasn't saying much.

"Come on, Tin," Magnolia whispered before giving him another breath.

Had his eyelids just flickered?

Rodger pushed down one more time, and Michael's pale lips parted, disgorging a stream of water that smelled like raw sewage. Magnolia moved back to give him room and waved Rodger off.

"Tin," Layla said frantically. "Tin, are you okay?"

"Are you ever going to stop calling me that?" Michael

mumbled. He reached up and swiped a curtain of soaking hair out of his face.

Layla gave a laugh of pure joy and bent down to wrap her arms around him.

"Let him breathe!" Rodger said.

"Sorry," she said, pulling back.

Michael managed to put an arm around her. "Where...where am I?"

"*Deliverance*," Rodger said.

"Wha...How...?" Michael asked. He blinked rapidly, as if struggling to focus on the faces around him. Then he suddenly leaned over and vomited up more water.

"*Ugh*," he said, wiping his mouth.

"We gave you something to make you puke," Layla said. "Now, drink this syrup. It'll kill whatever nastiness is still in you."

No sooner had Michael glugged down the beaker of clear liquid than a violent jolt rocked the divers, tossing them across the floor. Magnolia slid away from the others, reaching out for something to hold on to but finding nothing. She crashed into a bulkhead with a thump that took the air from her lungs.

"Warning, threat level critical," announced the same monotone female voice.

"Timothy!" Magnolia shouted.

"I'm working to address the issue," he replied calmly over the PA.

His voice had returned to the same smooth, calculated tone that Magnolia remembered from their first meeting back at the Hilltop Bastion. After his earlier meltdown, she wasn't going to complain. But she hadn't forgotten that he'd almost killed them.

The ship continued rocking, but it leveled out enough that she managed to get to her feet. Michael lay on his back a few feet away. Layla scrambled over to him.

Another bolt of lightning blasted the hull. The Klaxon screamed, and red lights flashed from recesses in the ceiling. The swirling color spread through the cargo hold as if a portal from hell had opened. Rodger put his hands on his ears, rocking back and forth.

"Threat level critical," the dry female voice repeated. "Please move to your designated shelter."

Magnolia helped Rodger up and followed Michael and Layla toward the row of safety harnesses hanging from the bulkhead. Quakes shook the floor, throwing them all off balance. *Deliverance* continued picking up speed, the thrusters propelling them downward through the storm clouds.

This baby was way faster than the *Hive*, at least. Magnolia couldn't help but marvel at the ship's technological superiority. The *Hive* would already have crashed and shattered on the surface, but *Deliverance* kept flying through the onslaught of lightning.

Michael was first to the harnesses. Layla helped him strap in as his hands fumbled at the buckles. Rodger and Magnolia were next. She took the harness on the far right, which gave her a view out the porthole. A wave of water splashed over the hull, spraying brown mist into the air as the ship lowered even farther.

"Holy shit," she said, hardly able to hear her voice over the screaming siren.

"Hold on, everyone," Timothy said over the PA system.

Magnolia grabbed the harnesses and gritted her teeth. Loose armor rolled and clattered over the metal floor. Michael's helmet smashed into a bulkhead, but the visor, built to handle blunt-force impacts, remained intact.

Thunder boomed like a grenade exploding. The vibration rattled Magnolia's bones, and her face shook from the g-forces. It felt a lot like diving through a storm.

"I...I think I'm gonna puke, too," Rodger said.

Yup, exactly like diving.

Magnolia looked out the porthole to her right. The ship lowered again, giving her an even better view of the water. They skimmed the surface, leaving a frothy white wake in the brown water. She closed her eyes, trying to keep her stomach down.

"Almost clear," Timothy announced.

The ship groaned as every strut and bulkhead flexed with the strain. They were going to break apart; she knew it.

When her eyes opened again, Magnolia could see terra firma below. The ship rocketed over an island, leaving both the swamp and the worst of the storm behind. Ten consecutive thunderclaps sounded in the distance, as if the storm were applauding their escape. She took a deep breath and relaxed in her harness.

"The shit never ends," she muttered.

Timothy's hologram reemerged in the center of the small cargo hold, his hands clasped behind his back.

Michael coughed again and spat on the ground. "How in the hell did you find us?"

"I received your transmissions but was unable to reply due to the electrical interference. I traced your last SOS. It appears I found you right in the..." He paused and brought a finger to the bottom of his close-cropped beard. "... *in the nick of time*, I believe is how the phrase goes."

"All that matters is you came back for us," Rodger said. "Thank you, Timothy."

The AI dipped his head politely. "It is my pleasure."

"Yeah, thanks, Timothy," Michael said, "but we're not out of this just yet. Can you put together a damage report?" He staggered across the hold to his helmet and armor. Layla held his arm to keep him steady.

The Klaxon had shut off, but the female voice continued to repeat, "Threat level critical."

"One moment," Timothy said.

"What are we supposed to do now?" Magnolia asked as the hologram disappeared again.

"Let's wait to hear how bad the damage is before we start worrying about what to do next," Michael said.

"Several secondary systems are offline," Timothy announced. "Lightning strikes damaged the stern. Several areas require patching."

The divers gathered around their commander, looking to him for guidance, but he could hardly stand. Vomit stippled the front of his dented armor, and blood trickled from a cut on his forehead. His long hair was matted to his shoulders, and he reeked of sewage.

As if all were just business as usual, he straightened and said, "Here's what we're going to do. Rodger and Magnolia, patch the hull while Layla and I work on getting the secondary systems online."

"And then what?" Rodger asked.

Michael turned to him with a look that told Magnolia they were going to do something bat-shit crazy.

"We're going to fly this ship as low and as fast as possible until we get to X's signal—or until we crash."

* * * * *

Les Mitchells held a glove up to catch a snowflake drifting down from the swollen clouds. Lightning split the sky in a brilliant arc. By the time the flash faded away, the flake had melted.

"Never thought I would see snow," Jennifer said.

"Radioactive snow," Les replied. He lowered his hand and checked his wrist monitor. The rads were in the yellow zone.

"Everyone, keep an eye on your suit-integrity monitor," Erin said.

"I don't think my warming pads are working," Ty said. "I'm freezing."

Les checked the temperature reading on his HUD: thirty degrees and dropping by the minute.

"It's probably because you're as thin as a beanpole," Jennifer said.

"Shut up and keep moving," Olah snapped.

Erin brought a finger to her helmet, shushing them. They had been following her across the barren wasteland for hours, stopping only to raid the supply crates and pick up gear. She moved slowly but without hesitation.

Les was more grateful than ever to have an experienced leader on the team, but after seeing Tom die in the first few minutes of the mission, he was worried that Phoenix would end up like Erin's old dive team. How many more of them would be killed down here?

Olah grunted as he dragged the ski-mounted supply crates over the snow. So far, he seemed to be handling the plastic boxes fairly easily. There wasn't much inside, just the chutes and gear they had salvaged from Tom Price—not that the stubborn militiaman would ever ask for help if they were too heavy.

They were moving toward their target, an ITC installation deep underground. Erin continued on point with the satellite dish from the supply crate strapped on her back. She cradled one of the two assault rifles.

Les put his hand on the grip of his pistol for reassurance, hoping the cartridges would actually work if he ever had to fire the ancient weapon.

He stumbled over a chunk of rubble. *Stay sharp, Giraffe.* He was still getting used to the night-vision optics, and it was damned hard to see where he was going in the green-hued darkness.

There was a reason people referred to the surface as hell. Human bones littered the ground almost everywhere they went. They were in some sort of industrial zone now, trekking around old-world vehicles that rose out of the snow. Some of them Les recognized from picture books: cranes, concrete trucks, bulldozers. Others looked like nothing he had ever seen before. The area had been largely spared from the nuclear fires, but the crumbling infrastructure had suffered in the harsh conditions of the intervening two and a half centuries. Most of the vehicles were pocked and riddled with holes, just like the decayed network of roads they had once been driven on.

To the east, streets stacked one on top of another led to a wilderness of steel and concrete. A carpet of snow covered the dead city like a layer of skin. A skeletal arm protruded from a drift to his right, and even though it was ancient, Les checked for tracks.

He saw nothing in the fresh powder aside from ski tracks and the boot prints of Erin and the other divers ahead of him, but that didn't mean there weren't creatures out here. Hunting, stalking…watching.

The divers halted at the edge of the industrial area when Erin raised her fist. Another road snaked through several blocks of pockmarked brick buildings. Their roofs had given way to the weight of snow over the years, the rubble bulging out of missing windows like bread that had overflowed its pan.

Erin motioned for Olah to join her at the front of the group. She pulled the satellite contraption off her back and handed it to him, then pointed to the largest building in the distance.

"Set up there and try to reach Command," she said. "Les, you and Ty take over the supply crates."

Les followed her finger toward a building that was nothing

more than a husk, with the exterior peeled away like the skin of an orange, exposing steel girders and a concrete stairwell. He was glad Olah was going and not he.

The overeager militiaman gave a stiff salute and said, "Yes, Commander." They all watched him jog through the snow with his rifle shouldered.

As much as he disliked the guy, Les didn't want to see him get killed. So far, they hadn't been able to get any messages through to the *Hive*, and while Erin claimed it was normal to lose contact sometimes during a mission, they were counting on Olah to make sure they could reach Command.

Circling back, Erin crouched in the snow and brought her wrist monitor up. Les, Ty, and Jennifer bent down to look at the map on the small screen.

"We're one mile away from the target location," she said, pointing.

She sounded nervous, or maybe that was just the distortion over the comms. Not that Les would blame her if she were. He was pants-pissing scared out here, his thoughts shifting from his family to all the things hiding in the radioactive landscape, waiting to feast on his flesh.

"Once we enter the facility, we're looking for an underground entrance," Erin continued. "I'll stay on point until we get there. Keep sharp, and if you see anything, tell me."

Erin moved out, shifting her rifle barrel from window to window. The divers fanned out on the next street, with Les and Ty keeping to the right, and Erin and Jennifer on the left. Jennifer carried a blaster, but Ty was weaponless. As a criminal, he hadn't been entrusted with a weapon. Les really wanted to ask him a few questions, but they hadn't gotten the chance to talk one-on-one, and it didn't look as if that was going to happen anytime soon.

They entered a tunnel with leaning concrete walls that looked precarious at best. If one of the slabs fell, it would crush them like ants. Erin studied the concrete beams for a moment before passing underneath. Les squinted to see what lay at the end, but could only vaguely make out a pair of metal doors bent outward.

A gust of wind swirled the powdery, poisonous snow around the divers as they made their way through the tunnel. A skeleton lay facedown in the snow ahead. Most of the clothing had been stripped away, leaving nothing but a pair of boots on the corpse.

Les looked back up at the storm clouds and then at the street, checking for any contacts that may have flanked them. But he saw only the same cold, dead world in every direction he looked.

They came to the end of the passage a few minutes later. Across the street, a sagging structure towered above them. Though decayed from centuries of neglect, it was still impressive.

"I think this is it," Erin said. "Can anyone make out that sign?"

Les tried to read the metal sign hanging above the double doors of the entrance. His eyes flitted up the ten-story structure. Black squares where windows had once been dotted the gray exterior.

Was that a flash of movement, or were his eyes playing tricks on him?

"Tech something," Jennifer said, straining to make out the words. "Industrial Tech Corporation?"

"We're here," Erin said. "Drop the crates on the landing." She moved across the road toward a wide concrete platform at the entrance to the building. The front doors were sealed shut. Les hoped this meant there was nothing nasty inside. He dropped the crates where Erin had pointed, and helped Ty unclip the towropes.

Erin brought her wrist monitor up again, letting her rifle sag across her chest armor while she wiped the screen.

Radio static crackled over the comms. "Phoenix One, this is Phoenix Four. I'm moving into position."

"Roger that," Erin replied. "We're about to enter the facility. Stand by."

She looked back at Ty and Les. "This place looks pretty massive. We'll need to split up. Jennifer, you're with me."

"Then, I guess that makes us buddies," Les said, turning to Ty. The former technician just stared at the doors of the ITC building.

The team advanced up the stairs, and Erin tried the doors. The handle snapped off in her hand, and she dropped it in the snow. She put her shoulder into it and, with the other divers' help, pushed the doors open to reveal a gloomy atrium littered with upended furniture.

Erin raked her helmet beam over a mosaic on the high ceiling. Many of the tiles lay scattered on the floor, but enough remained to show that it had once been beautiful. At the end of the room, a desk stood in front of what looked like some sort of artificial waterfall, long since dried up. He couldn't believe that people used to waste good water so foolishly.

The divers moved slowly through the room. Erin and Jennifer went left, where two doors led deeper into the building. Les motioned for Ty to follow to the right, where two more doors stood at the other end of the room.

"Good luck," Erin said. She grabbed the handle of the first door on the left and motioned for Jennifer to cover her. "We'll meet back here in one hour."

Les paused to watch the two divers creep into a stairwell. They angled their weapons up first, then down around another landing, before finally disappearing into the darkness. The door clicked shut behind them, the noise echoing in the open space. Silence quickly replaced it. Les could hear his own breath, loud and quick in his ears. A chill ran up his spine, and he swallowed as he set off for the open doorway at the end of the atrium.

"Hey, buddy," Ty said as they walked. He wasn't using the

comm channel, and Les could barely hear him. The thin technician pointed at the blaster on Les' hip. "Can I borrow that? Just in case we run into trouble."

After a glance to the holstered weapon, Les shook his head. "Sorry, man, but we were all told not to give you a gun."

"You're going to wish you had if we run into those things down here."

"Sirens?"

Ty's helmet dipped.

"If that happens, I'll gladly give you my gun. But for now, the answer is no. I don't know you or your story. Now, come on."

They continued through the dusty atrium. Les tried to guess what the mosaic used to look like. Blue tiles formed a swirl overhead, a bit like an ocean wave, but that was all he could make out.

He stepped on a broken tile, crunching it underfoot, and winced at the noise.

"Pay attention," Ty whispered.

Les kept his eyes to the floor, where he saw a red metal can. Several more were spilled around a toppled metal box about as tall as a man. He nudged one of the cans with his foot to reveal the words "Diet Coke" written on the side.

"What in the heck do you suppose that is?" he asked, not expecting Ty to answer.

"Seen those before. One of the divers brought a can like that back to the *Hive* years ago. Some kind of drink."

"You try it?"

"Tasted like battery acid," Ty said.

Les chuckled. "Guess I'll leave it be, then."

"We're moving down a stairwell," Erin said over the comms. "Keep this line open."

"Phoenix Two, copy," Les said.

Olah came online a moment later. "Almost in posi—" The hiss of wind, followed by static, cut him off before he could finish.

Les looked back and found Ty crouching near a pillar. "Looks like tracks," he said, pointing down.

Moving as fast as he quietly could, Les tried to stay calm. His fear quickly gave way to confusion. Ty was right, but the tracks didn't appear to have been left by some mutant monster.

"Looks human to me," Les said. "But how is that possible? I thought they hadn't found a survivor for over a century."

"Giraffe, or whatever they call you, you should really think hard about handing me that weapon. If someone or something is here, I'm gonna...we're going to need it."

Les unbuckled one of the buttons on the holster. He narrowed his eyes before pulling the weapon all the way out, trying to get a look at Ty's features behind his visor. His face was haggard, like that of a man who had seen too much in his life. Les' gut told him Ty was a good man, but he had to be sure.

"What happened between you and Captain Jordan?" Les said, holding the grip of the blaster.

Ty looked over at the open door of an elevator. The boot prints led inside, and a frayed rope hung down into the shaft. He shook his head and used the tip of his boot to kick at the ground, clearly frustrated with something.

"Jordan is a liar," Ty said, anger rising in his voice. He turned back to Les and took a step until he was standing right underneath Les' chin. The beam from Ty's helmet hit the mosaic overhead, and Les saw what it had been: a waterfall surrounded by trees. "He's hiding a secret."

"What kind of secret?" Les asked.

Ty snorted and tilted his helmet to direct the beam at the boot prints leading to the elevator. "About a man we left behind years ago—the same man I believe left those tracks."

Les followed the beam, not quite understanding what Ty had just said. He racked his brain to remember all the divers who had been lost over the years. There were so many. And how could any of them survive on the surface?

Before he could ask any questions, a crackle sounded over the comms. Olah's frantic voice hissed over the channel.

"Phoenix One, Phoenix One, this is Phoenix Four. I've got the satellite set up, but we've got company. I can see them, but I don't think they know I'm here."

"Stay where you are and hunker down, Phoenix Four," Erin said. "Radio silence from here out, everyone, unless you're face-to-face with a hostile."

In the background came a noise vaguely like the emergency sirens on the *Hive*. Les found his hand moving back to the holster. He quickly pulled out the blaster and handed it to Ty.

"Don't make me regret this, man," he said.

"X," Ty said, pointing to the tracks. "It was Xavier Rodriguez that Jordan left behind on the surface, and I believe those are his prints."

SEVENTEEN

X gunned the motorcycle down the highway. He didn't bother using the night-vision optics; his eyes were accustomed to hunting in the dim blue glow of the incessant lightning.

Adrenaline rushed through his veins, and the tightness in his throat loosened. For the first time in months, he could breathe through his mouth. He sucked in air through the filter in his helmet, not daring to look over his shoulder at the high-rise he now called home. Doing so would have broken his heart, knowing that Miles was there, waiting, pacing, and probably whimpering.

Leaving the dog all alone was one of the hardest things X had ever done. It sparked a memory, just a fragment of an image that entered his mind. The moments before a dive in the launch bay of the airship. A boy with a foil hat waved at him from the crowd. He had just given X a note, but X could no longer remember the words—only that the memory made him sad.

The otherworldly calls of Sirens sucked him from his memories. His focus returned to the sky, where the monsters were flying in circles. Something had drawn them out of their nest. It was unusual to see this many in the open air, and he wasn't going to waste this prime opportunity to sneak into ITC Communal 9 and search for the cancer drugs that could save his life.

Thunder disguised the sound of his motorcycle as he entered the city. He hoped the beasts wouldn't see him coming. If they did, his rifle was scabbarded to the bike, and his blaster was holstered at his side, both within easy reach.

He twisted the throttle, giving the bike more juice as he shot over the raised bridge that would take him into the heart of Miami. Two massive ships were still docked in the harbor to his right. Most of the white paint had been stripped by hurricanes and wind-borne sand over the years, leaving them a grimy rust color. Black slashes like wounds from a whip marked the sides of the hulls where lightning had struck. The largest ship had broken in half, exposing its guts.

X steered the bike around a missing hunk of bridge, careful not to snag the blades protruding from his wheel hubs. The beach continued to glow as the plants fought off the Sirens. He glimpsed a Siren on the horizon, flying low over the black ocean, a squirming vine in its talons.

Easing off the throttle, he reached for the grip of his rifle with his left hand and continued watching the Siren. It flapped to the west and vanished behind a scraper, its wail fading away like a waning Klaxon after an emergency.

He navigated around several charred vehicles blocking the road ahead. The tires jolted hard over the broken concrete, threatening to twist the handlebars out of his grip. The bridge had taken a real beating over the years.

X weaved the bike carefully through a gap between two cars. A skeleton sat in the front seat of the one on his left, skull propped against the steering wheel. In the back, a smaller set of bones lay strapped into a plastic seat.

A child. Just a goddamn kid who never got a chance to live life.

It made him want to scream. Why had humans done this? Why had they destroyed everything? And why the hell was he still alive to see it?

He squeezed through the gap, the bladed hub scraping a long gash in the rusted metal. Finally clear of obstacles, he gunned the bike down the final stretch of road, accelerating hard enough to bring the front tire off the ground for a second. It reconnected with a jolt, and X sped toward the buildings along the shore.

He approached the fishing ship that had gotten wedged between two buildings. Chipped red paint still coated the stern, but the rest of the hull was the same burnt-flesh color as the rest of the city.

He drove at twenty miles per hour, eyes flitting from the road and buildings to the sky. He had studied the Sirens closely during his time in hell. The males seemed to be the ones with wings, while the females typically stayed on the ground or by the nests. They weren't the only threats out here, though. Giant snakes and fish prowled the waters, and monster lizards came out of their lairs from time to time to hunt smaller, bird-like beasts. There were also the poisonous plants and trees that had sprouted roots inside the city. Here and there, cock-roaches the size of a man's hand scuttled between cracks and piles of debris.

Miami was the most active ecosystem X had ever seen in his years on the surface. Even the ship dry-docked against the two buildings had sprouted a colorful garden of foliage from the hole in its hull. No doubt the plant would be poisonous or have acidic sap, making it as deadly as everything else down here.

X couldn't help but feel the weight of being the only man in the mutated wasteland. In the past, this feeling of loneliness had consumed him—broken him, even—but not today. Perhaps it was the adrenaline, or perhaps it was his finally accepting that the people in the sky were never coming back, that he would never see another human.

It's just me, he thought. *I'm the only one who will ever see this, and I'll never get to tell anyone.*

He roared through the streets, feeling free for the first time in years. His heart raced as the speedometer steadily ticked up. The oversize tires navigated the cracked terrain nicely, and the suspension made the potholes barely noticeable. It felt like flying.

The wail of a Siren rose over the thunder, snapping him back into survival mode. He considered reaching for a weapon but kept his hands on the bars when he saw the beast flap around the side of a building. So far, the noise of his bike hadn't attracted the beasts. They seemed focused on something else. But what had drawn them all out of their dens? X hadn't seen anything that might interest them besides the flashing trees on the beach. That was the only explanation.

He checked the minimap in his HUD. ITC Communal 9 was two blocks away. Looking to the road, he saw that it was flooded about a quarter mile away. He steered left onto the next street and drove under two buildings that leaned against one another other like men too drunk to stand on their own. A huge section of one had crashed to the street, blocking the route.

X cursed and wheeled around, back onto the main road, and went left at the next intersection. He couldn't see beyond the arched bridge, but the facility was somewhere on the other side.

Twisting the throttle, he zoomed up the ramp. The first injection was already starting to wane. His eyelids felt heavier, and his heartbeat had returned to normal. Pain ripped through his tightening throat. He sucked in air through his nose and focused on the top of the bridge. As soon as he was over it, he would stop and give himself another shot of adrenaline.

His eyes teared up as he increased the bike's speed. The wide tires thumped over a crack in the road right before he crested the top.

"SHIT!"

The cry of shock came when he saw a flash of motion barreling up from the other side. He swerved to miss a Siren bolting up the road. The sharp veer almost cost him control of the bike, but he managed to straighten out, the rear tire chirping before regaining traction.

He threw on the brakes and, in a swift movement, pulled his blaster. Twisting in the seat, he fired a shot that took off a piece of the monster's head in a spray of bone and gore. He holstered the gun and then turned back to the downward slope—where two dozen of the female beasts were making their way up the road on all fours.

All at once, their infernal cries blasted X with a barrage of high-pitched electronic noise. Instead of retreating and pulling his rifle, he turned the throttle to give the bike more juice.

The rear tire fishtailed with a screech, and the bike lurched down the road to meet the monsters head-on. The foot-long blades welded to the wheel hubs were supposed to be for cutting through vegetation, but he was going to test them on flesh and bone.

The monsters moved like a herd of wild animals, mouths chomping and angry cries splitting the air. One of the beasts had a ten-foot lead. It increased that lead, galloping straight for his bike. The front tire plowed into the monster, crushing its skull and flinging it aside.

X let out a whoop as the other creatures came together in a V formation. The wide front tire bucked the beasts that came at him headlong, and the blades cut through the others trying to attack from an angle—severing heads, hacking off feet and forearms, shredding flesh. An arm caught in the spokes, thumping halfway around before the blade sheared it in two.

It was all over in seconds. X eased off the gas and looked over his shoulder at the trail of devastation he had left behind. One of the female beasts crawled across the ground using its elbows, dragging a lower half that hung on by the spinal column and a narrow strand of sinew.

Leaving the carnage behind, he sped off toward the next bridge. The ITC facility was on the far side. Now all he had to do was find a way in.

The wails of the dying creatures filled the intervals between thunderclaps. Cresting the next bridge, he shot a glance over his shoulder to make sure none of them were following. His eyes flitted from the corpses to the skyline, where hundreds of tiny black dots flapped to the east.

Oh, shit.

His heart went back to thumping like an automatic weapon, but after a few seconds of watching the beasts, he relaxed a degree. The Sirens weren't flying to help their mates. They were heading toward a light on the horizon.

X stopped the bike on the top of the bridge and pulled out his binos. On the shoreline, the lighthouse turret was glowing a bright red, and the light was flashing over and over.

He centered the binos there for several seconds, blinking to make sure it wasn't an optical illusion caused by the lightning.

It wasn't. Something or someone had activated the beacon, and the Sirens were flocking like moths toward the light.

* * * * *

PRESENT DAY

Captain Leon Jordan slapped the cover of the book shut with such force, dust puffed up from the yellowed pages. He was tired of reading about lighthouses, boats, and all manner of bullshit that didn't make any difference to him, twenty thousand feet up in the sky. This was exactly why he had ordered the militia to raid the library. Books like the one he had just read were nothing more than legends, written to keep people believing in something that no longer existed.

He flicked on his touch screen and pulled up the audio clip his team had intercepted. Static crackled from the speakers for several minutes before a faint voice broke through.

"Timothy, this is Commander Everhart, reporting our coordinates." There was another flurry of static, then a broken message. "We need you...fly *Deliverance*..."

Jordan tapped in his credentials and pulled up the *Hive*'s confidential records. He searched for "Deliverance" in the database, but there were no results. He thought a moment, then typed "airship" and "ITC Communal Thirteen" into the search bar, and found a record of a smaller airship that was created sometime after the *Hive* and stowed at the Hilltop Bastion before the bombs went off.

"You son of a bitch," Jordan said, scooting up to the screen. An image of an airship filled the monitor. He clicked on the audio to play a short narration clip.

"In 2051, ITC designed a faster and lighter prototype airship with thrusters and turbofans. Engineers removed the helium gas bladders to save on space and outfitted the ship with a state-of-the-art artificial-intelligence system."

Jordan had read about these ships before but had believed they were all destroyed in the war that wiped out civilization. Apparently, one had survived inside the Hilltop Bastion and the other divers were calling it *Deliverance*.

He folded his hands, thinking of the implications. An idea formed in his mind. He stood as it began to materialize, grabbed his freshly sharpened sword, and left his office. There were so many questions that he wanted answered. First, who was this Timothy? And second, where was *Deliverance* now? He wasn't going to find the answers by sitting in his office.

Jordan walked out onto the platform above the bridge and motioned for Ensign Ryan to join him at the top.

"Follow me," Jordan said. He nodded at Hunt. "You have the bridge, Lieutenant."

"Aye-aye, sir," Hunt replied.

Ryan pushed his glasses up and followed Jordan through the hatch into the connecting corridor. Several militia guards were standing sentry, crossbows cradled over their riot gear.

"Sir, it's not safe out here," Lore said, holding out an arm to stop him. Jordan hadn't recognized the soldier with his helmet on.

"I thought everyone was inside their assigned shelters," Ryan said.

Lore shook his head. "There were a few that didn't follow orders."

"That's why I have *this*." Jordan half-unsheathed the blade. He led the ensign down the passage, where they could speak in private.

"Have you been able to determine the source of Michael Everhart's transmission?" Jordan asked.

"Not yet, sir. I'm working on it but so far haven't been able to lock on. We've been busy with so many other things at the—"

"This is your priority," Jordan interrupted. "Get it done."

Jordan walked away, leaving Ryan alone in the middle of the passage. Lore and the other militia guards ran after him to catch up.

The dark passage was lit by multiple emergency lights. Red swirled across the bulkheads and overheads, capturing the freshly scrubbed bare metal on each pass.

"Sergeant Jenkins, this is Jordan. Do you copy?"

"Roger, sir. Do you have an update on my—on the divers?"

"Negative, Sergeant, but I want a sitrep from you."

There was a short pause. "I'm currently patrolling outside the trading post to ensure that everyone is where they are supposed to be. Everything seems to be okay, sir."

"Good. I'm headed out for a walk."

"I wouldn't advi—"

Jordan stopped at a porthole and ducked down to watch the lightning blast through the clouds. The storm continued to grow, expanding toward the ship.

He pushed his headset back to his lips. "Hunt, make sure you put a safe distance between us and that storm."

"Roger, sir."

"Where are we headed, sir?" Lore asked.

Jordan ignored the soldier and kept walking. He didn't have a specific destination—he simply wanted to see what the ship looked like now that the work was done and the bulkheads were scrubbed clean of graffiti.

He wandered the corridors for a half hour before stopping in the officers' wing, outside room 789. He ran his fingertip over the rough metal hatch. The stone castle he had sketched as a child was gone. He let out a sigh that was more relief than anything else. The ship was cleansed and purged of the past. They could now focus entirely on the future.

"Come on," he said to the soldiers.

They moved faster through the next corridor, Jordan's mind racing the entire time. He stopped when he saw a silhouette at the end of the passage. A moment later, another figure emerged. Two teenage kids, wearing brown sweatshirts with hoods up, turned in his direction. One held a paintbrush.

"Stop!" Jordan shouted.

The boy took a step backward before taking off running with the other kid. Jordan ran after them, with the two militia guards right behind. He slowed when he saw what the boys had been painting. The image of an officer in a white uniform was crudely splayed on the bulkhead. Red paint dripped from the man's neck.

It was a painting of Jordan with his throat cut.

"Stop them!" he shouted.

Lore took off running, and Jordan followed a moment behind. But the kids were much faster than Jordan and the soldiers weighed down by riot gear. They lost them around the next corner. After another few minutes of running, Jordan finally stopped, panting, outside the medical ward and put his hands on his knees.

"Find…them," he said between gasps for breath.

He shot a sidelong glance at the medical ward entrance. Since he was here, he might as well pay a visit. He straightened his jacket and walked inside, heart pounding, not just from the stress but because of what he was about to do. Bradley Huff, the oldest doctor on the ship, met him inside the lobby.

"Captain, are you hurt?" Huff asked.

"No, I'm here to see Katrina."

"Oh." Huff stood there for a moment, his dewlapped throat quivering as if he wanted to say something else, and then gestured for Jordan to follow.

As they passed through the ward, Jordan avoided the gazes of the dozen or so patients dying from cancer. The beds were bolted to the deck, and straps kept the patients restrained in case of turbulence. Several nurses were walking freely through the space. They were out of all the cancer-fighting drugs from the surface and had been for months. The only thing left to treat these people were archaic forms of chemotherapy and radiation.

Huff led him into a wing of isolation rooms where they kept people with contagious ailments.

"She's in there," Huff said, pointing. "I thought she would be better off with some privacy, considering what happened."

Jordan didn't reply. He simply opened the door and walked in. There was hardly enough room inside for him to stand next to the bed. Katrina, restrained by straps, squirmed when she saw him.

"I don't want to talk to you," she growled.

Jordan watched her struggle, conflicted emotions gripping him. "I just came to deliver a message," he finally said. "One I think you're going to want to hear."

She stopped struggling and met his gaze, anger burning in her eyes.

"Michael Everhart is still alive, and he's found a new airship." Katrina shook her head. "You're lying."

"Why would I lie?" Jordan folded his arms across his chest. "I'm telling you this because I think I know where he's taking it."

Katrina's eyes widened.

"No guesses?" he asked. When she didn't reply, he continued, "He's trying to find X."

"Xavier's still alive?" Her words were just a whisper, but Jordan heard them clearly.

"In a way, Janga was right. A man *will* lead us to a new home. But not one on the ground. *Deliverance* will carry us into the future."

Katrina fought against her restraints again. "You're crazy, Leon. Do you realize that? You're insane—oh, and you're also a murderer."

Jordan ran his thumb under the bottom of his nose, scratching an itch. His eyes flitted to Katrina's midsection. She followed his gaze.

"I'm not the one that killed our child, Katrina," he spat, remembering the tray of food she had thrown against the wall of her cell. He was certain she had intentionally stopped eating out of spite. "You're the murderer. I'd kill you myself, but I'd rather you lie here strapped to that bed and remember what you've done, for the rest of your days."

He turned away from the bed but then stopped and waved Dr. Huff inside.

"If she won't eat, give her a feeding tube," Jordan said.

EIGHTEEN

The lift door to the cargo bay creaked open, and a metal ramp extended to the ground. Michael took a sip of water from the straw inside his helmet and swirled it around his mouth. No matter what he did, he could still taste the rancid swamp water. Hopefully, the pills would keep any infection at bay, but he wasn't so sure. His gut felt sour.

The ramp slid out, the metal sinking with a gurgle into the muck. Michael heaved a sigh. *Deliverance* was docked on the same island where Timothy had dropped them off less than twenty-four hours ago. The graves of his family weren't far from here.

"You sure you're feeling okay?" Layla asked, stepping up to the edge of the ramp.

"I'm fine, don't worry." Michael held his arms out to check his armor one last time.

"How's your suit?" she asked.

"We got most of the dents out, and my battery seems to be fine. It's still got a seventy-seven percent charge."

"You're lucky, Tin."

"I know."

He motioned for Layla to follow him down the ramp and out onto the dirt. The fresh graves were about a hundred feet to the right. On the smallest mound of earth, the wooden elephant Magnolia had placed there stood vigil.

"I hope Timothy doesn't lose his shit again," Layla said.

"He seems okay, and he did come back for us. Saved my life. We owe him."

She didn't respond, which told Michael she either didn't want to argue or was worried about the AI overhearing them. In truth, Michael wasn't sure about him, either, and he planned on keeping a close watch.

Michael held his rifle scope up to his visor to study the crumbling infrastructure of the city on the hill. Between the ship and the city stood an old building with an island of concrete pumps outside the entrance. A single charred boat rested upside down in the dirt, showing off its rusted belly.

"Timothy, do you copy?" Michael said into his comm link.

"Yes, Commander."

"Scan the area for contacts again."

"Already done, sir. The sensors have not detected anything in the general vicinity. I will inform you if that changes."

"Thank you," Michael said. The AI seemed back to normal, maybe even a little annoyed at the constant requests from the divers. Could a computer program get annoyed? Michael didn't understand enough about the advanced technology to know.

He continued to scan the buildings, not trusting the ship's sensors. The Sirens were still out there somewhere, and the poisonous vegetation was patiently waiting for them to step into its trap. This time, he wasn't going to let that happen.

Yes, they were back to square one, as Magnolia kept pointing out. But they all were alive, and that was what mattered. They could still fight another day and continue the search for X.

"Looks clear to me," Layla said.

Michael agreed and led the way past the old gas station. To the east, storm clouds belched lightning.

"Keep an eye on the storm, too, Timothy," he said.

"Yes, Commander." The AI definitely sounded annoyed.

Michael wanted to see how Rodger and Magnolia were doing on the hull repairs. Although Layla still had a limp, she was moving faster than Michael and quickly outpaced him. His skull pounded with a mean headache, and his gut roiled with every step.

It took several minutes just to walk around the massive ship. Michael looked up and studied the exterior as they walked. Hundreds of portholes marked the center line of the dark-gray ship. Two wings stuck out from the top of the stern, and another two jutted from the bottom. The thrusters were centered in the back, near the propeller and underneath the belly, where turbofans lined the bottom like suction cups. The landing gear was the size of a person, but it still didn't seem big enough to prop up the ship, especially on muddy terrain.

"There," Layla said, pointing up to the crest of the ship.

Two figures were working, their armor illuminated in the blue-white glow of a blowtorch. The divers were repairing the hull where lightning bolts had lashed it.

"*Deliverance* has one hell of a thick hide," Layla said.

"Hopefully thick enough to get us across the swamps. We should have tried that the first time." Michael continued to replay the journey in his mind, questioning his earlier decisions. Layla must have noticed, and she put a hand on his shoulder.

"Don't beat yourself up. Timothy advised us to go in on foot."

"Yeah, but . . ." Michael still felt guilty. X was out there, and every second that passed put them one second closer to losing him. He closed his eyes against the terrible specter of finding X dead—or crazy, which in some ways would be worse.

He's alive, and you will find him. But will he remember you?

Shaking his head, Michael snapped his eyes open to look at Rodger and Magnolia. They were welding a panel over a damaged section of hull. Neither seemed to notice Michael and Layla watching them.

"Timothy, do you have an update on the systems?" Michael asked.

The AI replied instantly. "Life support is at eighty-five percent, sir. I've managed to get the main valves back on, and the nuclear reactor is functioning at seventy-five percent. Drain valves and liquid hydrogen fill are working, and the oxygen flow is back at optimal levels."

"That's great," Michael replied.

Magnolia and Rodger were both standing now, waving at them.

"How are things going?" Rodger called out.

"Listen for yourself," Michael said.

Timothy continued relaying updates over the channel. "Distribution lines are mostly clear, but we have some blockage in compartments thirteen through sixteen. One of you will need to open those manually."

"I can clear that valve," Layla said. "I'm the smallest of us."

Michael looked back up at Rodger. "How much longer until you guys are finished up there?"

"A few hours."

"You have one hour," Michael replied. He turned to Layla. "Let's go get those valves cleared."

They walked back toward the open ramp leading to the bow, their boots sinking into the muddy terrain.

"I . . . I really thought I had lost you earlier," Layla said suddenly.

"It's going to take more than that to kill me."

She stopped and grabbed his hand, stepping up close so their helmets were just inches apart.

"You're always trying to be tough, like X, but you don't have to be. I miss you. I miss being with you."

Michael gripped her hands. "I know, but it's not as if we've had much time." The excuse sounded flimsy even to him. "I'm sorry. Come on, maybe we can take a detour on the way to that valve."

She chuckled. "How romantic."

Michael led her back into the ship, already imagining the two of them slipping into a cabin and feverishly removing each other's armor and suits. It might not be romantic, but he needed to touch her, to be touched. He needed the human connection.

Lightning corkscrewed over the shattered city in the distance, and Michael glimpsed what looked like a statue perched on one of the rooftops.

"Timothy," he said into the mike, "do another scan."

"Yes, Commander." A second later, the AI reported that the area was clear of contacts. Unconvinced, Michael aimed his rifle and zoomed in using his night-vision optics.

"Do you see something?" Layla said, following the angle of the barrel.

The statue—or what he had thought was a statue—suddenly moved, extending long limbs and climbing down the side of a building and out of sight.

"A Siren," he said, lowering his rifle.

Timothy reported the contact over the comms.

"Rodger, Mags, they're out there, so stay sharp," Michael said. "Layla, change of plans. You go fix the valve. I'll stay here and make sure those Sirens don't get the drop on us."

She hesitated, her hand lingering on his arm, and then nodded. He watched her walk up the ramp. When she was gone, he sighed again and checked the magazine in his rifle. It was fully loaded. He charged the weapon by pulling back the slide to chamber a round and then set off to patrol the area for contacts.

*   *   *   *   *

Team Phoenix had gone silent over the comms after the Siren sighting. Olah hadn't reported anything since then, and the quiet was making Les crazy. He tried to stay calm, but his hands were shaking and he was cold, which made his thin body spasm.

Gritting his teeth, he held up his wrist monitor. Cords connected the device to the control panel of the steel bunker door. Ty stood a few feet behind him, pacing with his blaster leveled at the dark corridor, helmet light raking back and forth.

"Should we hail Commander Jenkins?" Ty asked.

"Not yet."

"What about Olah? Do you think he's okay?"

"I don't know, man," Les replied. He tried not to snap at Ty, but his nerves were getting to him and the questions were hurting his head—both the ones Ty was asking out loud and the ones Les was asking himself. He still had no idea whether Ty was telling the truth about X. Had Captain Jordan really left the legendary diver on the surface after learning that he was still alive all those years ago? And if so, why?

Ty shifted his light to the open door at the other end of the corridor. A sign marked the wall there, but Les couldn't make it out. He looked back at his monitor. Three of the five numbers had solidified on the screen. Breaking the lock's code was taking far longer than he had anticipated.

"Come on, you piece of crap," he muttered. Both his arms were shaking now, and he dropped his pistol hand to his side. The fourth number flashed on the screen. Only one more to go.

Les alternated his gaze from the screen to the hallway, where he could see the rope hanging in the elevator shaft.

"You really think X was here?"

Ty shrugged. "Who else would these tracks be from?"

Les took a moment to think. His mind was full of burning questions. "Why the hell would Jordan leave X behind? It made no sense. He was one of the best divers in history."

"Simple," Ty replied with a snort, as if Les were a little thick for not figuring it out sooner. "Katrina."

"Huh? What's she got to do with anything?"

"They had a thing, X and Katrina, long time ago."

Les shook his wrist, trying to keep the blood flowing. "Why would that matter now?"

"You really don't know shit, do you?" Ty turned toward Les, and his helmet beam hit him in the face.

"Get that light out of my eyes."

"Sorry," Ty said. He moved to point the light at the steel door they were trying to open. "Jordan and Katrina got together. Thought they were keeping it a secret, but it was obvious to anyone with eyes, especially when she got pregnant."

"No shit?"

A nod from Ty. "So when we got the SOS from Hades that proved X was alive, Jordan decided to leave him down there."

Les shook his head. "Jordan abandoned X just to keep his woman?"

"Mostly. That and the fact X had survived so long in a place Jordan doesn't think is habitable. Reckons if it got out he was alive and had been for years, people would demand that he land the ship."

"Well, now that I've seen what's down here, I'm with Jordan. Our future is in the sky."

"Doesn't change the fact that Jordan left X down here to die," Ty said. "That's not right. He was a hero."

Les didn't reply, because he didn't know what to say. If the story was true, then Jordan was a liar and potentially a danger to everyone on the *Hive*. Les was a follower, not a leader, and he wasn't about to try to overthrow someone who wouldn't flinch at having him jettisoned from an air lock. He had his family to think about.

The fifth number finally appeared, and the locking mechanism clicked. The heavy steel door slowly opened. Les moved out of the way and pulled the patch cords free from the control pad. He stuffed them back in his vest as he stepped back and raised his pistol. Ty kept his blaster leveled at the door. White helmet beams shot through the inky darkness, touching the edges of what looked like silos rising toward a vaulted ceiling.

"Who's first?" Ty asked, clearly hoping it was not him.

Les held in a breath and stepped inside, moving his light back and forth over the massive chamber. Tubes with glass covers lined the sides of the silos like perfectly shaped eggs. He angled his light at the ceiling, where a crane hung on a metal track fifty feet above them.

"This ain't a supply warehouse," Ty said quietly. He stepped up next to Les and shined his beam over a tower of capsules.

"Then what the hell is it?"

"A tomb," Ty said. "We gotta get out of here."

"Why?" Les directed his helmet beam at Ty. The man's features were clenched, and sweat dripped down his forehead.

"This is where the Sirens came from," Ty said. "I heard Jordan talking about it with Katrina. Those monsters…they evolved from genetically modified humans in places like this."

Les shifted his beam back to the towers. "So why the hell was X here?"

"Don't know, and I don't much care." Ty was already walking away, but Les stood his ground and examined the silos. There had to be thousands of the capsules.

He took a few more steps over the dusty concrete, toward the silos. Dust motes floated down as his beam cut through the darkness. Were those really people frozen inside? If so, could they be woken up?

He flinched at the crackle of static from his earpiece. "Phoenix Two, this is Phoenix One. Do you copy?"

"Roger, this is Phoenix Two," he said.

"Where are you, Phoenix Two?" Erin's voice was low, as if she didn't want to be overheard.

"We're in some sort of cryo chamber. Over," Les replied, following her lead and keeping his voice low. He looked over his shoulder to see Ty standing in the open doorway, waving at him to hurry up. Les shook his head, signaling for Ty to calm down.

"Get out of there and head back to the atrium," Erin said. "We need your help loading supplies. We hit the jackpot."

Les felt the tickle of a smile. *Looks like we're going home,* he thought.

"On our way, Phoenix One," Les said.

He started to back away when his light flitted over what appeared to be a broken capsule about three rows back and halfway up a tower. He pulled out his binoculars and focused on the tube while keeping the light angled on the silo.

"Move it, Giraffe," Ty said.

"One of those is broken," he said, pointing.

"That's why we need to get the hell out of here," Ty grumbled. "Come on, man, or I'm leaving you down here."

Les tucked the binos back into his vest and turned to leave, his awe at what he was seeing finally overtaken by raw fear of what it might mean. He and Ty grabbed the doors and heaved them shut. Now they knew why X, or whoever had beaten them here, had locked the chamber. Something had awoken early from its artificial sleep.

After securing the lock, Les and Ty made their way back up the stairwell. The twenty floors to the surface gave them plenty of time to talk.

"Sirens were people once, huh?" Les asked.

"From what I overheard."

"But how did they turn into those monsters?"

Ty stopped on the next landing to catch his breath. "It took years. All those genetic modifications did something funny to them. Or maybe it was the radiation from the bombs. Hell, maybe it was both."

Les tried to wrap his mind around that, but it was almost too much for his brain to handle. He swallowed and kept moving up the stairs. By the time they made it back up to the atrium, both divers were winded, and Les had a dozen more questions rattling around in his skull. He hurried through the space, his heartbeat ramping up from more than the exertion.

Across the room, Jennifer and Erin were stacking ITC boxes. They had already dragged the *Hive*'s supply crates inside. The front door was wide open, allowing flurries of snow to blow in.

"You guys find anything?" Erin asked when they arrived.

"Nothing useful," Les said. "I'll tell you more later. Let's help you get these into the crates."

"There's more downstairs," Erin said. "I want to make sure we get as much as possible. Ty, come with us. Les, you stay here and stand guard."

She started to hand him the machine gun but held it just out of his reach.

"Just flick the safety off, aim, and shoot if you run into trouble. Simple as that. Okay?"

"Yeah...okay."

She raised a brow, apparently reconsidering her order. "You're sure you can handle this?"

"Yes, I'm sure." Les holstered his pistol and grabbed the barrel stock of the gun. The weapon felt surprisingly light in his grip. He watched the other divers return to the stairwell before walking over to the open front door. A light carpet of snow had collected over the tile floor. He shut off his helmet beam and chinned on his night-vision goggles.

"Phoenix Four, this is Phoenix One," Erin said over the open channel. "How's it looking up there?"

Les flicked the safety off before stepping out onto the landing, listening to the conversation as he scanned the street.

"All clear, Phoenix One. The Siren I saw earlier is long gone. I've got the satellite ready. Just give me the word and I'll relay a transmission."

"Roger, Phoenix Four. Contact Command and give them our coordinates. Tell them we're sending up two full crates and will be coming back up in the next thirty minutes. Phoenix One, over and out."

Les crouched down behind a low wall for cover and brought the scope of the rifle up to his visor. He zoomed in on the tower Olah had scaled, but didn't see the diver.

A jag of lightning streaked across the skyline like a shooting star, illuminating the area. Shadows bent beneath the cloud cover, and the bones of buildings seemed to move in the flickering light. He moved right for a better view, trying to decide whether his eyes were playing tricks on him, or there were indeed Sirens hunting up there.

Another fork of electricity shot over the city, backlighting the horizon enough for him to see that it was clear of Sirens. He relaxed and moved across the landing to scan the street. Purple weeds grew out of the shattered road, whipping back and forth. A beetle with antennae the size of pencils scuttled in front of his boots and into a hole in the concrete.

Creepy, he thought. *Wait till I tell my boy about that!*

The clatter of metal and plastic came from inside the building, and Les peeked back inside. The other divers were returning with more crates, some of them marked with biohazard symbols. Erin had explained before the dive that the supplies might not seem like much for a ship packed full of nearly five hundred people, but the compressed synthetic food would feed them for months, and the cancer drugs would heal dozens of dying lower-deckers.

Les found himself smiling for the first time on the dive. Maybe being a diver wasn't so bad. Then again, they still had to make the return trip. And Ty's revelations about Jordan made him wonder what they would find if they did manage to get back to the ship.

After loading each crate, two divers would carry it outside and put it down in the middle of the street, all the while keeping a close watch on the precious cargo.

"Phoenix Four, Phoenix One. Did you reach Command?"

"Yes ma'am. They're moving into position to pick us up."

"Good," Erin replied. "Now, get down here. We're preparing to deploy the crates."

Les handed the rifle back to her and unholstered his pistol. He stood sentry with Jennifer and Ty while Erin readied the boxes. She hadn't said anything about Ty carrying a blaster, but Les had caught her looking at the weapon, so she must be okay with it.

"Make some room," Erin said.

She bent down and typed a passcode into the control panel on the side of the first supply crate. Two balloons popped out of the external boosters and quickly filled with gas, and the crate lifted off the ground. She punched the code into the second box and stepped back as it rose into the air, carrying the valuable supplies heavenward.

Olah arrived just as the crates vanished into the cloud cover.

"You see anything on your way in?" Erin asked.

"No ma'am. If those things are out there, they aren't showing themselves."

Erin pulled her binos from her vest and glassed the sky in all directions.

"Looks clear," she said. "Let's get into the air, but remember to keep your distance from each other. We don't want to get tangled."

The divers all fanned out until they were about twenty feet apart. Erin pointed at Jennifer. "You're first," she said. "Ready?"

Jennifer stood stock-still as Erin punched the booster over her back. The canister fired, filling the balloon with helium, and up she rose, just like the supply crates. She let out a yelp and reached for the toggles, her feet kicking at air as she lifted off the ground.

"Don't fight it," Erin said. She watched for a few seconds before moving over to Olah and Ty. She punched their boosters, and the two men followed Jennifer into the sky.

Erin stopped beside Les. "Good job today," she said. "Now, get home safe."

"Thank you, ma'am. I plan to."

She punched his booster, and the canister fired. He looked up over his shoulder as the balloon rose behind him. Erin ran to put distance between them before hitting her own booster. Within a minute, all five divers were floating toward the *Hive*, nearly four miles above them.

Les straightened his trajectory, then let go of the toggles and pulled out his binoculars. He wanted one last look at the remains of this metropolis, where people had once lived under the bright, beaming sun.

Sunken streets, crumbling scrapers, and block after block of flattened houses filled his view. Snow covered the graves of thousands, maybe millions, who had burned up when the bombs exploded.

Les held the binos on a spot of red in the white landscape. It took him a second to realize that it was their DZ. Blood marked the spot where Tom had fallen, but when Les zoomed in, he didn't see the body.

After a quick scan of the area, he located an arm, and a trail of red streaking away from the site. He followed the path to a crater, where a frenzy of motion surrounded a pool of gore. Three Sirens ripped and tore at Tom's remains.

"Contacts," he choked out. "Three, half a click from our DZ at six o'clock."

"They didn't see us," Erin said. "Stay quiet and steady. We're about to hit the cloud cover. They won't follow us into it."

Static broke over the channel—the electrical storm, already messing with their electronics. Any minute, his night-vision optics would flicker off, leaving him blind.

A voice crackled through the white noise.

"Commander, uh...I seem to be losing altitude."

It was Ty, his voice calm but shaky.

Les scanned the sky. He spotted Jennifer and Olah to the west. To the east was Erin, and about three hundred feet from her was Ty. He appeared to be about twenty feet below the other divers. But how was that possible if he had been the second to take off?

"Check your helium levels," Erin replied.

Ty's reply was strained. "Must have a leak in the lines or the balloon."

Erin muttered a curse—a rare break in her calm demeanor.

"I can hear it hissing out," Ty said, his usual drawl taking on a panicked edge.

"Listen very carefully," Erin said. "Pull yourself up by your risers and find the leak. As soon as you find it, patch it with the kit in your vest."

Ty twisted and reached up for the balloon. "I can't reach it!" he yelled.

"Hold on, I'll come to you," Erin said. She used her toggles to direct her body toward Ty, dipping down slightly.

An alien scream sounded in the distance, and Les knew exactly what had made the noise. The beasts had taken to the air.

"We got c-company," he stuttered. He pulled out his pistol and thumbed back the hammer. The divers were almost to the clouds. Lightning bloomed in the west, but the flight path overhead looked clear.

"Help!" Ty yelled over the comm. "I'm falling!"

"Shhh," Erin said. "Just stay calm. I'm on my way."

She sailed through the air, knees bent and hands on her toggles. A few seconds later, she reached Ty and bent down to inspect his balloon. All the while, he continued slowly sinking back to the ground.

Les felt his heart jump a beat when he saw more of the Sirens to the south. The beasts were flapping away from towers and climbing at an alarming speed.

"Ty, listen to me," Erin said. "I need you to—"

Her instructions were lost in static. Les aimed his pistol at the bat-like creatures stalking them. The first group was a hundred yards out. He could see their shriveled skin and frayed wings now, but it was their oscillating wails that chilled his blood. He fired a shot, and the gun kicked in his hand.

"Hold your fire!" Erin shouted.

Too late, Jennifer's blaster sent a flare arcing through the darkness and lighting up the sky around them. As if in answer, lightning flashed.

In the eerie light, Les saw the eyeless face of a Siren—and the mouth full of jagged teeth as it unleashed a blood-curdling wail.

It wheeled toward Ty, clawed hands reaching up for his boots.

An instant later, Ty opened a private channel between him and Les and looked up at Les.

"Don't forget what I told you about Jordan. You're the only one who knows the truth now. You have to—"

The first Siren wrapped around Ty's body, engulfing him in its membranous wings. A second grabbed his legs, and a third slashed the deflating balloon.

Thunder boomed, drowning out Erin's anguished cry as she lost the second member of her team that day. The green hue of Les' optics flashed off as he broke through the floor of the cloud cover. The comms crackled offline, but the surviving members of Team Phoenix were forced to listen to Ty's screams as the Sirens ripped his falling body apart.

NINETEEN

Jordan splashed cold water on his face and slicked his dark hair back against his scalp. Wearing a freshly pressed uniform, polished boots, and his sword, he stepped into the hallway. An entourage of heavily armed militia waited, led by Ensign Del Toro.

"Ready, sir?"

Jordan answered by setting off down the dimly lit passage. Passengers were already flooding the corridors, the curfew having been lifted hours earlier. The crowds didn't concern him. He had soldiers with crossbows posted at every intersection, and the most experienced men carried pistols, with orders to use extreme prejudice to keep violence from breaking out.

In the past, Jordan would have worried about a stray bullet puncturing a gas bladder, but right now he was more worried about a mutiny.

So far, the show of force seemed to be working. Everywhere he walked, people fell silent and parted to make way. Lower-deckers in their tattered clothing retreated, pressing their backs against the bulkheads. Jordan could smell them as he passed: body odor, shine, and piss. The scents disgusted him.

But at the next passage, several lower-deckers stood their ground. At the head of the group stood Cole Mintel, muscular arms folded across his chest, sleeves rolled up to expose his clock tattoo.

Del Toro reached for his baton, but Jordan shook his head. "Is there a problem, Mintel?"

Their eyes met, but Rodger's father looked away first. "It's not right," he muttered. "You can't—"

"In a few hours, everyone on this ship is going to be very happy," Jordan interrupted. "You'll all be praising my name. In the meantime, step aside."

Cole watched him pass, and Jordan let him look. He wasn't going to waste his time on an old clockmaker. The soldiers closed in protectively around Jordan, and he began to relax as he walked, putting the anger and worry out of his mind. He was focused on his goal. He would find the new ship and save humanity. Nothing else, not even Katrina, was more important than that.

By the time he got to the launch bay, a crowd had gathered outside the doors. The few people who managed to squeeze past the guards jostled for a view, pushing each other against the portholes.

"Should we push them back?" Lieutenant Hunt asked.

Jordan scrutinized the grubby faces pressed up against the glass. Men and women, young and old—they were here to see which divers had made it back and what treasures they had found on the surface. According to the last radio transmission from Olah, the divers had come back with quite a haul.

The launch bay doors screeched open, and Jordan stepped inside. Staff in red and yellow jumpsuits surrounded the two reentry domes. A grappling hook had already pulled the plastic roof off the first, exposing two supply crates that had recently been scrubbed for contaminants.

A team opened the crates and pulled out boxes marked with biohazard signs. Those contained the rare cancer drugs and other medicines that would heal dozens of otherwise doomed people. Still more boxes bore the symbol of a bread loaf, indicating synthetic food.

A little boy wriggled past Jordan, his lower-decker father right behind him. The child pointed through the window and asked, "Papa, what's in those boxes?"

His father lifted the boy up to give him a better view. "Medicine for Mama," he said. He glanced at Jordan and added, "Thank you, Captain."

The unexpected words of gratitude made Jordan pause. He couldn't remember the last time a lower-decker had shown him any respect.

"You're welcome," Jordan said.

"Sir," Hunt called from inside the launch bay, "shall I clear the passage outside?"

"No, I want them to see this."

Jordan continued into the room. He had lifted the shelter curfew so people could see the synthetic food, cancer drugs, and supplies being unloaded. It was amazing how fast people forgot their grievances when their bellies were full and their loved ones were healed.

The hiss of air filled the launch bay as he approached the dome in the center of the room. Sergeant Jenkins was waiting near the crowd of support staff.

Through the fence of red and yellow jumpsuits, Jordan glimpsed four divers inside the reentry zone. That was good. One accidental death and one problem dealt with. They were still hanging from the balloons that had pulled them into the air. A metal floor clanked shut, and one by one, the divers dropped to the floor.

"There's only four," Jenkins said, his voice panicked. "What happened? Who's not here?"

"We must have lost another diver on reentry," Hunt said.

Jenkins elbowed his way through the crowd, pushing technicians and engineers aside to see whether his daughter had made it home. The sergeant's muscular body visibly relaxed when he learned that Erin had returned. Jordan joined him to get a better look.

White mist hissed into the reentry tube, covering the divers inside. Technicians, Dr. Huff, several nurses, and other personnel crowded around the dome. Jordan made his way over to a burly bearded man.

"How are things here, Samson?" Jordan said.

The chief engineer wiped his mustache with his greasy fingers. "Not good, Cap. We lost Ty."

"That's a shame," Jordan said, giving his best rueful frown.

Pulling out a handkerchief, Samson dabbed his forehead. Jordan wasn't sure how anyone could be overweight aboard the airship, but Samson had somehow managed it. His jowls shook as he spoke.

"I don't know what he did to earn his time in the brig, but he was a damn fine technician." He shook his head. "We can't keep losing people that are impossible to replace, Cap."

"I know that." Jordan held back the dressing-down he wanted to give Samson in front of his engineering staff. The engineer disgusted him, but he would be vital when they took over the other airship. "How much longer until they're done?" Jordan asked, gesturing toward the decontamination tube. The mist continued swirling inside, shrouding the divers. Seconds later, jets fired, coating the ghostly figures in white foam.

"Depressurization is complete; now we're sterilizing. Shouldn't be too long." Samson shook his head. "Can't believe we lost Ty."

Jordan pretended to share the chief engineer's regret. Ty had seen too much and guessed too many of Jordan's secrets. Now the problem was dealt with, and Jordan could relax a degree.

Floor vents inside the dome clicked on, and white mist vented out of the ship. A second jet sprayed the divers with water, rinsing the foam off their armored bodies. Jordan found Jenkins again in the crowd. The sergeant moved from side to side to get a view of his daughter.

"She's okay," Jordan said. "And she did a fine job."

"Thank you, sir."

A team of techs carried the first of the cargo crates out of the room. Several militia soldiers armed with crossbows followed. Jordan could no longer hold back a smile. Team Phoenix had returned with an impressive haul for their first dive, and he had one man to thank for giving them the location. *X was the gift that kept on giving.* The thought soured his smile.

At the portholes along the wall, dozens of lower-deckers were still peering in, their grubby faces expectant, eyes on the crates.

"Not chanting about wanting a new captain now, are we?" Jordan muttered. He wondered whether the teens who had defaced the bulkhead with his effigy were out there watching. It was only a matter of time before the militia found them, and when they did, he would make sure no one tried such a thing again.

The lift clanked down over the dome. The technician controlling the device expertly pulled the plastic roof off the divers.

"Jenkins, have them meet me in the ops room after they finish decon," Jordan said.

He clapped Samson on the shoulder and walked away from the crowd, continuing to the operations room, where he unclipped his sword and placed it on the table. He glanced over at the pictures on the black bulkhead, stopping on X last. It had been a few days since the legendary diver haunted his dreams. Maybe that was because Jordan no longer feared the man. After losing his child and Katrina, the only thing he had left to lose was his command. And if the people wanted that, they would have to kill him.

Fifteen minutes later, the door opened and Jenkins walked inside. Erin, Jennifer, Les, and Olah followed him in, their hair still wet from the showers.

"Welcome back, Team Phoenix," Jordan said. He took the seat at the head of the table and motioned for them to sit.

The door clicked shut, and the sergeant stood in front of it, hands behind his back. He looked at his daughter, but she kept her sharp brown eyes on Jordan. She had performed well under pressure on the surface, it seemed, but he wondered how she had handled listening to Ty's death screams. After the botched sabotage of Magnolia's chute, he had been more meticulous with Ty's booster. Still, he would have preferred not to put Miss Jenkins through the emotional stress of losing another team member after the disaster that claimed her previous crew.

The divers looked exhausted and horrified—especially Jennifer, who shivered and stared blankly ahead.

Les Mitchells sat calmly, hands clasped on the table. Olah, pale and sweating, smiled proudly when Jordan looked at him.

"You have done well and should be proud of yourselves," Jordan finally said. "I'm here to congratulate you on one of the most successful dives in recent memory."

Erin fidgeted in her chair but didn't say a word.

"I'm sorry about Tom Price. I didn't know him well, but he seemed a good man. As for Ty, well, perhaps I made a mistake in sending him to the surface. Before we proceed, I need to ask you all a few questions about him."

Jordan scrutinized the divers' reactions. Mitchells seemed agitated. He unlaced his fingers and picked at a nail. Jordan read the subtle clues in the man's expression, his movements. Even the slightest hesitation in a response would tell him when someone was lying.

"Did Ty say anything to any of you that could be considered treasonous?"

Jennifer, still shivering, managed to shake her head. "I never talked to him. Cagey son of a bitch—begging your pardon for my language."

"How about you, Commander?" Jordan asked.

"No sir. He was quiet the entire dive. Except when . . . well, except at the end."

"A tragedy," Jordan said. "I'm sure you did all you could."

"The only person he was alone with was Les," Erin added.

Jordan watched Les' Adam's apple bob in a dry swallow. He focused on the tall man.

"Anything you'd like to report, Les?"

"He asked me for a weapon when we heard the Sirens," Les said. "And I'm sorry, but I gave him my blaster. I was scared, sir. I thought, better to have us all armed if we were forced to fight."

"I approved it," Erin said. "That's on me."

The ship groaned, distracting Jordan. He looked at his wristwatch. Right on time.

"Are we moving?" Jennifer whispered.

Jordan ignored her. "Did Ty say anything else?"

"No, sir."

There was no hesitation, and Les didn't look away. Deep down, Jordan felt a flood of relief. He couldn't afford to kill Mitchells. The man was an engineer and now a Hell Diver. Samson was right. They couldn't afford to lose people like that.

"Good," Jordan said. "Despite his history, Ty sacrificed himself for the good of everyone, as did Tom Price. For that, we honor them."

"We dive so humanity survives," the divers said quietly.

"And you will continue to do so. That's why I called you here. There's been an exciting development." Jordan pushed his mike to his lips and said, "Hunt, direct full power to the turbofans and rudders. Full speed toward *Deliverance*."

"Roger that, Captain," came the response in his earpiece.

Jordan stood and clipped the sword back onto his belt, wanting to present an impressive image for his big announcement—after leaving the divers in suspense a moment longer.

"The reason we are changing course is confidential. It does not leave this room. Understood?"

Four immediate nods, and a fifth from Jenkins.

"I've been informed Commander Everhart and some members of Team Raptor survived at the Hilltop Bastion. Those traitors managed to find another airship, which they have commandeered."

Jennifer stopped shivering and sat up in her chair. Olah's brows scrunched together, and Les stopped picking at his fingernail. Erin was the only one who didn't react.

Jenkins paced away from the door.

"We're going to find that ship," Jordan said. "I firmly believe that our future will continue to be in the sky for the next two and a half centuries. This new ship will serve as backup in case something happens to the *Hive*. It will be imperative to our survival as a species."

"How do you expect to find her, sir?" Erin asked.

Jordan smiled. "I can't tell you that. But when I do find *Deliverance*, you're going to help me take it from Team Raptor."

Silence filled the room. Jenkins scratched at the back of his neck and glanced at his daughter. She stared at Jordan with an unreadable expression on her face.

"I'll brief you when I know more," Jordan said. "Go see your families and get some sleep. You deserve it. Just don't mention what we discussed here. Dismissed."

Jordan held up his hand before Les could leave. "Not you," he said.

The diver backed away from the door and turned to face him. Les was a foot taller, and Jordan had to tilt his head back slightly to meet his eyes.

"I sure hope you're telling me the truth about Ty," he said. "Because if you're not, I'm going to be very disappointed. Are you sure there's nothing else?"

Les hesitated a second and then nodded.

"Don't forget that Trey is being held in the brig," Jordan said.

"Not likely to forget that," Les said, then added a belated, "sir."

Jordan regarded him for a long moment, trying to find the lie hidden behind the taller man's wary expression. "That's all. Dismissed."

"Thank you, sir," Les replied.

Jordan watched him leave. Les knew something, and he was going to find out exactly what it was.

*　　*　　*　　*　　*

ONE YEAR AND NINE MONTHS EARLIER

Xavier brought his rifle up, the buttstock nestled in the sweet spot against his shoulder, and scanned the hallway of the underground ITC facility. After slaughtering the female Sirens on the bridge, he had put another needle in his vein. The second dose coursed through him now, warm and intense. He could feel his pulse pounding in his neck, and his vision had narrowed as if he were seeing the world through a pair of binos.

X was ten floors belowground now, making his way toward the medical center—one of the most dangerous parts of any

ITC facility. He had been in enough bunkers over the years to know the layout. The smooth concrete shells, narrow corridors, and massive warehouses all looked essentially the same outside and inside.

The medicine he sought was likely stashed next to the cryogenic chambers, in the heart of the facility, where the Sirens often returned for fresh meat.

He stopped to rest on the next concrete landing, blinking to clear his vision. Sweat rolled down his forehead, and his throat burned. The cancer was eating him alive. It didn't seem any better than being torn apart by Sirens. The monsters killed you quickly, at least.

He started to move when he spotted slime on the stairs. He shined his helmet light on the glistening goo. The Sirens had been here—recently.

Keep moving, X.

Cryogenics couldn't be much farther. He hoped the female Sirens he had killed with his motorcycle were the only ones that lived in this facility. With luck, he could get in and out without another fight. But he also knew not to count on luck. X put his faith in bullets and medicine.

A sound rose over his labored breathing. Somewhere high above him, a screech of metal echoed through the abandoned building. Or had it come from below?

X paused on the steps to listen, then eased over to the steel door on the landing. It was unlocked, and he slowly pushed it open. The long hallway led to another door, marked COMMUNI-CATIONS. Inside were radio equipment and computers. Nothing of use to him.

After closing the door, he waited another few minutes, then continued down the stairs. The Cryogenics lab was three floors below. As he suspected, the door was wide open. The medical ward would be close, maybe even the next floor down. But first he had to pass the open doorway.

He shut off his helmet light and left his NVGs off, for fear that the battery would attract the Sirens. He took two very cautious blind steps. Once he knew he was past the open door, he stopped and reached out for the wall and used it to guide him across the next landing.

Faint scratching came from the other side of the wall, like a child dragging fingernails down a bulkhead. Grunting followed. Animalistic, almost sexual.

X shivered, but not from fear. He was running a fever again. Whatever was on the other side of the wall was preoccupied for now, though he had no doubt it would happily slaughter him if it noticed his presence.

Don't ... stop ... moving.

His fingers felt along the wall until he reached the edge of the stairs. As he slowly took a step down, his rifle scraped the wall.

The sounds shut off like a light switch, and silence filled the stairwell. He froze with his boot in midair.

He closed his eyes and waited, heart pounding, blood singing in his ears. Trying not to breathe audibly. Trying not to move at all. His leg began to shake after a few seconds, and he slowly brought it down to the next step. His boot touched down with a soft thump.

A high-pitched alien cry replied.

He didn't waste any time in reaching up to flip on his light. The beam shot out and captured an eyeless face staring up at him from a few steps below. The sinewy white-gray flesh of a Siren hurtled forward, clawed hands reaching for his throat.

The adrenaline rushing through his system saved his life. X matched the monster's speed, bringing up his rifle and firing a burst through its rib cage. Shrieking, it slammed into the wall.

X loped down to the next landing, looking desperately for the medical center. He tried the door, but this one was locked.

Enraged wails rang out above, spurring him on. He continued around the corner, sweeping his light and rifle muzzle over the stairs. His vision flickered, red suddenly washing over everything. He blinked, and the red faded.

Shit. Not good.

The stairs were chipped and broken, but clear of contacts. The sight of the medical symbol, two serpents coiled around a winged staff, got him moving like a man half his age.

He cleared the corner and turned to make sure the beasts above him weren't following. Their wails continued, but they weren't in sight. He flung open the door and burst into the passage with his rifle out front and his finger on the trigger. *Clear.*

He closed the door and ran for the next one. Letting his rifle hang from the strap, he pulled his pistol and fired into the lock. The report filled his helmet, drowning out the rush of blood in his ears. Moving into the room, he swept the pistol over a space furnished with islands and workstations. His beam captured the freezer and several storage areas—the most likely places to start looking.

Halfway across the room, a wave of dizziness washed over him, and sharp pains raced up his left arm.

Was this the moment when his heart finally gave out?

He eyed the cabinets not a hundred feet away.

X waited for his heart to slow from automatic gunfire to a fairly normal pace. It was taking too long. Sweat crept down his scalp.

He ignored the wails above and focused on his breathing, inhaling for a count of five, exhaling for a count of seven. The rhythm gradually calmed his racing heart, and he felt steady enough to move. He crossed the room and began raiding cabinets.

Ten minutes into the search, he found a freezer, still powered by a generator somewhere deep beneath the ground. The second drawer contained cancer meds. X stuffed them into his backpack and went back out into the hallway. He listened for beasts at the door but heard nothing.

The facility had gone quiet again.

He slowly opened the door and moved into the stairwell. Sure enough, it was empty. With the precious cargo on his back, he headed up the stairs. With each step, the grunting and crunching noises he had heard earlier grew louder. This was nothing like the normal emergency-alarm screech the Sirens made. He came to the carcass of the female he had killed on the way down, and nudged it with his boot.

At the next landing, he turned off his helmet lamp and flipped on his NVGs. He peered around the corner and into the open cryogenic chamber. Once his eyes adjusted to the green light, he scanned the massive room filled with silos like the one where he had found Miles. Hundreds of capsules lay shattered and empty. Several rows back, however, motion flickered around one of the towers and up the side.

X's breath caught when he saw them.

Hundreds of creatures were scaling the silos like ants. Smaller than the usual Sirens and hideously pale in the green hue of his optics.

Children.

At the top of the tower, several adults broke the glass of a capsule and tossed a full-grown human from the chamber to the floor below, where it landed with a sickening thud. The genetically modified human lay on the floor in a puddle of fluid mixed with blood.

The young Sirens scampered around it, grunting and pushing each other out of the way. Then one of them—an older child, judging by its size—bounded forward and clamped down on the human's leg. It took a bite, ripping flesh from the ankle.

The man jerked awake screaming in a voice that chilled X to the core.

All at once, the other juvenile Sirens joined the feast.

X didn't wait around to watch. He bolted across the landing and up the stairs. The beasts, intent on their feast, must not have seen him. He ran past the communications door, but something stopped him. It had been months since he thought of the people in the sky and the warnings he had sent them. But what if they were still out there? What if they tried to raid this place and encountered the nest?

He had given up on the people in the sky years ago, but the thought of them walking into a trap made him pause. Instead of moving up the stairs, X went back to the communications center to relay what could be his final message: a warning to stay away from ITC Communal 9.

The distant wails of the monsters continued as X worked to bring the radio back online. Fortunately, the facility's nuclear-powered backup generators, installed to preserve the cryo chambers indefinitely, also powered other critical equipment. It took an hour to activate the radio and relay his message. By the time he finished sending the transmission, the eerie echoes had faded away, leaving him in silence.

X used the time to search a row of lockers, to make sure he wasn't leaving anything valuable behind. He found a sealed bottle of stimulants and a few dead batteries. The bottle went in the bag.

As he closed the locker and turned to head back aboveground, a metal banging froze him in place. The noise reverberated like a gong throughout the facility.

The electronic cries of Sirens rose in reply. Dozens of them, all at once. The discord rose into a loud cacophony.

But it was the next sound that made X freeze.

Gunshots.

Could they be real, or was this just his mind playing tricks?

X moved slowly back to the door and peered down the hallway. Beams of green light jumped across his field of vision. He shut his NVGs off and the green lights turned white. They darted back and forth, hitting the walls and ceiling of the landing at the end of the passage.

Another gunshot rang out, and this time there was no mistaking it.

Enraged Sirens answered the noise. Had they learned how to fire a weapon? It was the only explanation, unless...

X blinked rapidly, trying to grasp what he was hearing. Was it possible that the people from the sky had heard his message and come down?

No. There was no way they had heard it and come for him this fast. Whoever these people were, either they had already been inside the facility or they slipped past him while he was in the radio room.

He crept into the hallway, keeping the rifle pointed at the landing. He knelt and waited, the rifle wobbling in his shaky hands.

The beams grew brighter, and a hulking metal figure strode past the landing and rounded the corner, dragging something meaty over the stairs.

X reared back at the sight. It was the first human he had seen in... He realized he no longer knew.

Metal clattered like a can being tossed against a wall, as more people in heavy armor trudged up the stairs. The light beams danced back and forth over a mesh wire net two of them were dragging.

Inside the net, three Sirens thumped up the stairs, all unconscious or dead. The wails continued from below, where more gunfire rang out. Whatever was happening had started when he was inside the radio room, but he hadn't heard anyone or anything slip past the steps outside.

Curiosity pushed him to his feet, and he moved a few steps forward, his rifle still aimed at the landing where the lights continued flitting across the stairwell.

The metallic clanking grew louder, and voices rang out. They were muffled but undeniably human, although he couldn't understand a word they were saying. Whoever these people were, they didn't speak his language.

He considered retreating to the radio room to hide, but the voices were almost on top of him. Another armored hulk of a man crossed onto the landing, and X moved his finger to the trigger. But the figure kept moving, hauling another mesh net full of young Sirens. One was still conscious, clawing and shrieking and flopping about.

Melancholy wails answered. The adults were searching for their missing children. Gunshots held them back.

A third man in an armored suit stepped onto the landing and pointed a long weapon with a spear-like muzzle at the Siren. An electric bolt flashed into the naked beast. It screeched and jerked violently on the ground for several seconds before going limp.

X held in a breath and took a step backward, his metal armor scraping the concrete wall.

The sound drew the men's attention. A helmet with two almond-shaped eye covers turned in his direction.

"¡Contacto!" the man yelled. "¡Peligro!"

X had the man at point-blank range, knowing he should pull the trigger, but for some reason he hesitated. These were *humans*. The first people he had seen in years.

The armored figure raised the electrical rifle, and a blue arc leaped out and hit X in the chest before he could get off a shot.

He crashed onto the concrete landing, jerking spastically. Unable to move, he watched boots crossing toward him. The same stifled voices came from all directions as the men surrounded him. Loud, angry voices. His hesitation would likely cost him his life, and that would be the end for Miles, too.

"No," X mumbled, thinking of his dog. He tried to push himself up, but another jolt ripped through his body, and he went limp on the ground.

TWENTY

"This is…*cough*…Xavier Rodriguez. I'm currently…" The voice on the channel coughed again. In the mess hall aboard *Deliverance*, Magnolia listened over the PA system to the strained, scratchy voice of the man they were looking for. X gave his coordinates and then said something she wasn't expecting.

"Stay away from ITC Communal Nine."

Magnolia frowned as the message concluded. It was like hearing the hoarse murmurings of a ghost. Timothy played it a third time, as if they might unlock some secret by listening to it over and over again.

The divers sat at one of the twenty white tables in the mess hall, listening intently as X's voice rang out from the speakers. A day had passed since they landed on the island. After discovering another problem with the electrical system, Michael had kept them grounded for repairs. Now he wasn't sure what to do.

"X sounds sick," Rodger said.

There was a moment of silence as they considered the implications of the message and the state of the man who had transmitted it. X had warned anyone listening to avoid ITC

Communal 9 in Miami, and he did sound ill. Had they come all this way for nothing?

"This was two years ago?" Michael asked. "How come this is the first time we're hearing it?"

"Twenty months and twenty-two days ago, to be precise," Timothy replied. "This is the first time I've detected the transmission. The last one was simply an SOS."

"Is it possible the *Hive* could have received it as well?" Magnolia said.

Timothy's translucent form looked pensive. "Perhaps. But the electrical storm centered over this region may be interfering with radio communications, so unless the *Hive* is close, they likely won't hear this transmission."

"Thank you, Timothy," Michael said. He heaved a sigh, and Magnolia watched him curiously, wondering what he was thinking.

This changes nothing," he finally said. "X is still alive, and we're going to find him. Now, eat up. We're going to need the energy."

Magnolia could only pick at the gelatinous hunk of what was supposed to be meat. It jiggled like the flesh of a living creature. She forced down several bites anyway as Timothy appeared in front of the table, virtual hands clasped behind his back.

"All secondary systems are online, sir. The ship is ready to depart."

Michael stood and looked at his team. "Once we start flying into that storm, there's no turning back. Are you all sure you're up for this?"

"Beats those boats and sea monsters," Magnolia said.

"I'm ready," Layla said.

Rodger nodded. "Good to go, sir."

"Okay, then," Michael said. "Grab your gear and meet on the bridge."

A half hour later, the team gathered in the command center.

They were all wearing their armor. Magnolia carried her helmet in the crook of her arm. Most of their equipment was in the cargo hold, ready to be deployed as soon as they landed in Miami, but she already had her lucky blades sheathed and strapped.

On the bridge, Timothy's hologram stood at the helm, between the wall-mounted monitor and the circular command island. Screens glowed at each station, waiting for the crew that should be flying a ship this size. Instead of a full complement, it had four divers and an AI. The divers strapped into the comfortable leather chairs facing the helm.

"Initiate systems checks," Michael said.

Magnolia, in charge of navigation, touched the screen and brought up their current location. "Online."

"Comms online," Rodger said.

"Life support online," Layla added.

After a brief pause, Michael nodded and said, "Fire her up, Timothy."

Deliverance growled to life, and the clatter of electrical relays and mechanical equipment raced through the ship. Vibrations shook the bridge as the nuclear-powered engine engaged, and Magnolia cinched up the harness across her chest.

Rodger looked over, his usual joking manner gone. Sincere brown eyes behind thick glasses met her gaze.

"Everything's going to be okay," he said.

Impulsively, Magnolia reached out and grabbed his hand, feeling the rough calluses of a man who had been a woodworker all his life.

"We're online," Timothy reported. "The engine is fully operational. Turbofans and thrusters are functioning at ninety percent power."

The numbers were good—even better than when they found the ship at Hilltop Bastion. All their work had paid off.

Magnolia relaxed in her leather chair and looked over at Michael—*Commander Everhart*, she reminded herself. It was up to him now.

"Get us off this mud pie, Timothy," he said.

The turbofans kicked on, and the ship creaked and hummed in response as it climbed into the sky.

"Goodbye," Timothy said. He bowed his head slightly and then looked back at the wall-mounted screen as a view of the ground came online. The small graveyard that served as the resting place for the real Timothy Pepper's family emerged on-screen. Magnolia thought about saying something, but decided to pay her respects in silence.

All sense of motion vanished for a moment, as if they were hovering in darkness. Everything seemed peaceful, but Magnolia knew what was coming. Clanking echoed from under the floor as the landing gear retracted into the belly of the airship. When it finally stopped, Michael tapped on his monitor, directing power to the turbofans.

Then they were rising toward the heavens, the massive airship groaning and creaking like a prehistoric beast waking after a long hibernation. Recessed lights flickered along the ceiling, and the main screen at the helm changed from a view of the island they were leaving, to the storm ahead.

"There she is," Layla said.

The massive storm glowed an eerie yellow with a faint hint of orange, as if the clouds were on fire. Patterns of swirling blue marked the center.

"The mother of all storms," Rodger said, fidgeting nervously with his taped glasses. He put them back on and Magnolia reached over and squeezed his hand.

"Don't forget what you said earlier," she said.

"I won't forget. We're going to find X, and we're going to get back to the *Hive*, and I'm going to see my parents again." Rodger seemed to be talking to himself as much as to Magnolia, and she didn't reply. She knew how much his family meant to him.

This mission was also for X's family, in a way: Michael, Layla, and herself. She missed X more than she had ever admitted. Since she was a child, Magnolia had lost everyone she ever cared about, every man she admired, looked up to, and loved. The thought that she might get to see X again was almost too much to deal with, so she went back to studying her monitor and the wall-mounted screen. *Deliverance* was already at five hundred feet. Far below, the cameras showed spurs of land and sporadic islands dotting the endless swamp.

"Bringing the thrusters online," Timothy announced.

Magnolia finished the scan of her screen and looked over at Michael and Layla. This was the first time in as long as she could remember that she felt close to anyone. Team Raptor was like a family, and that scared the hell out of her.

She gripped Rodger's hand harder, and he grinned at her. "Hey, Mags," he said.

She smiled back. "Hey."

"Thrusters are all online, sir," Timothy announced.

Michael said, "Take us in."

Deliverance lurched, and the harness pushed against Magnolia. She let go of Rodger's hand and held on to the straps across her armor. The other divers did the same thing while staring ahead at the monitor. Thunder rattled the hull. The vibration reminded her of the battle drum they used to mark the beginning of a boxing match in the lower decks of the *Hive*. What she wouldn't give for a glass of shine right about now.

"Keep us as low as possible, and as fast as possible," Michael ordered.

Timothy's hologram vanished, but his voice boomed over the PA system. "Roger that, sir."

A fort of storm clouds in the distance flashed with pulsing blue light like a beating heart. The orange tint in the middle brightened as they flew toward the monstrosity. Was that the sun bleeding through the ceiling?

Timothy reemerged in front of the divers. He put two fingers on his chin, watching the video screen as if in deep thought. The fiery center of the storm looked like a portal that was about to suck them into another dimension. Lightning blazed across the sky, and the thunder that followed boomed like a shotgun.

"Don't you kill us, Timothy Pepper!" Rodger shouted.

Magnolia shook her head wearily. What the hell was she going to do with him? He'd probably have a few ideas, but Magnolia still wasn't sure what she wanted. Right now, she just wanted to get through the damn storm in one piece.

Deliverance dipped slightly, but the thrusters pushed them to twenty and then twenty-five miles per hour. Thirty seconds later, they were nearing forty. The airship was designed for a maximum speed of sixty, and Magnolia had a feeling they would be pushing that soon. At that speed, it would take them only twenty minutes to reach Miami, but in this storm, twenty minutes was an eternity.

Lightning raked across the screen, so bright that the blue flash dazzled Magnolia's eyes. When her vision cleared, they were completely surrounded by the massive, brooding storm. Clouds swirled and bulged in all directions.

The ship lowered again, the bow dropping to two hundred feet. A view of the swamps came back on-screen. A large stretch of land turned and twisted through the water below like a massive snake. Some sort of bridge? The area looked nothing like any of the old-world maps in *Deliverance*'s databases.

"Full power to thrusters," Michael said.

Deliverance heaved, and Magnolia jerked forward hard enough that the harness dug into her neck. She grabbed the armrests on her seat, eyes flitting from her monitor to the front screen.

"Entering the central mass of the storm in T minus one minute," Timothy said.

The clouds overhead seemed to part like the gaping mouth of some monstrous sea creature. Magnolia thought of the documentary she had watched as a child of a whale swallowing smaller fish whole.

We're the little fish today, she thought.

A barrage of blue bolts speared downward like rain. Turbulence rocked the airship, the bulkheads creaking and cracking.

"I don't know if she can take this for twenty minutes," Rodger said.

"She can take it," Michael said.

They were moving at fifty miles an hour now—an amazing speed for a ship this size. Magnolia tried to relax in the comfortable leather seat. She closed her eyes, trying to zone out, but a moment later, her eyelids sprang open with the first strike to the ship.

The blast licked the starboard hull with a raucous crack. A warning sensor chirped, and the female operator's voice came over the speakers.

"Threat level critical," said the maddeningly blasé voice. "Please get to your designated shelters."

"Can't you shut her up?" Michael asked.

"With pleasure, sir," Timothy replied. The woman's voice cut off in midsentence, and Timothy continued. "Entering the center of the storm in ten, nine, eight, seven, six, five, four, three, two…"

Magnolia reached for Rodger's hand again.

"Hold me, sweet thing," he said.

She looked over to see him grinning. This time, she did laugh. But her nervous chuckle was short-lived.

"One," Timothy said as another blast of lightning hit the port side of the ship. A monitor behind them exploded, sparks flying over the bridge.

"Oh, my G-God," Rodger stuttered. The grin was gone, and his eyes were squeezed shut. He wasn't the only one feeling sick. Magnolia had to will her food to stay down, even though she had eaten very little.

"Take us lower," Michael said, his tone still measured and calm.

"I am unable to descend beyond the minimum safe distance," Timothy replied.

Magnolia watched the spurs of land on the screen. Hills and ruined buildings reached up dangerously close to *Deliverance*'s belly.

A recessed red light switched on, and the Klaxon wailed its high-pitched alternating tones. Movement danced around the room in the swirling red light, the divers casting shadows that looked like Sirens.

Two bolts of lightning struck the bow, and an explosion followed somewhere deeper in the ship. Timothy's hologram reappeared on the bridge.

"Fire detected in compartment fourteen," he reported.

"Seal it off!" Michael yelled, his measured tone forgotten.

Ten minutes into the journey, and the ship was already on fire.

Another monitor fell off the bulkhead, shattering on the floor.

"Lower, Timothy!" Michael ordered.

"Sir, I would highly recommend—"

"Just do it!"

Magnolia looked at her monitor. They were just fifty feet above the water now and fast approaching a land mass.

"Contact at one o'clock!" she shouted.

"Readjusting course," Timothy replied. The ship veered left, the fins cutting through the air. Lightning illuminated an island about a mile away, silhouetting the shells of old buildings. For the next few minutes, they flew under the storm without suffering a single strike, but the turbofans were skirting dangerously close to the jutting towers below.

"The fire in compartment fourteen has been isolated," Timothy said. "We are three minutes from target."

Another bolt of lightning slammed the starboard hull, and Magnolia gritted her teeth as the ship jolted violently. The Klaxon screeched on and on, filling the bridge. On-screen, the entire sky seemed to light up at once. Magnolia squinted against the brightness.

Nearly blinded, ears ringing, she looked down at the monitor, where dozens of contacts blinked on the radar.

"Shit!" she yelled, unsure whether anyone could hear her over the alarms. "We've got multiple objects ahead!" By the time she looked back at the main screen, the obstacles were already looming into view. The buildings lined the horizon like teeth on a Siren's jaw.

"Are those scrapers?" Rodger asked.

"More of them than I've ever seen," Layla replied.

"That's our target," Timothy said. "We are two miles out from Miami. Everyone, hold on!"

Magnolia watched the screen, flinching when a flash of electricity hit the stern. She saw the strike with perfect clarity as it lanced like a bullet into the ship. The screen of her station exploded, sending glass, circuitry, and pieces of metal flying into the air. Shrapnel sliced her cheek, burning as it cut through her flesh.

Rodger reached out for her. "Mags!"

Flames danced from the destroyed console, as if reaching out for her body. Michael unbuckled his harness and grabbed an extinguisher. She tried to get out of her harness, but the clasp wouldn't release. The heat from the flames singed her hair, and she pulled back, screaming.

"Mags!" Rodger cried again as he shucked off his own harness. He reached through the flames, his arm catching fire as he unfastened her belt and dragged her away. White mist suddenly coated the station, suffocating the fire in a single blast. The spray turned on Rodger and Magnolia next.

"One minute to target," Timothy said over the comms as if nothing were happening on the bridge.

Smoke from at least three fires on the bridge choked the air. A voice was calling out to her over the Klaxon's blare.

"Magnolia, are you okay? Please, Mags!"

She turned toward the sound and found Rodger's pleading eyes.

Managing a nod, she blinked away the sting of smoke and focused on the main view screen. The skeins of lightning died away. Below, she saw what was once a great metropolis. And beyond the shells of towers was something she had longed to see again.

The ocean.

The ship jolted again, and Rodger helped Magnolia strap into another seat.

"There are fires in compartments four and five," Timothy said. "Sealing them off now."

Deliverance rocked so violently that the front monitor cracked. Magnolia could still see the ocean, though. And something else: a red light flashing from the top of a tower. Was that a real light or a product of shock?

"Taking us down," Timothy said.

The monitor fell to the floor, shattering before she could get a good look at the source of the red light. She reached up and put a hand to her face, gently probing the wound. Her fingers came away bloody.

Then they were descending again, slowly, like an elevator.

Michael finished blasting the fires with the extinguisher, and vents sucked the smoke out of the room.

"Prepare for landing," Timothy said.

* * * * *

ONE YEAR AND NINE MONTHS EARLIER

X woke up shivering. He forced a heavy eyelid open to a blurred version of the world. He couldn't see much besides rusted brown metal. His face was pressed against a cold metal surface.

Groaning, he tried to move onto his side, but his body wouldn't respond. He could move only his eyelids, and even those felt heavy like metal hatches.

Was this some sort of a dream?

He drew in several long breaths and then pushed at the ground. His arms wobbled, and he fell back to the cold metal. A fence of bars obstructed his view, but through the gaps he could make out a candle burning on a bulkhead, spreading a glow over a pitted surface streaked with brown.

He was in a cage inside a larger room. But how had he gotten here? And where was Miles?

Fear gripped him when he realized he wasn't just alone, but also shirtless. The resulting surge of adrenaline enabled him to push himself up, stretching clenched muscle fibers.

At the sound of voices, his eyes flitted across the room to a metal hatch with a spin wheel.

No, it can't be. You're dreaming.

More of the voices echoed, faint and muddled. It took several moments of listening for X to realize that he couldn't make them out, because he didn't know the language.

A vague memory raced through his mind. In it, he was back at the ITC facility, where he heard the same language being spoken.

That was basically the last thing he could recall.

He wrapped his arms across his chest, shivering in the cold, and trying to think harder. In his mind's eye, he pictured the flashlights inside the stairwell, and then the men in bulky armor, with long cords hooked to oxygen tanks. They were dragging nets full of Sirens out of the facility. That was the last thing he remembered before blacking out.

Wait...no...There was one other memory...the image of a man with oblong eye coverings on his helmet. He had fired some sort of electrical weapon. The blue jolt was the last thing X remembered.

At least Miles was still safe in their hideout. X had to get back to him, but he had no idea where he was or who these people were.

One thing he was certain of: they weren't from the sky—at least, not from the ship of his memories. And since they had captured him and thrown him in this cell, they weren't good people, either.

"I fucking hate humans," X said quietly. Even the croaking whisper sparked the raw pain in his throat, and he remembered why he was ever in the ITC facility to begin with.

Shit, the cancer meds!

The reminder gave him a spark of energy, and he managed to crawl over to the bars. He still wore the bottom half of his suit, but the upper half had been stripped, along with his armor.

X crawled along the edge of the cage to look for his gear. He finally spotted it on a pile across the room. Using what little energy he had, he moved over to the edge of the bars and reached between them. His filthy fingernails just narrowly missed the bag containing the cancer meds.

He tried again. Letting out a breath, he took a moment to rest, trying to ignore the pain in his throat.

Stay focused. Stay alive. Breathe, Xavier. Just breathe.

He searched his pockets for anything useful. His captors had patted him down pretty well, removing everything from his cargo pockets. Or maybe not everything…

He pulled out the small syringe from the bottom of a cargo pocket. Holding it up to the glow of the candle, he saw it was an adrenaline shot, with some liquid still left in it.

Footfalls echoed from outside the hatch across the room, and X wasted no time jamming the shot into his leg. He kept the syringe in his hand, holding it flat against his forearm, while his eyes rolled up into his head. His veins constricted, and red flashed across his vision.

He gritted his teeth again, and this time one of them cracked from the pressure. When his vision finally cleared, the wheel on the hatch was spinning. It creaked open and slammed into the bulkhead, disgorging a burly figure that bent down to clear the overhead.

X blinked and tried to focus on the huge man wearing one of the bulky armored suits. He carried his helmet under his arm. The glow of the candle spread over his caramel skin and shaved head.

A helmeted figure, cradling a rifle, followed him into the room. He stopped next to the open hatch and turned his oval eye slots on X.

The man with a shaved head lumbered over to the bars, boots clanking on the deck. He crouched beside the cage, and X shifted his gaze from the Siren skull crests on his shoulder pads, to his face in the flickering light.

The man licked his thick brown lips, dark eyes narrowing beneath a circular scar on his forehead, and above a nose whose missing tip provided a window into his nostrils.

Hot breath that smelled of barbecued meat hit X in the face.

The man grinned, opening his mouth to expose a row of sharpened teeth. Then he spoke approvingly in a deep voice. "*Sabrás rico a la parrilla.*"

X shook his head. "I don't understand."

"*¿No Español?*"

"English," X replied, realizing that "*Español*" was the language he had been hearing. He didn't remember it from school as a kid, but then, he didn't remember much else these days, either.

The man just stared at X for a moment, then pointed to the center of his muscle-shaped chest armor, where an octopus had been engraved in the metal.

"El Pulpo. King of the Cazadores."

X raised a shaky finger to his chest and said, "Xavier." He had a hundred questions in his jangled brain, but he settled on the first one that came to mind. "What do you want with me?"

"The Cazadores need more."

X tried to make sense of it. How did the *Hive* not know of their existence? Unless these people had absolutely no radio contact—which was possible now that he thought about it.

"Where is your home?" X asked.

His captor ignored the question and posed one of his own. "How many of you?"

X thought of Miles again. The dog was out there waiting, probably frantic. And judging by this guy's teeth, he would likely eat a dog.

"Just me," X said.

El Pulpo reared his head back and laughed. The man at the bulkhead chuckled, his voice raspy through the breathing apparatus.

"You lie," el Pulpo said, turning back to X with a stone-cold face.

X shook his head. "I'm the last man—or I was, until I met you."

"YOU LIE!"

Hot breath hit X in the face. El Pulpo snorted out his third nostril and then calmly said, "Tell me where the others are."

X blinked and hesitated, then raised a finger to the ceiling.

"In the sky," he said.

El Pulpo narrowed his dark eyes again.

"No more lies. Time to feast." He pulled a machete from a leather sheath on his belt. Then he retrieved a key from a pocket and unlocked the gate into the large cell. X scrambled backward, the adrenaline shot still rushing through his veins.

The man at the bulkhead said something in Spanish and pointed at X.

"No jefe, está enfermo. Mátelo, nada mas y se lo dejamos a los tiburones."

El Pulpo hesitated, towering over him with the blade drawn. X tried to glean something from their conversation, but he couldn't understand a damn word. The man at the hatch kept repeating, "No lo comamos. Nos asqueará."

Clicking his tongue, el Pulpo silenced the other man.

"He says you're sick, no good to eat," el Pulpo said, turning back to X. Now he knew why the man's breath smelled like barbecue. These barbarians wouldn't stop with eating Miles; X was also on the menu.

The Cazadores were cannibals.

El Pulpo grabbed X under the arm and yanked him to his feet.

"NO!" X shouted, squirming in the powerful man's grip. The cold, dull machete blade touched his bare neck, and rancid breath almost made him gag. X tried to fight, but the man was much stronger and had X in an iron grip.

"I guess we just kill you and feed you to the demonios," el Pulpo said.

It didn't take long for X to realize who the demons were. He was about to become Siren chow.

"Lo siento," el Pulpo said with raised brow.

As he began tracing the blade across X's throat, X stomped on his foot and pulled free of his grip. Blood trickled down his cold chest.

El Pulpo let out a roar. X pulled out his syringe and jammed the needle into the man's right eye. The machete clanked to the floor, and X snatched it up.

The man with the rifle was already moving toward the open gate to the cell. X shoved el Pulpo forward and then bounded around his side.

The barrel of the rifle hit X in the chest as he raised the blade. *Click.*

The helmeted man looked down at the gun.

Heart pounding, X didn't waste his lucky break. He swung the machete into the side of the rifleman's helmet and left it embedded in his skull. Then he grabbed up the rifle and smashed el Pulpo in the round scar on his forehead—which wasn't a scar at all, but a tattoo of the same octopus logo on his chest armor.

The massive man collapsed in a heap of armored limbs.

X pulled the trigger again, but the gun wouldn't fire. A bad round, perhaps, but he had no time to clear it. And it didn't matter, anyway. El Pulpo was out cold.

After locking him in the cage, X moved over to grab his gear. An animalistic grunt came from behind, and he glanced over his shoulder at the rifleman with the machete sticking out of his helmet. His legs were squirming, and he was making odd noises.

The sight gave him an idea. X didn't know how many Cazadores were in this building, but he would need a disguise to escape.

X walked over and yanked the machete free. Blood gushed from the man's head, and X removed the helmet to find another face with an octopus tattoo on the forehead.

X continued to strip the dead man. Once he had put on new clothes and the armor, he grabbed his pack containing the cancer medicine. There was only one thing left to do before he escaped this wretched place: find a map or any information he could get about where these barbarians lived.

TWENTY-ONE

This was it. The moment Michael had been anxiously awaiting. In a few minutes, Team Raptor would leave the ship and begin the trek through Miami to find X.

Breathing in filtered air, he used his headlamp to navigate from the bridge to the cargo hold. Timothy had silenced the alarms, but it didn't matter. Every creature in Miami would have seen them coming in hot over the swamps.

Weapons ready and suits functioning at 100 percent, the four divers stepped into the cargo hold, ready for whatever awaited them outside. The door creaked open at Michael's command, and Timothy's hologram emerged by the exit.

"Good luck," he said politely. "I hope you find what you are looking for, Commander."

"Don't move from this location," Michael ordered. He set off down the metal walkway with his AK-47 out and up. To the divers, he said, "NVGs on."

He chinned on his optics and moved out into the field that Timothy had chosen as their LZ. A circular structure taller than the ship surrounded them on all sides. Thousands of seats, blasted and melted almost beyond recognition, lined the sloping walls, all facing the field. Michael had no idea what the space had been used for in the old days, and he didn't really care.

The ramp to the cargo bay retracted as they cleared the area for contacts. Fingers of smoke rose from the airship's battered hull, still sizzling from a dozen lightning strikes. At least he didn't have to worry about Timothy abandoning them out here. *Deliverance* wasn't going anywhere until it got some major repairs. From the looks of it, they were lucky to have made it here at all.

Magnolia shook her head and muttered, "Hope you have a plan to get us out of here, Commander."

"I think I know what this place was," Rodger said. "They used to play games here."

Lightning flayed the ground in the distance. The boom silenced Rodger. Michael gestured for the divers to fan out and find the closest exit. He hurried to take the lead, knowing that whatever happened, he could count on his friends. Layla, Rodger, and Magnolia were prepared for what came next, and he trusted them to have his back.

The plan was simple: navigate through five city blocks and find the source of X's last transmission. His message had mentioned two locations: one to avoid, and one where he had been holed up two years ago. It felt almost as if X was still watching out for him.

He knew that the odds of finding X alive and mentally stable weren't great. But he had to know, had to give it this one last shot.

Thunder boomed overhead. Michael strained to hear the wails of Sirens or other beasts over the noise. Neon patches of weeds shifted in the dirt ahead, their pulpy limbs flashing as the divers approached. Michael moved around the clusters, careful not to get close to the suction cups on the longer tendrils.

He made for the first row of melted seats and climbed over

a wall covered in orange moss. Then he reached back and helped Layla.

"You good?" he asked.

"My ankle's much better. You okay?"

A nod. Michael reached out to help Magnolia next. A bandage covered half her face. The shrapnel had slashed deep. Her cheek really needed stitches, but there was no time for that.

She hopped over the ledge without his help. Rodger followed an instant later, and they moved up the concrete steps toward the first concourse. Inside were little booths that reminded him of the market on the *Hive*, each marked with faded letters announcing what they had once sold: POPCORN. BEER. PIZZA.

"*Pie-zah*," Rodger said. "What do you suppose that is?"

The rest of the team, ignoring the old-world signs, made their way to a balcony where they could look out at the city. The metal scrapers rose in a jagged line across the sky. Gutted, stripped of paint, and full of black gaps like the mouth of a lower-decker. Flashes of lightning backlit the structures as well as the red vines cascading out the windows. Weeds grew along the sidewalks and in open spaces that had once been parks. There was even a cluster of dark-gray mushrooms, each the size of a man, growing out of the broken concrete in the lot below.

The entire city was infested with mutant foliage, and what wasn't covered in vines was submerged under brown, swampy water. Why the hell had X picked *this* place?

Michael held up his wrist monitor, and did a double take when he saw the rads. "The radiation is off the charts," he said. "Timothy, are these readings correct?"

Static crackled, and the AI replied, "Yes, Commander. I also detect a high concentration of toxins in the air."

Michael took a sip of water from the straw in his helmet and used the stolen moment to think. If any of the divers got even a small tear in their suit, they would be compromised and would likely suffer an awful, painful death.

"Don't worry, sir. We're with you," Rodger said, showing an unexpected flash of awareness.

Hearing the vote of confidence, especially from such an unlikely source, was helpful. But Michael still feared the journey ahead. They had two miles of rough terrain to cover, and who knew what threats to face.

"Damn, X sure picked a shithole to retire in," Magnolia said.

Rodger chuckled, but Michael could see his brown eyes tight with fear. He waved the divers onward, toward a metal stairwell. It led them to a concrete open space with dull-blue tables. Beyond was a parking lot full of destroyed vehicles, with more of the purple weeds and the huge round mushrooms growing in the spaces between them. Several skeletons, now covered in orange moss, lay on the ground right where they had fallen centuries ago.

Michael checked the nav marker on his minicomputer for their target and then set off across the parking lot. The street beyond had sunk and filled with water. Foam the color of a flesh wound lapped against the edges.

He zoomed in with his binos on a massive yellow frog perched on a concrete ledge covered in red weeds. A single eyeball glared at the water, and a tongue shot out of its mouth. It pulled a small fish out of the stew and swallowed it. Another flash of motion came from the weeds. A six-foot-long snake, mostly camouflaged by the foliage, shot forward and swallowed the frog in a single gulp.

Michael lowered the binos. Even a glimpse of the food chain here was enough to make him want to turn around and hide aboard the airship. Instead, he pushed back the fear and led the others onward.

For the next hour, they moved cautiously through the city. Unlike most of the places where they had scavenged over the years, there was no sign of snow. The temperature was a comfortable seventy-two degrees, but the radiation remained high. The climate here was different, and the mutant flora and fauna seemed to thrive in the warm, moist environment.

They trekked along the sagging network of roads, many of which had been swallowed by the earth and were filled with stagnant water. Glowing weeds writhed as they passed the shattered storefronts. Rodger and Magnolia kept their eyes on the higher floors of the buildings, while Michael and Layla kept their rifles trained at the ground level. "We're being watched," Magnolia said. "I can feel it."

"Me, too," said Layla.

Michael looked up at the buildings towering above them but saw nothing in the green hue of his night-vision goggles. So far, the camouflage Rodger had designed to reduce the energy output of their suits seemed to be working.

They were about halfway between the LZ and their target when a noise stopped Michael in his tracks. It sounded like many multilimbed creatures skittering over the concrete. The other divers took cover behind a brick wall covered in red vines.

"Stay away from those plants, and stay put," Michael whispered. "I'll take a look."

Without waiting for a response, he moved around the corner, keeping low. He dashed to a fallen billboard that stuck out of the dirt like an ax stuck in wood.

The clanking and scratching sounds grew louder. He peered around the sign at another road, slanting into a pool of water. No, not a pool—a *lake*. Two scrapers rose out of the water in the distance. He stood cautiously and moved around the corner, looking at the shoreline, which seemed to be *moving*.

His finger went to the trigger guard of his rifle as he watched hundreds of beetles the size of guinea pigs consuming the carcass of a fish on the concrete shore. They reduced it to a skeleton as he watched.

A voice behind his shoulder made him flinch. "That's disgusting," Magnolia said.

Rodger and Layla showed up a moment later, weapons lowered as they watched.

"This city...it's alive," Rodger said.

Layla nodded. "There's an entire ecosystem here. It's like nothing I've ever seen."

"And I'm guessing we haven't seen the half of it yet," Michael said. He scanned the area for higher ground and directed them toward an elevated street that turned into a bridge. The heat-warped hulls of vehicles clogged the road, providing plenty of cover—hiding spots for beasts.

Using hand signals, he told the divers to spread out. Rodger took point on the right side, and Michael took the left. The bridge rose several hundred feet over the water, providing a view of the city. To the east, beyond the fence of scrapers, lay the seemingly infinite stretch of black water.

And something else. Something that didn't seem to belong in this wasteland.

"Do you see that flashing red light?" Magnolia asked over the comm channel. She had her binoculars up to her visor.

A brilliant web of electricity flickered overhead, spreading a cold blue light over the wasteland. The thunderclap sounded as Michael squeezed between two vehicles and stood next to Magnolia.

"What is it?" he asked.

She handed him the binos. "Take a look for yourself."

Michael peered through the glasses at a silo rising out of the beach. Red and white paint swirled up the walls. It reminded him of one of the candy sticks his dad used to buy him from the trading post on the *Hive*. The lookout at the top was flashing a bright red glow.

"It's a lighthouse," Magnolia said. "Same thing I saw on my dive to the Hilltop Bastion. I thought I recognized it on the way in, but…"

Rodger looked through his own binos. "How the hell is that thing still working? It couldn't have been running all this time, could it?"

Layla shrugged. "ITC facilities have backup power, so why can't that tower?"

"Here's a better question," Magnolia said. "Why is it flashing? Lighthouses used to warn ships away from rocks, right? I remember reading about—"

"I don't know, but we need to keep moving," Michael said. He handed the binos back to Magnolia and set off across the bridge before she could respond.

Right now his priority was finding X, not figuring out the lighthouse. His nav marker put their target just two blocks away. But the bridge took them right into another flooded street. He held up a fist at the edge of the water. Dipping his boot in, he found that it came up only to his ankle.

Another quick scan around told him this was their best route.

"Let's try it," he said.

Another hand signal ordered Team Raptor into the muck. They moved through the shallow water until they reached an intersection. To the east, a mountain of debris blocked the street. The west was a delta that fed out into the lake he had seen earlier.

"Great," Michael said, cursing.

"Look at that." Magnolia pointed at a ship wedged between two high-rises to the north. "Weird."

Michael checked his nav marker again. Thanks to their detour and the blocked street, they were still two blocks from the source of the signal. He looked up at the buildings to the east, beyond the wall of debris. One of them was the place where X had transmitted his SOS. Michael resisted the urge to scope the windows, searching for some sign that their journey would be worth it, and instead waved the group toward the wall. As they waded, the red foam floating on the surface clung to his legs. It looked like frothy, blood-flecked spittle.

"Michael," Rodger said. "Uh, sir..."

Michael glanced over his shoulder. The other divers had halted and were looking back the way they had come. Ripples moved across the surface, away from the lake. A fin emerged, cutting through the water like a knife.

"Move," Michael rasped.

Rodger let out a yelp and nearly tripped as he turned away. Layla and Magnolia followed him, but Michael held his ground, watching in horror as six more scaly dorsal fins broke through the murky water. He considered firing on them before they breached the surface, but didn't want to risk drawing more unwanted attention.

Forcing himself to look away, he moved after the rest of the team. The closer they got to the wall, the deeper the water became. Soon it reached his knees, then his thighs. By the time he was halfway to the sloping barricade of brick and concrete, he was nearly waist deep.

Michael stopped and raised his rifle. They weren't going to make it, and he couldn't risk an attack from the fish or snakes or whatever the hell was swimming under the dark surface. Memories of the ordeal in the swamps haunted him. He refused to go through anything like that again.

He brought his rifle up, but hesitated when he saw a smooth head and a dorsal fin break the surface. This wasn't a snake—it was a fish. Moving his finger toward the trigger, he prepared to spray the water with bullets.

A shadow suddenly swooped around the building to his right, and he pulled the scope away from his visor to see frayed wings beating the air. An electronic wail followed, and a Siren scooped a fish the size of a small child out of the water. It flapped away, holding the squirming creature in its talons.

If Michael had learned anything from his time on the surface, it was that Sirens hunted in packs. He shouldered his rifle and fired over Rodger's head, sending a three-round burst into another beast, which had swooped around a building, with its eyeless face centered on Layla. The creature spiraled out of control and smashed into a two-story building.

"Come on!" Michael yelled, thrashing through the water as fast as he could move. Magnolia and Rodger continued wading toward the wall. The fish darted off in all directions, dorsal fins retreating under the surface as the apex predators flew overhead. The sky had come alive with the bat-like shrieking monsters.

Michael fired on full auto, raking the weapon in an arc to keep the Sirens back. The magazine went dry in a few seconds. He ejected it and slammed a fresh one in as he moved.

"Covering fire!" he yelled.

The crack of a rifle came over his shoulder. Rodger and Magnolia had made it to the wall, and one of them was firing. It wouldn't be long before the noise attracted every beast in the city. They had to get to cover. He turned and helped Layla through the water as she stumbled on her weak ankle, eyes flitting from the water to the sky.

Rodger and Magnolia were both firing from the wall of debris now, the crack of their weapons punching through the screech of the Sirens. Lightning blossomed behind the wall, illuminating their armored silhouettes. Booming thunder, screaming monsters, and the crack of gunfire raised an earsplitting din.

Layla reached the wall and pulled herself up onto the slope. Michael stopped to fire on the creatures trying to flank them. There were a dozen, maybe more, most of them swooping down on the water to pluck out fish.

But a few Sirens were focused on bigger prey.

A pair of the larger monsters made a run for the divers, but the covering fire was working. They wheeled away, blood dripping from multiple wounds.

"Take my hand, Tin!" Layla shouted.

He waded toward the fifty-foot-high pile of debris. She was crouched on the slope, balanced on a slab of concrete. His fingers had just met hers when something sliced into his leg.

Michael let out a cry of pain as teeth ripped through the gap in his armor between knee and thigh. He let his rifle sag over his chest, pulled out his knife, and brought the blade down on the fish that had clamped on to his leg. The tip cracked through bony plates and plunged into flesh, freeing him from the beast. He stowed the knife, grabbed Layla's hand, and climbed up onto the wall.

"Hurry!" Rodger yelled. He was frantically loading new bullets into the cylinder of his pistol, losing several in the process, while Magnolia kept firing her rifle. Empty shell casings rained down onto the concrete.

Michael tried not to look at his leg, but he couldn't help himself. Blood sluiced down his knee and armored calf guard.

His suit had been compromised. He was as good as dead.

Layla saw it, too. "We have to patch it!" she yelled.

He shook his head. "Not now. MOVE!"

They scrambled up to the top of the mound. There, he leaned on Layla before following Rodger and Magnolia down the other side. A narrow street lined by four-story buildings was relatively clear for the next block, but a dome-shaped steel cage as wide as the road blocked their escape at the bottom of the slope.

"We're trapped!" Magnolia shouted.

The Sirens were banking in formation over the water, ignoring the fish and turning their eyeless faces toward the divers.

"Fire!" Michael shouted. "Hold them off!"

The divers raised their weapons. The beasts came in all at once, a flying wedge of cadaverous flesh and sinewy muscle. He counted at least a dozen of the beasts, but they moved so fast it was hard to tell for sure.

Otherworldly wails sounded from the west as more Sirens joined the hunt. Michael emptied his magazine and turned to see another cluster flapping around the tower where X had sent the SOS.

He changed his magazine and turned back to the nearest group. One of them penetrated the wall of fire and swooped toward Layla. She ducked and brought her rifle up to fire three rounds into the monster's spine.

A cracking noise came from behind, but it wasn't a rifle. By the time Michael realized what was happening, it was too late. The scree had shifted under the weight of the four divers, sending bricks and concrete tumbling to the street below. Rodger and Magnolia were already caught in the landslide, Magnolia shouting curses as she fell toward the cage.

Michael and Layla went next, sliding on their backs. The entire fall took less than five seconds, but the momentum resulted in a hard landing inside the open door of the cage. His helmet smacked onto the street.

Red lights broke across his vision. His leg burned like nothing he had ever experienced in his life, as if someone were jabbing a hot needle into his flesh. He blinked through the pain and pushed himself up. Motion flashed from all directions, disorienting him, but he managed to focus on Magnolia. She stood at the other side of the cage, shaking the bars.

Layla was firing at the Sirens on top of the pile they had just slid down, raking the mound with bullets. Once they were down, she scrambled over to Michael and reached for her medical kit.

"We have to get you patched up," she said, handing him her rifle. "You hold them off!"

Four Sirens clambered to the top of the hill. The only escape was up the slope and past the beasts. But Michael could see that it wasn't going to be easy.

The monsters squawked and screeched at the captive divers.

"Shoot them!" Michael yelled. He fired a controlled burst at a beast perched on the mound. It darted away, and he looked over his shoulder to see why Magnolia and Rodger weren't shooting. She was still at the bars, looking at a pack of Sirens approaching them from the street to the east.

They were being surrounded.

"I'm out," Michael said.

Layla finished patching his leg, leaving a hasty dressing over the suit. Then she pulled out her blaster and Michael unholstered his pistol. She helped him to his feet and they stood together, side by side, aiming through the open door at the monsters above.

One of the beasts took to the air, screeching an alien wail. A flare lanced into the sky, catching the Siren in the right wing. It yelled louder and flapped away, wings catching fire as it climbed. Engulfed by the flames, it finally cartwheeled through the sky and landed in the water on the other side of the mountain. Michael heard it sizzle as it hit the surface.

Two more flares shot toward the top of the hill, and the other Sirens darted away. Magnolia and Rodger had finally snapped back into action.

Michael turned to look, but held in a breath when he saw the two divers standing weaponless and staring at the two figures approaching the cage from the east. In the red glow of the flares, Michael saw that it wasn't more mutant creatures after all.

It was a man and a dog.

TWENTY-TWO

Les had planned to see his family first thing after he returned to the *Hive*. He had imagined scooping up his daughter, gently embracing his wife, even holding his son Trey's hand through the hatch of the cell.

Instead, he found himself desperately searching for the nearest head.

The single-hole bathroom was just barely big enough for him to fit inside. He closed the hatch, bent down, and threw up into the bowl. As soon as he caught a drift of what was plastered to the tube, he gagged and tossed up the rest of his last meal.

He wiped his mouth and stood, banging his noggin against the overhead.

The moment he stepped back out into the corridor, he was faced by a crowd of over a dozen people. They all watched him with curious eyes. Hushed voices spoke of the dive and the loot that Team Phoenix had brought back.

Roberto, a short, bearded fellow who lived near Les' family, smiled and said, "Good job down there, Giraffe!"

"I heard you found some cancer meds," said Crystal, a farm worker who was good friends with Katherine.

"Did you find any antibiotics?" someone asked.

"How about yarn?" another yelled. "Or bulbs—did you get any bulbs?"

"Any fuel cells?" asked another.

Les moved away in a daze, not answering any of the questions or responding to the praise. His height, along with his distinctive red coveralls, apparently made him an easy target.

"Did you see any Sirens?" someone asked.

The question made his guts churn. He turned around and said, "Leave me alone. All of you."

Several people backed off, but some continued to follow him down the corridor. His quarters weren't far, and he broke into a jog after he rounded the next corner. That was when he noticed the bulkheads. Where there had been murals and graffiti, there was now matte-gray metal. Jordan had done it after all. He had ordered the entire ship scrubbed clean.

He knows I know, Les thought. *Jordan knows I'm lying.*

More passengers blocked his way in the next hallway, almost all of them firing off questions that he wouldn't—couldn't—answer.

He looked around for a different route home. Instead, he saw militia guards. Two of them, hanging back but focused on him. Watching him. Following him?

It was paranoid to think the captain would have him followed, but if everything Ty had said was true, then maybe he was being watched.

"Everyone get back!" one of the militia soldiers yelled.

Les shoved his way through the small crowd and bolted down the corridor. He lost the guards in the next hallway, squeezing through an old shortcut between some pipes. When he finally got to his quarters, he drew in a breath, ran a hand through his thinning red hair, and stepped inside.

The single lightbulb blinked on in the center of the room, illuminating his wife and daughter. Katherine was in bed with her back propped up against the bulkhead. Phyl got up from the bedside chair and toddled over to Les, wrapping her arms around his waist.

"You're back," Katherine said, her voice cracking.

The feelings of darkness and worry evaporated at the sight of his girls, and Les felt a sense of peace now that he was back with his family.

"Baby, I missed you so much," he said. He crouched down to kiss her on the cheek, but she pulled back and coughed into her hand. A deep rattle crackled in her chest.

"Don't," she protested.

Then Phyl started coughing, too.

Oh, God, no, Les thought.

The respiratory illness wasn't terribly contagious, and he had hoped his daughter's immune system would fend off the infection.

"You're going to be just fine," Les said.

"I'm so glad to see you," Katherine said. "I was so worried you wouldn't come back."

"We lost two divers," Les whispered.

Phyl looked up at him. "They got lost down there? Why didn't someone go and find them?"

Les hesitated. He knew she was old enough to understand, but he spared her the details. No other words need be said. Les knew by the look in his wife's eyes how frightened she was. And for good reason. Without treatment, the cough could eventually kill them. If he wanted to save his family, he had no choice but to keep diving.

"Who knows about Phyl?"

"No one, I think," Katherine replied.

His daughter coughed again, and he forced a smile in her direction. "It's okay, baby. You're going to be just fine, I promise."

He turned back to his wife and kept his voice low. "Did they bring you your first dose when I was on the dive?"

Katherine shook her head. "Dr. Huff said medicine wasn't going to be authorized until you came back."

"*What!*" Les said in a voice loud enough to scare Phyl.

Her eyes widened and Les reassured her with another forced smile. He clenched his jaw to hold back his anger at the broken promise. The medicine was supposed to have been delivered to his wife the moment he stepped into a launch tube. He dived, so his family survived. That was the deal.

"Must have been some sort of a mistake," he said calmly, not wanting to alarm his family. "I'll find out what's going on."

Katherine coughed into her ragged sleeve. It sounded worse than before, crackling as if her lungs had fluid in them.

"Have either of you eaten today?" Les asked.

Phyl shook her head, and Katherine stared blankly at the overhead. "We're out of our rations," she said quietly. "The baby's hungry, and I…"

Her voice trailed off. Les knew he was close to losing her, and now his little girl was sick, too. The decisions he made in the next few hours would determine whether they lived or died.

Where there should have been raw fear, he felt determination. He was going to get them the medicine they deserved, even if he had to fight and dive and kill for it.

"I'm going to the medical ward and then to the trading post to get you something to eat," he said. "I'll stop by and see Trey, too."

"I want to go, Daddy. I haven't seen Trey for…" Phyl looked up at the dangling lightbulb, then back at Les. "I don't know how many days."

"You have to stay here, sweetie," he said.

"Come here," Katherine said, reaching out.

The girl shook her head. "No, I want to go with Daddy."

Les met his wife's gaze. He longed to hold her, but he couldn't risk getting sick—assuming he wasn't already. They needed him healthy for what came next.

"I'll be back as soon as I can," he said. He opened the hatch and kept going, knowing that looking back would break him. He hurried through the halls, ignoring everyone and everything— even the fear of being followed.

His first stop was the medical center, where he demanded to meet Dr. Huff. The man didn't look happy to see Les when he stepped out into the lobby. He carried a clipboard under his arm.

"Where's the medicine for my wife?" Les asked before the doctor could say anything. "It was supposed to be delivered already. I want it, and I want it right now."

Huff pulled out the clipboard and flipped through the pages. "Ah, yes. I see there's a supply meant for your wife, but command has yet to authorize it...No, wait. That's odd."

"What's odd?"

Huff looked up from the paper. "The medicine was authorized but then put on hold. I'm sorry, Les, but I can't give you anything until Command reverses the hold."

"Son of a bitch," Les muttered.

"Take this up with Lieutenant Hunt. I'm sure it's just a misunderstanding." Huff began to walk away, but Les grabbed his arm. The doctor's eyes flitted to his hand, and then up to meet his gaze.

"Please let go of me," Huff said, clearly agitated.

Les took a deep breath and let go of Huff's arm. "Fine, Doc. I'll go see Hunt."

"Good luck," Huff said.

Yeah right, Les thought as he turned away. He raced through the corridors toward the bridge. A trio of guards armed with crossbows were waiting outside the black hatch. Ensign Del Toro raised his hand, and Les slowed his approach.

"Can I help you?" Del Toro asked.

"I'd like to see Lieutenant Hunt," Les said, trying to sound polite.

Del Toro pushed a mike to his lips and relayed a message.

A few minutes later, the doors whispered open and the XO walked out. "Why are you—"

"I'm here to get the medicine my family was promised," Les said, cutting the lieutenant off.

Hunt blinked but didn't reply.

"Jordan made me a promise. If I dived, my wife would get medicine for her cough and I would get my boy out of the brig. Neither of those things have happened. So where is the medicine?"

"*Captain* Jordan modified the agreement after you returned."

"You have to be fucking kidding me," Les said. "My wife is fading away, and my daughter—"

Hunt raised a brow. "Is she sick now, too?"

"Yes," Les replied, knowing he had no option but to tell the truth. "They need those meds."

"I'll see what I can do." Hunt started to turn away but hesitated. His stiff manner relaxed a fraction, and there was genuine sympathy in his eyes. "I'm sorry about Katherine and Phyl."

Les and Hunt had grown up on the same corridor, and despite their very different positions on the ship these days, Les trusted the man to be as good as his word. Hunt was just following orders—just like everyone else who obeyed Jordan's commands out of fear for their own families.

"I'll talk to the captain as soon as he has a few minutes," Hunt said. "Go spend time with your family, but make sure you follow the proper protocols. We can't afford you getting sick, too."

Exhausted, angry, and starving, Les turned and made his way back through the ship. They had let him go home, at least. For a second, he was worried they would keep him from his family.

No way in hell they are keeping me from my baby and my wife.

His mind churned with the things Ty had told him on the surface. Jordan wasn't just a lousy captain—he was a liar and a murderer. The *Hive* would be better off without him. In fact, his reign was a threat to the very future of humanity.

But every way he could think of to overthrow Jordan ended the same way: with Les joining his son in the brig, and his wife and daughter dead.

He needed help, someone he could trust, if he was going to try to take the captain down. Someone in the militia or in Command. But who? Hunt was too highly placed, and a childhood friendship was insufficient reason to commit mutiny. He snapped from the thoughts when he reached the brig. Sloan, the stone-faced woman posted at the front counter, frowned.

"What do you want?"

"I'm here to see my boy, Trey."

"It's not on the register," Sloan replied, not bothering even to look at the paper on her desk.

"I was promised a visit after my dive. Don't tell me you didn't get the message, because I'm having a really bad fucking day."

Sloan finally looked up. She seemed to stare at his red coveralls for a moment, then her lazy eye roved toward the hatch. She unlocked it and led him down the dark passage until they got to the second-to-last cell.

"Arms up," Sloan said.

Les did as ordered and allowed the guard to pat him down. When she had finished, she unlocked the hatch.

"You've got ten minutes." She flipped on a light inside the cell. It spread over the thin silhouette of Trey, his fourteen-year-old son.

He stood and whispered, "Dad, is that you?" Then his eyes widened. "Is that a *Hell Diver* jumpsuit?"

Les nodded. "Yeah. Had my first dive today."

"Don't tell me you joined because of me."

"How are they treating you?" Les asked in an effort to change the subject. "Do you have enough to eat?"

"I'm fine, Dad, and I'm really sorry."

"Stop, Trey. You stole to help our family, and I'm diving to help us now. I'm going to make sure you get out of here soon."

Trey sat back on his bunk and laced his fingers together. "How's Mom and Phyl?"

Les looked at his boots.

"Dad?"

"They're sick. Both of them now."

Trey cupped his head in his hands and shook it from side to side before looking back up at Les. Tears streaked down his filthy face.

"I need to get out of here. I should be with them."

"Let me worry about that," Les said. "Don't lose hope. I promise I'll get you out. Now, come give me a hug before Sloan drags me out of here."

"Sloan? She's harmless. Honestly, she treats me better than anyone. Katrina too, before..."

Les resisted the urge to look over his shoulder to see whether Sloan was watching. Knowing she was being good to his son helped ease some of his concern.

Trey wrapped his arms around Les, and Les squeezed his son hard. It felt as though the lad had lost weight from his already skinny frame.

Clanking came from the corridor outside the cell. Les looked out the small porthole to see Sergeant Jenkins pushing a female prisoner down the passage.

It was Katrina. Back from the medical ward, apparently.

"Just kill me!" she shouted. "Jordan sure doesn't have the balls to do it."

Les reluctantly let his son go and patted him on the shoulder, but the boy seemed to be paying more attention to the small window in the cell hatch.

"Jordan is a monster," Trey whispered, "and Sloan and other members of the militia know it."

Les kept his hand on his shoulder. "You heard her say that?"

"Not in so many words, but basically."

"Keep this to yourself. And be strong, son."

A nod.

"I love you, Trey, and I'll be back as soon as I can."

Trey wiped a tear away and nodded back. The hatch opened a moment later, and Les left his boy inside the dark room. As Sloan escorted him out of the brig, an idea stirred in his mind. Maybe there was someone who would help him after all. Maybe there were people who hated the captain even more than he did. All he had to do was find a way to get Katrina out of here and enlist the help of some of the militia to help him cut out the cancer.

For a third time, Jordan studied the maps spread across the desk in his quarters.

"They're trying to find, X, those sons of bitches," he said, looking up at Hunt and Ryan. "You're sure this is where they landed?"

Lieutenant Hunt nodded firmly. "Almost certainly. Ensign Ryan triangulated the signal, and—"

"*Almost?*" Jordan said, holding up his hand. "I'm not interested in almost. I want the precise location."

Ryan stepped up to the maps. "The other ship is—"

"*Deliverance,*" Jordan interrupted. "She's called *Deliverance.*"

"Yes, sir." Ryan waited a second before continuing.

"*Deliverance* has been put down in the ruins of Miami. It does not appear to have moved for several hours."

"How's that possible?" Hunt asked. He took off his glasses and rubbed his eyes. "Most of Miami is a red zone, and the storms there are severe."

"*Deliverance* is far more advanced than the *Hive*," Jordan said. "She can handle heavier storms and radiation. That's why I want her."

"Well, we'd better hurry," Hunt said, "because my guess is, they won't be in Miami for long. Even if the ship can survive the radiation, they can't."

"How long until we can get there?"

"It's about a day's flight, Captain," Ryan said. "That's at our current speed. I could have Samson push the engines, but he won't like it."

"I don't give a damn what Samson likes."

Ryan and Hunt exchanged an uneasy glance, but Jordan didn't blame them. Ryan had drawn a red circle around Miami, indicating the size of the storm. It was massive—one of the biggest he had ever seen.

"We can't fly through it," Jordan said. "So we'll have to go above it. That's one of Ash's old strategies that actually worked."

"And then what?" Hunt asked. "We can't send divers through those clouds to the surface."

Ryan nodded aggressively. "No one could survive that in a free fall."

"They aren't going to dive," Jordan said. "I'm sending them down in the pods."

"Pods?" Hunt asked.

Jordan smiled. "Follow me, gentlemen."

They left his office with a team of militia soldiers. Jordan checked his watch while they navigated the corridors, ignoring the onlookers.

Right on time.

They descended a stairwell into a compartment connected with Engineering. The sound of machinery filled the narrow passage. Jordan loosened his collar, feeling the heat of the lower deck. At the bottom landing, he opened a hatch and stepped into an expansive cargo bay. Flickering lights illuminated piles of spare parts, plastic, metal, and trash.

It was, essentially, the *Hive*'s junkyard, and it was run by a lone man named Nelson, who carefully recorded every piece of scrap that entered or left his domain. For that reason, he had been given the nickname "the Accountant." He sat behind a desk, gray wispy hair falling over his forehead as he checked a column of numbers.

"Ten, fifteen, nineteen," he muttered. "Not fifteen. Fourteen."

Jordan snapped his fingers, drawing Nelson's attention. The thin man shot out of his chair and threw a salute. Grubby brown overalls covered his grubby body.

"Hello, sir," Nelson said. "I wasn't expecting visitors, but it's a pleasure to see you. How can I assist?"

"I'm here to see the new pods," Jordan said.

The accountant gave a toothless grin and limped around the desk. Nelson never let anything go to waste, not even the metal post that served as his prosthetic leg.

"Follow me, sir," he said.

Jordan motioned for the guards to remain at the stairwell. Ryan and Hunt joined him as he followed Nelson through the massive space, navigating mountains of scrap that had been neatly sorted using a system Jordan couldn't begin to understand. A blue glow came from the other side of the mounds, and the sound of grinding metal filled the space. The air reeked of grease and oil, and it was hot enough to make Jordan sweat through his uniform.

He hated this place, but he wanted to see what Samson had built for him. When they rounded the next pyramid of scrap, he finally laid eyes on the two metal cylinders, tapered to a rounded point on one end and with four longitudinal fins at the other. A pair of engineers stopped their work and flipped up their face shields. One of them was Samson.

"Captain," he said, stopping to cough and wipe his forehead before setting down his welding equipment.

"I wasn't expecting you to be here," Jordan said. "How are the pods coming along?"

"What the hell are those things?" Hunt asked. He ran his hand across the metal surface, which was covered in drawings of fluffy white clouds. Jordan stepped up and examined the other pod, noting the exterior hatches soldered onto the side. Waves and sea creatures decorated this one.

"Were these...?" Ryan began to say.

"The hatches from the upper decks," Hunt said, glaring at Jordan.

The captain replied with a proud grin. "We're going to put them to good use on the next dive."

Samson coughed into his glove again and took a drink from the water bottle attached to his duty belt. "They're almost ready to go, Captain. Each will hold five people, as promised."

He opened the hatch and gestured inside.

"Multiple layers of insulators will protect the divers in the storm," Samson said. "Once they're through, the automatic system will deploy chutes."

"Genius," Hunt said. He smiled at Jordan, and for a moment the captain felt a sense of comradeship with the man. Ever since Katrina's betrayal, Jordan had been without a confidant. Perhaps Hunt could be trusted with the full knowledge of his plans. It would be good to talk it through with someone who understood what Jordan was trying to do and who shared his goal of saving humanity.

"Sir, there's something I don't understand," Samson said. "You didn't request boosters for the pods. How will the divers get back up to the *Hive*?"

"Leave that up to me," Jordan said. His smile grew as he touched the side of the pod, tracing his finger over the faded image of the sun hiding behind a cloud.

If all went to plan, he was going to be the proud owner of a new airship very soon.

TWENTY-THREE

When X first saw the airship screaming over the city, he thought it was a dream—until Miles started barking at it.

The people in the sky were real.

They had finally returned.

But the airship wasn't as he remembered it, and the people in front of him weren't any he recognized. His dog growled at them, and X trusted Miles more than he did his own faulty memories.

He brought his rifle up at a Siren swooping in from the east. A pull of the trigger sent a burst that made the beast go limp in midair. It splatted into the pavement, and X used the stolen moment to examine the four newcomers. One was severely injured and screaming in pain.

"It burns! It burns!" the man kept saying between screams.

"Hold on, Michael!" replied the female holding him up. Her voice was frantic, and by her tone X could tell she loved this man. After all these years of isolation, the raw emotion in her voice was as foreign to him as the Cazadores' language.

But it also helped X understand why he felt compelled to help them now. After watching them cross the city, he decided they weren't hostile like the bastards that had captured him inside the ITC facility and then tried to cut his throat. These people had come from the sky, and the sky was where his home had once been.

He went back to scanning the area to look for an escape. Brick-and-steel buildings framed the road on each side, blocking exit routes to north and south. The cage he had set to trap the monsters was blocked by the mound of debris to the west, leaving the humans only one option: to head east, where his home towered above them.

But thirty Sirens were closing in from all directions, and he didn't want to lead them back to his lair. In the air, on the ground, climbing out of broken windows—the abominations were everywhere, and they were determined to feed.

"Conserve your ammo!" X yelled. It had been a decade since he fought alongside anyone, but some things a man never forgot. He fired calculated shots, knowing that each bullet would determine the fate of these people—and, more importantly, of his dog.

"They're everywhere!" yelled one of the men.

"Keep moving," X said, his voice cracking.

The gutted building he called home was just ahead, but Sirens circled the structure. These people had brought the monsters right to his doorstep. Why were they even here? To kill him, to save him...or to raid his supplies?

The distant red flash of the lighthouse reminded him that time was of the essence. They were running out of it—along with bullets.

"Come!" he yelled, waving his arm.

They followed him down the final stretch of street, using the center of the road and navigating the maze of old-world vehicles. His dog barked and darted between the rusted heaps of scrap along the familiar route.

"Wait up!" one of the women yelled.

The man with the glasses turned to fire a pistol. The shot punched through the chest of a beast that had been perched on the top of the cage, trying to open the gate. Several more carcasses lay inside.

The trap was one of many set around his home. The next one was just ahead—a mesh net covering the stairs up to the scraper he called home. A pair of Sirens swooped down to cut them off, triggering the cord on the trap. The net twitched up, snaring them inside and pulling them up over the front entrance of the building. They hung there, squirming and struggling. Easy targets.

Raising his rifle, X fired twice, and the trapped abominations went limp. He brought up the barrel and tracked another Siren sailing around the upper floors of the building. He led it in his sights, and was about to fire when a voice made him hesitate.

"X—Commander Rodriguez—we have to help Michael now!"

He turned and tilted his head at the woman propping up the injured man.

"Please!" she yelled. "Tin is going to die!"

Tin. The word meant something to him, and he tried to resurrect a memory. The grating shrieks of the abominations pulled him from a memory of a boy wearing a strange, shiny hat.

Keep moving. Never stop moving! X thought, cursing himself for forgetting his motto.

These people were going to get him killed if he didn't pay attention. He squeezed off shots at four more Sirens flapping toward the group with talons extended, ready to scoop them off the ground.

Motion down the street revealed another three, galloping toward them.

X aimed his rifle at the pack. "Shoot!" he yelled. "Shoot them!"

The man with glasses and the other woman squeezed off

shots, and he moved over to provide covering fire. They formed a phalanx around the injured man, bullets lancing in all directions.

X let his rifle strap sag and pulled out his blaster. He shot a flare across the street to keep the creatures on the ground at bay, then fired a shell at a beast sailing overhead. The pellets tore through its wings, and the creature spun away.

"I'm out," said the one with glasses. The woman beside him slung her rifle over her shoulder and reached over his back to draw two curved knives. "Me, too," she said. As she pulled the blades, X saw the image of a bird on her helmet.

He stared at the emblem. *Raptor,* he thought, though he didn't know why, and that scared him more than any Siren in the sky ever could.

His eyes flitted away from the logo and back to the Sirens assailing them on the ground. A dozen strong circled them on foot, and another dozen waited to strike from the sky. The woman with the curved blades charged at a beast galloping in on all fours from the left. In two swift strokes, she beheaded the creature and then stabbed a monster on her right, impaling it and using her boot to push the dead monster off her blade.

Her quick, brutally efficient moves reminded him of someone from his past. An image of a young woman surfaced in his mind. Could it be the same person? He tried to get a better look, but a bandage on her cheek masked her features.

Keep moving, X!

The motto snapped him from his past and back to reality. He fought the confusion and brought his rifle to bear on the creatures in the sky, thinning them out while the others killed those on the ground. The thin man with glasses had pulled out a hatchet. He opened a Siren's belly, screaming, "You won't take me again, asshole!" Looking in X's direction, he brought the hatchet back, and flung it through the air.

X hardly had enough time to flinch, let alone raise his rifle. All he could think was how stupid he had been to trust these people.

The hatchet sailed past his visor and crunched into something behind him. An enraged wail sounded, and X turned just as a Siren dropped to the ground, with the cleaver stuck in its skull.

"You're welcome!" the skinny man yelled.

Miles barked wildly as X went back to firing at the beasts in the air, his mind a tumbling mess of past and present. Who were these people from the sky, and why had they come here now after all this time?

The woman with the blades continued to cut down any beast that made a run at their position. But more of the creatures emerged on the rooftops to the north and south, and even more came from the skies. There was only one way out of this that didn't end with X, his dog, and these idiotic new humans becoming Siren fodder.

He reached into his vest and pulled out something he'd been saving since he found it in a military bunker almost five years ago. The grenade felt light in his hand. It was strange that something so small could wreak so much destruction. He fingered the live button twice and shouted, "Everyone down!"

The others pulled the injured man to safety behind a rusted vehicle just as the explosion rocked the street, blowing pieces of meat in all directions. Smoke and flames burst into the sky. Over the ringing in his ears came the high-pitched wails of the beasts. Those that weren't dead or dismembered bolted off on foot or took to the air.

"Hurry," he said. He stood, but a hand grabbed his arm.

The injured man gripped him with a blood-soaked glove. "X," he croaked. "I finally found you."

The young man's face looked familiar. Had he been . . . a friend? But no, that didn't make sense. The face X was thinking of belonged to the distant past.

"Who...who are you?" he asked.

"It's me, X. Michael Everhart."

When X didn't react, the diver added, "It's *Tin*."

The memories crashed over him like a wave. Two tears dripped from his eyes as long-forgotten people and events flooded his mind.

The monsters retreated, and the humans gathered close around him.

And X remembered.

He remembered Tin, and his father, Aaron, and the *Hive*— the airship they called home. Michael looked so familiar because he resembled his father, who had been X's best friend. For years, X had given up on this day ever coming, but here it was. This wasn't a dream.

"We have to go," he said in a hoarse voice. "Before they come for us."

"The Sirens?" Tin asked.

X shook his head. "Different monsters. Worse than these."

* * * * *

Les stood in front of his quarters, staring at the militia soldier who stood guard outside the hatch. Del Toro wasn't letting him in. His family was inside, and Les was prepared to do just about anything to see them before he dived again.

"Del Toro, if you don't move, I will rip that helmet off your fat head and beat you with it until you're dead."

Del Toro blinked. "Les, I'm sorry. I want to let you in, but I'm under orders from the cap—"

Les reached out with both hands, stopping just short of Del Toro's throat. The soldier flinched but held his ground.

"Open the goddamn hatch."

"I can't do that."

"I'm not going to tell you again, you son of a—"

A voice on the other side cut him off. "Daddy, is that you?"

Del Toro wavered at the sound of Phyl's voice, and Les grabbed him by the shoulder and shoved him out of the way. The guard righted himself and pulled his baton. Les raised his fists, and Del Toro raised his baton.

Before violence could erupt between them, Captain Jordan came jogging down the corridor, flanked by Lieutenant Hunt and Sergeant Jenkins. In his right hand, Jordan gripped the hilt of his sword. In his left, he carried a small plastic box.

"Stop this nonsense," Jordan said. He was looking at Del Toro, not Les. "Put the baton away before you hurt yourself."

Puzzled, Les slowly lowered his fist. The militiaman seemed equally confused. Del Toro dropped the baton back into its belt ring.

"Here," Jordan said, handing the box to Les. "My sincere apologies for the delay. There was a mix-up about the medicine. When you're done giving it to your family, meet us in the launch bay. We're preparing for the dive."

Les took the box, eyeing it suspiciously. Was this some sick game, or was the captain being sincere? He didn't trust the man; that much was certain. But it didn't matter right now. He was just anxious to get the medicine to his family.

Del Toro, frowning, backed away from the hatch, and Les hurried inside his quarters. Phyl was waiting there and grabbed him around the waist, hugging him tightly, but Katherine remained in bed, hardly able to raise a hand in greeting.

"Les," she croaked. "Is that you?"

"Shhh," he said, moving over to her bedside. He opened the box and pulled out two vials of blue liquid, handing one to Katherine. "Drink this. It'll make you better."

Katherine downed the vial, and Les helped Phyl do the same.

When they had finished, he sat next to his wife on the bed and, for the first time in a month, bent down and kissed her on the lips.

"Everything's going to be fine, baby," he said, even though his pounding heart told him things were still far from okay. In a few hours, he was going to dive again, and this time he wasn't heading to a green zone.

    *   *   *   *   *

Magnolia waited on the landing inside the gutted tower, listening for any sign of Sirens or the other monsters X had mentioned on the street. Rodger and X carried Michael up the next flight of stairs, with Layla trying to keep it together behind them. On rear guard, Magnolia twirled the blades, ready to slice anything that followed them.

The dog waited with her, and she could see the tail wagging inside its suit whenever she looked down at it. It reminded her of Silver and Lilly, the two huskies from the *Hive* that had died years ago, the last of their line. She never thought she would see another dog.

She hadn't been sure she would actually see X again, despite Michael's faith in their mission, but here he was, alive and, from what she could see, reasonably lucid.

Moving left, she peered through an open door on the landing and down the connecting corridor. Doors lined the hallway, and a window at the end flashed red from the distant lighthouse. A Siren flapped by, its leathery hide obscuring the view for a second.

Magnolia jogged up the stairs to catch up with the others. The dog loped beside her, anxious to rejoin its master. The group had stopped on the next landing, and X motioned for Layla to open a steel door with a key he pulled from his vest. Her hands were shaking so badly, she dropped the key on the floor. She scrambled to pick it up and inserted it in the lock.

X mumbled something to Michael, but Magnolia couldn't hear it. He still hadn't said a word to her. Did X not remember her?

Sure, she was a few years older and had laid off the black-market makeup she used to wear, but she hadn't changed so much that her old friend wouldn't recognize her, even with her short-cropped hair and the bandage on her face.

Unless he really is crazy.

Layla opened the door to reveal a tiled room with plastic curtains covering the walls. A row of showerheads hung from the ceiling. Rodger and X helped carry Michael inside and laid him gently on the floor.

"Can't..." He reached up, wheezing. "Can't breathe."

Layla started to take off his helmet, but X reached out to stop her. "Everyone has to rinse off first."

"No," Layla said. "We've got to get Tin stabilized before the poison stops his heart!"

Michael squirmed on the ground, clutching his leg, barely lucid. He gasped for air as the poison began to affect his lungs.

"Decon first," X said. "Keep your voices low. They know we're here now."

He turned a knob on the wall, and a line running up to the showerheads filled with a white liquid. It sprayed down in a mist that coated their bodies and dripped onto the tile floor, running into the floor drain along with Michael's blood. He let out a cry, his whole body jerking.

"Tin," Layla said, eyes pleading to X for help. "We're losing him. You have to help him right now."

Bending down, X pulled back the patch and dressing that Layla had covered the wound with. The flesh around the cut looked foul, already turning orange and leaking pus. He tossed the bloodied patch on the floor and took a syringe from his vest.

"Gotta risk it," X muttered.

"What is that?" Layla said, reaching out to stop him.

"An adrenaline-steroid mix. Saved my life."

Before Layla could object, X stuck the needle directly into Michael's wound. He sat straight up and roared in pain until he ran out of air. He fell back to the floor, eyes rolling up in his head.

"Help me get his clothes off," X said. He coughed and looked at the other divers. "The rest of you, strip down to your underwear."

"You're kidding, right?" Rodger asked.

Magnolia cut her eyes at him. "Do it."

The divers took off their armor and then everything but their undergarments. Rodger put the discarded items in a pile while X and Layla helped pull Michael's clothes off. Rodger kept his eyes on the floor, but Magnolia still folded her arms across her chest, slightly embarrassed. This wasn't exactly how she had imagined Rodger seeing her undressed.

She shivered in the cold spray of chemicals and stared at the man everyone had written off for dead. The burly leader of Team Raptor was gaunt now, but his bones were still covered in lean, ropy muscle. Scars crisscrossed his flesh like roads and rivers on a map. A thick gray beard covered his face but didn't quite obscure the long scar across his neck, where something or someone had cut him from ear to ear. The evidence of the pain and suffering he had endured was written on every part of his body.

He turned as if sensing Magnolia's gaze on him. He opened his mouth to bark an order, revealing chipped teeth. Amazingly, most of them were still white. X had always had a killer smile.

"Open that," he said, indicating the plastic sheet behind Magnolia. She pulled back the drape, revealing another steel door. She grabbed the handle and opened it. There was only darkness beyond.

"Light," he said, pointing at the floor.

Magnolia went in and bent down to turn on the lantern. The

light spread over a small room with a metal dresser on each side. Supplies were stacked neatly on metal shelves.

"Next door," X said.

Magnolia crossed the space with the lantern and pulled back a hatch that opened onto a living space. The room connected to a kitchen with an island covered in some sort of water purification equipment. Stacks of crates, a large metal table, and two chairs furnished the living space, and a second door led to an open bedroom, where Magnolia saw blankets and pillows piled on the floor. Various weapons were propped against the walls.

Rodger and X picked Michael up and moved him over to the table in the living area. They sat him down carefully, and X grabbed a medical kit from his stash, along with a canteen. He swirled some water around his mouth but didn't offer a drink to anyone else.

"Miles," X said, jerking his chin toward the dog. "This is our home."

"It's very nice," Magnolia said uncertainly.

He locked eyes with her. "You ... What's your name?"

"You don't remember me?"

X's eyes went unfocused, as if he were looking at something far away. He seemed unable to form an answer to her question. He turned and busied himself with Michael's injured leg.

"Is he going to be okay?" Layla asked.

"Wound's deep. Poison and rads making things worse."

No one said a word. They just watched X treat the wound. With Layla's help, he cleaned it and began stitching it up. Unable to stand the silence, Magnolia walked over to a pair of rifles set up against the wall.

"Help me with these, Rodger," she said.

She tossed him a rifle. They were both still in their underwear as she stalked back into the other room to check the dressers for clothing, with Rodger in tow. She found plain brown coveralls that looked as though they would fit okay.

"You think he's going to make it?" Rodger asked as he dressed.

"He's strong, but he's been through a lot over the past few days." Rodger looked at the ground, shoulders sagging.

"It'll be okay," she said. "Come on, let's get back out there."

As they walked back into the living area, she heard X talking. "Took you long enough to find me," he was saying. "It's too bad, though. If I saw you coming in, then the floaters saw you as well."

"The floaters?" Rodger asked. "You mean the Sirens?"

X gestured toward the black plastic tarp covering the balcony. Several hazard suits were folded on the floor beside the exit, along with a pair of binoculars. "See for yourself."

Magnolia and Rodger put on the suits and stepped out onto a balcony covered by a cage of bars like the one that had blocked their way earlier, protecting them from airborne Sirens. She taped the black tarp back in place to seal off the light from the apartment, then turned to look out over the city.

"Holy moly," Rodger breathed. He stood stock-still, staring through the binos.

Magnolia studied the massive ship docked at a concrete pier stretching out into the dark waters. Several other ships had capsized on the shoreline, their bellies burst open like dead sea animals. But the ship on the pier didn't seem to have any damage. Just a coat of rust covering most of the hull.

"No way," Rodger said. "No freaking way…"

"What do you see?" Magnolia asked. Her eyes flitted to the lighthouse where Sirens circled the flashing tower. She nudged Rodger impatiently and held out her hand for the binoculars. He slowly handed them over, still looking out toward the ocean.

Raising them to her visor, she then dialed them in on the flashing lighthouse. The Sirens flapped around the light. There were dozens of them drawn to the beacon and more still coming from the city.

"Do you see what I saw?" Rodger asked.

She lowered the binos to the shoreline where she finally saw the reason for their erratic behavior. Aboard the ship docked on the pier she saw movement. She zoomed in further on a person in heavy metal armor standing at one of the ship's turrets.

"It can't be…" she said, gasping.

Rodger looked over, eyes wide. She quickly pushed the binos back into position to scan the ship that appeared to be decked out for the end of the world. Which, she supposed, it technically was. Tarps covered the stern, and rusted sheet metal formed a roof over the middle section, with several lookout towers jutting out at intervals.

She focused on old-world vehicles parked on the deck. Another person emerged at one of the turrets. The figure grabbed a mounted swivel gun and fired a harpoon into the air, skewering one of the Sirens circling the lighthouse through the back. The beast fought for altitude, but the man reeled it in like a fish.

"Who are they…?" Magnolia muttered. She knelt and pulled Rodger down, out of view.

"Are those really *people*?" he asked.

Magnolia nodded.

Layla stepped out on the balcony. "X insisted I see this, too. What is he talking about?" She glanced back toward the tarp covering the door, clearly irritated at having to leave Michael, even for a second.

"We're saved," Rodger said, his voice low.

Magnolia handed Layla the binoculars. She brought them up and then lowered them a few moments later, silent.

"See, we're saved," Rodger said excitedly.

"No," said a gruff voice behind them. "Get back inside."

X held the plastic curtain open and gestured for them to

return to the apartment. When they were all back inside, he zipped the curtains back up.

"They aren't here to save us," X said. "You must trust me on this."

"Who are they?" Magnolia asked. Her body shivered with excitement, and fear. After all of this time, these were the first humans she had seen in her life besides people she knew from the sky.

"X, who are they?" she entreated.

"Monsters," X said. "That's all you need to know."

He went back to work on Michael without saying another word, Layla joining him at the table. Magnolia and Rodger stayed behind and exchanged a glance. X definitely knew more than he was telling them about these mysterious boat people, and while Magnolia wanted answers she knew the most important thing they needed to focus on right now was saving Commander Everhart.

TWENTY-FOUR

Jordan stood in the launch bay, surrounded by officers, support staff, technicians, engineers, and militia soldiers. Anyone without an active role in the launch was outside in the crowded corridors. Hundreds of faces—nearly everyone on the ship—tried to get a look at the pods the engineers had pushed through the narrow passages an hour ago.

The captain was looking at those pods now, admiring the quick work of Samson's team. He might not like the chief engineer, but the man did good work. If only he could learn when to keep his opinions to himself.

"We're almost in position," Hunt said in his ear.

"Good." Jordan walked over to the two groups of men and women preparing for the dive. On the right was a small team of militia soldiers, Sergeant Jenkins among them, donning armor and black hazard suits. Jenkins was a valuable asset to the *Hive*, but Jordan couldn't risk sending anyone less experienced to retake *Deliverance*—and kill Xavier Rodriguez.

Team Phoenix stood beside the pod on the left. Together, they would kill or capture the traitors and then board *Deliverance* and fly her from Miami to a rendezvous point safely away from the storms.

Samson strode through the crowded room, wearing a combat suit that barely contained his sagging belly. Other than Jenkins, he was the most important man on this mission. They needed the chief engineer to help operate *Deliverance*, especially if the airship had sustained damage in the storms.

Les Mitchells would assist him and serve as backup in case something happened to the chief engineer. That was the reason Jordan had personally delivered the medicine to Les' family just hours ago. The *Hive* needed the electrician, too, even if he was compromised by the lies Ty had fed him.

"Everyone other than the dive teams, clear the room," Jordan ordered. He grabbed the hilt of his sword while technicians and support staff hurried away from the pods. Both hatches were open, providing a view inside. It would be cramped, but then, the divers wouldn't be in the pods long.

Sergeant Jenkins and the militia soldiers saluted as Jordan approached. He returned the gesture with a firm salute.

"Today is one of the most important days in the history of the *Hive*," Jordan said. "*Deliverance* will help preserve our fragile existence until we can safely return to the surface in the distant future."

He scanned each face in turn, starting with the divers. Erin, Jennifer, Olah, and Les all stood with straight backs, eyes ahead. It was remarkable how quickly Miss Jenkins had managed to whip them into shape. The young woman had a future on the *Hive*—or possibly on *Deliverance*.

To their right were Del Toro, Lore, and Sergeant Jenkins, all of them decked out in bulkier armor than they wore on the ship. All members of the two teams carried automatic rifles, blasters, and combat knives. Samson also had a duty belt around his wide waist, stuffed with tools.

"Twenty-nine thousand feet below us is one of the most intense electrical storms I've ever seen," Jordan continued, "and beneath that, the city that was once called Miami. Make no mistake, there will be countless threats on the surface. The traitors we once called friends have taken over *Deliverance*. Your job is to take it back from them."

He paused to think of the most convincing lie or half-truth. "Michael Everhart will claim he was abandoned down there on the surface. If you see him, do not be deceived. Do not negotiate with him. He and the other traitors are armed and dangerous. Don't hesitate to fire. They surely won't hesitate if they have you in their sights."

Sergeant Jenkins slung his rifle over his shoulders. "Don't worry, sir. I'll take care of them."

Jordan scrutinized the sergeant, still unsure how far to trust him. Hell, he wasn't sure he could trust *anyone* anymore. But that was why he had one last test up his sleeve.

"Hunt, bring in Bennett and Donnie," he said.

Hunt hurried to the launch bay doors while Jordan sized up the divers and soldiers in front of him. Everyone looked frightened, but for different reasons. Jordan had a feeling Jenkins was more worried about his daughter's life than his own. Families made reliably good leverage. But Jordan was going to add another incentive just in case any of them weren't as loyal as they seemed.

The launch bay doors screeched open, and he turned as Hunt and a pair of militia guards led two teenage boys into the room. These pimply-faced wastes of *Hive* resources were the ones who had defaced the bulkhead with their effigy of the captain with his throat cut. The militia had finally ferreted them out, and now it was time to make an example of them.

Hands bound and wearing orange coveralls, the two prisoners shuffled forward, eyes burning with rage.

"On your knees," Jordan said.

Bennett slowly got down, but Donnie remained standing, defiant. One of the militia soldiers kicked him in the back of the leg, forcing him to one knee.

Hunt spoke. "You have been charged with, and found guilty by a jury of your peers, the crimes of vandalism, conspiracy, and threats against the captain of the *Hive*. You are hereby sentenced to five years in the brig with minimal rations—or conscription into the Hell Divers."

"Five fucking years!" Donnie spluttered. "It was just a *joke*, man." He looked at Jordan and spat on the deck. "You're a pig. You think we're stupid? We know you're a liar and a—"

In a swift motion, Jordan drew his sword and traced a line across Donnie's neck before the boy could finish his words. Blood spattered the shiny metal floor and flecked the toes of Jordan's boots.

"No!" Jennifer shouted.

Les wrapped an arm around her shoulders and she turned away, burying her face against his side. Erin watched, expressionless, as the boy reared his head back, bloody bubbles gurgling out of his mouth.

"You were saying?" Jordan said, raising a brow. He looked at the edge of the blade. "She's sharper than I thought."

"Please . . . please, don't kill me," Bennett said as Donnie slumped to the deck, his body still fighting to scavenge a few more precious seconds of life.

"I'll join the divers," Bennett said. "I'll do whatever you want!"

"Of course you will," Jordan said. He turned to the others. "This is what happens to traitors, and this is what you're all going to do to Michael Everhart and his comrades when you find them. Got it?"

The divers and soldiers all nodded at once.

"Good," he said. "Now, go get me that ship."

*   *   *   *   *

Les looked out the porthole as the launch bay emptied. A pair of soldiers dragged Donnie's limp body away, leaving a broad smear of blood. Another soldier hauled Bennett outside, presumably to return him to the brig.

"I can't believe he did that," Jennifer mumbled for what seemed like the fiftieth time.

Les put a gloved hand on her armored shoulder but didn't reply. Erin's helmeted head was downcast, silent, but Olah was smirking.

"He wanted to cut Jordan's neck, so Jordan cut his," he said. "Seems fair to me. That's what I call karma."

Olah fastened his harness across his chest armor. If karma was real, then Les was really looking forward to the moment Olah got what was coming to him.

"Quiet, all of you," Erin said. "Fasten in and prepare for launch."

The divers all finished belting into their seats while Erin made sure their weapons and gear were secured by mesh nets attached to the bulkheads.

A technician in a yellow jumpsuit knocked on the porthole, and Erin gave the man a thumbs-up. He returned the gesture and then secured the hatch over the thick glass window, sealing the divers in darkness. Then two LEDs in the top of the pod warmed to life, spreading red light over their armored bodies. Erin belted in and reached up to the control panel to prepare the operation systems.

Les chomped down on his mouth guard, preparing for the rush. Part of him was glad they were taking the pods down. He liked having a thick layer of insulation between himself and the storm. But what if something happened with the chute? What if this was just an elaborate plot by Jordan to get rid of him?

Snap out of it. You're going to be fine. Katherine, Phyl, and Trey will all be fine.

"Preparing for launch in T minus one minute," said an automated voice.

"All systems look good," Erin said.

"Sit back and enjoy the ride," Olah said with a chuckle.

"You're sick, man, you know that?" Jennifer said. "This ain't no game."

"Aw, lighten up," Olah sneered. "I'll be sure to watch your back once we get down there."

"Cut the shit," Erin said.

"Thirty seconds," said the same automated female voice.

The seconds ticked down on the mission clock at the upper right corner of his HUD. Les tried to focus on the task ahead. Over 470 people were counting on them. Even if Ty was right about everything Jordan had done, Les and the others had no choice. They had to take *Deliverance* back from Commander Everhart.

He just wished there was a way to do it peacefully. Killing Sirens and monsters was fine. It was a clear choice: shoot them or get eaten. An easy decision. But the thought of killing another human made his guts churn. Les imagined having to tell Trey that he had shot Michael Everhart. He pictured the look of hurt and betrayal in his son's eyes that his father had killed one of his role models. If the order came to pull the trigger, he wasn't sure he could do it.

"Ten seconds," repeated the female voice.

The red lights in the pod shifted to a cool blue as the clock on his HUD hit the end of the countdown. Les took a breath that smelled of plastic. His heart hammered, and the blood rushed in his ears. The launch process was different from a free-fall dive, and he wasn't prepared when the clock hit one.

Something clanked below them, and they were falling into darkness. Les imagined them plummeting through the clouds, gaining speed with every passing second.

"Good luck," said Jordan's voice over the comms. "Do not come back without my ship. The future of the human race depends on you."

"We dive so humanity survives," Olah replied.

Erin repeated the motto, but Jennifer and Les remained silent. He anxiously watched the altitude and speed on his HUD. It occurred to him that the top of his helmet nearly touched the roof of the small pod, and he tightened his straps to make sure a jolt didn't earn him a broken skull.

The comms crackled, and Lieutenant Hunt came online. "Entering the storm in ten seconds. Prepare for turbulence." The transmission cut out, and Les wondered whether it was the last time he would ever hear from someone on the *Hive*. Death would be bad, but failure would be worse—Jordan might take it out on their families. He had no doubt that if the mission went sideways, he wouldn't be coming home.

Don't think like that. You're going to see your family again.

He bit down on his mouth guard again. The distant rumble of thunder was muted by the pod's walls, with their multiple layers of insulation against the lightning. But there was nothing the engineers could do about air pockets and turbulence.

The pod rocketed through the first five thousand feet in no time at all. Then Les heard the most frightening sound he could imagine: the hiss of air leaking from one of the seals. He looked desperately around for the source.

"What is that?" Jennifer called out.

Les didn't have time to reply before they entered the storm.

NICHOLAS SANSBURY SMITH

303

A gust of wind slammed into the side of the pod, tossing it like a ball. The straps did their job, holding Les secure in the seat, but his long body jerked and his head rattled.

A hundred and fifty miles per hour. Holy shit, we're dropping fast.

The first lightning bolt struck the metal cocoon a moment later. It sounded as if a blaster had gone off inside Les' helmet. Jennifer screamed, and even Erin cried out as they were once again tossed through the sky. The hissing noise increased as air was sucked out of the pod. It had to be the porthole. The rest of the pod was basically an oblong canister of sheet metal welded to a steel frame.

"Everyone, just breathe slow," Erin said, her voice back to its normal self-possessed calm.

Les tried to follow her example. He closed his eyes and breathed deeply through his nose. His destiny was no longer in his hands. Either they would survive the drop, or they would all die screaming.

Cut it out, he thought, as images of Tom Price's semiliquefied corpse flashed through his mind.

Another bolt blasted the side of the pod and sent them rolling. The forces on his body warred with each other, trying to toss him this way and that, and his skin warmed like what he imagined a radiation burn felt like. Banging sounded on the outside of the shell, as if some flying monster were trying to get in, but it was the wind. It ripped the hatch completely off the window, giving them an upside-down view of the storm. It seemed the fins on the pod were too small to keep it upright.

A brilliant blue light arced across the bowl of sky. The clouds had coalesced into a dense mass, with no margins to differentiate one from another. Overlaying the roar of blood in his ears and the buffeting of the wind, he heard an endless roll of thunder.

Ten thousand feet and two hundred miles an hour.

"We have to right the pod before we can deploy the chutes!" Erin yelled as she reached for a control panel above her head.

Les watched the webwork of lightning outside. Another blast hit the pod, and the gear in the mesh net dumped onto the ceiling below them. Weapons, including several sheathed knives, clanked by his head. The next strike sent it all flying about the pod. A pack hit Les in the chest, and a rifle smacked Jennifer's helmet. He heard the crack, followed by a yelp of pain.

"Jennifer, are you okay?" Les shouted, fearing that her visor was cracked.

She managed to raise a hand and nod. He looked over at the exposed glass porthole. Cracks spiderwebbed across the surface, but at least, the lightning had righted them—mostly.

Still, Les knew that the chutes could be compromised if the pod didn't rock back into a stable position. A diver wouldn't deploy his chute with his back to the ground, for fear of being enshrouded. Doing so now with the pod's chutes could tear even the strongest suspension lines.

"Almost got it," Erin said, straining to reach the button. "Brace yourselves!"

An auxiliary chute fired on the outside of the pod and pulled them back into a stable position. Les breathed a sigh of relief that quickly turned to a gasp of shock.

"My God," he said.

The storm swirled around them like a tornado, lightning slashing the darkness in every direction. Les glimpsed the other pod. It looked so small against the backdrop of the storm.

"Three thousand feet, almost clear!" Erin shouted. She reached up, waiting for the right moment to punch the button for the main chutes.

The numbers ticked across Les' HUD. His eyes flitted from

the display to the soldiers' pod in the distance—just before a brilliant bolt enveloped it in a curtain of blue.

A voice cracked over the radio as someone shouted, "Holy shit!"

"The other pod just got hit!" Les said, pointing at the window.

Erin's helmet turned. "Dad..." she murmured. She strained for a better look, but the pod had been swept away beyond the narrow view from the porthole.

"I'm sure they're okay," Les said.

Erin waited another beat, then reached back up and punched two buttons in a row. "Hold on!" she yelled.

The main chutes fired, jolting Les' stomach down to his feet, or so it felt. He kept his eyes on the porthole. The noise of the air leak had dwindled from a teakettle shriek to a low hiss as their air pressure neared equilibrium with that outside.

The first view of the Old World came into focus below: husks of scrapers backlit by a stroboscopic display.

"Prepare for landing," Erin said.

Les looked up at his HUD. Only two hundred feet to the surface. They were almost home free.

He saw the scraper leering up at them a moment too late. There was no time to warn anyone, and no way to avoid the crash. Holding in a breath, he grabbed his harness as the pod caromed off a steel girder.

The chutes went taut, jerking them again, and the violent motion again made projectiles of the spilled gear. A cry rang out, and Les slammed his helmet on the ceiling. His vision went dark, and his entire brain ached.

Another scream sounded, different from the first. It sounded like Erin, but he still couldn't see much besides stars flitting across the darkness.

The pod continued to fall, slowly leveling back out as the ruined city rose up to meet them. He bit down on the mouth guard, trying to lessen the pain in his head. His vision returned, and he got a blurry image of Erin reaching toward Jennifer, just before the pod hit something else, this time with a much more dampened impact. For a moment, Les didn't know what they had hit, until Olah started shouting.

"We're sinking. We have to get out of here!"

Les stared as the brown expanse outside the cracked porthole resolved into a lake of murky water. The faulty seal, instead of leaking air, was now letting the water in. He looked over at Jennifer, whose head was tilted at an odd angle, like a rag doll tossed carelessly on the floor. Erin was trying to wake her up, but she didn't respond.

"She's gone!" Olah shouted. "Her damn neck's broke. We have to leave her."

Les unbuckled his harness and crashed to the floor, hands slapping into a foot of brown water. Olah grabbed a rifle and a bag and splashed his way over to the hatch.

"Hurry!" he yelled. Then he palmed a red button, blowing the hatch off its hinges. Water poured in, and Olah pulled himself out.

"Come on!" Les yelled. He yanked Erin away from Jennifer's body and pulled her into the water as it quickly flooded the pod.

"No!" Erin shouted. "No, she's still—"

Les glimpsed Jennifer's right hand twitching just as he pulled Erin out of the pod and into the choppy water. He chinned on his night-vision goggles and kicked upward toward the surface, breaking through a second later. Olah was already swimming toward shore. Les and Erin swam after him even though every instinct told Les to turn back and try to help Jennifer.

She was still alive, damn it. Maybe hurt bad, but still moving.

Olah reached a slab of concrete on the shore and crawled up. He turned to help Erin out of the water, then grabbed Les.

"On your feet, Giraffe," he said.

Together, the divers stood on the concrete pad, watching the pod sink with most of their weapons and gear—and Jennifer.

Les kept telling himself there wasn't anything he could do for his friend, but it didn't work. If he wanted, he could jump in and try to pull her out of the sinking vessel. Instead, he watched in silence—a coward abandoning his teammate in a hostile wasteland.

TWENTY-FIVE

Michael awoke to darkness. He tried to sit up, but a hand pushed down on his chest. His muscles were tight across his back, and raw pain shot up his leg. He held back a groan and struggled against the hand holding him down.

"Easy there, Tin. You're safe."

Layla's sweet voice soothed him, but he still had to grit his teeth against the pain as he lay back on the hard mattress.

"Where is he?" Michael asked.

"Who, X?" Layla said. "He's outside with Rodge and Mags." She turned on a lantern by the bed and smiled at him in the glow. He reached up to her freckled face with the back of his hand, running it over her soft skin. He had almost forgotten how beautiful she was without a helmet on.

"I thought I was never going to see you again," he whispered. He pulled his hand away and closed his eyes for a beat, trying to remember what had happened to him. The last thing he could recall was X jamming a needle into his leg. Everything after that was a dark blur.

"You've had two close calls. I just don't know what I'm going to do with you."

"A kiss would be a start."

She leaned in and pressed her lips against his, holding them there for a moment before sitting back in her chair. It figured that the first time they were alone together in ages, he was too banged up to do anything about it. He looked down at his bandaged leg to assess the damage, wondering whether he would even be able to walk.

"It's not as bad as it looks," she said. "We got you all stitched up and we have you on a strong regimen of antibiotics. X also used something to neutralize the poison."

"How long have I been out?"

"Twelve hours," Layla said, looking at her watch. "Give or take."

"Has anyone contacted Timothy?"

"Not yet. I was waiting for you to wake up. X strongly urged against sending any radio transmissions."

"Now that we've found X, we should get moving. Wait...Why did he say not to send any transmissions?"

"I'll let him tell you." Layla frowned as he tried to sit up. "Seriously, stop moving. You need to rest."

"I'm fine. I need to get up and talk to X about—"

A distant screech cut him off. A dog's growl followed. Next came the zipping of a plastic curtain, and the creak of the bedroom door opening.

"Layla, get out here," Magnolia called out.

Michael managed to press his back against the wall and use it as a brace. "What's going on out there?" he said, trying to get a view.

"Sirens—lots of them," Magnolia said. "And the floaters."

"Floaters?" His eyes darted to Magnolia, then Layla. Noise came from the adjoining room and Rodger poked his head in the open door.

"Hey, he's awake!" he almost shouted.

"Keep your voice down, idiot," X growled, coming up behind the group.

Michael had to chuckle, although it hurt. The angry old man in front of him was the same X he remembered from a decade ago.

"Honestly, I expected *you* to be the blabbering idiot," Michael said. He shook his head, smiling incredulously at the sight of the frail yet strong man in front of him. "I can't believe you survived down here all these years."

X ran a hand over his short-cropped hair but didn't return the smile. For a second, he simply studied Michael, as if trying to remember something. Then he walked over to his bedside and knelt down. He slowly reached out and flicked Michael's shoulder-length hair like a dirty piece of laundry.

"I'm still picturing you with your tin hat, kid. What's this dog tail?"

Yup, this was definitely the X that Michael remembered from his childhood. The man who was always busting his father's chops and who could always be trusted to speak the brutal truth. The warrior who never stopped fighting. He had saved them out there on the street, and he had saved Michael from the envenomated bite wound on his leg.

But X had paid dearly during the decade-long battle for survival. His voice sounded as if he had been smoking home-made cigarettes every day of his life, and scars covered his flesh like macabre tattoos.

"Help me up," Michael said. "Let's go talk in the other room."

X grabbed Michael's hand and squeezed it, then helped him to his feet. Before X could protest, Michael wrapped his arms around the legendary diver. In that moment, he felt less like a strong warrior and more like a feeble old man.

Michael pulled back, scrutinizing X up close. Behind the ragged beard were hollow cheeks, and wrinkles and scars formed ravines across his forehead. He looked far older than his fifty-five years.

They made their way into the living area outside the bedroom.

Michael limped but managed to walk without support. He needed to prove to the others he was okay to leave this place. They had to get back to *Deliverance*.

X took a seat in a chair, and Miles sat on his haunches beside him while the other divers sat around the metal table in the center of the room.

"Where do we start?" Michael asked, sighing.

"You can start by telling me why you're here," X said.

"For you," Michael said. "When we found out about your transmissions, we raced to find you. I'm so sorry, X. We didn't know you were down here all this time."

X didn't say a word—maybe because he didn't believe him, maybe because he was waiting to hear more.

"Captain Jordan knew about your transmissions but kept them a secret," Michael continued.

"Captain *Jordan*?" X asked. "What about…?"

"Captain Ash passed away from throat cancer not long after you were left behind. If she had known you were alive, she would have rescued you. But Jordan…"

X reached up to touch the scar on his neck.

"Bastard," Magnolia growled. "I'm going to kill him."

X lowered his hand from the scar and stroked his dog's head calmly. Michael wasn't sure what to expect, but the man seemed to be taking the news rather well.

"If he got my messages, then why didn't he send someone to find me?" X asked.

Magnolia looked over at Michael, clearly eager to talk, but Michael had to be the one to tell X. It was his responsibility.

"Katrina," he said, locking eyes with X. "Jordan and she were together, and she's pregnant with his child. I think he was still jealous of you."

X didn't say anything, and Michael couldn't read the expression on his weathered face. If the news shocked or upset him, he didn't show it.

Michael hurried to fill the dead air. "I also believe he was relying on your messages to find places to raid. So in a way, you were still helping the *Hive* all these years."

The old diver's lips tightened into a grimace, and his nostrils flared. After a moment, his features returned to normal, and X looked over at the black sheet covering the balcony.

"Enemies in all directions," he said. "The sky, the land, and the sea." Silence filled the room until he cleared it with a sigh. "I'm not worried about that chickenshit Jordan *or* the Sirens. It's the floaters that are the problem."

"What floaters?" Michael asked. He looked at Layla again, then Magnolia, and finally back to X. "What the hell aren't you guys telling me?"

"The men on the ship," X said. "They come every six months to the lighthouses and trap Sirens and other creatures, then take them back out to sea. I've seen them carrying cargo away from the ITC facilities, too."

Michael shook his head in disbelief. He paused to think a moment before asking the obvious questions. "Are you telling me there are *survivors* down here? How is that possible? The *Hive* or one of the other airships would've detected them years ago."

X just shrugged.

"That's why the lighthouse was blinking," Michael said, realization setting in. His gut sank at the implications. "We have to find them," he said. "We have to figure out where they're fr—"

"No," X said, cutting him off. His fingers reached up to the scar on his neck again.

Magnolia broke the silence. "I saw a lighthouse at Charleston, too. Wondered why it was all lit up."

Again the room was silent, and everyone looked to the

legendary Hell Diver for answers. He scratched at his beard and sighed.

"I'm not sure who they are," X said, "but they come from the sea, and they're dangerous." He went back to petting Miles as if this explanation were enough. The distant cry of a Siren rang out, and the dog's hackles rose.

"Maybe they have a home on an island or something, where the radiation isn't bad," Magnolia said.

Layla looked at X. "You said they trap the Sirens. Do they eat the god-awful things?"

X shrugged again. It seemed he was done telling stories for now, or maybe he was simply feeling the strain of talking so much, to so many people, after his long isolation. But Michael had a feeling there was much more to this story—something X was hiding. Still, now wasn't the time to pressure him to talk. Not after what he'd been through. If anyone should have questions, it was the man who had been left behind for a decade.

"I want to go home," Rodger said. "When are we leaving?"

X raised his bushy eyebrows. "Leaving?"

"We came to take you home," Michael said.

"This *is* my home now," X said. He pulled a flask from his vest and took a slug of whatever was inside. Magnolia massaged her forehead, her frustration and disappointment bleeding through. Clearly, Michael wasn't the only one who remembered the alcoholic version of X from ten years ago. Somehow, he had managed to make his own shine here or else had found a stash somewhere.

"You belong on the *Hive*," Michael said. "But we're going to need your help taking it back from Jordan."

"Fuck that," X said, wiping his mouth on his sleeve. "I'm better off on my own."

Miles let out a whine, and X patted his head. "I didn't mean without you, boy."

Staring in disbelief, Magnolia said, "Jordan *left* you down here."

"Yeah, I heard you the first time," X said. He took another slug from his flask.

"Honestly, I'd rather not go back to the *Hive*," Layla said, speaking up for the first time. "Why can't we just stay on *Deliverance?*"

"No," Rodger protested. "I can't leave my parents behind."

"Humanity is counting on us," Michael said, turning to Layla. He couldn't believe what he was hearing. She of all people was supposed to have his back.

"I'm sick of humanity," Layla said with a shrug.

"And I've got unfinished business with Jordan," Magnolia chimed in. "I'm going back to the *Hive* with or without you guys, and I'm gonna strangle Leon with his own guts."

Michael shook his head, frustrated. They had come all this way to get X, but the stubborn jackass didn't want to leave. On top of that, Layla was dragging her feet about returning to the *Hive*.

A chirping sound came from across the room, and everyone looked at the handheld radio in the pile of their gear and armor. Magnolia walked over and picked up the radio, then gave it to Michael. He brought it up to his lips.

X slowly got up from his chair, watching warily. "That on a private channel?" he asked.

Michael nodded. "Why?"

X shook his head and settled back into his seat. Michael narrowed his eyes, trying to figure out why the hell the floaters scared X so much. After all the man had been through, humans should be the least of his concerns. The speakers crackled, and the AI's voice came online.

"Commander Everhart, this is Timothy. Do you copy? Over."

"Copy you, Timothy. Go ahead."

"Sir, I apologize for breaking radio silence, but I have a problem. There are people approaching *Deliverance*, and they are armed with automatic rifles. What should I do, sir?"

"Your friends?" X asked.

Michael shook his head. "It's just us down here."

"Shit, it's got to be the floaters," X said, getting back up from his chair. Miles stood and looked up, as if awaiting a command.

Michael wanted to ask a dozen questions, but whoever these people were, only one thing mattered. "We can't let them take our ship," he said, looking to X. "Please, X. Will you help us?"

X started to bring the flask back up to his lips, then slid it back into the slot on his vest. He shook his head wearily, like an old man who didn't want to get up for the day's chores.

"Ah, fuck it," he said. "Miles and I don't have anything better to do."

*   *   *   *   *

Rodger followed the other divers down a dark stairwell to the garage under the building. In the middle of the space was a motorcycle with wide tires, hitched to a trailer.

"Nice bike," Michael said.

X pointed at the trailer, "Everyone in the back."

Rodger examined the vehicle before getting in. The wheels on both the bike and the trailer sported extra-wide tires and had metal blades protruding from the hubs.

"You want us to get inside *that*, and let you drive us across the city like livestock being shipped to slaughter?" Rodger asked. "No, thanks."

"Just get in, man," Michael said.

Magnolia turned to look at him. "Come on, Rodger Dodger. I'll save you a seat."

Rodger gave an uneasy smile and followed the other divers toward the open trailer. X and Magnolia had already loaded the crates of supplies and weapons they would need on the journey. Rodger went over the plan again in his head. It was simple. They would drive through the city to an area a few blocks away from *Deliverance*. From there, they would move in on foot and engage any hostiles trying to steal their ship.

"Once we're on the open road, I'm going to haul ass," X said in his raspy voice. "Your ship is about ten minutes away. Your job is to shoot anything in our way, without hitting Miles or me."

Michael dipped his helmet in assent. Somehow, X had taken over command of the mission. Rodger wasn't sure letting the man lead them was a good idea, but once again no one seemed especially interested in his opinion.

"The others are heavily armed," X said. "Mags and I will take them down."

"Won't they hear us coming?" Rodger asked.

X shook his head. "I've modified the mufflers and engine. She purrs, but she don't scream." He swung his leg over the bike. "You guys ready?"

The divers, crammed into the trailer among the crates and weapons, nodded. Miles thumped his tail on the floor.

"I'm Rodgeman," Rodger whispered again. The words had become a nervous habit.

The bike choked to life as X revved the engine, and the trailer lurched up the ramp toward the surface. Magnolia pressed her leg against Rodger's and flashed a smile at him. He swallowed and moved his rifle out of the way.

As soon as they were clear of the garage, he scanned above

for Sirens. The creatures had flocked to the south shortly after Timothy's message. Something had drawn them away, and Rodger had a feeling it had to do with the armed men now approaching *Deliverance*.

The trailer jolted over a pothole when they hit the main street, and Rodger twisted to grab the metal railing for support. It was a rocky ride, but X was right—the bike hardly made any noise. They sped through the ruined city, navigating around the ancient vehicles and mutant plants with calculated precision. It seemed this wasn't X's first time driving these roads.

Rodger looked back up at the sky again. His parents were up there somewhere, and he longed to see them again. His heart hurt at the thought that the reunion might not happen. Michael and Layla were good people, but they weren't family. And Magnolia ... Well, he could never figure out what she was thinking.

Sometimes, she seemed to want to get close to him, but then she would run away again. Someday, maybe soon, he would just tell her how he felt. No more longing glances, no more awkward flirting. Just put his heart out there and let her do with it as she pleased. His mother liked to say that if Rodger met a girl he liked, he should marry her and start making babies as soon as possible. He grinned, imagining a couple of blue-haired, bespectacled toddlers running around the *Hive*.

"What's so funny?" Magnolia asked.

"Oh, n-nothing really."

A raindrop splatted on his visor, and a second later the storm clouds dumped. Rodger wiped his visor and bent his head down to keep the water from blinding him. The bike slowed, and the trailer jolted over another bump in the road.

Lightning struck a scraper in the distance, and the following blast of thunder shook the metal trailer. A crevice in the pavement rocked them from side to side as they sped over it. With no way to communicate with X, the divers remained silent, putting their faith in the hands of a man most of them barely knew.

The rain continued to batter them as they wove through the windy streets. X drove up a bridge, giving Rodger a view of the swamps. The lighthouse continued to flash on the horizon, but he didn't see any Sirens circling the tower.

So where were they? Rodger felt a growing lump in his gut as he thought about it.

On both sides of the road, vines and mushrooms glowed. The blades on the bike and trailer hubs sliced through them, painting the sidewalk with purple and green sap. Plants shriveled back into their cracks in the torrential downpour, and a lone beetle skittered for cover. Everywhere he looked, the city's vast poisonous ecosystem was alive and functioning. How could X possibly have survived out here? What kind of man would want to make his home in a world like this?

Rodger watched the back of X's head as if he might see into the man's troubled mind. X's helmet panned constantly and moved from road to sky, constantly alert for threats.

Rodger thought about Janga's prophecy, the one that told of a man who would lead humanity to a new home in the sea. Rodger had half believed that X would turn out to be that man, but now he wasn't so sure. X didn't seem to care much whether humanity lived or blinked out forever.

Maybe it was these "floaters" that would lead humanity to a home in the sea. But Rodger didn't know who or what they were, and X seemed frightened of them. He shook away the questions and focused on the mission.

They turned around another corner, and the bike slowed to a crawl. Rodger and the other divers readied their weapons as X pulled off to the side of the road and under a slanted rooftop that provided cover from the rain. Magnolia opened the liftgate and let the divers out onto the street.

"Your ship should be two blocks from here," X said. He pointed at the walled stadium.

"Timothy, do you copy? Over," Michael said over the comm.

Static crackled for several beats before the AI came online. "Roger, sir."

"We're moving into position. You got eyes on these soldiers?"

"They are moving into the concourse, sir."

"How many?"

"The sensors are detecting eight contacts of human size."

"Any other contacts in the area?" Michael asked.

"I will do another scan and report back. Over."

Michael ducked under the awning to look at the sky. Rodger followed. He still didn't see anything out there, but he could hear the distant hunting cry of a Siren.

"We're splitting up," Michael said. "X and Layla with me. We'll enter on the left side of the stadium. Rodger and Magnolia, take the right side."

X put a hand on Michael's shoulder. "Listen, kid, you should sit this one out. You're injured. Let me handle these guys."

"I'm not the kid with the tin hat anymore," Michael replied. "I'm the leader of Team Raptor." He pointed to the logo on the top of his battered helmet.

X didn't reply right away, his gaze fixed on the Raptor emblem. "You can hardly walk," he finally said.

"I can walk just fine."

X shook his head. "Fine, suit yourself, but I'll take point. You stay behind me. Got it?"

Two beats passed before Michael finally dipped his helmet. The interaction reminded Rodger of his father, who had always tried to protect him, even when Rodger didn't need the help.

Even after all this time, X was still trying to look out for Michael. But maybe there was nothing X could do to get them out of this city alive.

*   *   *   *   *

Magnolia and Rodger bolted across the street. She was anxious to return to *Deliverance* and get off this apocalyptic obstacle course. The view of the ocean had been satisfying for all of an hour. Now she just wanted to leave the mysterious "floaters," the Sirens, and the man-eating trees behind. If all went according to plan, she would soon be strangling Jordan.

The thought made her smile.

With her rifle up, she ran in front of Rodger, toward a brick building. The entire city block consisted of ruined structures, most of them eroded down to their foundations. An exfoliated scraper formed a mountain of scree to their right. Debris covered the street and the storefronts on the left side. This section of the city had been spared from the nuclear heat wave that flattened most of Miami to the west, but the centuries hadn't been kind to the structures that remained. Most of them were covered in a skin of orange lichen and red moss. It looked innocent enough, but Magnolia didn't trust the moss not to dissolve her armor on contact or to release flesh-eating spores.

The radiation was also a threat. Fortunately, X had given them pills that would mitigate some of the effects, but even these wouldn't save them from full-on exposure. He had found the pills in the same place where he found the cancer medicine that saved his life almost two years ago. The man was the archetype of a survivor, having thrived for a decade in a place where death ruled.

Magnolia studied the next intersection, where a pair of old-world vehicles rested in the street, their shells rusted and covered in more of the suspicious orange lichen. After raising a fist, she got down to scan the area. Rodger knelt behind the wreckage of a truck. They would have to cross the open space to get to the next block, and from there it was just a short trek to the stadium. She could already see the circular wall in the distance.

A chilling wail sent her diving to the ground. The Siren flapped into view a few blocks away, fighting for altitude, with some sort of stick or barb protruding from its wing.

"Let's go while it's preoccupied," Magnolia said.

Rodger followed her through the intersection. They kept low, using the vehicles for cover as they crept down the street.

"Moving into position," Michael said over the comms.

"Copy that," Magnolia replied.

"Radio silence from here out."

The comms went dead. The vehicles thinned out, and the two divers left the open street and took to the sidewalk, moving along the shattered storefronts. The stadium towered over the paved lot at the end of the street. She scanned the area around the building, looking for contacts.

The last transmission from Timothy had put all the soldiers inside the stadium and approaching *Deliverance*, but she still approached cautiously, keeping an eye out for lookouts or snipers.

A shiver ran up her back, and the hair on her neck stood up the way it did just before a lightning strike. But no bolt came from the sky. She brought up her rifle and aimed it at the stadium. Something was off.

The silence felt heavy, charged with expectation. Not a Siren could be heard.

Nor could she hear Rodger behind her.

She spun around to look for him but saw only the dusty concrete sidewalk where he was supposed to be standing. Her eyes naturally flitted to the sky as she prayed not to see a Siren carrying him away. Nothing. Had he spotted a piece of wood in the rubble and run off to salvage it?

A crunching behind her made her freeze, and she caught a glint of movement reflected in a shard of glass. She whirled with her rifle raised, finger on the trigger, only to be rocked by a crashing blow to the side of her helmet.

The world went red, and Magnolia collapsed on her back. She blinked at the shades of light, trying to get a look at whoever had just attacked her.

Voices sounded, muffled and strained as if heard through a breathing apparatus. She tried to move, but her body wasn't cooperating.

A man bent down into her line of sight. A metal helmet covered his face, and he looked at her through two almond-shaped mirrored eye visors that reflected her helmet with a dent in the side.

The man tilted his head to the side, like a wild animal assessing its prey. His massive shoulders were topped with jagged white pads. It took her a moment to realize that they were actually the eyeless skulls of Sirens.

Magnolia tried to scoot back, away from her captor, but gauntleted hands grabbed her shoulders from behind. She craned her neck to see two more armored men, though these lacked the skull epaulets. The men began to drag her across the concrete.

"No," she mumbled, a string of drool coming out of her mouth. Her head pounded, but her visor didn't appear to be compromised, at least. She gritted her teeth against the pain.

A voice crackled over the comm channel. "Mags, Rodge, where are you? We're in position."

The man dragging her had heard the transmission. He leaned down with a knife, placing it in the space between her helmet and chest armor. The muffled voice spoke again from behind his mask, but she didn't understand the words. They were unlike any she had ever heard before. Still, she didn't need to understand the words to guess their meaning. If she replied to Michael, the man would cut her throat.

"Magnolia, Rodger, do you copy?" Michael asked.

The man picked her up under her armpits and slung her over his shoulder. The world went topsy-turvy, and then she was staring at the ash-covered sidewalk.

Head pounding, she fought to remain conscious as he carried her down the street. A few minutes later, she was tossed inside the back of a vehicle. She hit the floor and rolled over to see Rodger on his side, visor cracked and eyes shut.

Magnolia tried to squirm toward him despite the pain in her head, but one of the beastly men smacked her helmet with his rifle butt. The pain returned, more intense than before.

She stared for several seconds at Rodger's chest. Satisfied that he was still breathing, she looked around. They weren't the only cargo in the back of the vehicle. There were dozens of capsules, stacked and held down by ropes. The same type of capsules she had seen in the cryogenic lab back at the Hilltop Bastion.

Each one was filled with a naked human body.

TWENTY-SIX

Team Phoenix and the militia soldiers had the airship surrounded. Thunder boomed in the distance as Les and the other divers raced down past the rows of blasted, melted seats. They kept their rifles trained on the massive ship, but Les kept looking around in awe at the terrain.

The landscape here looked far different from his first dive. Huge mushrooms, patches of weeds, and other poisonous things grew in the lumpy dirt. A giant insect darted across bare ground.

The radioactive wasteland—and the thought of killing Michael Everhart, a man who had served as a role model to Trey—made Les want to puke. But it was the image of Jennifer sinking into the muck that he couldn't shake. She had still been alive; he was sure of it. He closed his eyes for a moment, trying to will away the memory of her final moments.

When Les opened his eyes, he was looking at *Deliverance*.

The ship was magnificent. At two-thirds the *Hive*'s size and without the vulnerable and unwieldy gas bladders, it was a sleek design with thrusters and turbofans built for speed and maneuverability. Judging by the smoky creases in the hull, the ship had taken one hell of a beating on the flight into Miami. But the lights on the undercarriage told Les it was still operational. With Samson's help, they would be able to get her into the air.

Hair-raising wails came from the sky, where Sirens wheeled over the arena. They kept their distance, but they were hunting.

Across the stadium, Sergeant Jenkins flashed hand signals down the rows. Del Toro, Lore, and Samson followed close behind. Most of the group had never seen the surface before, and they all moved with extra caution, darting glances all around like nervous children entering a dark room.

The soldiers continued down the east side of the seating area while Erin led Olah and Les down the western rows. Relying on their night-vision optics, they kept all lights and headlamps off. So far, the only sign they had seen of Commander Everhart and his comrades were boot prints leading from the bottom of the ship across the field. There were four sets, meaning four members of Team Raptor were still alive.

Les hoped they had missed the rogue divers. He was still praying for a peaceful resolution. Olah and the militiamen, however, looked hell-bent on carrying out the captain's orders.

"Samson, you know where the door is to this ship?" Jenkins asked over the comm channel.

"Should be a ramp underneath."

Jenkins motioned for the engineer to stay put at the bottom row of the stadium's shattered seats. Then he flashed signals across the field to Erin. She looked over at Olah and Les, giving them a nod.

Reluctantly, he leveled his blaster at the ship. He had no idea whether it would even fire after being submerged in the water. After some thought, he holstered the weapon and pulled out his pistol. He thumbed back the hammer with a click and continued down the steps after Erin and Olah.

At the bottom row, Erin raised a fist, and everyone stopped. She and Olah ducked down behind the low wall, and Les followed suit as best he could, folding his rangy frame into a ball just as a Siren swooped over the stadium. The eyeless face scanned the field. Soaring away, it let out a screech that was equally terrifying and heartbreaking.

That thing isn't so different from us, he mused. *Just trying to survive and care for its young. Its ancestors were as human as we are, after all.*

"Hold your fire," Sergeant Jenkins said over the comm channel. His raspy breathing told Les he was nervous—and for good reason.

Lightning struck the upper seats. The tremendous thunder crack that followed seemed to come from all sides at once. A second creature answered the call of the first, the sound reverberating like an emergency siren over the waning boom of thunder. Les tried harder to tuck his body behind the wall.

"Stop where you are and come no farther!" shouted a voice from the field.

He glanced over at Erin, who raised a finger—a single contact. Olah looked over the ledge and shouldered his rifle.

"On the fucking ground!" Olah shouted.

Les and Erin both stood and angled their weapons at the shimmery figure hovering over a ramp that had extended from the belly of the ship.

"What the hell?" Les muttered. It looked like a ghost, but that was crazy. *No crazier than Sirens, though.*

"Please do not shoot," the man said, raising a hand. "I wish you no harm."

"Who are you, and where is Commander Everhart?" Jenkins demanded. The soldiers hopped over the wall and trotted out onto the field.

"I am Timothy Pepper. Commander Everhart is no longer here."

"That's the AI Jordan was talking about," Olah remarked. He jumped over the wall before Erin could object.

"Come on," she said to Les.

Timothy held up both hands and retreated several steps.

"Stay where you are!" Jenkins ordered.

Timothy halted on the ramp. "I do not wish you any harm," he repeated, "but I will be forced to use the ship's weapons systems if you do not lower your firearms."

"Fuck that," Olah said, "he's bluffing. I say we pump this guy full of lead."

"He's a hologram, you idiot," Les muttered.

"Erin, Les, go stand sentry with Samson," Jenkins said, looking in their direction.

Erin hesitated and then jerked her helmet at Les. She was no longer in charge down here. The militia soldier was calling the shots—literally, it seemed. Olah linked up with his comrades and continued toward the AI. By the time Les and Erin reached Samson, the soldiers had the AI surrounded.

"We've come for the ship, Commander Everhart, and any other surviving divers," Jenkins said. "Tell us where the divers are, and I'll make sure Chief Engineer Samson doesn't wipe your consciousness from the hard drive when we board this ship."

The AI suddenly vanished, and the hydraulics on the ramp hissed, raising the platform.

"Stop!" Jenkins shouted. He bolted forward as another shout rang out—a gruff voice that Les had never heard before.

"Drop your damn weapons!"

A man in a black jumpsuit, with armor similar to a Hell Diver's, emerged on the top of *Deliverance*, with a rifle trained downward on the militia soldiers.

"Don't move," said a voice right behind Les. He lowered his

pistol and slowly turned to see two more Hell Divers at the top of the concourse, their rifles aimed at him, Erin, and Samson.

Now *they* were the ones surrounded.

Jenkins kept his aim on the man on top of the airship but instructed the other militia soldiers to look at the stairs.

"Start walking," the woman behind him said.

A brilliant flash of lightning illuminated the stadium, and Les saw who had the drop on them. It was Michael Everhart and Layla Brower.

Samson recognized them, too. "Holy shit, Michael! It's me, Samson."

"I see you," Michael said coldly. "Now, start walking onto the field."

"Go to hell," Olah shouted, raising his gun.

"Drop your weapons or Samson gets one to the head!" bellowed the man from the top of the airship.

"What?" Samson said, shocked. "Please, you can't..."

"Shut up, Samson," Layla snapped. "You shouldn't have come down here."

Les strained to see the man perched on *Deliverance*, but he already had a feeling he knew who it was. It had to be Xavier Rodriguez. No one else would have been so brazen.

The legend was real after all, and he appeared ready to unload a magazine into the men who marooned him all those years ago. Les didn't blame him one damn bit for wanting revenge.

The entire thing had been a trap, with the AI serving as the bait.

"We don't want any trouble," Samson said, raising his hands.

"Bullshit," Layla said. "You came here to steal our ship."

"Jordan's orders," Erin said, turning to look at Layla.

Jenkins and his men kept their weapons pointed in both directions. It would take only an inopportune twitch for a firefight to erupt. With Sirens hunting in the area, Les had a feeling that things were about go downhill very soon.

"Surrender, and I'll make sure you get a fair trial once we get back into the sky," Jenkins said.

"Hah!" Layla said. "That's funny. Jordan's idea of *fair* is pushing anyone he doesn't like out of a launch tube."

Jenkins didn't reply. He couldn't. There were plenty of rumors about the things the sergeant had done under Jordan's orders. Intimidation, beatings, and worse.

The two groups on the field were maybe a hundred feet apart, but the man in black remained on the top of the ship, keeping his gun on Jenkins.

"It doesn't have to be like this," Michael said. "There's still time to join us. To take back the ship from—"

"Fuck you, traitor," Olah said. "Jordan is the only person keeping humanity alive."

Layla pointed her rifle at his chest. "Say one more word and you're Siren shit."

Samson turned to Michael. "Please, son. You're an intelligent, reasonable man. I promise I'll do everything I can to fix this."

"There is no fix when it comes to Jordan," the man in black said. "That bastard left me down here for a decade. The only fix I can see is my dog eating his face."

Lore and Del Toro began to lower their rifles, but Jenkins kept his gaze on the figure up top. It was definitely X. All the pieces fit. Ty had been right all along. Les scanned the area, looking for this mysterious dog. He remembered the ship's dogs from his childhood, and he would very much like to see one again.

"You're a traitor just like the rest of these assholes," Olah said to X. "Captain Jordan was right to leave you behind."

"Dad, Michael and Layla are right," Erin said. "Please, let's all just lower our guns."

"Stay out of this, sweetheart," Jenkins snapped. "We have orders to—"

A pair of Sirens flapped over the south end of the stadium, distracting everyone for a moment—everyone but Olah. He fired his machine gun at Layla, knocking her down in the blink of an eye.

The screams and gunfire agitated the monsters, and they soared away as Layla crashed to the ground. Michael screamed and fired off a blast. Les tried to move, but he was paralyzed. He could only watch as the battle raged all around him.

X and Jenkins had both opened fire. Bullets cut into the dirt to the right of the sergeant, who unleashed a salvo into the top of the ship. X held his ground and fired another burst, catching Jenkins in the center of the chest.

"Dad!" Erin screamed.

Jenkins managed to squeeze the trigger once more, but Les couldn't see whether X was hit. The diver stumbled and fell over the side of the ship, vanishing from view.

Michael had opened fire at Olah, who dived for cover just in time. Del Toro and Lore fanned out, but Michael quickly turned his barrel on Lore and shot him three times in the side. The soldier crumpled to the ground. Del Toro took a knee and aimed at Michael, but the diver was too fast. A shot punched through the center of Del Toro's visor.

Olah had taken cover behind a massive leg of the landing gear. He popped out and aimed at Michael, firing a shot that took him down.

Michael hit the dirt hard a few feet from Layla. Both of them writhed in pain as Olah emerged from his hiding spot. He approached cautiously, weapon shouldered.

Erin ran over and knelt beside her father. He locked hands with her, still alive but gasping for air. "Dad," she sobbed as she draped herself over him. "Daddy, please…don't go."

Les searched for X, but he was nowhere in sight. He glanced down and saw a pistol lying in the dirt. Had he dropped his weapon, or was it someone else's? He bent down to pick it up.

Olah strode over to Layla and Michael, weapon angled down. He kicked their weapons away.

"Stop!" someone shouted. The hologram had reappeared on the ramp as it lowered back to the dirt. "Please, please don't kill them. They are my responsibility."

"Captain Jordan's orders," Olah said. He moved his finger to the trigger.

Without even thinking, Les brought up the pistol and fired two shots into the side of Olah's helmet. The rounds punched through metal and skull. The soldier fell like a board, dead on impact.

Les lowered the gun and stared at it in his shaking hands.

"Tin," Layla groaned, reaching out for Michael. His hand gripped hers and he squirmed closer to her.

"Drop it," said a voice. Les saw a figure limping toward him. A second creature, on all fours, moved by the man's side. It took Les a moment to figure out that the thing in the oddly shaped helmet and rad suit was indeed a dog.

Les let the gun fall in the dirt.

Samson held up his hands but didn't say a word. He moved over to Layla and Michael. The commander was on his knees now, a hand clamped over Layla's stomach. Blood gushed from a hole in her armor.

"Michael, you okay?" X asked.

"My armor stopped the bullet, but Layla's hit," he said. "We have to stop the bleeding."

X looked at the sky. "We have to get out of here before those Sirens get brave."

Erin walked over, tears streaming down her face. "You shot

my dad, you bastard!" she yelled, reaching for X as if she wanted to strangle him. He grabbed her hands as she swatted at his helmet.

"I'm sorry, but he was on the wrong side of this," X said.

Les held Erin back while X helped Michael and Layla. "We all were."

"Where are Mags and Rodger?" X asked.

Michael shook his helmeted head. "I don't know. They aren't responding."

"Let go of me!" Erin shouted.

"You have to be quiet," Les replied. He slowly loosened his grip, watching her to make sure she didn't attack X.

Everyone fell silent, shocked by the violence. Erin had stopped sobbing, but her gaze was locked on her dead father. X and Michael picked Layla up and carried her to the ramp, with Timothy leading them to a cargo bay. The dog trotted after them, glancing back at Les, Erin, and Samson, who remained in the dirt where they were.

"What are we supposed to do?" Samson asked.

"You can stay here, for all I care," X said.

"No," Michael said. "We'll need them to help us capture the *Hive*."

*　　*　　*　　*　　*

Lieutenant Hunt burst into Jordan's office. "Sir, we made contact with Samson on the surface," he said.

Jordan, who had just dozed off, snapped alert. "Did they take *Deliverance*?"

A smile on Hunt's exhausted face told Jordan the mission had been a success. But the smile quickly faded. "We lost a lot of people on the landing. Apparently, their pod hit the water, and the only survivors were Samson and Sergeant Jenkins."

Jordan massaged the side of his head. He didn't have a strong liking for either Del Toro or Lore, but they were reliable and would be missed.

"So Erin and her team were able to complete the mission."

"Yes, sir. They killed Commander Everhart and Layla, but Sergeant Jenkins and Olah were both mortally wounded in the battle."

The news surprised Jordan enough that he didn't reply immediately. He imagined the fight on the surface and found it grimly satisfying.

"Erin, Samson, and Les survived," Hunt said, "but there's no sign of X, Rodger, or Magnolia."

Jordan folded his hands on his desk and considered the implications. They had lost several experienced soldiers but gained an entire airship—a prize well worth the cost.

"Sir, *Deliverance* has been damaged, but Samson and Les are working on getting it in the air. They want to dock with the *Hive* so our engineering team can perform more repairs."

"How long until they arrive?" Jordan asked.

"Samson thinks he can have her in the air in a few hours. We should start flying in their direction."

"Make it happen," Jordan said. "I'll meet you in a few minutes. Until then, you have the bridge."

Hunt nodded and left Jordan in the dimly lit room. He sat there in silence, considering all that had happened and how to move forward. There was much to do to prepare for docking with *Deliverance*.

Jordan stood and grabbed the sword off the wall. He stepped out onto the bridge and looked at his officers. Soon this place would be mostly empty, and Jordan would have a new command center aboard a new vessel. He couldn't wait to see her.

He strode out over the metal platform with his hands behind his back. He wished his child could have been around to see their future home. And Katrina, too, for that matter, but he had other plans for her.

"Listen up, everyone," Jordan said. He waited until he had every officer's attention. Eyes filled with hope and fear looked at him. For the first time in the history of the *Hive*, he could promise these people a new home—a better home. He would be remembered forever for what he was about to do.

"In a few hours, we will rendezvous with the airship *Deliverance*. All operations will eventually move to the new ship, which is faster, safer, and more advanced than the *Hive* in every way. She will indeed be our *Deliverance*. I promised to guide you to salvation, and that's exactly what I've done."

All around him, officers exchanged glances. Ensign Ryan stood at his station and clapped once, then twice. Several other officers joined in, and after a beat, the entire room erupted in applause.

Jordan had finally won. All the traitors were dead, and he had secured the future of the human race and her name was *Deliverance*.

*   *   *   *   *

Rodger woke up to find himself lying on a hard surface, staring up at black clouds. White lines like a spiderweb stretched across the sky. He groaned, trying to remember where he was and why his head felt as if someone had put it in a vise and tightened it a couple of turns.

His heart stuttered when his vision cleared enough to see that the cobwebs weren't high above him in the sky but, rather, cracks in his visor shield. He sucked in unfiltered air through the gaps. It tasted like salt and barbecue and was laced with a lethal dose of radiation. His throat and eyes burned. He tried to reach up to the visor, but his right hand wouldn't move. Neither would his left. He lifted his head slightly to find that his arms, hands, and legs were bound and bolted to the rusty deck of a ship. A few feet away, Magnolia lay in a similar state, her body limp.

"Mags," he mumbled. "Wake up!"

Footfalls sounded, and a figure in full-body armor approached, carrying a machine gun.

The floaters, he realized. The memory of the men catching him outside the stadium rushed through his mind. They had been hiding in a storefront, and when he passed, they had yanked him inside the dark room.

They were soldiers of some sort, but what did they want?

The man with the machine gun strode forward. His massive metal-clad frame was an intimidating sight in itself, but the humanoid skulls he wore as shoulder pads made him all the more terrifying. Rodger's eyes widened as the warrior's almond-shaped, mirrored visors centered on him.

"G-get away," Rodger said, kicking. He looked over at Magnolia. "Mags, you got to wake up, you…"

His strained voice trailed off as the man with the machine gun bent down. He spoke in a foreign language that Rodger didn't recognize, but whatever it was, he sounded angry. So Rodger kept his mouth shut.

The man kicked him in the side. It hurt like hell. Then he walked away, his boots clanking across the metal deck. Rodger watched him go. He looked around him at the massive ship, hoping to find some clue as to where they were or how to escape. Several old-world vehicles were parked on the deck: a truck with oversize tires and a mounted machine gun in the bed, and three cars covered with armor plating. They all appeared to be in working order, with petrol tanks and oil canisters sitting beside them. There were also fuel cells on the deck to power the trucks that didn't run on the archaic fuel.

Beyond the vehicles was a metal garage with two wide doors, both of them half open. Inside were more cars, a few motorcycles, and gigantic shipping containers. More people in the armored suits were loading what looked like cryogenic capsules into the containers.

Rodger turned his head the other direction, straining to see more. Tarps covered bulky shapes along the bow. One of them wasn't tied down properly, and he caught a glimpse of what lay beneath. Cages, dozens of them. Several barrels burned along the railing on the ship, spreading an orange glow over the occupants.

No way. Nobody's that crazy.

Chained Sirens, all of them apparently unconscious. The cages were stacked like crates, three high and who knew how many deep. This was some sort of cargo ship, and Rodger had a feeling he and Magnolia had been added to the manifest. But what the hell would these people be doing with captured Sirens, not to mention him and Mags?

His answer came a few minutes later, when one of the armored soldiers opened a cage and dragged a Siren across the deck. It slowly came to, head cranking from side to side to look at its captors. It clawed at the air, but the man with the chain yanked the beast to the deck as two more soldiers strode forward with machetes. They hacked the creature to pieces without even bothering to kill it first. Blood spattered the rust-coated deck as it let out an inhuman wail.

When the men had finished butchering it, they brought pieces over to the barrels and set them on grates over the top. Rodger's stomach churned. Now he knew where the barbecue smell was coming from. He had to get out of here before he and Magnolia suffered the same fate.

The red glow of the lighthouse drew his attention. It flashed several times, then went dark. A horn sounded, and the armored men stopped what they were doing. They looked up at the tower that rose above the metal roof amidships.

Screaming in the foreign dialect came from all directions, and Magnolia finally stirred. The alarm sounded again. Footfalls came toward him, and the man with the machine gun and the skulls on his shoulders crouched down between him and Mags. He looked at Rodger first, and Rodger saw that the man had only one working eye behind the almond-shaped visors. The other eye was milky white.

"You speak the English, yes?" he said in his deep voice.

Rodger nodded warily. He noticed an octopus engraving on the breast of the man's chest armor. Was it some sort of symbol like the raptor?

The man checked Rodger's bonds with his good eye, making sure they were tight. "You will no get away like the others," he said in broken English. He paused to look up at a man who had emerged in the lookout tower above; then he looked back at Rodger. "They call me el Pulpo. I am king of the Cazadores."

"I'm Rodgeman," Rodger said, trying to be polite. "I'm from the *Hive*."

The man tilted his helmet as if trying to figure out what to make of him. Rodger did the same.

"Who are the Cazadores?" Rodger asked.

"Last of the humans." He raised a long metal-clad finger at the containers. "We come every six months, save those frozen ones we can and bring back to our metal islands. We breed them there."

"And what do you want with us?" Rodger asked, hoping it wasn't the latter option, especially for Magnolia's sake.

"You see soon." He stood and slung his rifle over his back. "Live long enough, you see the sun!"

"The *sun*?" Rodger said, uncomprehending. He wanted to ask questions, but he was so terrified he could hardly form a sentence.

Was it really possible that these barbarians were taking him to an island where the sun would shine?

El Pulpo turned his working eye to Magnolia and leered. "Pretty. Not many as nice as this one on our island." He laughed—a humorless cackle that made Rodger shiver. "Big plans for this one."

"Leave her alone," Rodger said. "Don't touch her, or I'll—"

The man looked back at Rodger and laughed again. The deck suddenly vibrated, metal groaning as the gargantuan ship began to move. The Klaxon sounded a third time, and the anchor chain clanked onto the deck on the starboard side.

The ship was setting sail, and Rodger had no idea where it was headed.

TWENTY-SEVEN

The street raced by in gray and brown flashes as X gunned the engine of his motorcycle. Miles, apparently unconcerned by the speed, sat calmly in his custom seat, enjoying the ride.

Les had volunteered to come along and help find Rodger and Magnolia, but X told the others to stay behind. The ship needed repairing, and Layla needed saving. Michael had refused to leave her side. Seeing the young man's pain brought back a feeling that X had suppressed during his long exile on the surface. It was an emotion that he shared easily with Miles, but he hadn't felt it for another human in a very long time.

Hell, X had never been good at loving people.

Another emotion swirled through him as he drove. An emotion he *was* good at feeling. Anger.

He was angry at Jordan. He was angry at the militia soldiers he had been forced to gun down, including his old friend Sergeant Jenkins, who had apparently sold his soul. And he was furiously, righteously angry at the Cazadores who had kidnapped Rodger and Magnolia. He wanted to dismember them alive for daring to steal his friends away so soon after he had found them again.

Focus, old man. Save them first, then worry about getting payback.

The bike zoomed toward the coast, swerving around debris and jolting over cracks in the pavement. As soon as X and Michael had carried Layla into the airship, the ship's AI had shown them the video feed of an old-world truck racing away from the area where Rodger and Magnolia had vanished. X had a feeling he knew where the seagoing bastards were taking his friends. The lighthouse had stopped blinking several minutes ago, and a horn signaled that the others were preparing to leave the harbor.

He didn't have much time.

If he didn't get to the ship, Rodger and Magnolia would be lost forever—assuming they were still alive now. X continued to debate whether he should have told the divers the truth about the cannibals. He knew from his own experience in captivity just what they planned to do to his friends.

He had always wondered whether there were people on the surface, but these were not the sort of people Captain Ash had hoped to discover. Somehow, these pirates or barbarians or whatever they were had gone undetected by the *Hive* and other airships all this time, and X had wanted to keep it that way.

But now the bastards had his friends.

He stared at the tower in the distance. Since his captivity, he had learned much about these people, mostly by watching and studying them from afar. Many years ago, the Cazadores had left their home in the metal islands and used the lighthouses to lure human survivors of the wars. People who had surfaced from bunkers or ITC facilities to repopulate the earth. Later, when stocks ran low, the Cazadores had turned to the next best thing: Sirens. Then to the people and animals still frozen in the cryogenic chambers.

And now Rodger and Magnolia were on the menu, although

X had a feeling they would use Magnolia for other purposes. The Cazadores had clearly sacrificed their humanity on the altar of their own survival. Now they were animals, barely more human than the Sirens they hunted.

It was precisely why X had lied to Michael and the other divers. They didn't come from some utopian society basking under the sun. The pirates came from a dark world where men ate whatever meat they could find, including their own species.

At the next bridge, X twisted the throttle and sped up the ramp, finally getting a view of the beach. The ship was already pulling away from the pier. The speedometer ticked up to ninety miles per hour over an open stretch of road.

The sky was remarkably clear, with not a Siren in sight. Chances were, the Cazadores had captured and killed most of the beasts that were stupid enough to come out of their lairs. But there were always more out there, hiding and waiting.

X steered onto another road at the bottom of the bridge, weaving between charred hulls and melted vehicles. He reached a hundred miles per hour on the final stretch to the beach.

The ruined coastline stretched northward. Tsunamis had leveled this area centuries ago, crushing the buildings and washing away everything but the foundations. Destroyed boats, sheets of metal, amorphous hunks of plastic, and other debris littered the beach.

X parked the bike behind a brick wall and unbuckled Miles. The dog jumped out, and X grabbed the backpack he had designed for carrying the dog in unusually dicey situations. Then he grabbed his assault rifle and a noise-suppressed long rifle, which he slung over his shoulder, flattening the backpack against him. Next, he shouldered the machine gun as he ran out into the junkyard, barrel pointing at the deck.

Several Cazadores manned machine-gun nests on the ship's

deck, keeping an eye out for Sirens in the sky. The junkyard would provide plenty of cover, but he and Miles would have to make it quick. He darted around the mounds of sheet metal and concrete slabs, running faster than he had thought possible, his dog at his heels. Lightning cracked across the sky like muzzle flashes from an automatic rifle.

He eyed a metal ladder running down the side of the ship. A guard manned the nearest turret above the deck, but his eyes were on the clouds. If he looked in X's direction, he would have him and Miles dead to rights in his kill zone.

X swapped the assault rifle for the long rifle and knelt behind the split hull of a boat. He brought the scope up and centered the crosshairs right between the two almond-shaped lenses in the guard's helmet.

With the noise-suppressed barrel lined up, he waited for a bolt of lightning and the following thunderclap. A flash speared the sky, nearly a mile away, and he counted four seconds until the thunder boomed, pulling the trigger with the noise.

As soon as the shot was away, X lowered the rifle and started running again. The man slumped over, blood trickling out of his helmet and onto the deck below.

X sprinted from the beach and onto the concrete pier. The ladder wasn't far, just two hundred feet, but the ship was picking up speed.

X slowed, unslung his weapons, and strapped Miles into the custom pack and onto his back. A moment later, X was running with the weapons hanging over his chest, and Miles high on his back.

The massive ship was slipping out into the dark ocean. Waves slapped the pier behind X, water sloshing over the concrete platform. He reached out and grabbed the ladder, his boot sliding on the metal rung for a heart-skipping moment. Gritting his teeth, he climbed toward the railing fifty feet above. He flattened his body against the ship when a helmeted head appeared to his right.

Had they found their dead comrade?

X waited, straining under the load. Miles was only fifty pounds, but along with the weapons and armor, it was a lot to haul up a ladder. He could feel the blood pulsing in his carotid arteries and his temples.

When he risked looking up again, the man was gone.

Wasting no time, X grabbed another rung and kept climbing. At the top, he whispered to Miles to keep quiet and then peeked over the side, giving the area a quick scan. To the right, several armored soldiers were standing around a barrel while something cooked over a metal grate. Neither of them seemed to be aware of the dead man in the nest above, but X could see the blood striping down the turret. The left side was open deck between the rail and the middle of the ship.

He got over the railing and bent down to let Miles onto the deck. The center of the ship was a metal garage and storage area for containers. He had spent days studying the layout from his apartment after the bastards caught him over a year ago, just in case he ever tangled with them again.

Now was his chance to even the scales.

Hugging the pocked metal wall and keeping low, he moved with the assault rifle shouldered. This weapon had no suppressor, and any gunfire would surely attract every soldier on board, but he was ready for a firefight. He had never been much for sneaking around.

He stopped when he got to the edge of the garage. The doors on the right were open, and inside were more vehicles and the shipping containers. The bow was clear of contacts, but several crates were stashed along the deck, blocking his view.

Just as X was about to move into the garage, Miles nudged

him. The dog's head was pointed at the crates, keying on something that X had apparently missed. Crouching down, X studied the rust-darkened metal before finally glimpsing the silhouettes of two figures strapped between crates.

It had to be Rodger and Magnolia.

He reached down to pat the dog's head, glad he had lugged him up the ladder.

X pulled a knife from his vest and raised his rifle in his other hand, prepared to make a run for the divers. But he didn't get the chance. A Klaxon screamed overhead, and the sound of men yelling in Spanish came from all directions. Cursing, he sheathed the knife.

"Stay," he said to Miles. Then he stepped around the side of the garage with his rifle up and the safety off.

Let's see if you've still got it, old man.

He squeezed the trigger and fired a burst at each of the three men standing outside the shipping containers. Two of them went down right away, but the third staggered until X shot him through the helmet.

X ejected the spent magazine and pulled another from his vest, slapped it in, and did a quick scan of the garage. Two more Cazadores came around the other side of the entrance to see what was happening. He raised the freshly loaded rifle and fired just as one of the men stopped and raised his hands in the air.

A three-round burst sent the man buckling and he collapsed in a limp heap onto the deck. The next burst hit the second soldier. He fell backward over the rail with a muffled scream and a splash.

Return fire ricocheted off the deck beside X, and he rolled for cover. He came up on one knee and fired at the turret on top of the garage. The bullets pinged off the side of the armored wall, and X waited until a helmet popped up again to pull the trigger. This time, the round punched through a visor slot, finishing the job with a small spray of blood.

As X looked for the next target, Miles barked, but not at him— he was barking at the two men flanking them from the bow. They had been hidden by the crates, and now they were slinking toward Magnolia and Rodger with machetes.

The men both darted for cover as X brought up his gun. He ran after them, firing as he moved and hitting one in the back. The second vanished in the maze of crates. X stopped to pull out his blade again and cut Rodger free.

"Thank God you found us," Rodger said. "They were going to ea—"

"Shut up and call Michael for evac," X said. He looked over at Magnolia. "You okay?"

She managed a nod, but the two dents in her helmet told X she had taken a beating. At least, she was still in one piece.

"Go!" X shouted as soon as they were free.

Keeping his rifle tight, X moved toward the crates, sweeping for contacts. He pivoted around the first crate with Miles on his heels, wondering whether they should abandon the hunt. He wasn't sure how many of the ghouls were still left on the ship. It might be better to get Mags and Rodger to safety while he had the chance, but he also didn't like the idea of turning his back on someone armed with at least a machete.

"Bark when you see 'em, Miles," X ordered. He jumped up, grabbed the lip of the crate, and then hauled himself to the top. From his new vantage point, he saw movement around the next crate. The man had his machete up and was moving directly for Miles. Cords hung over his shoulders like metal dreadlocks, connecting his helmet with the tanks on his armored back.

X whistled from above, and the man looked up in time to

catch two rounds to his helmet and a third in the tank on his back. One of the cords disconnected, hissing and jettisoning air.

"Help!" came a scream. He whirled back to the center of the ship, where a hulking Cazador held a saw-toothed blade pressed to Rodger's throat. Magnolia was backed against the gunwale, eyes wide behind her visor.

"Let him go!" she snarled.

Two more Cazadores were moving on her. One of them unslung a shotgun.

"Drop it," shouted the man holding Rodger captive. It was then that X noticed the crushed Siren skulls on his shoulders.

El Pulpo.

The scar on his neck itched as he looked at the leader of the Cazadores. The bastard wouldn't hesitate this time; he would kill all three of them and barbecue them right alongside the Siren still grilling over the oil drum. X steeled himself to make a call that would haunt him for the rest of his life. There just wasn't enough time to save them both.

His heart ached when he made his decision.

Bringing his rifle up, he fired several bursts at the two men approaching Magnolia, hitting the one with the shotgun first. He dropped from a head shot, but the second man took a round to the chest and kept moving with his cutlass raised, apparently determined to take Magnolia with him.

Maybe if X had dispatched them both with head shots, he would have had a chance to save Rodger, but he was forced to spend another second killing the man with the blade.

Three bullets sent him crashing into the railing.

Magnolia was already running toward el Pulpo as X pivoted, finger on the side of the trigger.

They both were too late.

El Pulpo loosened his grip on Rodger and then thrust the

blade into Rodger's back, lifting him off the ground. Magnolia screamed, holding up her hands and freezing, as if she might fix what had happened if she could just hold still enough.

Rodger squirmed, his feet kicking. "Help!" he croaked. "Someone help me!"

El Pulpo pulled the blade free from Rodger and unslung his machine gun as Rodger toppled onto the deck. X fired first, aiming for the eye he had destroyed with a needle nearly two years ago. But his labored breathing threw off his aim, and the bullets punched into armor below the elbow. The machine gun clattered onto the deck.

El Pulpo let out a muffled roar and ran for cover as X continued firing until his magazine went dry. Miles barked ferociously and gave chase, with his master right behind him. X dropped the empty machine gun and unslung the long rifle as he ran. Bringing it up, he fired two rounds at the escaping cannibal leader. A window shattered and a tire went flat, but El Pulpo disappeared before X could take him down for good.

"Miles, back!" X shouted.

The dog returned, and X hurried over to Magnolia. She was on her knees next to Rodger, cradling his helmet. X scanned for contacts again, keeping his barrel on the garage.

"We gotta move," he said, his voice even gruffer than usual.

Rodger wheezed, peppering the inside of his helmet with blood. He held up a gloved hand to Magnolia and said, "Sorry I never…" His words trailed off in a coughing fit.

Magnolia grabbed Rodger by his chest plate, trying to lift him up. "You're going to be fine. Come on, get up."

"We got to go, Mags," X said. He looked down at Rodger. How could he apologize to the man for choosing Magnolia?

Rodger coughed again, more blood flecking the inside of his cracked visor. His suit had been compromised, and the rads here were off the graph. Rodger seemed to understand this. "Too late for me. Could already feel myself getting sick."

Miles nudged up alongside Rodger, nuzzling his arm and whining softly.

Rodger looked up at X, his eyes clear and steady. "Tell my parents that the good chisel set is in my footlocker. And...Magnolia, I always..." His eyelids fluttered, and his hand fell away from Miles' head as his body went limp.

X grabbed Magnolia and pulled her away, though she fought him at first. They moved to the railing. The ship had left the pier, and they were in the open ocean now. More shouts came from the bow as Cazador soldiers streamed up from the lower decks in response to the gunfire.

A voice that had to be el Pulpo's roared behind X. He grabbed Miles under one arm and took Magnolia's hand with the other.

"C'mon, Mags. Let's dive."

*   *   *   *   *

Michael stood next to Layla's bed in the medical ward. She was sedated and sleeping peacefully, but she had lost a lot of blood. As soon as they reached the *Hive*, she would need surgery, assuming she made it that long.

Michael was still struggling to understand what had happened on the ship. X had brought Miles and Magnolia back, all of them dripping wet, but Rodger wasn't with them.

Magnolia sat in a chair nearby with her battered head cupped in her hands, spiky black and blue hair like a storm cloud around her head. Timothy was there, too, monitoring Layla's vitals.

"Where's X?" Michael asked.

Timothy paused a moment, apparently tapping into the ships video system.

"He's watching Samson, Erin, and Les make their final repairs in the engine room."

"Final repairs?" Michael asked. "They're almost done?"

"It would be more accurate to call them the final repairs before the ship is airworthy. More work will need to be done once we get clear of the storm."

Michael looked at Layla, his mind in a fog. He ran his finger along the back of her hand, but she remained unconscious, unmoved by his touch.

"Mags, are you okay?" he asked.

Her pale face was blotchy with dried blood from the head injuries she had received and the tears she had shed over Rodger. But it was the radiation exposure that worried Michael the most. But for the medical supplies X had brought in his bike trailer, she would likely have died from it, and Layla would have never made it this long. Neither woman was out of danger yet, though.

A voice came over the PA system. "Timothy, this is Samson. I've fixed our biggest problem, which was a venting issue. Engine should be good to fire up now."

Michael glanced at the wall-mounted monitor, studying the data. The secondary systems were mostly functional, but he was concerned about the hull's integrity. A few more well-placed lightning hits could send them crashing back to the surface.

"Waiting for your orders, sir," Timothy said.

Michael nodded. "Fire it up."

The AI vanished from the room, leaving him alone with Layla and Magnolia. Michael knew they could have used his help below-decks, but he didn't want to leave her side.

Magnolia joined him and put her hand on his shoulder. "She's going to be okay," she whispered.

Michael could tell by her tone that she wasn't convinced. The ship vibrated as Timothy brought the engine online. For a few minutes, they waited there in silence.

The hatch opened, and X strode inside. He had trimmed his beard and was wearing black fatigues and a tactical button-down shirt that hung loosely over his lean frame.

"How's everybody doing?" he asked, his gruff voice almost a bark.

Michael forced a half smile. "Layla's hanging in there—a real fighter," he replied. "Are Erin, Les, and Samson still in engineering?"

"Don't worry, Miles is watching them," X said. He jerked his chin at Magnolia. "How are you, kid?"

Magnolia shrugged a shoulder. "Alive."

X then reached forward, hesitated slightly before making contact, and put a hand on Magnolia's arm. Michael suddenly wondered how long it had been since X touched another human being.

"I'm sorry I couldn't save Rodger," he said quietly.

Tears fell from Magnolia's eyes. She wiped them away quickly but didn't reply.

A glowing column of light solidified between X and Michael as Timothy's form took shape. Michael's stomach dropped when he saw the expression on the AI's normally calm features.

"Sir, we have a problem."

Michael cursed. "What now?"

"Sirens," Timothy replied. "Hundreds of them, all flocking toward the ship."

Magnolia brushed a bright-blue lock of wet hair from her swollen eyes. "The engine. It must be attracting them the same way they're attracted to the batteries in our suits."

"Watch Layla," Michael said to Magnolia, knowing he had no choice but to act now. He kissed Layla on the cheek. "I love you, and I'll be right back."

Layla's eyelids fluttered, but she remained unconscious.

"You're with me, X," Michael said.

They hurried outside and through the corridor toward central command. The passages still smelled like smoke, and stains from the white fire-suppressant foam covered the destroyed stations inside the bridge. Monitors on the central island flashed data.

"Sitrep, Timothy," Michael said. He made his way over to a secondary monitor.

"Secondary systems are operational, and the engine is online," Timothy replied.

"Bring up the video feed."

The monitor on the starboard side of the room came online, and Michael instantly saw what had the AI so concerned. The camera zoomed in on a vortex of Sirens flapping into the sky above what Michael assumed was the ITC building. They nearly blotted out the horizon as they made their way toward *Deliverance*.

"Get us into the air," Michael said. He rushed over to the captain's chair, took a seat, and brought the comm link to his lips.

"Everyone, this is Commander Everhart. Buckle in and prepare for a bumpy ride. We're leaving Miami." Although he wanted to be at Layla's side, her life depended on his staying here and monitoring the flight.

"Mags, take care of Layla for me," he said, finishing the transmission.

The turbofans clicked on below the ship, and the entire vessel vibrated as it lifted off the field.

"Retracting landing gear," Timothy said, working through his preflight announcements methodically, with no apparent sense of urgency.

"Just get us out of here!" Michael yelled.

He watched the Sirens on the screen as they approached, their frayed wings and pale naked forms moving ever closer, flapping like huge albino bats.

"Can they get inside?" X asked, taking the chair next to Michael's.

Timothy nodded from his position next to the central island. "There are multiple areas through which they could access the ship, including the port exhaust conduits, the—"

"Not now, Timothy," Michael groaned. "Just get us the hell out of here."

Lightning bloomed across the skyline, backlighting the creatures homing in on the ship. Michael closed his eyes briefly and then looked at the screen, hoping they would be spared from any lightning strikes. So far, they had managed to avoid the worst of the storm.

The Sirens weren't so lucky. Several cartwheeled to the ground, their blackened carcasses smoking. *Deliverance* rose into the sky, but if they went much higher, they would be too close to the storm clouds.

"Keep us low and punch it!" Michael said, his voice hoarse from yelling so much.

"Bringing on thrusters three and four," Timothy said.

A loud clanking sounded, but the ship didn't lurch forward. The whining that followed told Michael something was wrong, and an alarm confirmed it a moment later.

The Sirens were closing in, having grouped themselves into the V-formation that Michael knew all too well. He could almost hear their high-pitched wails.

"Thrusters three and four are offline," Timothy said unnecessarily.

Another clank sounded, echoing through the ship as the turbofans kept them hovering. Without thrusters, they would have to go right into the flight path of the Sirens if they wanted to leave Miami. It was either that or use the turbofans to take them into the storm, which was suicide.

"Engage forward thrusters," Michael said.

"Thrusters one and two are online."

The turbofans shut off, and the powerful thrusters propelled them away from the stadium and toward the coast. X fastened his harness, and they both watched the screen as *Deliverance* rose over the ruined buildings and raced toward the oncoming Sirens.

Michael swallowed hard and grabbed the armrests as the hundred-strong flock soared toward the massive airship, traveling at fifty miles an hour on a collision course with the flapping wall of pallid, diseased flesh.

Timothy announced, "Contacts in three, two..."

Michael focused on the screen, watching the beasts in awe. The formation broke at the last second, the creatures fanning out to either side of the ship.

Clank...clank-clank.

The sound of the Sirens crashing into the hull echoed inside the bridge. X let out a chuckle, but a blast of lightning ended it and he followed Michael's lead, grabbing the armrests.

"Warning, threat level criti—"

Timothy silenced the automated female voice and turned off the Klaxon as they raced over the city, turning away from the shoreline and back the way they had come. The Sirens circled after them, but the airship sped away, leaving them in its exhaust trail.

Deliverance slowly did a 360-degree turn, in the process taking another lightning blast to the starboard hull. A distant boom roared through the passages and into the bridge.

"Timothy, sitrep!" Michael yelled over the noise.

"Fire in compartment six," he replied. "I am sealing it now."

Through the chaos, Michael managed to keep his eyes on the screen. They were heading out over the ocean as they continued to turn. In the distance, he glimpsed what had to be the rusty Cazador ship carving through the swells. It was the last thing he saw before the screen and the entire bridge went dark.

TWENTY-EIGHT

Jordan stood in the bridge of the *Hive* with his hands clamped to the oak wheel. The countdown ticked away in his mind. He couldn't wait to see his beautiful new ship. The ship that would keep humanity alive and thriving for centuries to come and would ensure that every child who grew up in the sky knew the name Leon Jordan.

"Sir, we're receiving a broadcast," Hunt reported from his station.

"Relay it to my headset," Jordan replied.

His earpiece crackled, and Samson's voice boomed, "Captain Jordan, this is Chief Engineer Samson, do you copy?"

"Good to hear your voice," Jordan said, pulling the headset away from his ear to escape the deafening volume. "What's the condition of *Deliverance*?"

There was a short pause, long enough to fill Jordan with anxiety.

"Sir, we took a beating on the way out of the city and are down to one thruster and three turbofans. But the engine is holding steady, and we should be able to make all necessary repairs in the skies."

Jordan breathed out, his nerves settling. *Deliverance* had survived the storms, not that he had any doubts about her abilities.

"Excellent news, Samson. Stay safe, and we will see you soon."

He shut off the comms and slowly turned the wheel toward the updated coordinates marking *Deliverance*'s position. The dark clouds swirled on the wall-mounted main display, and he scanned them for the first signs of the airship.

"How far out are we, Ensign Ryan?" Jordan asked.

"About five minutes, sir," came the reply from the station above.

Jordan nodded, eyes flitting from the screen to the monitor displaying altitude, speed, and systems data. It was hard to contain his excitement. After all his sacrifices, they were finally entering a new era of human history. Today would mark a new beginning for the survivors of what had once been the dominant species on the planet. And someday, long after he was dead, his legacy would live on through their descendants, when *Deliverance* and the *Hive* finally set back down to repopulate Earth.

"Should be getting a visual in a minute or so," Ryan said.

Hunt walked down the ramp and stood next to Jordan. "Sir, I just wanted to say…"

Jordan looked over at his second-in-command. "Yes?"

"To say thank you and that I'm proud to serve with you," Hunt finished.

A quick scan of the room revealed officers from all directions looking down at Jordan, excitement and something else in their gaze—something that Jordan hadn't seen for a very long time.

Hope.

He nodded proudly and turned back to the screen. He pushed the mike back to his lips and ordered Hunt to open a shipwide transmission.

"To every soul on the *Hive*, this is Captain Jordan speaking. In a few minutes, we will be docking with the airship *Deliverance*. This ship is newer, faster, and better in every way than the *Hive*, and I'm proud to bring her home to us in the skies."

What he didn't tell them was that not everyone would be moving over to the new airship. The lower-deckers, the sick, and any other undesirable passengers would stay on the *Hive*. And while the two ships would remain in the skies together, they wouldn't be connected.

"In the coming months, we will deploy more Hell Diver teams to the surface to retrieve the parts we need to make *Deliverance* a second lifeboat for humanity," Jordan continued. "Once our engineers have retrofitted *Deliverance*, we will have the ability to grow more food, recycle more clean water, and provide a better standard of living."

He left out the part about where the Hell Divers would come from and how many would likely die in the process. All that mattered—and all that these people needed to hear—was the promise of more food and nicer accommodations.

Jordan thought of Katrina, and then of their child, who would never get to see *Deliverance*. But this time his heart wasn't filled with sorrow. The sacrifices were all worth it. And best of all, Janga had been wrong all along. There would be no man to lead them to a new home under the water or in the water.

There was just one man—Leon Jordan—the hero who had found a new home for humanity in the skies.

Several voices rang out behind him, and he followed Hunt's finger to the wall-mounted monitor.

"There she is," he whispered.

The smooth hull of *Deliverance* was the most beautiful thing he had ever seen. Every porthole in the central section of the ship glowed white, and on the top, red lights flashed—a beacon of hope in the darkness.

———

Magnolia sneaked a glance through one of the portholes as the *Hive* came into focus. She had seen the ship from the outside dozens of times during her dives, but now that she compared it to *Deliverance*, she could appreciate just how battle scarred and rickety the old ship was.

"Keep away from the windows," Michael said. "They must have removed the hatches over the portholes for some reason."

"I told you," Les said. "Jordan purged the ship of the past."

"That doesn't make any sense," Magnolia said. "There's no way he'd get away with something like that. The people would riot."

But would they really? People got used to things, even terrible conditions, if they were downtrodden long enough. Part of Magnolia wondered why they were even bothering to rescue the *Hive* from Jordan's control.

Because Rodger's parents are still on board. The Mintels are worth saving—and I still have to kill Jordan for what he's done.

She wriggled in the oversize armor that had come from Del Toro's corpse. X was brilliant, retrieving the gear and weapons from the field in Miami before *Deliverance* took to the sky. It was odd wearing the suit of a dead man, but if it got her close to Jordan, it was worth it. The idea of throttling him was the only thing keeping her going.

They hadn't been able to retrieve Rodger's body. He was out there on that terrible ship, floating toward the metal islands. Magnolia wished she'd been able to bring him home to his parents, but she could at least tell them that he was brave to the end.

Magnolia looked over at Michael, who was wearing Lore's armor. He looked so young standing next to X. It was strange to see the current and former commanders of Team Raptor side by side. X was wearing the armor he had taken from Sergeant Jenkins—a fact that had Erin on edge. She stood near the hatch with Les and Samson, and although the rest of them carried automatic rifles, none of the three standing up front were armed.

"Remember, Samson," Michael said, "as soon as we dock, you go straight to engineering and take control of the systems. Les, you get your ass to the brig and release Katrina—and your boy, too, while you're there."

"Understood," Samson said.

"You got it, Commander Everhart," Les replied.

Magnolia cast a wary eye over them. Samson was brilliant, but he was also part of the system. She barely knew Les, although he seemed a decent enough man. And as for Erin, she had just lost her father. But even before that, there had been something off about her. Ever since she came home from the mission that killed most of her team, she had been withdrawn. Back in the good old days, Magnolia had gone drinking with her a few times, but after that last dive, she had stopped socializing with Hell Divers. Magnolia wasn't sure she could trust any of them.

She looked at Michael next. Could she trust him to lead them on this mission when Layla was fighting for her life back in the med ward?

Of course you can. He's never let us down before.

Magnolia hated herself for even thinking it, but her nerves were getting to her. The pain from Rodger's death was making her loopy. She couldn't stop thinking about all the things that had been left unsaid between them, all the things she would have done differently if she had known that their days together were numbered.

X cleared his throat, snapping Magnolia from her thoughts. "Once the militia boards the ship, we're only going to get one chance at taking down Jordan. You've got to keep calm."

Magnolia gave him a solid nod. "Can't wait."

"I'm good, X," Michael said.

"I know," he replied.

"Remind me how this is going to work," Samson said. He folded his arms over his belly. "Because I really don't think you all blending in is going to work."

"Jordan's not stupid," Michael replied. "He'll send in the militia to search *Deliverance*. When they board, we'll move over to the *Hive*, pretending to be the crew he sent over. The armor we bagged off Del Toro, Olah, Lore, and Jenkins will disguise us long enough to get aboard the *Hive*. By the time anyone knows what's going on, we'll be on our way to the bridge."

Erin turned to glare at X, rage in her eyes. "You shouldn't be wearing his armor."

"I'm sorry about your dad," X said. "But—"

"Maybe we should just let Les and Samson go over first," Magnolia interrupted.

"You can trust me," Erin said. "I hate Jordan as much as you all do, but I'll never forgive you for what you did."

"Fair enough," X said. "Not asking your forgiveness. Let's just get this done."

Magnolia scrutinized Erin for a lie, but she turned back to the hatch that would connect with the *Hive* before Magnolia could get a solid read.

Timothy's voice sounded in Magnolia's earpiece. "Preparing to dock with the *Hive* in T minus two minutes," said the AI.

Michael drew in a deep breath and released it inside his helmet. He looked at everyone in turn, taking extra time to study Erin and Samson.

"You all ready?" he asked.

Everyone nodded. A countdown sounded at one minute. Les, Erin, and Samson all stepped up to the hatch. An enclosed walkway clicked and clacked as it extended from *Deliverance* into the blue.

"Stand by for docking procedures," Timothy said. "Connecting in three, two…"

A jolt rocked the ship as the walkway connected with the air lock on the *Hive*. Michael, X, and Magnolia took up positions in the quarters they had picked earlier, down the corridor from the bridge. Miles was waiting for them inside, tail wagging. They readied their weapons and moved to the side of the hatch.

The air lock clicked open farther down the passage, and voices sounded in the tunnel. Jordan's soldiers had boarded *Deliverance*.

Michael and X pressed their backs against the bulkheads, and Magnolia aimed her rifle at the hatch. The footfalls grew louder, then passed by outside.

"A team of five engineers and three militia soldiers has boarded the ship," Timothy said over the private comm channel that fed into their helmets.

"Copy," Magnolia whispered.

"Three more soldiers just boarded," Timothy added. "One appears to be an officer with the rank of lieutenant."

"Hunt," Magnolia said quietly.

Michael nodded back. He checked his HUD for the time. "We need to give Les a few more minutes."

They waited in silence, Magnolia's heart thumping so hard she could hear it.

"The boarders have moved to the first and second quadrants of the ship," Timothy announced.

Michael gestured toward X. He nodded back and opened the

closet door. After herding Miles inside, he bent down and told the dog to stay. Miles whined and licked X's hand as he shut the door, watching him until the last second. Magnolia hoped the dog wouldn't start barking at the wrong moment and blow their cover, but X seemed to think Miles was smarter than the average Hell Diver.

Magnolia grabbed the handle on the hatch and slowly opened it. She backed away and let X take point. Her head and heart ached, but in a few minutes, she was finally going to get the revenge she had been craving ever since Jordan sabotaged her chute.

"Commander Everhart," Timothy said, "I am detecting movement outside the hatch on the *Hive*. There appears to be additional soldiers."

"Changes nothing," Michael said. "Just stay focused on the approach. "The *Hive* doesn't have cameras like *Deliverance*. Jordan can't see us coming."

A chill ran through Magnolia's body. Something felt wrong—like walking into a trap.

She kept the hunch to herself and took a deep breath to calm her nerves as they approached the open hatch leading to the tunnel. X was first to round the corner and move into the enclosed space.

Two soldiers were standing sentry on the other side, backs turned, facing the corridors of the *Hive*—probably to keep back any passengers who wanted to see the new ship. X and Michael moved quickly and took them both out with blows from their rifle butts.

"Go, go, go!" X croaked.

Magnolia darted past the unconscious soldiers. Michael was limping, but he moved fast enough to keep up with her and X. Maybe that meant they were slowing down in their old age. The bridge wasn't far. It would take them only a few minutes to reach the command center—maybe even less, with the corridors this empty.

Wait... Where the hell *was* everybody? This place should be teeming with passengers.

X held up a fist just before they reached the final turn that would lead them to the bridge. He readied his rifle and peeked around the corner. Then he pulled back and held up two fingers, signaling the number of guards outside the hatch.

This was it. Either their ruse worked and they would be able to walk onto the bridge unimpeded, or all three of them would be gunned down in the next thirty seconds. X walked around the corner, calmly cradling his rifle. Michael and Magnolia followed, trying to look as though they belonged here.

"Hey, guys, Lieutenant Hunt told us to come back with the thing we found on *Deliverance*," Michael said, pitching his voice half an octave lower.

The guards exchanged a glance.

"Didn't hear nothin' about that," the man on the right said.

"You got to check it out, man," Michael said. "I didn't think this shit still existed."

The guard tilted his head. "Frank, is that you?"

"What'd you find?" the other militia soldier said.

Michael gestured toward X, who strode forward and raised his rifle.

"I'm back," X said, smashing them both in the face before either could react. They crumpled to the floor, and X pushed the button to open the hatch. Magnolia strode onto the deck with her rifle raised, finger along the trigger guard. She was prepared to shoot if someone got in her way, but she didn't want to kill anyone besides Jordan.

"Everyone down!" she shouted.

Michael and X fanned out to the right and left, covering the room with their rifles.

"Where's Jordan?" Michael demanded.

Ensign Ryan raised his hands from his station. "Who...who are you?"

X pulled his helmet off.

"It can't be," someone gasped.

Ryan shook his head. "No...you're dead."

"I should be," X said. "Guess I didn't get the memo. Jordan sure went to a lot of trouble to make sure I didn't come back."

A voice crackled in Magnolia's helmet as she scanned the room for the captain—the man responsible for the deaths of Rodger, Weaver, Ty, Pipe, and so many others. He needed to be brought to justice, and by her.

"Commander Everhart, we have a problem," Timothy said over the comm link.

Magnolia froze. *Shit*, she thought. *Jordan isn't here. The fucker outflanked us.*

"Captain Jordan has just boarded *Deliverance* with a crew," Timothy said, confirming her fear. "They are carrying bags with them."

Magnolia turned and bolted out of the room. X and Michael ran after her.

The sneaky bastard had tricked them and was about to steal their airship. She had felt something was off, but she put it down to her grief over Rodger. X had taught her to trust her gut, but she had second-guessed herself.

It didn't matter now.

All that mattered was getting back aboard *Deliverance*.

She raced through the corridors, leaving Michael and X behind. Halfway there, the PA system came online.

"Passengers of the *Hive*, this is Captain Jordan speaking.

Tonight, I've done what I promised. I've brought you a new home called *Deliverance*. I'm boarding her now, and I must say, she is beautiful."

Magnolia ran faster, anger fueling her as she listened Jordan's voice.

"Unfortunately, we have been betrayed yet again by the Hell Divers. They are on the *Hive* now, attempting to lead a mutiny against me. We cannot let them succeed."

"Hurry!" Magnolia shouted over her shoulder. A quick glance showed X close on her heels, but Michael was falling behind. There was a wild, panicked look in his eyes, and sweat dripped down his too-pale face.

"Layla," he gasped.

Magnolia cursed again. Layla was defenseless. If Jordan and his goons got to her first, he'd have no problem murdering an unarmed woman in her hospital bed.

A distant clanking noise sounded ahead, and Magnolia's heart nearly stopped when she realized it was the bridge connecting the two ships. The platform was already retracting.

"You have to stop them, Timothy!" Magnolia shouted.

"I have been locked out of the system by the engineers," replied the AI. "Captain Jordan has control of *Deliverance*."

Magnolia pushed her body to its limit, lungs and muscles burning. The intersection that would lead them to the tunnel was just ahead, but she feared they were already too late.

No, it doesn't end like this!

"Until these traitors are captured and killed, I will be taking *Deliverance* to a safe distance," Jordan said. "It would be in the best interests of everyone aboard the *Hive* to find the mutineers and stop them using whatever force is necessary. Until then, good luck."

Magnolia stopped at the hatch to the tunnel. The two uncon-scious guards still lay there. All along the corridor, confused passengers emerged from their shelters, talking in hushed voices. Several of them looked at Magnolia, Michael, and then X. And then they noticed the two motionless bodies on the floor.

"They killed the guards!" someone shouted.

"There!" yelled one of the lower-deckers. "Those are the traitors!"

Magnolia turned her attention to the porthole windows and saw movement on *Deliverance* as it slowly pulled away. Jordan was there with Hunt and several militia soldiers, watching the two airships separate.

She pounded the glass so hard it hurt her hand. The filthy passengers closed in around the trio of divers.

"Stay back!" Michael shouted. "Jordan's lying. He's the traitor!"

"Everyone back!" X yelled.

"Is that Commander Rodriguez?" someone said.

Another person gasped, "He's a ghost!"

The PA system suddenly clicked back on, Jordan's voice coming online. "No," he said. "It can't be."

Magnolia pivoted back to the porthole window, thinking he had somehow seen X.

"Stop them!" Jordan shouted.

Everyone crowding around Michael, Magnolia, and X stopped, looking up at the wall-mounted speakers. Others crowded around the portholes for a view of the other ship.

Magnolia squinted at motion in the passage aboard *Deliverance*. A tall man aimed a pistol at Jordan, and a woman...Not just any woman, Magnolia realized. It was Katrina. And she was holding a sword to Jordan's neck. He had his hands up, and the other militia soldiers were all standing with their hands on their heads. Sloan from the brig and a teenage boy were watching over them.

"Is that...?" she started to say when Michael finished the thought for her.

"Trey Mitchells and Sloan," he said.

Magnolia, trying to make sense of what was happening, made a conscious effort to slow her breathing. Jordan hadn't seen X after all. He was talking about Les and Katrina. They had made it back onto *Deliverance*, and they had Jordan in custody. She wanted to be the one to kill the captain, but seeing Katrina with the sword to his throat was still satisfying. As long as she got to be there when Katrina spilled his blood on the deck.

* * * * *

Les held the same gun he had shot Olah dead with, but this time it was pointing at Captain Jordan. Les' son, Trey, was there, too, along with Katrina and Sloan. In the end, it was the hard-faced woman running the brig who had been the key to taking down Jordan.

"You can't do this!" Jordan shouted at them. "I've saved us all. I saved humanity!"

"No," said Katrina, coldly. "You're nothing but a *cancer* to humanity."

"I've stood by and watched your reign of terror for too long," Sloan said. "Today it ends."

Les checked the militia soldiers to make sure none were trying to maneuver on them. All three men, as well as Lieutenant Hunt, were now facedown on the deck, hands tied behind their backs. He looked through the porthole windows at movement on the other side, aboard the *Hive*. Michael, X, and Magnolia were surrounded by a growing crowd of lower-deckers. "Hit the bridge button, Sloan," Les ordered.

She moved over to the bulkhead and hit the button. The clanking of the platform sounded as it reached back out toward the *Hive*.

"I should make you suffer," Katrina said. "I should skin you alive and then dump your body back to the surface so you can see it for yourself." She pushed the blade deeper, nicking his neck and drawing blood.

He reared his chin back, crazed eyes focused on Katrina.

"You never deserved me you selfish b—" His eyes widened even further as Katrina let out a scream of rage. She pulled the blade away from his neck and thrust it into his chest.

Jordan let out an astonished croak, his mouth agape. He grabbed the hilt and pulled her toward him. Around the blade, a crimson bloom spread outward across the white uniform jacket.

Katrina shoved the sword deeper, until the blade pushed through and out his back, hitting the bulkhead with a clank. Impaled on his own sword, Jordan wore a mask of shock, rage, and fear. She leaned closer until she was just inches from his face.

"What have you done?" Hunt said from the deck.

"Shut up," Sloan said, giving the lieutenant a swift kick in the ribs.

"I—I loved you," Jordan stuttered.

He fell to his knees, and Katrina calmly put her foot against his chest and pulled the sword free. He toppled onto his back and pressed his hand down on the wound, his lips moving as he tried to speak.

Les looked over as the bridge clanked and connected with *Deliverance*. The hatch opened, and the other divers moved away from the portholes on the *Hive* to cross the enclosed bridge.

When Les looked back at Katrina, she was calmly wiping the blade on Jordan's white trousers, first one side and then the other. The captain stared up at her in disbelief, his feet squirming. No matter how hard he pressed, his hand couldn't stop the gushing blood. It bubbled out of his mouth, his lips still moving as he tried to speak.

Magnolia was the first one onto *Deliverance*. She slowed and looked at Jordan as he let out a final sigh. There was no smile on her face, just a stern look of justice delivered.

*   *   *   *   *

"Jordan's dead," Michael said into the comm mike. His voice got louder as he repeated the message. "Captain Leon Jordan is dead!"

The passengers from the *Hive* made their way over to *Deliverance*. A bottleneck formed on the bridge just outside the hatch where the first of the lower-deckers had stopped to gawk at the gory scene.

"Back!" X said. "It'd be a real good idea to stay the hell back!"

Blood continued to pool across the deck around Michael's feet. He swallowed, part of him disgusted, part of him filled with a grim satisfaction at the sight of the captain's corpse.

Katrina dropped the blade onto the floor and sobbed when she saw the other divers.

"Kat!" Magnolia said, enveloping her in a hug.

"I thought you were dead," she said, gripping Magnolia tight.

Time seemed to slow and then stop altogether as dozens of passengers pushed past X. He gave up trying to hold them back. Within minutes, thirty turned into fifty, and then a hundred. Young, old, sick, healthy—all of them staring in awe at the clean, warmly lit corridors.

"Welcome to your new home," Michael said to the people he had known his entire life. "Welcome to *Deliverance*."

Both Trey and Les nodded at Michael, who nodded back and then turned away as the other divers celebrated. Sloan hauled off Lieutenant Hunt and the soldiers who had helped Jordan escape. Seeing this, some lower-deckers began to cheer. Several claps turned into a din of shouts and applause.

X pushed his way out of the clogged passage and vanished.

Michael followed him, anxious to check on Layla. He made his way through the throngs of filthy passengers, only to freeze when he saw Timothy's translucent form.

"I'm sorry, sir, but I couldn't stop her," he said.

Michael tilted his head at the AI. Then he saw her. Layla was resting against a bulkhead, one hand on her gut.

"Layla!" Michael shouted. He ran over to her, taking off his helmet as he ran. "What are you doing here? You're supposed—"

"And miss this?" she said, reaching out to him. "Not a chance."

"Les, get Dr. Huff over here now!" Michael yelled over his shoulder.

"On it," the tall diver replied.

Michael gently put her arm over his shoulder.

"Is it really over?" she asked. "Are we really home now?"

Michael nodded, looking at the shiny bulkheads of their new home, unable to think of anything profound to say. Instead of saying anything, he kissed her on the lips and helped her toward the hatch leading to their old home.

"Come on, let's get you to the medical bay," he said.

The passengers continued to flood onto *Deliverance* as the two divers made their way back toward the *Hive*. X emerged around the corner ahead, with Miles trotting alongside. They stopped to watch from the shadows as the awestruck lower-deckers marveled at the new ship.

Michael knew right away by the distant look in X's eyes that he wouldn't be staying. While Michael and Layla were home, X was not. His home was no longer in the skies. He belonged down there.

EPILOGUE

Xavier Rodriguez was still recovering from his decade on the surface. Regaining weight and sleeping uninterrupted through the night had strengthened him for his next journey, and he was ready to go.

The ship no longer felt like the home he had once known. Many of the people who had been his friends were frightened of him, and he was just as anxious around most of them. Some spoke in hushed voices behind his back, using such words as "ghost" and even "demon." That wasn't the main reason he decided to leave in the end, but it had helped make the decision easier.

Miles trotted after them as they walked toward the tether connecting *Deliverance* with the *Hive*. All around them, bulkheads sported fresh paint. X slowed to look at the porthole hatches. Fluffy clouds, a brilliant sun, and star-filled skies covered nearly every square inch of metal.

The art that Jordan had stripped from the *Hive* was quickly replaced with newer and more vibrant images. Just ahead, kids were scribbling on a bulkhead with chalk, laughing as they tried to draw animals they had never seen. One of the kids, a boy no older than six, looked in his direction and waved.

"Hey, there's Ghostman and his wolf!" the boy exclaimed. "I'm gonna draw a picture of the wolf next."

X waved back and clicked his tongue at Miles, who wagged his tail excitedly as he trotted after his master.

Cole Mintel and his wife were supervising construction of a memorial in the next corridor, and X stopped to pay his respects. A wooden statue of a Hell Diver was displayed outside the launch bay. Cole was putting the finishing touches on the helmet.

X cleared his throat, and Cole turned around. "I didn't know Rodger well," X said, "but he was a good man, and brave."

"Thank you," Cole said. He seemed to consider saying something else but then shook his head, eyes glistening with unshed tears, and turned back to his work.

X looked at the statue for another moment, remembering the divers who had lost their lives over the years. Maybe someday, no more men and women would need to dive to the surface to save humanity. Maybe there would be no more need for memorials to lives cut short. Either way, X wouldn't be around to find out.

Two militia soldiers stood guard at the hatch leading to *Deliverance*. The one on the left opened it and let him through with a nod. Taking in one last breath of the familiar recycled air, X left the *Hive* behind, knowing that he would never be back again. He led Miles across the enclosed walkway.

Engineers were retrofitting *Deliverance* using supplies that Les, Erin, Michael, X, and several new Hell Divers had retrieved from the surface over the past two months. Their work showed in every passage, from updated wiring to reinforced hull metal and shiny new bolts—all materials taken from ITC facilities west of Florida.

X passed one of the most impressive new sights: the water

treatment plant, which was nearing completion. He paused to look inside the open room with a vaulted ceiling. Three empty silos were tucked against the starboard bulkheads. They would eventually serve as the water supply. Engineers worked on a pair of empty pools in the center of the space. When finished, the treatment plant would be more sophisticated than the *Hive*'s, allowing for a higher percentage of water to be recycled.

He continued down the next passage toward the farm, where another militia soldier stood sentry. The man smiled and gave a cheerful wave. X couldn't remember his name, but then again, he couldn't remember most of the people here.

"Mind if I take a look inside?" he asked.

The soldier checked both passages for anyone who might be around to see him break protocol, and said, "Fine by me."

X and Miles walked into a clean room walled off by plastic sheets, to look through the window into the open space beyond. The mission to retrieve the dirt was one of the longest he could ever remember. It had taken the divers two days to dig enough to fill the farm. Then another two days to get the dirt aboard the ship. Timothy had been able to land *Deliverance* on the surface, which made transport much easier, and it had also allowed them to get the water silos and other major equipment from the nearby ITC facility onto the ship. Still, it had been backbreaking work for an old diver like him.

Every cubic inch of soil inside the farm had gone through a rigorous decontamination process. Several farmers were already planting hybrid seeds into the brown expanse. In a few days, the first seeds would sprout, providing new food for the still-hungry population.

X stopped at the armory next. They had finally found a way to unlock the vault and had been rewarded with a bounty of weapons and ammunition. Enough to wage a war—or end a world. Again.

Dozens of nuclear bombs and missiles were still armed, and so far engineering hadn't been able to find a way to unlock the weapons system. If it were up to X, he would dump them all into the ocean if he had the chance.

He sighed and pushed on to his destination. The clean white bridge bustled with staff, closely monitoring the screens. Officers surrounded the island in the middle of the room while others worked at stations along the bulkheads. New monitors and other equipment, salvaged from the surface, flashed data and images to the men and women running the airship.

Michael and Magnolia were standing at the helm, watching the main display with their backs to the entrance. Katrina was there, too, sitting in the captain's chair. Voted in unanimously, she was calling the shots these days.

The room quieted as X strode toward the central island.

"Sir," someone said, saluting.

X nodded back and forced a smile when Michael and Magnolia turned. Layla got up from a radar station, gritting her teeth against the pain. It was good to see her on her feet again after spending a month in the medical ward.

"We're ready," X said, glancing down at Miles.

Katrina hesitated, then nodded. "Let's go." On the way out, she looked over at Lieutenant Les Mitchells, her new XO. "You have the bridge."

The former XO, Lieutenant Hunt, was currently serving time in the brig with Ensign Ryan for conspiracy. Their excuse of "just following orders" hadn't gone over well with Katrina. She had wanted to execute them both, but Michael saved their lives, arguing that they needed to save every warm body they could now that Jordan's reign of terror was at an end.

X wasn't so sure, but it wasn't up to him. His time as a Hell Diver and citizen of the *Hive* was over.

He walked out of the bridge and took a ladder to the lower decks, where the cargo hold was full to the brim with technicians, engineers, and other support staff, all of them working on the boat that would serve as his new home.

It sat on a track near the cargo doors, ready for launch. X examined the vessel for several minutes, admiring the excellent job the crew had done on it. When he had seen the ITC model on a raid several weeks ago, he knew it was the vessel he would take out onto the open seas. The twin hull was maximized for stability at high speeds in versatile conditions. It also sported a broad deck, perfect for walking around when not in the command center.

"She's a beauty," Samson announced. He walked over with a wrench in his hand and a wistful look in his eyes. "Fully equipped with two turbocharged engines and battery power that will keep you charged for extended periods. She's even got two heads on board."

Miles sat on his haunches, watching as an engineer finished welding on a panel to the hull—the final step to completion. The rectangular metal slab was painted with a silhouette of a Siberian husky, and the name "Sea Wolf"—X's idea.

"That's you, boy," X said, crouching and pointing.

The dog tilted his head and looked up at X. His eyes were the color that the sky and the sea had once been. Someday, when the storms finally cleared and people returned to the surface, the whole world would be wrapped in that shade of blue. He patted Miles on his head and noticed that the dark fur was starting to turn gray.

We're both getting old, he thought.

Samson smiled and dragged a sleeve across his sweaty forehead. "The *Sea Wolf* is one hell of a vessel, if I do say so myself. Those thick hulls will protect you from radiation and will manage smoothly in rough waters."

"I just hope it's as stealthy as it looks," X said. "If I'm going to reach those metal islands, I'll need to sneak up on the Cazadores."

"And what about once you get there?"

X shrugged. "Guess I'll kill 'em all."

"That's why I keep telling you to bring someone else with you," Samson said. "But Miles will help, right?"

The husky wagged his tail and barked excitedly. Magnolia, Katrina, Layla, Michael, and Les gathered around to admire the boat. After a few minutes, the room slowly cleared, leaving the divers alone with Samson. They met in front of the thick glass windows built into the bow, where a command center would provide X with all the navigation tools he needed to find the metal islands.

The ship would do what *Deliverance* and the *Hive* couldn't, traveling low enough to find the Cazadores' fabled homeland, where the sun still shone.

"You're sure I can't change your mind about staying?" Michael asked.

X turned away from the boat to look at Michael. The skinny kid in the tinfoil hat had grown into a fine young man over the past decade. And now he was going to help Katrina lead humanity into a fragile, but hopeful, future.

"Nope," X said. "It's time for me to head out. Leave saving the human race to you young folks."

Michael frowned. "You talk like you're a hundred years old."

"Besides, I kind of like it better down there than up here," X said.

Katrina looked over at him. There was concern in her gaze, but nothing more. They were lovers once, but their time had long since passed. Her duty was to stay here and keep the remnants of humanity safe while he searched for a home on the seas. She reached forward to shake his hand, but he gave her a hug instead, patting her gently and kissing her on the cheek.

"Good luck, Captain DaVita," he whispered.

"You too, Commander."

Layla hugged X next. She sniffed and wiped her eyes on the back of her hand as they pulled apart. "I'm still mad at you for leaving," she said.

"I know. Take care of Tin for me, will you?"

Then came Les. They shook hands and X said, "Thank you for everything you did."

The tall lieutenant smiled. "Just following your lead, sir."

He looked back at Michael, then reached out to embrace him. The boy had grown up strong, both mentally and physically. X wished he had been there for him while it was happening, but Tin had turned out okay anyway.

"You remind me of your dad," X said, cracking a smile. "He'd be very proud of you. And so am I."

They separated, and X heaved a long sigh as he looked at Magnolia. But instead of reaching out to embrace him, she grabbed a large duffel bag from Les.

"What are you doing?" X asked.

She grinned, and some of the old sparkle returned to her eyes. It had been dimmed by Rodger's death, but nothing, not even the end of world, could keep Magnolia Katib down.

"I'm coming with. You didn't think I was going to let you get payback for Rodger without me, did you?"

Miles looked up at X, then at Magnolia, apparently as confused as X was. X wasn't sure how he felt about having human company, but he could tell by the look in Magnolia's eyes that she wasn't going to take no for an answer.

An announcement played over the PA system, warning everyone to get to their safety shelters. Timothy's holographic form emerged after the message. He smiled warmly.

"*Deliverance* will undock from the *Hive* in five minutes," he said. "Please prepare for descent."

"Thanks, Pepper," X said. He looked at the divers one last time and then picked up Miles. He carried the dog over to the ladder and climbed up to the deck.

After letting Miles down, he reached over to take Magnolia's bag.

"What the hell do you have in here?" he asked, grunting as he lugged it onto the deck.

"Oh, stuff," she replied.

Chirping sounded throughout the cargo hold, and a vibration rippled through the bulkheads as Timothy lowered *Deliverance* toward the ocean twenty thousand feet below. Standing on the deck of the boat, X caught a glimpse of the *Hive* through the starboard windows.

"Goodbye, my old friend," Magnolia said.

Once the beetle-like hull had vanished from sight, they moved belowdecks and explored the quarters. Magnolia claimed one of the small cabins, and X put his bag down in the other. Every storage locker was packed full of gear, clothes, and weapons. After they had finished getting settled, they made their way to the bridge. They were greeted in the command center by a warm orange light gleaming over panels of instruments and monitors.

"Greetings," said a familiar voice. "Welcome to the *Sea Wolf.*"

It was Timothy. Part of his consciousness had been downloaded to the boat, and while his main program would stay on *Deliverance*, they would also be taking the AI with them on their journey.

Magnolia took a seat in one of two leather chairs. X sat next to her and motioned for Miles to sit on the small bed to his right. The dog curled up, already content with his new home.

Beyond the windows, all the divers waved goodbye. X felt a tear tickling his eye, but he didn't bother wiping it away. Instead, he brought up a hand, a final farewell to the boy he had thought he would never see again, and to his old friends who had believed him to be a ghost.

The divers cleared the room as a red warning light spread over the cargo bay. *Deliverance* lowered through the skies, bringing them just over the ocean.

"All systems online," Timothy said. "We're ready to launch."

The cargo bay door creaked open, revealing nothing but darkness outside.

"Lights," X said.

The powerful front beams blazed out of the bow, carving through the darkness. X checked their altitude. They were almost to the surface, and a few seconds later he saw the first sign of the ocean swells below.

"You're sure about this, kid?"

"I told you not to call me kid," Magnolia replied. "I'm forty-three years old. And I'm more than sure."

X put his hand on the throttle. The tracks beneath the vessel clicked on, jolting them closer to the open door.

"Ready to launch when you are," Timothy said.

X studied the whitecaps and wondered what beasts hunted beneath the inky surface. He had conquered the skies and he had conquered the surface. Now it was time to conquer the seas and find a place where humanity might be able to start over, before it was too late.

Pushing down on the throttle, he launched the boat out of the cargo hold and into the water, ready for wherever the waves took him.

"We sail so humanity survives," X said.

ABOUT THE AUTHOR

Nicholas Sansbury Smith is the *New York Times* and *USA Today* bestselling author of the Hell Divers series, the Orbs series, the Trackers series, the Extinction Cycle series, the Sons of War series, and the new E-Day series. He worked for Iowa Homeland Security and Emergency Management in disaster mitigation before switching careers to focus on storytelling. When he isn't writing or daydreaming about the apocalypse, he enjoys running, biking, spending time with his family, and traveling the world. He is an Ironman triathlete and lives in Iowa with his wife, daughter, and their dogs.

Join Nicholas on social media:
Facebook: Nicholas Sansbury Smith
Twitter: @GreatWaveInk
Website: www.NicholasSansburySmith.com